Praise for Martyn Waites

'Grips, and squeezes, and won't let go . . . Martyn Waites' lean, exhilarating prose is from the heart and from the guts, a   hat's exactly where it hits you' Mark Billingham

'A reckless energy which demands attention and respect' *Literary Review*

'   tal, mesmerising stuff' Ian Rankin

'   n, mean and machine-like, with a pacy narrative and   rp, staccato dialogue . . . His male characters are tough   complex, a throwback to the no-nonsense, near-mute   risma of *Get Carter* or *Point Blank*' *Scotsman*

'   n evocative, gripping and angry novel' *Newcastle Evening Chronicle*

'An   bitious, tautly-plotted thriller which offers a stark ntidote to PD James' cosy world of middle-class murder' *Time Out*

'A gripping read; Waites juggles a complex plot with astute urban commentary' *Jack*

'Waites' writing is lean and taut, while his eye for detail gives his prose a vivid immediacy' *Ink*

Martyn Waites was born and brought up in Newcastle upon Tyne. Before becoming a writer he was an actor. He has written five novels – *Mary's Prayer*, *Little Triggers*, *Candleland*, *Born Under Punches* and *The White Room* as well as short stories and non-fiction. He has held two writing residencies, one at Huntercombe Young Offenders Institution and, most recently, HMP Chelmsford. He currently runs arts-based workshops for socially excluded teenagers.

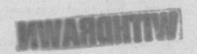

THE MERCY SEAT

Martyn Waites

POCKET
BOOKS

LONDON • SYDNEY • NEW YORK • TORONTO

First published in Great Britain by Pocket Books, 2006
An imprint of Simon & Schuster UK
A Viacom company

Copyright © Martyn Waites, 2006

1 3 5 7 9 10 8 6 4 2

Simon & Schuster UK Ltd
Africa House
64–78 Kingsway
London WC2B 6AH

www.simonsays.co.uk

Simon & Schuster Australia
Sydney

A CIP catalogue record for this book is available from the British Library

ISBN 141650222X
EAN 9781416502227

Typeset by M Rules
Printed and bound in Great Britain by
Cox & Wyman Ltd, Reading, Berks

To Linda, again

Hope in reality is the worst of all evils,
because it prolongs the torments of man.
FRIEDRICH NIETZSCHE

Then he shall kill the goat of the sin-offering
. . . and bring his blood within the veil, and . . .
sprinkle it upon the Mercy Seat and before the Mercy Seat;
And he shall make an atonement . . .
LEVITICUS 16: 15–16

PROLOGUE
A SECRET AFFAIR

Tosher opened his eyes. And tried to breathe.

Something was covering his mouth, his face, something tight, constricting. He gasped frantically, tried to put his hands up, remove it, but couldn't. His hands, arms, wouldn't move. Panic rose in his chest; he forced his heart to slow down, his mind to remain calm, process his situation, his surroundings. He attempted deep breaths, felt the new second skin suck wet and clammy against his own.

He tried to move. Couldn't. He was tied to some kind of chair — big, sturdy, bolted to the ground — restrained by cords round his arms and legs. His body was naked. He shivered.

Tosher knew who was responsible for this. It wasn't a comforting thought.

His breathing began to quicken again; he tried through nose and mouth simultaneously, forcing air into his body, smelled only old, sweated leather, his own stale breath. The sound, amplified by the mask, was like that of a wheezing asthmatic.

Breathe out: his vision fogged, cleared slightly. Fogged, cleared slightly. But still dusty, opaque. He blinked: once, twice. Didn't clear. The opacity was external.

Tosher looked around. The building was old, dark. Dirt-streaked brick walls, high, rough-beamed roof. A warehouse, or something similar. He was sitting in a pool of light, dust motes dancing before him, as if spotlit on stage. Beyond the light, in the shadows, he could make out figures in mist vision, two of them, both looking at him. On seeing him stir, one stepped forward to the edge of the light.

'Back with us, Tosher?' he said. 'Good.'

Tosher looked at the speaker. The tailored business suit and expensive haircut couldn't hide the meanness about him, the unrefined street-fighter in him. The danger. Tosher was aware of that. Had understood it the first time he had met him.

Tosher's heart began to race again. He began frantically to pull against the restraining bands.

'Struggle all you like,' the man said; 'you're in the mercy seat. You're not going anywhere.'

Tosher stopped struggling, became aware once again of the smell and sound of his own breathing.

'Know what a mercy seat is?' the man asked, then continued, not waiting for an answer. 'Check your Bible, if you've got one. Bloodstained altar where you made sacrifices. Listened to instructions.' He nodded. 'Sounds about right.'

Tosher looked at the other figure, the neatly bearded and blazered man. Half hidden by shadow, standing away from the speaker, his body language shouting he was not really part of the proceedings. The man was sweating.

'You've spotted him?' said the dangerous man. 'That's my partner, Dr Faustus.' He laughed, as if he couldn't quite believe what he was saying. 'Yeah, Faustus. That makes me Mephisto, apparently.' He turned to Faustus. 'Right?'

Faustus shook his head, turned away. Mephisto caught the action, looked at him.

'You don't like these names?' he said, laughing. 'They were your idea. Like everything else here.'

Faustus shook his head again. 'I . . . I'm not going to be part of this,' he said. He started walking for the door. 'This is . . . this is . . .'

'All your idea,' said Mephisto, his voice sharp and hard. 'Now stay where you are.'

Faustus stopped moving, did as he was told. Mephisto

turned back to Tosher. 'Now, you seem to have a problem doing what you're told. Taking instruction.' He stepped nearer, into the light. His heavy, spicy aftershave penetrated Tosher's mask. 'We can't have that, can we?'

Mephisto snapped his fingers. From out of the shadows came another man. Big, wearing workboots, jeans and a white long-sleeved T-shirt. Beneath the shirt was a muscle-pumped, steroid-assisted body. Tosher could make out trails and swirls through the material: black-ink tattoos looking like veins and arteries. His head was shaved. He was holding something in his hands.

'This is our companion,' said Mephisto. 'We call him Hammer. You'll find out why.'

Hammer smiled. Revealed a blue-sapphire tooth.

Tosher struggled against his restraints. Much harder this time. He succeeded only in tightening them.

Mephisto laughed. 'Don't waste your strength.' He stood up, stepped back to the edge of the light. He held up his fist, raised his index finger.

'Three questions. Who did you tell?'

Another finger.

'What did you tell?'

A third finger.

'And what are they going to do about it?' Mephisto smiled again. 'Want to tell me now? Save the unpleasantness? Or want to see Hammer's party piece?'

Tosher said nothing; his breathing became faster, more laboured.

Hammer picked up a wooden block out of which was sticking a six-inch nail. The nail was showing over four inches. Hammer placed the block of wood on the ground in front of Tosher. Across his knuckles: FEAR, LOVE. He kneeled before it, concentrated. Then brought his fist down hard.

The nail was plunged right into the wood. Mephisto

crossed to it, bent carefully down so as not to get his suit dirty, tried to pick it up.

'See that?' he said. 'Solid. Right through the wood into the concrete.' He stood up. 'Guess whose turn it is next?'

Mephisto grabbed Tosher's right hand, held it down over the arm of the chair. Tosher struggled, tried to cry out. His words were lost behind the mask. He had no time to feel beneath his palm, register how many splintered holes were already there in the hard, thick wood.

Hammer produced a nail, held it over Tosher's right hand. Hit it.

Tosher screamed. The mask absorbed most of the sound escaping, reverberated in Tosher's own ears.

Mephisto stepped back, not wanting blood to arc on to his suit.

Faustus turned away.

'The other one.'

Mephisto and Hammer moved to Tosher's left side.

Repeated the procedure.

Tosher felt his vocal cords strain and tear. His hands and arms felt like liquid fire was running up them. He struggled, tried to lift his hands up. The pain increased.

'Ready to talk yet?' asked Mephisto. 'Any sacrificial offers to make?'

Tosher screamed. Whimpered.

'What's that?' said Mephisto. 'Didn't quite hear you.' Mephisto looked at Hammer. 'Do his cock.'

Hammer produced another nail, held it over Tosher's groin.

Tosher screamed even louder.

Faustus threw up.

Tosher opened his eyes. And tried to breathe.

He didn't know how long he had been sitting in the seat.

He could have been there days. Or hours. Minutes, even. He had lost all track of time. Of pain.

He had passed out, he knew that. They had brought him round. And continued.

Every time.

They had been thorough. Hammer had enjoyed his work. Tosher could tell. He had broken his body, his spirit, his mind. Systematically, piece by piece. Until he was no longer a man.

Until he was less than nothing.

'He's back.' Hammer's voice.

Mephisto came over. Looked at him. 'Well, Tosher,' he said. 'Ready to talk now?'

Tosher nodded slowly, vision behind the mask blurred by tears, snot and spit.

'Good.'

Mephisto removed the mask. Tosher gasped gratefully at the air.

'Question one,' said Mephisto. 'Who did you talk to?'

'Name's . . . Donovan . . .' Tosher spoke in slow, fractured gasps. '. . . Joe . . . Donovan . . . reporter . . . *Herald* . . .'

'Very good. Next question. What did you tell him?'

'Everything . . .'

'Everything?'

'Everything . . . I . . . knew . . .'

Tosher looked at Faustus. The blazered man was ashen-faced, shaking, near collapse. He couldn't look at Tosher, turned away from him.

'And how much do you know?'

Tosher told him.

'And what is Joe Donovan going to do with this information you gave him?'

Tosher tried to laugh. It came out as a guttural, painful bark. 'Use it against you . . .'

Mephisto smiled. 'I doubt that.' He motioned to Hammer, who stepped forward, replaced the mask on Tosher's face. Tosher made no attempt to stop him.

'Very good, Tosher,' said Mephisto. 'Very good. See, you can do it if you try. Now, that's everything we wanted to know. We're finished with you now. One last question – are you going to talk to this Joe Donovan? Or anyone else?'

Tosher shook his head, let out a groan that could have been a 'no'.

Mephisto smiled. 'Good man. I believe you. But you know what it's like – a few months down the line you start feeling brave again, think, That wasn't so bad; I'll make them pay for that. We can't have that, can we?'

Tosher let out a groan that could have been 'I won't'.

'Risky, though. Not a chance I'm willing to take.' He began pacing again, appearing to think about it. He stopped, turned. 'I'm going to let you go. Show mercy. But I'm going to make sure you don't talk to anyone.'

Something in his tone stopped Tosher from feeling relief.

Mephisto circled Tosher, his soles and heels like whipcracks on the cement floor.

'Know much about history, do you, Tosher?' asked Mephisto. 'Military history, I mean? Recent stuff?'

Tosher said nothing. Heard only his desperate, broken breathing.

Mephisto sighed, shook his head. Kept walking.

'Course not,' he said. 'Russia. Early 1990s. The old Soviet Union breaking up. The death of socialism, the triumph of capitalism. All the old Eastern Bloc countries breaking up, the comrades wanting McDonald's and Levi's. Boris the Bear having trouble holding on to the territories. So what did he do? In his vodka-soaked state? Sent the tanks in. Everywhere.'

He stopped pacing, faced Tosher.

'And the most uppity of them all was Chechnya.'

Mephisto laughed, resumed his walk.

'Don't know why I'm telling you all this. Wasted on scum like you. Anyway, what the Red Army used to do—' He turned to Tosher, looked him directly in the eye '—the Red Army, the most powerful fucking fighting force in the world, the army nobody fucked with—' He resumed his walk. '—well, they got pissed off with these Chechen rebels. So they fought dirty. They would capture them, make them talk. Then make sure they could never talk again.'

He stopped. Bent down, face to face.

'Know how they did that? Mustard gas. They would get a gas mask like the one you're wearing, strap a can of mustard gas to it and invite their prisoner to breathe in. After that . . .' He shrugged. 'You don't feel much like talking. Well, you can't, really.'

Hammer moved forward on command, began attaching a canister to the front of Tosher's mask.

Tosher began to cry.

Mephisto slapped him on the side of the head. 'Be a man,' he said. 'This isn't mustard gas. We couldn't get any. So we're using a compound supplied by Dr Faustus over there. It'll do the job just as well.'

Hammer finished his work, opened the valve on the can, stepped back.

Tosher tried to stop sobbing, tried to hold his breath.

'You've got to breathe sometime,' said Mephisto. 'Sooner you start, the sooner you'll get it over with.'

The gas was clouding Tosher's face; it felt like acid burning away at his skin, his eyes, peeling and bubbling.

'You bastard . . .' he sobbed, 'you sick bastard . . .'

His last words. And Mephisto couldn't hear them.

Tosher breathed.

PART ONE
THE SECRET KINGDOM

1

Jamal ran. Round Argyle Square, along St Chad's Street, down Belgrove Street. He stopped, shoulders hefting, body gasping for air, and looked quickly behind him. He made out people, crowds swirling and shifting in the cold, darkening late-autumn afternoon. Eyes darted over them, picked out, zoomed in like speed-binoculars, scanned, pinpointed; homeward-bound office workers, misplaced tourists, a smattering of students, foetally bagged beggars dotted in doorways, hustlers, pimps, dealers, whores. Just the usual. The ebb and flow around King's Cross, the human flotsam and jetsam.

But not him. He didn't see him.

Jamal stood, bent over, hands on thighs, grasping the respite. He breathed deep, chest burning from exertion, legs shaking from running. He checked the street again.

And there he was, barrelling around the corner, knocking pedestrians out of his path as if they were plywood and paper, pounding down the pavement, eyes burning with anger, face contorted by hatred.

Jamal turned and, still clutching his shining prize, ran.

Towards Euston Road. The 24/7 permanent building site. Construction dust competed with exhaust fumes, created a post-millennial London fog complete with post-industrial soundtrack. Traffic blared and raced, cars darting sleekly, lorries emitting crunching, heavy metal bounces over potholes, buses gliding like stately battleships, taxis creating new lanes, reimagining the Highway Code.

Jamal stared at the traffic, halted at the pavement's edge. A glance behind: the figure was still gaining. Jamal took one deep breath, two. Then ran into the road.

Horns honked, vehicles swerved. He slapped the bonnet of an Astra, salmon-jumping to avoid having his feet crushed, hurting his hand as he did so: he caused a bus to abruptly halt with an angry hiss of air brakes and a hail of abuse from the driver. But he wouldn't let go of his silver treasure.

He jumped, dodged, ran. A computer game character come to life. He reached the other side sweating and coughing. His pursuer wouldn't have followed him. Couldn't have. No way. He was safe. He looked back at the opposite side of the road, ready to shout a triumphant insult and disappear.

The taunt died on his lips. His pursuer was striding through the traffic in an unwavering line, causing vehicles to brake and swerve, ignoring them like they weren't there, like he was still on the pavement.

'Oh fuck,' said Jamal and ran.

He jostled and dodged, the pavement heavy with weary commuters pouring into King's Cross, Euston and St Pancras, filling up underground and overground, waiting to be deposited back in suburbia. The citizen world was an alien one for Jamal, always had been. One he didn't understand, couldn't relate to. And now here he was, hoping to blend in among them. Wrap that world around him like a child in a blanket.

No chance. He knew his pursuer was as much a citizen as he was. Knew both of them would stand out in a crowd. The only way the crowd might save him, he thought, was if the man chasing him was too afraid of doing anything bad when there were people watching.

He took another look around. The man was barging through the throng of travellers as if they didn't exist. Pile-driving his way towards his prey, zeroing in on Jamal like a heat-seeking missile.

Jamal sped, dodged, weaved. He feigned joining the crowds heading underground, peeled off left at the final minute. Ran towards the entrance of King's Cross mainline station, through the doors. He sprinted across the concourse, bobbing and ducking around swift-moving commuters and slower-moving, bag-heavy, board-studying long-distance travellers, feet slapping and slipping on the polished floor. Up ahead, a long-distance train had pulled in to a platform, was disgorging its passengers. On the shared platform next to it, another mainline train was taking on passengers. Jamal ran at the crowd, hoping the hither-thither flux of bodies would conceal him.

He danced up the platform, hid behind pillars, crouched aside weary luggage-laden trolley pushers. He looked around for the station police, who, whenever he didn't want them, were always there to move him on, threaten him with arrest or just verbally abuse him. He thought fast, prioritized, traded off lesser evils in his mind, half developed a desperate idea of turning himself in to them for protection, even causing a disturbance to get arrested, just to get away from his pursuer. He scanned and scoped: no uniforms to be seen. Typical. Mentally scratch that one.

Up the platform, bobbing and weaving, ducking and diving. A zigzagging, moving target. He didn't dare look around.

He reached the engine of the train, ran out of crowd to hide in.

'Shit,' he said aloud, gasping for breath.

He looked down the platform. He could make out a disturbance by the barrier. He knew who that would be. Slight hope rose within him. He had the advantage. He looked around again, assessed his options. His heart pumped extra adrenalin around his system. He looked around again. And jumped from the platform.

Being careful not to step on the rails in case they were electrified – because a kid in his children's home had died doing that on the underground – he moved gingerly but quickly, crunching on the soot-blackened stones, across to the train on the next platform. He gripped the concrete edge and pulled himself on to it.

He stood up, ignoring the dirt on his hands and clothes, and looked down the length of the train. Doors were closing, whistles preparing to be blown. Thinking fast, he ran to one of the open doors and jumped inside the train. There came a loud thump as the door was slammed shut behind him.

Jamal stood in the corridor, breathing heavily, body shaking, the sliding inner door opening and closing as he came within the ambit of its sensor. A voice over the speakers welcomed him aboard. Told him what time he was due to arrive at wherever he was going. Thanked him for travelling and advised anyone not wishing to travel to leave. Jamal didn't listen. Heard only his own rasping breathing. Another whistle. The train began to move. Jamal moved over to the right, looked out of the window. On the next platform along he could see his pursuer standing there, looking around. Anger emanated from him, the waves penetrating the train's hull, reaching Jamal. He pulled his face away in case he was spotted, then slowly inched round for another look. The man wasn't looking in his direction.

The train pulled out of the station.

Jamal had done it. He had escaped.

He looked down the length of the train. Passengers were storing luggage, finding seats, excusing themselves to others. Jamal was going to join them. But first he had to go to the toilet.

He wanted to throw up.

* * *

Jamal sat in his seat and stared out of the window. Concrete and brick had given way to countryside, which gave way to darkness, which left Jamal staring at himself. He looked away. Opposite him was a suited businessman, hair disappearing in exchange for an expanding stomach. He busied himself with papers and reports, made ostentatious, self-aggrandizing calls on his mobile, sat with the air of a man who believed himself to be a hero. Occasionally he would cast glances at Jamal, glances that began slyly then became knowing, finally working their way towards anticipatory. Jamal understood what they signified. He made a living from interpreting such looks.

He decided to ignore the suit, cast his mind back instead over the last few hours.

Nothing had given him an indication of what was to come.

He had been working his usual corner, the top of Crestfield Street, and just gearing up for his busiest time, rush hour. He was feeling fine about himself: he'd scored a couple of rocks in Burger King an hour previously, heard of an upcoming rave later that night and had managed to keep his Nikes box white for another day longer.

He saw his first punter. Middleaged, well dressed and so flushed he seemed to be having a heart attack. He moved slowly, nervously edging forward. Building up courage with each furtive footstep. A new one, not one of the regulars. Jamal knew how to handle him: carefully, like a bird he wanted to catch then eat. Gain its trust then pounce.

Jamal smiled at the man, winked. The man sweated even more. Up close, his face was cratered and pockmarked, his skin unlovable and unkissable. Jamal switched his body language to open, relaxed. Encouraged the man to make the first move.

'Are you . . .' The soon-to-be-punter gagged, cleared his throat.

Jamal waited.

'Are you working?'

Jamal was. He explained the rules – cash upfront and the punter pays for the room – and the price list. The red man nodded quickly, desperately, agreeing to anything.

Jamal walked to the Dolce Vita Hotel on Birkenhead Street, the man following eagerly behind. Once inside, he gave the nod to the fat old Greek sitting behind the glass mesh partition in what he claimed was the foyer but was in actuality a rattily carpeted, foul-smelling corridor decorated with brown patches on the walls and ceiling.

The red man paid for the room with trembling fingers, then followed Jamal up to the first floor. Once inside, Jamal asked for the money. The man handed it over. Jamal pocketed it, began unbuttoning his jeans and the punter asked the question Jamal had been waiting for:

'Huh – how old are you?'

The first few times he had heard that he had answered with the truth. But it wasn't what they had always wanted to hear. So he had started to ask them how old they thought he was. Now, he was so used to it he reckoned he could tell how old each punter wanted him to be.

'Twelve,' he said, losing two and a half years from his real age.

It seemed to be the right answer. The punter smiled, eyes glazed with a cloudy dreaminess, and began to hurriedly strip.

Later, business concluded, Jamal was washing himself off in the sink when he heard whispered footsteps behind him. He turned sharply. The red man, his contrasting fat, white little body now thankfully covered by clothes, was standing right behind him.

'Jesus, you gave me a shock,' said Jamal.

'Sorry.' The man kept his eyes fixed on Jamal's chest and shoulders. 'You're beautiful . . .'

'Yeah,' said Jamal, turning away, 'I am.'

The punter was still there. 'Look, can I . . . can I see you again?'

Jamal smiled. Either one extreme or the other. 'Sure,' he said, back still turned. 'I'm here every day. Same spot. Same time.'

'No,' stammered the punter, 'I meant . . . can I . . . see you . . .'

He reached out a hand to touch Jamal's cheek. Jamal saw it in the mirror, swatted it away, unable to hide the look of distaste on his face.

'Don't touch me, man,' he said.

The punter recoiled as if he had been slapped.

Jamal hated it when they did that. When they tried to be close. He accepted the fact that they had to touch him when he was working, but even then he kept it down to a minimum. He hated to be touched by anyone. Especially them. He wished he had so much money he never had to be touched by one of them again.

'Keep it business,' said Jamal, hiding what he really wanted to say. 'Now go, before they charge you another hour for the room.'

The punter hurriedly left.

Jamal looked in the mirror, checked that his hair looked good. It did.

He had been making a living from the street for over a year. He had grown up in a succession of care homes and foster homes ever since his mother had walked with him into Social Services in Tottenham one day when he was six and walked out without him.

He had never known his father but knew he was responsible for the black mix in his skin. He imagined his father an African chieftain, passing his noble warrior blood down along with his skin colour. He had told this to his mother, and she had never contradicted him on it. His mother had never mentioned his father to him at all.

One more pat of his hair, one more admiring glance at his Avirex leather, one last check to see there were no remnants of that tearful, snot-nosed scared little six-year-old looking back at him and he was ready to go.

He pulled the door closed behind him and began to move down the hall towards the stairs. As he went he tried the door handles of the other rooms. He always did. Occasionally he had been lucky; found a wallet stuffed with cash and cards or a watch and some jewellery left on a chest of drawers within easy reach and the owner too busy to notice. If anyone saw him or called him on it, he would front it, tell them he had booked the room and could they get a move on?

Usually it yielded nothing and had just become a habit.

But not today.

Pushing down on the handle of room seven, he found it open.

Jamal stopped walking, looked around. No one in the hall. He listened. No noise coming from the room. Cocky teenage adrenalin surged through his body. He smiled to himself, slowly pushed open the door.

And there, within easy reach on the chest of drawers, was a minidisc plus headphones.

Solid gold, thought Jamal.

He reached for it, rapidly calculating how many hits and highs he could get from it once he had fenced it on, when the door swung open further. And Jamal stopped, his arm extended in midair.

It must have been only a few seconds that he stood there for, but it felt like hours. Eventually he recovered from the shock, turned and, minidisc in hand, left the room.

And ran.

* * *

'Tickets, please.'

Jamal looked up, startled out of his reverie. A uniformed inspector entered the carriage carrying a ticket machine over his shoulder.

'Anyone not bearing a valid ticket will be asked to pay a full-price standard single.'

He spoke the words like a weary mantra.

Jamal looked up. Other travellers were delving into their pockets, their luggage, bringing out various-sized tickets, holding them aloft. He was angry with himself for not considering this eventuality. Usually he would hide or run or be ready to mouth off. But this time his mind was elsewhere.

He thrust his hand into his jeans pocket, brought out a mess of crumpled bills. He plundered his other pockets, began stacking a rough mountain of notes and coins on the table before him. His day's earnings, minus the burger, coke and rocks he'd bought in Burger King.

The inspector approached him. An apparition in purple and blue nylon. He looked down at Jamal, held out an expectant, yet not too optimistic, hand.

'Ticketplease.' Said as all one word.

'Where's this train goin'?'

'Newcastle.'

Meant nothing to Jamal. Was that in Scotland? Scotland was good. Miles from London. Safe. Jamal nodded.

'Yeah, yeah. There.'

The ticket inspector, whose gold plastic badge proclaimed his name as Garry and his job title as Customer Service Manager, sighed.

'I'm sorry, but I'm goin' to have to charge you full fare, sir.'

Jamal shrugged.

Garry didn't look sorry. He began to punch buttons on his machine.

'Eighty-eight pounds, please.'

'Child,' said Jamal.

Garry gave a patronizing smile. Course you are. 'Eighty-eight pounds.'

'Stitchin' me up? Yeah? Well, I—'

'Look, sir,' said Garry, cutting him off and straining civility through his teeth, 'take it up with customer—'

'Perhaps I could take care of the young man's ticket?'

They both stopped arguing, looked for the source of the voice. The businessman sitting opposite Jamal was smiling, opening his wallet.

'I don't think—'

'No problem.' Another suited smile.

Garry sighed. He knew what was going on, decided not to get involved. 'How far's he going?'

The suit looked at Jamal, smiled. 'All the way.'

Garry tiredly punched numbers, swiped the suit's card. Presented the ticket. Business transacted, he walked on.

'Ticketsplease . . .'

Jamal looked at the businessman, at the ticket lying on the table between them. He couldn't bring himself to thank him so he nodded. He began counting out notes, ready to hand them over.

'That's all right,' said the suit. He leaned forward and gave a lascivious, dominant smile. 'We'll come to some arrangement.'

Jamal emptied his eyes, his face, of emotion. Stared across the table.

'Oh come on,' said the suit. 'I got your number as soon as you sat next to me. I should know that look by now.' His voice dropped. 'I'm in Newcastle on business for a few days. Got a hotel room. Want to share it with me?'

Jamal stared.

'Hit a couple of clubs, maybe a restaurant . . .' He

shrugged. Then snaked a hand across the table, picked up Jamal's ticket.

'Mine, I think,' he said.

Jamal stared. He weighed his options. Eventually he sighed.

'OK.'

The man smiled. 'That's better. Now, shall I go to the buffet car? Get something to eat and drink? It looks like a long time since you've had something hot in your mouth.'

The man began to giggle, high pitched and obnoxious.

Christ, thought Jamal; one of them days.

Left alone while Bruce, which the suit had claimed as his name, ventured to the buffet car, Jamal glanced around, sat-isfied himself no one was watching him, took out the minidisc and looked at it.

He shuddered. Just looking at it brought back that hotel room. He ran a finger along the edge. It was chipped, worn, battered and scratched. Well-used looking. Less cash fenced. Shit.

He unwrapped the coiled wires, inserted the earpieces. And switched it on.

It wasn't what he had been expecting.

Bruce came back from the buffet car, apologizing about the delay, blaming the queue, showing Jamal what he had for him. But by then Jamal didn't hear him. Jamal didn't move.

Just sat there. Listening.

Jamal couldn't sleep.

Bruce's farting and snoring didn't help, nor did the ster-ile, unfamiliar hotel room with its blond-wood furniture, pristine white *en suite* and hard, unyielding bed. The drugs didn't help either. But it was more than that.

The minidisc.

Bruce had been as good as his word but extracted his money's worth; Jamal usually charged a lot more for a stay over but there had been some compensations. The restaurant, the drinks, the club. Not his music and too many gays, but he'd managed to score some decent coke and a couple of Es. Best of all, the shower and the fluffy, towelling robes. Jamal felt cleaner than he had in a long time, despite Bruce's best efforts to the contrary. Jamal had even given himself up willingly in return. But his mind hadn't been there. Even further away than usual.

The minidisc. It was still playing in his head.

Boring at first. No good tunes. No tunes at all, in fact. So boring he was ready to turn it off, stuff it back into his jacket. But something about it kept him listening. And listening. He struggled to keep up, rewinding and replaying sections until he was sure he understood them, but was eventually rewarded.

Bruce had thought he was just listening to music. Jamal encouraged him to think that.

By the end of the disc, Jamal had a strong suspicion that he knew why someone had tried to kill him. He was beginning to realize just how important the disc was. He remembered a thought he had had earlier that afternoon, another lifetime away:

He wished he had so much money he never had to be touched by one of them again.

This could be it. He just had to think what to do with it. How to make it work for him.

Jamal couldn't sleep.

By morning he had a plan.

'And this is Stephanie. She's six. And Jack, four.' Bruce smiled. 'Right little tearaway.'

Jamal hated it when they did that. Showed him pictures

of their kids. What was he supposed to say? They're nice, d'you fuck them too?

'And that's Susan.'

Then the wife picture. Looking a beat too long, the name always said with such conflicting emotions. Jamal sometimes counted, tried to separate them. Guilt was there, obviously. Rage, hatred, loathing, the last two usually prefixed by 'self', veneration, adoration. Betrayal. Take your pick.

Jamal would just look at them, nod, pass them back without really seeing them. Watch the punter stare at them for longer than he needed to then stuff them viciously back into his pocket, drop his eyes from Jamal. That always left Jamal with a sour feeling of retribution.

Jamal had wanted breakfast, but Bruce had told him he couldn't, they couldn't risk being seen together, what if a colleague from Bruce's company should be there?

'But I'll see you later, won't I?' Bruce had smiled. 'You won't be able to get back to London without me.'

Jamal had emptily promised to meet Bruce later, arranged a time and place, left the hotel and walked.

Newcastle was cold. Like edge-of-the-Arctic cold. And really unfamiliar. It had the same shop names, but everything else was different. And they talked funny. Not like English. He didn't know where to go. He pulled his Avirex round him, wished for something warmer. He smiled to himself. When his plan paid off, he would be in luxury for the rest of his life.

He found a phone box, called a 118 number, punched the given number into his mobile's memory. Then a decision to make. Payphone or mobile. Mobile, he decided. Harder to trace than a landline, he thought.

He ducked into a doorway, made his call. It was answered by a female voice.

'I want to speak to Joe Donovan,' he said to the voice.

'An' don't give me none a that "he ain't here" shit, right, 'cos this is a matter of life an' death am' talkin' about, y'get me?'

It took a while, but they got him.

2

Joe Donovan picked up the revolver from the table, felt the heft of it in his left hand, weighed his options. His chest rose and fell, his breath shallow and sharp. He slid a bullet into one of the six chambers. Clicked the barrel shut, spun it, replaced it on the table. He stared at it, his world reduced to that one piece of lethal metal. He breathed heavily – once, twice – then swallowed hard and, eyes screwed tight shut, picked the gun up, pointed it at his temple, pulled the trigger.

'Should be just over this ridge.'

'Well, let's hope so. That's what you said about the last two.'

Francis Sharkey swallowed his reply, looked again at the map in his lap. The bumps and swerves were giving him motion sickness. He looked up again, breathed deep.

'All these blasted B-roads look alike,' he said. 'Why couldn't he live somewhere nearer? Somewhere he could easily be found?'

Maria Bennett took her eyes off the road, glanced at him.

'I think you've just answered your own question.'

Sharkey tutted, gave up looking at his map. 'So what's this place we're looking for?'

'Ross Bank Sands. Very popular with naturists, apparently.'

Sharkey looked at the scenery. Rain was hitting the car so hard it felt like they were in the middle of a meteorite shower. The windscreen and windows seemed to have been turned into liquid, melting things. The Northumberland countryside rendered monochromatically drab, distant and barren.

'Too bloody cold for that. For God's sake,' Sharkey mumbled, sighing. 'This place is about as desolate as Norway in winter.'

'I don't think they come here in winter,' replied Maria Bennett. 'And we're not seeing it at its best. Apparently it's beautiful in the summer. A real unspoiled paradise. The Secret Kingdom, the tourist board calls it.'

Sharkey stared out of the window, tried to imagine.

'Secret? Only secret here is that they all sleep with their cousins,' he said miserably. 'Or is that Wales? Probably both.'

Maria Bennett concentrated on the road ahead.

They had travelled up from London the previous night, stopping in a hotel in Newcastle before picking up their hire car and heading into Northumberland.

'So what was he like, then,' Francis Sharkey had said at King's Cross, settling back into his first-class seat, with a gin and tonic and complimentary *Daily Telegraph* before him, 'this Joe Donovan?'

Maria Bennett sat opposite him, duplicate gin and tonic on the way to her lips.

'Best of the best,' she said, taking a mouthful and replacing her glass. 'Cliché, I know, but he was.'

She named a prominent Conservative politician who had been jailed on perjury and corruption charges.

'Remember him? Joe was on that team. His first assignment.'

Sharkey, despite himself, looked impressed.

'And there were more. Some high profile. One that he did on care homes even led to a change in the law. Had the makings of a great investigative journalist.'

'And then?'

Maria swirled her drink, watched liquid flow over ice, wondered why ice seemed to disappear faster in drinks on trains than in bars.

'I'm sure you heard,' she said. 'All that business about his son. Went off the rails, never got back on.'

'And this was . . .?'

'About—' She tipped her head back, frowned '—two years ago. About now, I think. Just coming up to Christmas. Yes, that would make him thirty-five. Same age as me.'

Sharkey smiled. 'Well remembered.'

'I'd just moved from dep. to editor. Not the kind of thing you're likely to forget. One of your best, going from reporting the news to being the news.'

'If he was that good, didn't you try to coax him back?'

'I did but . . . he wasn't interested. He wouldn't return my calls. And then he moved to Northumberland. Where he couldn't be contacted. I got the message.'

Sharkey gave a supercilious smile. 'Seems like someone was interested, though.'

Maria felt her face flushing from more than the alcohol. 'It wasn't like that,' she said, her voice trembling on the verge of anger and indignation. 'Joe was a very happily married man. Very happily married. What happened was a terrible thing. For everyone concerned.'

Sharkey shrugged and sat back. 'Whatever you say.' He took a sip of his drink.

Maria watched him smacking his lips, smugly surveying the carriage as if the passengers, the staff, the world revolved around him. Exuding the arrogance of the always right. He was middle-aged and greying, wearing his receding hairline, reddened cheeks and nose and expanding waistline as medals given for success and affluence. Voice as rich, dark and polished as old mahogany furniture. She was generally

mistrustful of lawyers and solicitors, and he seemed one of
the worst examples. But she had to work with him. If she
allowed her dislike of colleagues to contaminate her working
relationships, she would never have reached as far as she had
as young as she had. And that was what mattered most to
her.

The windscreen wipers were working furiously and
futilely. Sharkey, Maria noted, still held his arrogant bearing,
even wearing a Barbour, casual clothes and what he had
described as stout boots. He still managed to look and act as
if rain would bounce off him.

He looked across at her and smiled. She remembered
that same smile from the previous evening. The one that had
accompanied his advances at dinner. The one that had provoked the polite, yet firm, rebuttal. At first he had acted as if
he believed her to be joking, playing the hard-to-get
coquette. But the message had eventually penetrated. He
had shrugged, walked her gallantly to her hotel door then
returned to the bar. She didn't know what he had done for
the rest of the night. She hadn't asked; he hadn't told.

A patch of darker grey appeared through the windscreen.
'I think that's it,' she said.

'Let's hope so,' said Sharkey, 'because if it isn't I hope
whichever poor inbred peasant that lives there knows how to
make a decent cup of tea.'

Joe Donovan opened his eyes.

A great drumming and crashing sound: the rain, he
thought, lashing down on his cottage. He sighed, waited.
The crashing and drumming continued. With a groan he
realized it was inside his head. And it was worse.

The room blurred and spun, waxed and waned and
throbbed into flawed focus. He waited for it to settle, then
attempted to pull himself upright. No good. As soon as he

moved it began to spin again. He flopped back, panting, eyes scanning the room, looking for clues to fill in the black spots in his memory.

The upturned tea chest coffee table before him bore an empty bottle of Black Bush, the old revolver. He groaned, closed his eyes. Tried to piece together the fragments of memory. Build a chronology from blackout.

He remembered:

The noise in his head had started again, building, trying desperately to find respite, release. Like a JCB revving up, tearing up the tarmac with its fierce-toothed digger. He couldn't get rid of it, couldn't drive it out.

Then the images playing over and over again. David there, then gone. There, then gone. Hunting everywhere, trying to think of something – anything – that could bring him back. Something overlooked, a rediscovered memory, a previously unthought-of clue. Nothing. Just David gone and the JCB tearing up the tarmac. Too much.

Then the whisky became involved. From Black Bush to blackout. Sometimes it was enough. Most times. But every time was taking longer, requiring more booze to make the journey successful. This time it didn't work.

And then the revolver had become involved. He had found it hidden under the floorboards, left there by the pre-vious owner. It was old, but it still worked.

The pain building up so he couldn't think, see or hear . . .

He had taken it out, looked at it.

David there, then gone. There, then gone.

He had chambered a single bullet from an equally ancient box of ammo, spun . . .

The JCB tearing the insides of his head apart . . .

And fired.

Click. An empty chamber.

He had replaced the gun on the table, sat back and sighed

heavily. He shook from head to foot, felt hot sweat prick his body, breathed short, stabbing breaths. Then noticed.

The JCB had stopped. Silence in his head.

There, then gone.

He had lain down on the sofa then, knowing nothing until he had woken moments ago.

Donovan took a deep breath, attempted again to pull himself to a sitting position. With a groan he succeeded. He sat there, letting what he had done the night before sink in.

He had tried to kill himself. And failed. He looked at his hands. They were shaking from more than the whisky in his system. His actions terrified him but, more than that, thrilled him. He had been given a reprieve. He had cheated death. He remembered how he had felt before slipping away into sleep: at peace with himself. Satisfied.

He sighed, shook his head. He knew it wouldn't last.

He swung his feet to the floor and yawned. Tired, and he had just woken up. His head, stomach lurched then stabilized. He wasn't going to throw up. He thought of what he could do with the day. Thought of making a cup of tea.

Then came a knock at the door.

Donovan looked quickly around and felt a sudden stabbing pain in his head as if his brain were sloshing around in a bucket.

Must be a mistake, he thought. Ignore it.

Another knock, more insistent.

Donovan stared at the door, trying to see through it.

Another knock, this time accompanied by a voice calling his name.

No mistake. Someone wanted him.

His heart began to quicken. Perhaps it was news. Even after all this time he still had hope.

He slowly peeled himself off the sofa, made his way through the tiny towers of building materials to the front door and opened it. The noise of the wind and rain increased. Cold northern air blew into the cottage. Donovan felt it penetrate his clothes, hit his skin like hard, dry ice.

Before him stood two figures, one vaguely female huddled beneath heavy, brightly coloured outdoor clothing, the other a tall, middle-aged man wearing a Barbour and a miserable expression. He looked as cold as he was wet, and he was very wet indeed.

'Joe?' said the woman.

She tilted her head up. It took a few seconds, but Donovan recognized her.

'Maria . . .?'

He didn't know what else to say. He was stunned to see here there.

'Can we come in, please?' Maria said. 'It's freezing out here and soaking.'

Donovan numbly stood aside to let them in. He closed the door behind them. They stood there dripping on to the floor, tentatively undoing and removing their outer layers. He was aware of them looking around his living room, making judgements on both it and him as they were doing so. He looked, too, seeing it through their eyes.

It looked like a building site during lunch break: tools downed and waiting for the workforce to return and resume work. Dust accreted on ladders, paint pots and tools told of a long, long lunch break. Walls a jigsaw of exposed brick and crumbling plasterwork, light bulbs hanging from frayed wires like dolls from toy gallows. A sofa, armchair, table and dining chairs all vied for space with bags of cement and sand, piles of bricks and wood standing on the stained and dusty floorboards. A TV stood on two upturned plastic fishmonger's crates.

He didn't ask them to make themselves at home.

Maria forced a smile.

'You've been decorating, Joe.'

'Made a start.' His voice sounded strange inside his own head, like a car undriven for years, the gears harsh, grinding, rusted over.

'This is Francis Sharkey,' said Maria, pointing at the other man. 'He's a . . . work colleague of mine.' The man smiled, in approximation of a hearty greeting, stuck out his hand to be shaken. Donovan looked at him, nodded.

Maria turned around, patted her arms about her body, blew into her cupped hands. Donovan looked at her face, blank then quizzical. Then he understood.

'I'll put the heating on.'

He crossed to an old Calor gas heater in the corner, struck a match, held it. Hissing whoomed to blue flame. He turned, faced them.

'So what d'you want?'

Maria crossed space to be beside him. As she did, she glanced at the makeshift coffee table, saw the empty bottle. The gun. She looked back at Donovan.

Donovan's features hardened. His eyes became hot as lava, cold as stone.

'Why are you here, Maria?'

She looked back at him, fearful now, as if she was treading on an area of unsafe land, expecting an abrupt descent to quicksand at any second.

'We're . . . we need your help, Joe.'

A gust of wind threw rain against the window with machine-gun force. Donovan ignored it, stared at her. Waited for her to continue.

'Gary Myers,' she said. 'Remember him?'

Donovan nodded.

'He's gone missing.'

Donovan shrugged. 'So?'

'He was working on a story. Meeting someone who had something important to tell him. We don't know what, but something big. Very hush-hush. You know what he was like, played it close to his chest until he had the whole thing put together. Then, another piece of crusading journalism for us. Usual thing. Our trademark.'

Donovan waited. Maria stood uncomfortably.

'D'you mind if I sit down?' she asked.

Donovan shrugged, pointed to the sofa. Maria sat.

'Um . . .'

They both turned towards the door. Sharkey smiled at them.

'Do you have a loo I might use?'

Donovan told him where it was. Sharkey picked his way noisily through the debris.

Donovan looked out of the window. Beyond the smudgy monochrome of the deserted beach, the cliffs and the roiling North Sea, he saw the ghost image of himself staring back through the glass. Hair long, greying and unkempt, matted almost to neo-dreads, straggly-bearded, eyes dark and sunken. Old jeans and a jumper. He glanced back at Maria, sitting there all primary-coloured polyesters, and saw himself from her perspective. He hadn't just let himself go; he had become abandoned.

He crossed to the sofa, sat down next to her.

'What were you saying?'

She recoiled from him slightly. Stale booze-breath and unwashed skin would do that, he thought, almost touched by shame.

'Gary Myers,' she said, recovering her composure, 'missing. Along with this person he went to meet.'

'So? What's that got to do with me?'

'Because yesterday we got a phone call.'

'We?'

'The *Herald*. Reception. A voice telling us it had some information about Gary. Telling us how much they wanted for it. Telling us who – and only who – they were prepared to deal with.'

'Who?'

'You.'

Donovan smiled, almost laughed.

'Me? Has this person been reading old papers or something?'

Maria smiled. 'I doubt it. Too young.'

'What d'you mean?'

'Sounded like a teenager. Black.'

Donovan smiled again. Muscles straining in unfamiliar ways.

'Black?' he said.

Maria reddened. 'You know what I mean,' she said. 'Urban.'

Donovan nodded. 'Urban. Right.'

'You know what I mean. Anyway, he said he was genuine. He had something to trade and he would deal only with you.'

'Why me?'

Maria sighed. 'We don't know. We've been over it again and again. We can only think that whatever he has to trade has something to do with you. God knows what.'

'Is this serious, d'you think? On the level? Have you called the police in?'

'We . . . thought about it. Decided not to. Not yet. There's no evidence that a crime's been committed. Perhaps he's just working on something that he can't show us yet. You know what it's like.'

Donovan nodded, eyes lost to something beyond the room.

'Used to,' he said.

Maria said nothing, uncomfortable once again.

They both lapsed into a strained silence. He smelled her

perfume. It was wonderful, the first time he had smelled anything like that for months. It smelled like a glimpse into another world, a past and a possible future. She tried not to stare at the gun on the table. Eventually she sighed.

'Oh Joe . . .'

She hadn't meant to say anything. She looked quickly away.

'What?' He tried to look her challengingly in the eye, but he couldn't hold her gaze.

'I don't know,' she said. She turned to face him properly. 'Look, Joe, I'll be honest. I'm worried about Gary. Even when he's been working on something we can't see, in the past he's usually let us know where he is. Or usually lets his wife know, and she's not heard from him.'

'Is she worried?'

'Not yet. But she's getting there. And I've got a bad feeling about this, Joe.'

'I'm sure you have. You wouldn't have come all this way otherwise.'

'I know. And I know I'm asking you a lot, Joe, but . . .' She reached out, placed her hand on his thigh.

He looked at her, opened his mouth to speak.

Then: a noise from the back of the house. Falling wood. A door opening. Donovan stood up swiftly.

'Bastard!'

He ran to the back of the house, hangover slipping away. The door was open. The door to the one completed room in the house. He had closed it firmly when he left it. He always did.

He opened it fully. And stopped dead.

Sharkey stood in the centre of the room, staring at the walls, his features circular with amazement. He turned at Donovan's entrance. The look of anger on Donovan's face spread to his. He became defensive.

'Now, look, I was just . . . I had no idea . . .'

'Get out.' Donovan's voice was low. Like the rumbling and creaking of an old dam before cracking and unleashing a devastating tidal wave. 'Get out. Now.'

'I . .'

Donovan was on him. He pushed Sharkey to the floor, hands around his throat, squeezing hard.

'Bastard!' Donovan spat the word into his face. 'You had no right to be in here. No right!'

Sharkey clawed at Donovan's hands. It was no use. They were like a constricting collar of rock. The lawyer's face began to turn a deep shade of purple. His eyes rolling to the back of his head.

'Bastard!'

Sharkey's hands began to slip away. Feebly grabbing air, then nothing. His body began to still.

'Joe! For God's sake, what are you doing?'

Donovan looked at the man as if seeing him for the first time. Realization began to dawn on him. He pulled his hands away and, eyes staring, slumped against the nearest wall breathing heavily.

He was aware of Maria crossing to the prone body, trying to re-engage it with consciousness. She seemed to be succeeding.

Donovan felt hot, nauseous. His body felt like lead and stone, his arms water. He watched Maria break off from her ministrations, look around the room. Saw it through her eyes. Filtered it through her consciousness.

Panting, he stared. From the other three walls the same face stared back at him. A boy. Dark-haired, eyes bright. Sometimes playful, sometimes serious. Sometimes with either parent or an older girl. Any permutation. Sometimes alone. From birth to six years old. Ageing only so far and no further.

All photos: originals, blow-ups, scans. Snipped and grafted, placed in images both real and imaginary, collages of memory and remembrance, wish fulfilment and fantasy.

And among the photos, newspaper clippings. Preserved and yellowing, headlines screaming, riffing on the same theme:

Boy Vanishes without Trace
No Clues in Hunt for Missing Six-Year-Old
Tragic David – Why Did No One See Him?

Against the far wall, folders and box files, all labelled:

Police Reports
Missing Persons Reports
Results of Public Appeals

Whole housing estates contained within: dead ends, cul-de-sacs, blind alleys, all round the houses, round in circles, no entries.

Then back to the photos. An evolutionary pictorial life. Birth and home. School. Family and friends. David on holiday in Dorset, in France. Collages of memory and remembrance. David in Disneyland, on colour-supplement white-sand paradise beaches. Collages of wish fulfilment and fantasy.

Donovan panted, looked at the other two people in the room.

Sharkey seemed to be coming round, Maria helping him up on to his elbows. His face was scarlet, his eyes fearful.

'Sorry . . .'

Maria looked around again.

'Sorry, Joe . . .'

Donovan said nothing, stared ahead as if he was invisible, as if he couldn't see or hear the other two.

'No.' Sharkey was struggling to speak. His voice sounded raspy, broken. 'My fault. I shouldn't . . . I'm sorry.'

Sharkey tried to get to his feet. Maria, with painful slowness, helped him.

'I didn't realize it was so . . .' Sharkey sighed. 'It must still be painful for you.'

Donovan nodded slowly and deliberately.

'Yeah,' he said. 'Now fuck off.'

Maria nodded. 'Suppose we asked for that. Sorry, Joe.'

Donovan stared straight ahead. 'Just leave me alone.' His voice sounded small in his own head. Fragile and easily broken.

The other two turned to leave, Sharkey supported by Maria. As he reached the door he stopped, turned.

'I don't suppose,' he said, voice as shaky as his body, 'that Maria told you the deal?'

Donovan looked up slightly. Maria looked at Sharkey, frowning.

'Deal?'

'Yes,' said Sharkey, the ghost of a lawyer's glint returning to his eye, 'the deal. You help us to find Gary Myers, negotiate on our behalf, and we help you find your son.'

Donovan pulled himself swiftly to his feet, ignoring the reeling in his head.

'David? You know where he is?'

'No,' said Sharkey, 'I didn't say that. I said that if you help us, we'll do what we can to help you.'

Maria shook her head in disbelief. This was never part of the plan. She opened her mouth to speak. Sharkey, gently but firmly, placed a restraining hand on her arm, looked her straight in the eye, shook his head in admonition. Donovan, eyes only for Sharkey, missed the subtle gesture.

'How?' said Donovan.

'By giving you access to as many resources as we can,

access to files, the means to follow up leads and sightings . . .
What do you say, Mr Donovan?'

Sharkey smiled, seemingly back to his previous self.

Maria turned away, shook her head.

'Hmm? Have we got a deal?'

Donovan stared at him, hope rising behind his eyes.
'Yeah,' he said, 'yeah. We've got a deal.'

Sharkey stuck out his hand. Donovan took it. They
shook.

Donovan suddenly noticed the rain had stopped.

3

Jamal woke up, pulled his jacket around him, suppressed a shiver.

He unfolded his legs, cramp- and cold-hardened, slowly uncurled his body from its foetal shape, stretched the aches and pains away and yawned.

He didn't feel awake. He didn't feel like he had slept.

The BMW's back seat had been hard and unyielding at the start of its life, but a decade and a half of over- and misuse had left it spewing stuffing and thrusting, rusted springs, rendering it unfit to take the weight of bodies. But the choice for Jamal had been either that or the street. And he had spent enough time on the street to know that he should take whatever was on offer.

The car sat wheel-less in a yard at the back of an empty house on a Gateshead housing estate. The estate was long and narrow, each house more abandoned than the last, this one, charred and blackened with windowpanes of nailed-on, damp-warped plywood, at the furthest end. The fag end.

Jamal swung his legs to the floor. No longer box-white trainers crunched on broken glass, plastic. He stretched again, shivered, held his arms about him. He wished he had some weed for a smoke, a couple of rocks to get him going, anything. He felt the bulge in his inside pocket. The minidisc that would make him rich. He smiled. Drew strength from that.

He got out of the car, looked around. The yard had become a repository for the estate's casual discards, an open tip legitimized by consensus. Old plastic milk bottles, cans, fast-food packaging, an old sofa, a rotting, rusting fridge. An urban consumer graveyard.

He had stayed there one night. He couldn't take another.

Joe Donovan. The name on the disc. There had been no Joe Donovan at the newspaper he had called. So he mentioned the other name on the disc: Gary Myers. That opened doors. Features, then editorial. Then someone called Maria, who said she was the editor. He told her the names he had heard. Wouldn't give his own. The voice in his headphones at the start of the disc:

'Look, Mr Myers—'

'Call me Gary. If that makes it any easier for you.'

A sigh, then:

'All right. Gary . . .'

Shuddered at the memory of the hotel room.

Life and death, he had told her. Life and fucking death.

But it didn't come for free.

She had paused, played for time, said she had to find Joe Donovan, for Jamal to leave his number, get back to him. He wouldn't; he would call her a day later. Two days, she had said.

Then hung up.

He had scoped the city then, looked for comparable places to what he was used to. Found an arcade on Clayton Street. He had felt safe in the arcade; like home from home even in a strange city. But he had attracted looks. The kids, the adults, were all, apart from the Asian owner and a couple of Asian kids, white. He was the only black kid. No outright hatred in the looks, just curiosity, some suspicion. Like they had never seen a black youth in real life and were waiting for him to do something. Like they had never heard a London accent except for *Eastenders*.

Normally he considered himself light skinned. But not here. Here, he felt blacker than black, darker than dark. He

44   *Martyn Waites*

wondered again just where this city was. And how far from London he had come.

Yet for all that he had felt something like kinship with some of the players. He had caught another youth's eye occasionally, and a connection had been made. A commonality shared beyond skin colour, a two-way mirror: I know you. I know your life. I know the ways you get money.

About the same age but tall, blond and white.

'You Jermaine Jenas?' the blond youth had said.

Jamal hadn't known what he was talking about. And that accent. Not Scottish because he'd heard that one on TV. But not English either. Jamal had let the shutter drop; face blank, eyes flat.

'His brother, anyway.'

The blond boy had smiled. And Jamal had got that feeling again. That shared commonality that went beyond skin colour. Hustler to hustler.

'You rap? MC?'

Jamal had shrugged. 'Bit. Back at my ends, you know?'

'I'm Si.'

'Jamal.'

And that was it. Jamal scored some rocks off Si, smoked them with him in a park. Got that buzz, almost told him what he was planning. Si had asked Jamal back to his, a house he shared with friends, to stay there. Jamal had refused, something about the boy he didn't like. Besides, he had Bruce. And his hotel room.

He stayed with Bruce long enough to be fed and fucked. Then awoke early and left, lifting the sleeping sicko's wallet, leaving him to explain its absence when he eventually woke up.

Then he had walked. Over the bridges, the sun rising as he went, breathing clouds in the cold. On the Redheugh he had rifled the wallet, found a hundred and twenty pounds in notes, several cards and the usual shit. The Blockbuster card.

The store cards. The grinning family. He pocketed the cash and cards, dumped the rest into the Tyne. Watched the opened wallet plummet, a dying black crow slowly beating its old, leathery wings for the last time, into the water where it was welcomed with a soft splash.

Over the bridge to Gateshead.

A ghost town, he thought, but had found a McDonald's. Same shit the world over, he had thought, drawing comfort from that. He had a breakfast blowout, eating as much as he could, draining Bruce's money like cheap lager pissed away up a back alley wall. Keeping some for later, to score some rocks and weed.

He walked on, past a newsagent, a billboard banner head-line proclaiming:

Fears Grow for Missing Scientist

Jamal sighed. At least the scientist had someone missing him.

He had sat down then, by the bus station, watched what was happening around him. The place coming to life; buses in and out, passengers on and off, up and down the escala-tors to the Metro, going somewhere, coming back, moving with purpose. Jamal sat, watched, waited. Like a kid at an aquarium, seeing a whole different world before him. He never admitted it aloud, but sometimes he wanted to be in that world, going to work or school, coming home to a proper family, having his dinner, watching TV, going out with his mates, going to bed. But he could no more join that world than he could live underwater with the fish in the aquarium. So he sat and watched. And waited.

He marked his life by waiting. For punters. Money. The next high. To get dark so he could go raving. Waiting. To make a fucking phone call.

Sometimes in that stillness, that inaction, an emptiness opened up within him. And he was more alone than anyone had ever been.

He felt that emptiness creeping up, so had stood up and walked away.

And that had been his day. On his aimless travels, he had found the car in the housing estate, guessed it would make a safe place to sleep for the night. To hide. Bruce or the police wouldn't be looking for him there.

He started walking again, looked back at the broken BMW. Probably the same age as him. Used, abused, discarded. He wouldn't allow that to happen to him.

Soon, he would be able to afford a new BMW all of his own.

He headed back towards the bridges, back to Newcastle. To the arcade, the boy with the rocks.

Counting off time until he could call again.

As he walked, he smiled.

Used, abused, discarded.

He felt the minidisc in his inside pocket, the cash in his jeans pocket.

He wouldn't allow that to happen to him.

An electronic scream, a synthesized death rattle, a fall and then the figure quickly faded from existence. Failed in his mission. The screen flashed up: GAME OVER. The credits rolled. Jamal waited.

'Fuck.' An angry sigh.

He hadn't even made the top ten. Low, low score.

'Fuck.'

He walked, not waiting for the screen to flash, exhort him to play again, show him optimistic highlights of what he could be doing. He walked the aisles of the Clayton Street arcade, his home from home, face lit by the ever-changing

nauseous rainbow strobe of the machines, ears bombarded
with electro/metal/hip-hop signature tunes.

He found a machine to stand at, fed it a pound coin, began
to play. Hoped the optimism of cyber genocide would give
him a self-esteem-raising high score. High enough to chart.

He shot, killed, saw blood fly, limbs hacked off. Distanced
himself from dismemberment, rode only for kicks and high
scores. Then he became aware of someone watching him.
He turned, saw the blond boy, Si, from the day before. He
lost concentration and was killed. The blond boy smiled.

'Back again, Jermaine Jenas?' Si laughed.

He turned to the boy exasperated, anger beginning to
bubble within. 'Who's this Jenas guy, anyway?' he asked.

The boy laughed. 'Plays for Newcastle. You look just like
him. Could be his brother.'

Jamal nodded. The anger subsided.

Silence.

'So,' Si said, 'what you doin' here again?'

Jamal remembered the cards in his pocket.

'Sellin',' he said.

'Sellin' what?'

'Cards. Credit. Debit.' Jamal shrugged like it was no big
deal. 'You know.'

'Let's see.'

Jamal looked around. 'Not here, man,' he said. 'Why?
You interested?'

'Not me,' said Si, 'but I know someone.'

Si began to walk to the exit. 'You comin'?'

Jamal shrugged. 'Yeah,' he said as casually as possible and
followed the blond boy out.

Behind him the abandoned machine flashed, offered him
another life.

'So where did you say you got these?'

Jamal looked at the speaker. His first reaction on seeing him: fuck me, you're a fat cunt. Any more an' you be wearin' a dress. But he had kept that to himself. Because of the eyes. They didn't go with the body. They belonged to someone whom you knew not to fuck with.

Si had told Jamal as much on the way there, over a Big Mac at McDonald's.

'You're from London, aren't you? So what you doin' up here?'

Jamal slurped up his cola, felt a pinprick of pain between his eyes from the cold.

'Needed a change,' he said.

'You runnin'?'

Jamal looked dead-eyed, shrugged.

'You need somewhere to stay?'

The same question as the day before. He thought of the BMW. Just for one night. Then it's five star all the way.

'Yeah.'

'The bloke we're goin' to see,' said Si between mouthfuls, 'Father Jack. I'll put in a word for you, yeah?'

Jamal shrugged again, nodded.

'Howay, then.'

Jamal followed Si to the Metro station. They emerged from the tunnel, went over a concrete bridge high above a dwindling, weed- and garbage-decorated river, a strange, curving block of flats to the right of them, like a huge, multi-coloured wall with windows.

'Where's this, then?'

'Byker,' said Si.

They got off the train, left the station. The area looked derelict, boarded-up shops, rubble-strewn emptiness. Scary pubs and barricaded pawnshops the only things thriving. People moved around, went about their lives oblivious. Air close, sky dark, a weight pressing down. The kind of place

Jamal had seen on the news, a reporter standing in front of saying, 'And life gets back to normal after the shelling.' When he thought about it, the kind of place he lived in in London.

'Come on,' said Si.

He led them to a house in an old terrace which on closer inspection seemed to be two houses knocked through. Or three. The pebbledash and whitewashed façade now blackened and greying with dirt and moss, the ornamental grille work over the windows colonized by rust, like lime eating into bone. The houses on either side were boarded up. Weeds flourished in the meagre front gardens. The street was truncated, book-ended by low-lying thirty-odd-year-old housing estates, opposite some 1980s-built orange-red flats, designed with the same amount of flair and imagination as a modern prison.

Si pushed open a rusting front gate and walked up the short path.

'This is it. Now, remember.' Si looked suddenly serious, as if part of the grey cloud hanging over Byker had detached itself and was now haunting him. 'You might think he's funny lookin' an' that, but don't laugh at him. He'll make you sorry if you do.'

Jamal frowned. 'OK . . .'

They entered.

It looked like the *Big Brother* house for under-eighteens. Brightly lit, adequately furnished, a real mess. A flat-screen TV took up one corner of the front room, wires haemorrhaging from it; Play Station and two operating consoles sat in front. Video cassettes and DVDs lay on the floor and other surfaces, well used, not well treated. Jamal clocked the titles: the *Matrix* series, *Dog Soldiers*, *Jeepers Creepers I* and *II*, *Ghost Ship*, *The Lord of the Rings* trilogy. Class, he thought. Takeaway pizza cartons, empty soft drink cans left lying around, seemingly invisible. From somewhere else in the house, some rapper was challenging another one to see who was the hardest.

Jamal nodded. 'Yeah,' he said. 'Nice. Like my yard back home.'

Another boy slumped on the sofa, pizza crumbs down the front of his T-shirt. Thin and pale with prominent, yellowing teeth. A horror film played on the screen before him, a nubile young woman being screamingly sliced up, but his sleep-lidded eyes let the images just slide over him. Si pointed at him.

'This is Andy.'

Jamal nodded; the boy barely registered him.

'You get owt for us, then?' the boy asked Si, his voice a listless drawl.

'Later,' Si said.

'Fuckin' better 'ave an' all, you tosser.' There wasn't enough energy behind the words to turn them into a threat.

Si's response was cut off by a booming voice from upstairs.

'Is that Si I hear down there?'

'Yeah,' Si replied, 'and I've got something for you.'

'Then come on up.'

Si smiled broadly, but the affected bonhomie didn't reach his eyes. Fear lingered there.

'That means you too,' said Si. 'Let's not keep him waiting.'

'Look, our boy's back.'

Click. Click.

The camera was as near to the window as possible without being seen. A young Asian man, good looking, in designer jeans and a tight-fitting black T-shirt, trained his telephoto on the terrace opposite. On two houses knocked through. Or three.

'And he's got someone with him.'

A woman, young, with long blonde hair tied back, joined him at the window. They watched.

'Been recruiting again,' she said. 'Any idea who, Amar?'

Amar, the Asian man, didn't take his eye from the lens. 'New playmate, from the looks of it. Black lad.'

Click. Click.

He smiled. 'Quite cute, if you like that kind of thing.'

The woman gave him a stern, unsmiling look.

Amar felt it more than saw it, turned to her. 'Which I don't. Oh come on, Peta, it was just a joke, for God's sake.'

Peta's expression didn't change. 'Just shut up and keep watching. And be thankful I don't shove this camera up your arse.'

Amar smiled. 'Promises, promises.'

She sighed, shook her head. Allowed herself a small smile. 'Just keep watching. We'll get a break soon.'

'I know, but in the meantime . . .'

The smile disappeared. 'We keep watching.'

Click. Click.

Jamal followed Si up the stairs and into the master bedroom. All white, it was dominated by a huge bed. At its foot a wall-mounted plasma TV, beneath it a DVD and VCR. On the screen the writhing, sighing and grunting of a porn film. And on the bed one of the biggest, fattest men Jamal had ever seen.

Wearing a black-silk dressing gown that looked big enough to parachute with, the man sprawled across the bed, taking up so much space that another person would have been prohibited from joining him. He had faint, wispy, blond hair and dark, sunken eyes, like pebbles at the bottom of an algae-infested, stagnant rockpool. They lit up with a murky, green glow when they alighted on Jamal. Somehow,

Jamal thought, the man would find room on the bed for another.

'And who have we here?'

The screen was paused. A pained expression, gender indiscriminate, filled it.

'Jamal.'

'Jamal . . .' He almost purred the name. 'Lovely. Very . . . exotic. Come closer.'

Jamal approached the bed. The fat man smiled. Like a clam opening its jaws, waiting to catch an unwary fish. 'Mmm. A little coffee boy. Tell me, little coffee boy, do you ever take cream?'

The fat man laughed, high and effeminate.

Creep, thought Jamal.

'Has Si told you who I am?'

'Father Jack?'

'Well done. Very bright, little coffee boy. Father Jack. Not an ecumenical appellation, purely an honorary one. I'm father to all the children here. I look after them, nurture them . . . even love them. Don't I, Si?'

'Yes, Father Jack,' said Si too quickly.

'Si tells me you've got something for me.'

Jamal handed over the cards. Father Jack looked at them.

'And can they be traced?'

Jamal shook his head. Told him he had robbed someone. Didn't mention the hotel room. Or the rest of the money. Father Jack smiled.

'Good work. I could pay you and let you go on your way, or . . .'

'I told Father Jack you needed somewhere to stay,' said Si.

'Good boy. Yes, Jamal, I take all the waifs and strays, the runaways, and I give them a loving home. Do you want a loving home, Jamal?'

Jamal shrugged. 'Yeah.'

Father Jack leaned forward. 'Are you sure?'

'Yeah, I'm sure.'

Father Jack smiled. 'Good. Then you're welcome to stay.' He looked at the cards. 'I won't charge you. For now.' The cards were put into a pocket in the dressing gown.

'Got everythin',' said Si. 'PS2, Sky, everythin'.'

Jamal nodded, face blank, eyes stone.

Father Jack was smiling at him again. 'You been sleeping rough? You need a shower?'

Jamal shrugged.

'Si . . .'

Si showed him where the shower was, gave him a towel. Jamal stripped, Si watching him all the time. Jamal ignored him, kept his jacket in view throughout the shower, made sure the bulge was still there.

He barely felt the water on his skin. He barely felt anything.

He could guess what the setup was. He knew there would be a reckoning, a payment.

He hoped to be gone before that.

He focused on the jacket, the bulge in the pocket. Kept everything else under lockdown. He X-rayed through: saw the disc, concentrated hard until it turned into money, turned into a one-way ticket.

An escape to where they could never touch him again.

'Fat boy's moving,' said Peta. Her turn at the window.

Click. Click.

'In a wheelbarrow?' Amar looked up from the book he was reading.

'Moving slowly, admittedly.' She checked her watch. 'Nearly five thirty. Off to meet one of his clients.'

Amar stopped reading, looked up. 'Bring them back to the house?'

'Must be. He hasn't got one of the kids with him.'

'Let's hope we have more luck with a positive I.D. for this one.'

Click. Click.

Peta sighed. Frustration starting to show. 'We need a break. We need some leverage.'

'I know. Don't worry, we'll get it.'

'He's in the car now.'

Click. Click.

Peta pulled a face. 'Jesus, look at the state of that. He's sweating already. Looks like a melting lard sculpture. Think he's diabetic?'

'What, you going to run over there, hide his insulin? I can think of better ways to get to him than that.'

'Arms can barely reach the wheel. He'd be better off in an open cart pulled by a horse.'

'A fucking big horse. Fucking Indian elephant couldn't manage that. Speaking of which . . .' Another look at the watch.

She sighed again. 'Off you go, then. At least it's bringing in some money.'

Amar smiled. 'Don't worry, sweetheart, I'll think of you.'

She wrinkled her nose in disgust. 'You'd better fucking not.'

'Take care. You'll be all right, yeah?'

'Go on. I'll see you later.'

The door closed quietly.

Click. Click.

'You comin' down, man? Elise's got bare draw.'

Andy, the slack-jawed boy. Jamal's room-mate.

'Nah, man, I'm cool. Be down in a bit.'

'Safe, man. Whatever.'

Andy left the room, ambled downstairs. Jamal waited

until there was no noise from the top floor, crossed the room on tiptoe, closed the door. He silently removed his mobile from his jacket pocket.

The rooms were quite small, two beds each. There were six in all living there, including him. Four boys, two girls. And Father Jack. Jack didn't live there all the time, Si had explained, but he liked to know what was going on. His room was often in use most of the day or night. Jack brought round clients. Special clients with special needs.

Jamal looked at his mobile. He had switched it off, conserving power. His charger was in London and he needed another. He had thought of stealing one, but he couldn't be sure he would get the right one. And when he put his clothes back on, he found that Si had taken his money. Jamal had confronted him, demanded it back. Si had given him fifty pounds.

'House rules,' he said.

'That's my fuckin' money, man.'

'Not any more, it ain't. House money. You want more, you earn it.'

Jamal had stared at him.

'An' that's a nice minidisc player, man.' Si smiling. Knowing he was the favourite, knowing there was nothing Jamal could do about it.

Jamal began to shake with rage.

'Touch that an' you're fuckin' dead. I swear it, man, I will fuckin' kill you.'

Si, rattled by Jamal's sudden ferocity, left him to it. Jamal checked the disc. Still there. Air left his body in a big sigh of relief.

He had to do something, put it somewhere safe.

He took off his leather jacket, turned it inside out. Then pulled at the stitching underneath the collar until he had worried a small hole in it. He took the disc from the player, dropped it through the hole, dropped it down the lining to the bottom, then slowly worked it until it sat directly in the middle, resting at the base of his spine as he wore it. It wasn't perfect, but it was the best he could do.

He looked at the mobile. Two days wasn't up. He knew that. But he didn't want to stay in Father Jack's house a minute longer than he had to.

He pressed the button, powered it up. Waited. Shit. Only one bar left. A new charger. He needed a new charger.

On the screen: unheard messages, unread texts.

The door opened. Si stood there.

'You comin' down? Meet the rest.'

'Yeah. In a minute.'

He clocked the phone. 'Who you phonin'?'

'Guy I met on the train,' said Jamal quickly. 'One at the hotel. But I'm down in charge. You got a charger?'

Si looked at the phone. 'Nokia, yeah? No problem.'

Jamal grunted his thanks. 'Might have to go out for a while.'

'No problem. But Jack'll want his cut. Don't hold out on him.'

Jamal shrugged. 'Yeah.'

Si went to get the charger.

Later, Jamal stood shivering.

Grey's Monument. Newcastle city centre. Somewhere anonymous where he could phone from.

He had charged the phone, looked at the messages. They were all from one person: Dean. His friend from road. His blood, his bredrin. They both lived in the same house in North London, sometimes serviced the same punters. Dean must be worried.

Jamal didn't know whether to contact him or not. He weighed it in his mind, decided, yeah, he would call. If

Dean had taken the trouble to call him, then he should return that. Safe.

He dialled the number he knew by heart, waited. It was answered.

'Hello, yellow.'

'Dean, man? It's me, Jamal.'

'Jamal? Where the fuck you been, man? I been like worried about you. Thought you was dead or somethin'.'

'Nah.' Jamal laughed, touched that Dean was so concerned. It was good to hear his friend's voice again. 'I'm not dead, man. Just had to lie low for a bit, you get me?'

'Safe, blood. Where are you, man?'

'Newcastle. Fuckin' miles away, man. Nearly Scotland.'

Jamal told him about Bruce, the stay at the hotel. Tried to make light of it, play it back as a holiday.

'An' listen,' said Jamal, smiling as he said it, 'I got me a big boy deal goin' down.'

'Yeah?'

'Yeah. For real cash, man. With a guy called Joe Donovan.'

'Yeah? Well, listen, blood.' Dean's voice dropped. 'I dunno what you done, man, but it must be fuckin' serious, innit.'

Jamal's stomach turned over. 'What d'you mean?'

Dean's voice dropped even further. 'This big scary fucker. Big bald guy. Muscles an' tats an' this fuckin' weird blue tooth. Like a jewel. Came lookin' for you.'

Jamal felt his legs begin to shake.

'For real?' he managed to say. 'Oh shit.'

'Yeah, man, oh shit is right. He said you took somethin' of his from the hotel. Whaled on the old Greek who runs it till he gave up our address. Then came round here lookin' for you. An' scarin' the shit outta peeps. This your deal?'

Jamal could feel the blood hammering in his chest; hear nothing but the pounding of it in his own ears.

'Jamal? You there?'

'Yeah, man, I'm here. Listen, man. I gotta go, yeah? If that fucker comes round again, you ain't heard from me, right? You don't know where I am, yeah?'

'Yeah, sure man, safe.'

Jamal exhaled a large breath. He wasn't aware he had been storing it.

'Safe. Look, man, I gotta go. Take care, yeah?'

'You too, man.'

Jamal broke the connection.

Shit, he thought. They were on to him. But Dean wouldn't give him up, he knew that. Dean was safe.

But . . .

That was one scary motherfucker. He could fuckin' make Dean give him up whether he wanted to or not . . .

Jamal felt pressure building inside him, pressed his hands to his temples.

'Fuck! Fuck! Fuck!'

Passers-by stopped to stare. He didn't care, was oblivious to them. He walked round aimlessly, trying to make a plan, find something to do. He had to phone the newspaper, get the deal going, get Donovan on the line now, get rid of that fucking disc. Be free.

That was it. He tried the number for the *Herald*. Explained who he was, who he wanted.

'I'm afraid Maria Bennett is not here at the moment. Can I take a message?'

He hung up.

Fuck, fuck.

He walked round the city, expecting to see a bald head and a blue tooth chasing him at any second.

He saw another billboard:

Missing Scientist: Police Suspect Foul Play

He began to get cold, so he grabbed a kebab, made his way back to Byker and the house. Safest place, he thought reluctantly.

'You were quick,' said Si as he entered. The music was deafening: Kelis' Milkshake, a boy and girl grinding to it on the front-room carpet. 'Where's the money?'

'Got none. Didn't show.'

Si shrugged. 'Father Jack's waitin' for you upstairs. Got someone wants to meet you.' Si smirking as he said it.

Jamal went upstairs, knocked on the bedroom door, waited to be invited in.

'Ah,' said Father Jack as he entered. 'This is the boy I was telling you about. The new boy. Come in, don't be shy. We're not.'

Jamal closed the door behind him, checked the disc was still in place. Turned. Father Jack and another man were staring hungrily at him.

The last thing Jamal wanted.

'Listen, man,' he said. 'You don't want this.'

'Don't we?' said Father Jack, a hint of anger behind his words.

'Nah, man, you don't.' Jamal thought quickly. 'Herpes, man. Bad, bad breakout. Believe me, you don' want that.'

Father Jack looked at him, deciding whether he was telling the truth or not. He turned away from him, waved his arm dismissively.

'Out,' he said, clearly disappointed. 'Next time.' The words held more threat than promise.

Jamal closed the door behind him. Stood on the landing, breathed a hugh sigh of relief.

Next time.

He hoped to be long gone by then.

He had to be.

4

The department store is crammed with people, a bobbing, ebbing sea of humanity, all shapes and sizes, fabrics and fleshtones, levelled beneath dynabrite lighting. Joe Donovan squints, shields his eyes and smiles. Amid the crowd, warm waves of contentment begin in the pit of his stomach, radiate throughout his whole body. This contentment is what he has always wanted. He has never expected to find it, never believed he would enjoy it so much. He looks down at his son, smiles. David smiles back. Warm, warm waves of contentment.

This is how he remembers it. How he chooses to remember it.

His mouth moves, the same words every time:

'Right. D'you know what you want, then?'

A simple question. Accorded almost unreal, legendary status by memory.

David's smile: the same smile every time.

'Ghost,' he says. His voice rings and echoes away down a time tunnel.

The perfume department, a hall of chrome and mirrors, sales assistants painted to perfection. Professionally warm smiles greet them. Donovan matches them to his mood, responds. Six-year-old David looks around in awe, clutching his first wallet, lips moving, attempting to pronounce the words he sees. Givenchy. Issey Miyake. Versace. Donovan sees them both in a mirror, smiles.

He hears himself say those words again:

'My son would like to buy some perfume for his mother. Her birthday.'

A simple statement. No foreshadowing of tragedy.

The sales assistant smiles, looks to the shelves behind her then back to the counter. And the response again:

'Did you have in mind . . .?'

The question trailing off. Ordinary. So ordinary.

Donovan waits to hear the word. Ghost. It doesn't come. He turns.

David is gone.

He starts to look for him. Angry at first that he has run away, preparing admonishments for his return, words to disguise his relief. He walks round pillars scowling, calling:

'David?'

Nothing.

Panic swells. His body feels hot and cold, prickly and clammy.

'David!'

Nothing. Just chrome and mirrors.

Back to the counter, hoping to find him there.

No sign.

Asking the assistant, his heart thudding, breath beginning to catch:

'Have you seen him? Have you seen my son?'

The assistant frowning, shaking her head, cracking her perfect visage.

Then frantically looking around. First wading then diving into that ebbing sea of humanity, pushing out, swimming against the tide, ignoring the elbows, the shouts, his own voice fraying with worry, topping them.

'David! David!'

Then standing still, looking.

Nothing.

His behaviour alerts the security guards. They rush over, two of them, pleased to have something to do. He speaks; they listen. His words are self-deprecating, self-deluding:

'I'm sure he's all right. He'll have probably just wandered off. I shouldn't waste your time . . .'

His tone betrays himself. The security men move off, looking.

He stands impotent, willing his son to appear. People stare. The bright lights expose too much, reveal not enough.

And then he sees it, on the floor.

David's wallet, spilled open, coins scattered.

Ghost.

Emotion builds; a huge, wooden battering ram seeks release from his body. Tempest-tossed and marooned, trying to catch a glimpse of his son before he is borne away on the tide.

Then the figure of Donovan recedes. Becomes smaller and smaller as darkness encroaches, blocking out all sight, sound, activity.

Ghost.

Fading to black.

He opened his eyes, shivered.

Back in the cottage in Northumberland, weak light spilling into his bedroom, another harsh, chromatic sunrise, he presumed. He yawned, stretched, rubbed his eyes. The dream again. Always with him. He reached for the whisky, his habitual cure for night-time unrest. Located it, intending to neck straight from the bottle, then opened his eyes.

He was on the sofa. Laptop, mobile phone, disks, CDs and paper piled next to it. He looked around. Still light. And remembered. He must have dozed off while working.

'I'll need to see everything Gary Myers was working on,' he had said on his ex-editor's second visit, the day after the first, the day she had come alone.

'Of course,' she had said. 'Come down to the office.'

Donovan paused before answering. 'I don't think I'm quite ready for that yet.'

Maria reddened, averted her gaze. 'Of course not. Sorry.'

The weather had changed, brightened slightly. Maria had left off her waterproof. In jeans, boots and a fleece top she looked casual, relaxed. A city girl having a weekend off in the country. She looked good, too. Donovan couldn't help but notice how well her jeans fitted her. How flatteringly they accentuated her.

'What?' she said.

'Sorry?'

'You were staring.'

It was Donovan's turn to blush. 'Sorry. I didn't . . . I was, er, miles away.'

'Right.'

Silence hung between them. Neither looked into the other's eyes.

'I could get it sent to you,' Maria said eventually. 'The contents of Gary Myers' computer. I'll get a couple of techies to strip it down, get the disks and print-outs sent to you.'

'I don't have a computer. Not any more.'

Maria sighed. 'Then I'll get one sent to you.'

Donovan smiled. 'Ambassador, you are spoiling us.'

Maria laughed. 'You have been out of circulation a long time.'

The silence returned. And with it the awkwardness. He noticed her looking around the room. Probably looking for the gun, he thought. She wouldn't find it. He had hidden it away.

'Have you . . . seen Annie recently?' Maria asked eventually, her voice hushed and sombre, riding the awkwardness.

'No. I . . . not for a while. I used to, but . . .' He sighed. 'Abigail. It was uncomfortable. Rowing, sulking, practising to be a teenager . . . In the end Annie told me to just stay away. Better for both of them.'

'Until they've worked it out?'

Donovan shrugged. 'Whatever. Whenever.' He stood up, crossed the room, looked out of the window, his back to Maria. 'Annie and me just couldn't stay together after . . . afterwards. And Abigail, poor soul. It wasn't her fault. I mean, he was her brother . . .'

Donovan broke off, allowed his eyes to follow the sea-gulls. Swooping. Cawing. Scavenging for scraps. Not giving up hope of finding something.

Maria sat in silence.

'I can't blame her for what she thinks of me,' said Donovan. 'If I was in her position I'd be exactly the same. I still love her, though. I doubt she realizes it or believes me, but I do. She probably thinks I care more for him than I do for her, but I don't. Course I don't. And I suppose she thinks I should have stayed with them, looked after her, but . . .' He sighed. 'I can't explain. It's . . . you can't let go. You can't stay either. And the longer you stay away, the harder it is to go back.'

He turned to face her.

'I'm sorry. You don't want to hear this.'

'No, no . . .' Maria stood up, crossed to him.

'It's ages since I've . . . It's not fair on you to . . .'

'It's all right.' Maria stood right next to him.

'Sorry.'

'You've nothing to be sorry for.' Maria looked at his face, into his eyes. The emotion there was naked and raw, vulnerable.

Donovan looked back at her.

Each could feel the other's breath lightly stroke their cheeks. Naked. Raw. Vulnerable.

Donovan turned away.

'Anyway,' he said, voice too loud, 'this isn't getting Gary Myers found.'

'No,' said Maria, her voice tightly modulated. 'We've got work to do.'

She had been as good as her word. One phone call to the *Herald*'s IT department had resulted in Gary Myers' hard drive being stripped and the contents being sent to Donovan along with a laptop to play them on and anything they could find on paper.

'His diary would be handy, too,' said Donovan.

'On his laptop, I think,' said Maria.

'Which, of course, he had with him.'

'Of course.'

'I don't hold out much hope. Reckon he probably had most of his stuff on his laptop.' Donovan ran his hands through his hair. 'When's the kid phoning back?'

'Tomorrow. We'll get a mobile to you, give him that number so he can talk directly with you.'

'How much am I authorized to go up to?'

'Five grand. If he's got what he says he has. But try not to. And, of course, there's your payment. To come.'

'Did Sharkey OK that?'

Maria shook her head. 'John Greene.'

Donovan laughed. 'John Greene? I thought he'd retired.'

'Executive editor.'

'Meaning?'

'A weekly column and boring the arse off the staff with old Fleet Street war stories.'

Donovan smiled, taken back in time for a second or two. A happier, simpler time. 'So,' he said, pulling himself back into the present, 'Sharkey. What's the deal with him?'

'He's the company's lawyer. Very good at his job, one of the best, but . . .' Maria shrugged.

'A twat.'

She laughed. 'I was going to be a little more diplomatic than that, but the gist would have been the same. If he says he can do something, believe him. But don't trust him.'

'Interesting distinction.'

'I'm sure you'll see what I mean.'

Donovan nodded. 'So the police haven't been called yet?'

'No.'

'Why not?'

Maria remembered the phone call with Sharkey before she had arrived at Donovan's house that day. Where she had told him she was calling the police in.

'The police?' he had said. 'I say not. Not yet. I mean, this boy. Who is he? Does he know where Myers is? Is he holding him? Is this a prank? A hoax? We don't know. Gary Myers could be away working, and this boy has seen a chance to make some easy money. We just don't know. And we won't until your man has talked to him face to face.'

She had tried to speak, but Sharkey had overridden her.

'If we go to the police and Gary Myers turns up, we'll end up looking foolish. Our competitors will have a field day. No police. For now.'

She relayed all that to Donovan, who nodded.

'Well, let's hope he's OK. Spoke to his wife?'

'Same thing with her. We didn't want to alarm her unnecessarily.'

Maria had left out one part of the conversation with Sharkey.

'You promised to help him find his son,' she had said to the lawyer. 'I'd like to know how you propose to do that.'

Sharkey had sighed. 'We'll have to postpone this conversation until another time, I'm afraid. I'm late for an appointment.'

'Francis,' she had found herself almost bellowing into the phone. 'Joe is a very desperate and damaged man. If you have no intention of backing up your words with actions, then he'll be a very angry man. And you know what that's like.'

She heard him involuntarily clear his throat.

'So are you stringing him along? Or is there something concrete you can do for him?'

Sharkey had sighed again. 'We'll talk later. I really must go.'

And the line had gone dead.

'What?' said Donovan.

'Sorry?'

'You were staring.'

Maria reddened again. 'Miles away. Listen, I'd better go.'

And she had left. Donovan had watched her leave. Then, finding he couldn't settle in the house, had gone for a walk along the shore.

First thing the next morning a heavily laden courier had arrived at the door. Donovan had started work immediately. Time passed without him realizing, he was so engrossed in the work. He was looking for clues, triggers, anything that would bring back a memory, start the ball rolling again.

Nothing.

He rubbed his eyes again, checked his watch. Ten to five. He had worked the whole day up to his nodding off. He had missed lunch.

He stood up, stretched, looked around the room. Torn from his work on the computer, it was like seeing it anew. The place was a tip. Did he really live like this? He ran a hand over his face, felt the stubble growing like an untended garden. Felt his hair: greasy, long hanks. Looked down at his clothes: filthy sweatshirt and boxer shorts. And felt, for the first time in years, shame in his appearance.

Had he really sunk so low? Was he really living with so little pride?

He looked again at the computer screen, tidied the papers up beside it. His stomach rumbled. Time for dinner, he thought, and walked towards the kitchen.

He thought of Gary Myers. A hoax? An opportunistic prank? Maybe. He hoped the journalist was OK, even if it was just for the sake of the man's wife, ultimately. Donovan knew only too well what it was like to carry the burden of worry over someone you love going missing.

He thought of Maria, too, felt a curious sensation inside. What must she have thought of him looking the way he did?

He diverted his route to the bathroom instead.

Time for a bath and a shave and a change of clothes.

Time to sort himself out.

Gary Myers opened his eyes yet still saw blackness. A clammy, claustrophobic, itchy blackness.

The hood was still in place.

Using his free left hand, he moved it slowly up his face, stopping every quarter of an inch, expecting a harsh voice to bark at him, order him to pull it down again.

His heart was beating fast, fear pumping blood round his body . . . push a little further . . . he could hear his breath hitting the fabric before his mouth and nose, feel sweat along his forehead and neck . . . further, further . . . his mouth free, his nose . . . they had forced him to keep the hood on . . . a good sign . . . meant they intended him to live . . . further . . . meant there would be an end to all this, that they wouldn't keep him for long . . . a push, then stop . . . checking for the voice . . . then more . . . further . . . stop for another few seconds, waiting, expecting that voice . . . a punch even . . . then a little more . . .

But the voice never came. No one touched him. Gary continued pulling and rolling until the hood came free.

He quickly closed his eyes, blinked away the sudden light, the attendant hurt. He tried again, opening them slowly this time.

The place was dimly lit but seemed overpoweringly bright compared with his view inside the hood. He waited a few minutes, allowed himself to acclimatize, his vision to come into focus.

It looked like a disused garage. Small, no longer operational. And for some time. Wooden double doors to the front were chained up, access granted by a small, rectangular door inset in the right-hand door. That, Gary knew, was bolted and double-locked from the outside.

An ancient Granada sat on a ramp in the centre of the garage. Body flaking rust like dead, leprous skin, tyres flattened and sagging like flabby, middle-aged beer guts. Behind the car a workbench holding a collection of rusting, blunted tools. Tools that looked solid enough to hurt. Tools that, judging by the deposits left on them, hadn't just been used to mend cars. Piles of decaying engine parts dotted the corners. The walls and floor were dark with accumulated dirt and dust, the stickiness and stink of old, rancid motor oil.

Behind the workshop, glimpsed through a filthy half-glass door and wall, was the office. An old, scarred metal desk, a swivel chair that had long since ceased to offer comfort and now haemorrhaged its innards, a ransacked filing cabinet and a calendar of naked young women who must now have been of pensionable age.

And in the centre of the room, the chair.

The mercy seat.

His first memory of captivity, before they had handcuffed him to the heavy iron radiator on the wall of the old garage. It scared him to look at it, had scared him even more to sit in it.

He had woken up bound to it. The hood had stopped him seeing his captors' faces, but he had heard their voices; barking questions at him, hurting him when he didn't give the answer they wanted to hear.

His companion had fared even worse. He had known his captors, tried to talk to them using first names, engage with them on a human level. That had resulted in an even more savage and severe beating than Gary had been given.

Gary looked at his companion lying uncomfortably next to him, handcuffed to the other end of the radiator. Two old blankets and a stinking slop bucket between them. It was all right at present, but when it filled up the place would stink. That, he thought, was the least of his troubles.

Poor Colin, he thought. Tried to do what he thought was right and honourable and look where it had got him. A broken arm, possibly several broken ribs, severe bruising and, from the pain he had described, internal damage. He wasn't a young man either. He wondered whether Colin could cope with whatever their captives had in mind.

Gary wondered if he himself could.

He knew why they had been taken. They both did. After the blue-toothed skinhead had burst into the hotel room in King's Cross it had been obvious. Apparently his minidisc player had been stolen, and this seemed to annoy them most. They had stripped and destroyed his laptop, but the loss of the minidisc had left them very, very unhappy. And although Gary knew nothing about that, he had paid the price for it. After heavy persuading, they had reluctantly agreed with him.

So he waited. He looked at Colin. Sleeping. A fitful, uneasy sleep. His stomach turned over yet again. He winced at the pain, a combination of heartburn from the cheap fast food their captives provided, the beatings and fear.

Gary sighed. The air left his body in shuddering gasps.

Fear. He had never truly understood the meaning of the word until this moment. Fear. Just sitting.

Meant they intended him to live.

And waiting.

Meant there would be an end to all this.

And not knowing.

That they wouldn't keep him for long.

Fear.

Gary sighed again, felt more than air bubbling up.

Quickly he grabbed the bucket and, eyes closed and nose blocked, threw up into the mess.

He kept vomiting until there was nothing left inside him. Except fear.

5

'Seventy-seven . . . seventy-eight . . . seventy-nine . . . eighty . . .'

With the air exploding from her lungs, Peta Knight flopped back on the floor, sweating. She felt the familiar trembling ache around her lower stomach and down the fronts of her thighs, felt the sweat bead and prickle her hot skin. She breathed deep, her lungs red and raw. Her muscles felt worked, her body burning; she flexed and unflexed, the second skin of black Lycra moving with her.

She loved that feeling. But it wasn't enough.

Seven thirty a.m.: her regular morning exercise session half completed. Four hundred sit-ups, eighty at a time, alternating extended legs. Sixty push-ups, three sets of twenty. Then side bends, stretches. All aerobic. Four sessions with the small weights.

But it wasn't enough.

She missed her bag, the heaviness of it on her foot as she kicked it, the resistance when she punched it. She missed the gym, the machines, her sessions in the dojo. She missed running and cycling. She missed the free exertion, the exhilaration. The release of endorphins into her body, the only chemical change she dared allow herself these days.

She needed the strict regime, the drug-free self-abnegation. Going back to her old ways was not an option.

But she hated being stuck in the room with virtually nothing to show for it.

She checked her watch. Nearly ten to eight. He would be here soon.

Bending her left leg and straightening the right, holding it six inches off the floor, she breathed deeply once, twice, knotted and locked her fingers behind her head and started again.

'One . . . two . . . three . . .'

She reached fifty-four when the door opened. He stopped, stood there smirking.

'I heard all that panting on the landing,' he said. 'Didn't know whether to come in or not.'

'Piss off,' she gasped. 'Fifty-five . . . fifty-six . . .'

He entered carrying a paper bag, closed the door behind him. Yawned, then smiled.

'You know you should get out more,' he said. 'Enjoy yourself for a change.'

She ignored him, keeping her rate steady, uninhibited by his presence, until she reached eighty and lay flat on the floor, panting again.

'Like you, you mean?' she managed between gasps. 'Have fun, did you?'

The man smiled, took off his jacket, the leather soft and high grain, the tailoring several cuts above standard chainstore sweatshop wear. He draped it carefully over the back of a chair, folded his arms. He was in good shape, but there was narcissism to his actions; for his prone, gymhead partner a good body was an end in itself, but his was only a means to an end. However, he also practised martial arts and as such carried himself well, gracefully even, Peta had to admit.

He placed the brown-paper bag on the table. 'Coffee and croissant in there for you,' he said, taking out his own. 'Starbucks. Last night, right, business and pleasure? Can't beat it.'

She sat up, propped her body on her elbows, looked at him.

'You're going to catch something one of these days, you know that? Either that or get arrested.'

He sighed, bit into his croissant, brushed crumbs away from his thighs. 'Oh shut up and drink your coffee. It's just good fun, Peta. And it brings in the money. God knows we need that.'

Peta looked away. Said nothing.

'And anyway,' he continued, taking a mouthful of coffee, 'I'm just there to watch, aren't I, darling? Well, most of the time . . .'

Peta sighed. 'Amar . . .'

'And,' Amar said, 'most of them have never seen an Asian poof before. Well, not outside an arranged marriage, anyway.'

Peta stood up, wiped sweat from her body with the towel. She opened the bag, took out the coffee, had a sip. 'You had any sleep?' she asked.

'Nope. You?'

Peta shook her head. 'Well, on and off. Not much.'

'Go get some,' he said. 'I'll take over here.'

'You sure?'

'Don't worry.' He smiled, gave a mock sniff. 'Got something a little stronger than caffeine in my pocket. That'll keep me going.'

Amar knew she was looking at him, probably disapprovingly. He avoided her eyes. Kept his gaze on the window.

'So did I miss anything?' he asked.

'Not really,' said Peta, also looking towards the window. 'Fat boy's client left in the wee small hours.'

'Positive ID?'

'Not yet. Took a minicab. May have to take a chance, you know. Do a bit of shadowing next time he turns up.'

Amar nodded. 'Anything else?'

'Only that new boy. The light-skinned one.'

'What about him?'

'Went out again. On his own.'

'So? Don't they all?'

Peta frowned. 'Yes, but he was . . . furtive. He circled the block a couple of times. Hid and waited. Like he was up to something and wanted to make sure he wasn't being followed.'

Amar raised an eyebrow. 'Interesting. Where did he go?'

'Don't know.'

'And then he went back there for the night after he was finished doing whatever?'

Peta nodded. Amar looked thoughtful.

'Maybe there's more than one person we should be shadowing.'

Peta nodded, began to gather up her things. 'You going to be all right left here for a couple of hours?'

Amar smiled. 'I've got last night's action to play back and keep me warm.'

Peta grimaced. 'Spare me.'

'Hey, loosen up, ice queen,' he said in his campest voice. 'Does you good to let your hair down once in a while. You should try it.'

Peta shook her head. 'D'you need anything while I'm out?'

'No, mum. I'm all right, mum.'

Peta turned to go.

'Oh, there is one thing . . .'

She turned back to face him. He was smiling.

'If you see Brad Pitt on your travels, I'll have him.'

Peta shook her head, opened the door, went out, slammed it behind her.

Amar smiled.

'Hugh Jackman would do,' he said to himself, then returned his gaze to the window.

He sipped his coffee, finished off his croissant.

Something'll happen soon, he thought. Something's got to give.

He kept watching the house. The morning wore on.

Mikey Blackmore surveyed the crowd. About thirty of them, he reckoned. He shook his head. Surely they must have something better to do with their lunchtimes, he thought.

He waited until the last of them had made it to the top floor, waited until everyone had admired the 1959 Sunbeam Alpine, waited until they had admired the view.

Then went into his act, his spiel.

'Right, ladies and gentlemen, if I can have your attention . . .'

The crowd turned to face him. Showtime.

'Here we are,' he said, pumping up his fake enthusiasm. 'The highlight of the tour. Brumby's Demon King Castle.' He smiled. Most of them smiled in return.

'Now, we'll be moving inside the restaurant area, which, of course, as we know has never actually been a restaurant.' A little laugh at that. 'But first, if you'll all stand back, we'll have the scene where Glenda rescues Jack and takes him to see Brumby.'

The crowd moved back, knowing what would be coming next. A blonde actress walked to the car and got behind the wheel, starting the engine. An actor in a black trenchcoat came from within the crowd and got in next to her. The car went round a corner and up a ramp to the next level of the multi-storey car park, where it sat idling. The crowd followed, huddled around. The actress turned off the engine and, when the audience was in place, began her scene.

Mikey stood at the back, keeping his distance. Sometimes he couldn't believe what he did to make a living. Or one of the things.

The *Get Carter* tour had started by accident, a group of

film enthusiasts having a laugh with their friends, walking round Newcastle and Gateshead, reciting chunks of dialogue to each other in what was left of the old film locations and then heading off to the pub.

But it had grown; money was charged and professionally aspirant actors were employed to act out scenes. And a tour guide needed to ferry the punters round, set the scene. Once they had met Mikey and found out about his background – his pedigree, as they insisted on referring to it in the interview, oblivious to his discomfort – the organizers had almost begged him to take the job.

He watched the scene progress, noticed how the young lad playing Jack Carter had tried to lower his voice, narrow his eyes in approximation of Michael Caine's performance. Thought it made him a hard man, a killer.

Mikey shook his head. The lad had no idea.

Mikey pulled his old overcoat around him. Oxfam's finest, at least one size too large for his scrawny frame, but it kept the wind from his bones. The top of the car park could get cold. He ignored the holes in his trainers.

The scene played out, the audience applauded. Mikey took his cue, stepped forward.

'Well done,' he said, 'well done. The plot thickens, eh? Right, well, I'll give you a chance to get your photos taken with the car and then we'll move inside, into the restaurant for five more scenes.' He held up a finger. 'Number one: Brumby offers Jack five grand to get rid of Kinear.'

He held up another finger. 'Number two. Carter kidnaps Thorpey and returns to the boarding house. Number three.'

A third finger. 'Carter meets Margaret at the crematorium, then quizzes her on the Iron Bridge. You saw it on the way over here. Number four.'

A fourth finger. 'Back to Brumby's house. You're a big man, but you're out of shape . . .'

The inevitable cheer went up. Mikey smiled along with them, waited for it to subside, then held up the thumb of his right hand.

'Number five. Carter and Glenda. I know you wear purple underwear.'

A smaller cheer, accompanied by a more knowing laugh.

'Then it's back over to the Bridge Hotel for the final scene and a pint.'

He looked around again, paused to allow his words to sink in, then said: 'Any questions?'

Silence, then, when he was about to move on,

'Yeah. What's it feel like to kill someone?'

Mikey's head jerked swiftly round. The words hit him so hard, so fast and unexpected, that it was like being stung from a fierce slap.

'What? Who said that?'

A laugh this time, either of embarrassment or anticipation, then the same voice. 'I said, what's it feel like to kill someone?'

Mikey felt suddenly hot inside his overcoat. He could feel the eyes of the crowd on him, expectant, waiting. Even the two actors were looking at him, waiting for him to answer their proxy questioner, to answer the question they hadn't dared ask for themselves.

The feeling swelled within the crowd. Mikey sensed it. This was it, they seemed to be thinking, the real thing. Not actors playing Hollywood stars playing hard men but the genuine article.

Mikey's stomach turned over.

He located the questioner, sized him up immediately. A smug, southern student, well fed and educated yet dressed as if he couldn't afford decent clothes, his accent a ridiculously affected mockney.

Mikey stared him in the eye.

The student laughed, but it was a nervous snort.

The crowd waited.

Mikey stared even harder at the student, anger rising. He wanted him not just scared but terrorized. He wanted to show him what happened when you opened your mouth and asked a convicted killer such a stupid question. He wanted to slap him stupid in front of all these people, teach them all a lesson. He wanted the student never to do that again.

Mikey's gaze was unblinking, unflinching. The student began to look scared.

And Mikey sighed, broke eye contact, shook his head. He couldn't do it. Couldn't feel those things, think those thoughts again.

'Worse than you'll ever know,' he said. His voice held no trace of the hardness the crowd wanted.

Only regret and sadness.

The student looked away, relieved Mikey wasn't staring at him any more, confused by the response, even embarrassed that he had asked the question.

Mikey turned his gaze from him, let his eyes travel around the rest of the group. He felt he had failed them. Failed to live up to their expectations.

He didn't care.

'Right,' he said, aiming for lightness but his voice falling flat. 'Let's make our way up to the restaurant. Let's see how the drama unfolds.'

The crowd, feeling that somehow the atmosphere had deflated, the excitement gone, began to make their way up the ramp.

Mikey waited until they were well ahead, then followed them.

Turnbull looked at the woman in front of him. And his heart went out to her. As a detective sergeant with the

Northumbria police, he knew all about professional detachment. Practised it most times. But a pretty girl in distress needing comfort and closure, looking towards him to provide it, was the perfect victim. And he needed a victim. His focus demanded it.

Turnbull saw the world in terms of moral absolutes; everything was black and white. There were victims. There was a good guy. Him. There were bad guys who had to be caught. By him. And anyone who stood in the way of that was on their side. Monochromatic and proud of it, even down to his dress sense. Black suit, white shirt. He could almost be taken for a rabid Newcastle United fan. And was.

He sat forward on the sofa, legs apart, black and white check tie hanging down. He wore what he hoped was a sympathetic expression. His senior partner, DI Nattrass, was doing most of the talking. He nodded occasionally to show he was listening.

Nattrass, stocky and plain-looking enough to be a lesbian, Turnbull thought, had on her soothing voice, the one she used to impart delicate information. Bad news or no news. No news, in this instance.

'We've found a sighting of him on CCTV at Newcastle station, and then a similar camera at King's Cross. And then nothing more, I'm afraid.' She leaned forward, eyes locking with the other woman's. 'Do you have any idea at all what he could have been doing down there?'

Caroline Huntley sighed. And Turnbull got a picture of her as she would have been a week ago: back and forth to work as head of personnel for a city bank, dinner dates with a boyfriend, nights out with girlfriends, nights in with a DVD, a glass of wine and a bar of fruit and nut. Two-week holiday in Greece or Portugal. A normal life. A happy life. A life unaware of nightmares.

She was trying her best to hold herself together. Her

fingers, curling and uncurling the edge of a newspaper in front of her until it was shredded, gave her away. So did the unwashed, long blonde hair, the clothes unchanged for the last couple of days. She would have been very attractive under normal circumstances, Turnbull thought. Her situation just increased that attractiveness.

She shook her head. 'No . . . He never . . . no . . .'

'We've spoken to his work colleagues,' said Turnbull, 'but they can't tell us anything either.'

Caroline nodded. The two police officers said nothing.

'Don't . . .' Caroline stared at the paper before her, the headline telling of the hunt for the missing scientist. 'Don't they say that the first forty-eight hours are crucial in missing persons cases?'

'They do, yes,' said Nattrass. 'But that doesn't mean to say you have to give up hope. We're doing all we can to find your father.'

Caroline nodded. He had been gone over two days now. And, barring a sighting in King's Cross, there was no trace. He had left behind no clues and a distraught daughter.

Turnbull looked around the room. The block of flats was 1960s built, all Le Corbusier angularity, and Caroline's décor was a twenty-first-century version of that, with the added warmth of earth tones: wood, creams and browns. Both modern and homely. All around were bouquets of flowers, most of them wilted, dying.

His eyes alighted on a photo by the TV. Caroline, Colin Huntley and a woman who was presumably her mother. There was a happiness in the photo as if they were good people and nothing bad would ever happen in their lives. And here they were: the father missing, the mother dead from a nasty form of cancer and the daughter before them.

Turnbull felt her pain all the more.

Her face when she had opened the door, despair and hope

fighting each other for prominence. The disappointment when they told her of the CCTV footage. The hope that it might lead to a discovery. The fear of what that might be.

They talked for a while longer, inconsequential stuff, Nattrass reassuring Caroline that they were doing all they could to find her father.

'Don't worry,' said Turnbull, 'we'll find him.'

Both Caroline and Nattrass looked at him. Nattrass shook her head.

Then they left.

Outside the block of flats Nattrass turned to Turnbull.

'You can put your tongue back now,' she said.

Turnbull looked angry. 'What d'you mean?'

'I saw the way you looked at her.'

Turnbull felt himself reddening. 'I didn't—'

'And what was all that about? "We'll find him"? What if we don't?'

Turnbull shrugged. Kept what he had been about to say to himself.

'Professional detachment,' said Nattrass with only a hint of condescension. 'Remember that.'

She turned, walked away to the car.

Professional detachment, thought Turnbull, walking behind her. You can shove it up your arse.

He watched. She had no idea.

He watched her get up in the morning, get into her Beetle, drive to work. Brave the slug-slow snarl-up once she reached Jesmond's Osborne Road, then down into Newcastle city itself.

Park. Heels clack-clacking, echoing round the all-but-deserted multi-storey as she walked towards the lift.

Any time, he thought. He could have taken her any time at all.

Had he wanted to.

He knew her lunch friends, her lunch haunts, her lunch menus.

He knew which days she drove, which days she took the Metro. Which bars, clubs, cinemas, restaurants she frequented after work.

But not tonight.

The day had dissipated, night rolling in. He sat opposite her block of flats in Jesmond, his car hidden by overhanging trees, outside the radius of the streetlights.

Watching. Waiting.

No going out for her this week. Just stuck in her flat, frantic with worry, praying for good news. Any news.

Watching. Waiting.

He saw callers come and go, stay with her, leave. He imagined the conversations, the platitudes. The inane, useless platitudes.

Don't worry, pet. You'll hear from him soon. It'll be all right.

Probably just gone away for a few days. He'll be in touch.

Perhaps it's a fancy woman he's got. You never know. He's not that old.

Inane, useless platitudes. White noise to block up her ears, to stop her receiving truthful broadcasts from her heart:

He's in trouble. Something's happened to him.

Something bad.

And the police had called. Personal assurances. Doing all they could, everything in their power, but . . . And then a shrug. The papers carrying it, too.

He continued watching the window. Imagined her in there, unable to watch TV, to listen to the radio or a CD, to read a book or a magazine or a newspaper. Unable to relax, to think straight.

And felt excitement at the thought of that, power. If he

wanted to he could just walk up to Caroline Huntley's front door, buzz her flat and tell her everything. Give answers to all her questions.

If he wanted to. Which he didn't.

He enjoyed that power. Conducting the orchestra of her despair.

He thrived on it.

The living room light went out. Shortly followed by the bedroom going on.

'It's no use trying to sleep,' he whispered, voice gentle as if he were at her bedside. 'Sleep won't come until your mind is at rest. And your mind won't be at rest for a long, long time . . .'

The bedroom light went out. The flat fell into darkness.

He smiled again, the streetlight glinting faintly off his blue-sapphire tooth, his shaved head. He inserted the earpieces of his iPod, pressed PLAY.

Mayhem: *De Mysteriis Dom Sathanas.*

Pure Norwegian death metal.

'Funeral Fog', the first track, kicked in and his mind floated away. He rested his hands on the steering wheel, tapped along.

Mayhem: they sacrificed animals on stage. When their lead singer, Death, committed suicide, the drummer made a necklace from his skull fragments. The guitarist cooked and ate pieces of his brain and was then killed by the bassist.

Music as pure darkness. If he loved anything, he loved them. Loved the way they made him feel.

His mind floated away, but his eyes stayed locked on the flat.

He settled down for the night.

The phone rang. The noise startled Donovan.

He looked at it lying there on the sofa. Such a small

thing; such a big decision. He swallowed hard. Took a deep breath, then picked it up.

'Joe Donovan,' he said after a moment's hesitation.

Silence on the other end of the line.

Donovan waited.

He heard breathing, experimental, as if trying out different phrasings, modulations, then: 'Joe Donovan, yeah?'

The voice was young, hesitant.

'That's me.'

Donovan waited.

'Got somethin' for you, man. Took me bare trouble, yeah? So I think I should be well rewarded.'

Donovan smiled, felt a surge of excitement that had lain dormant within him for years.

'Let's talk,' he said.

6

The housing estate was bleak to start with; the rain made it even worse.

Monolithic and crumbling, the remaining futurist 1960s urban parkland towers looked more like blocks of Soviet totalitarian prole containment. In their shadows, ground-level replacement community housing had degenerated into a maze of darkened walkways and alleyways, post-apocalyptic play areas, burned out and boarded-up shells. Now a quick-fix dumping ground for those consensually agreed to be socially undesirable. Thatcher's twenty-year-old remark that there was no such thing as society used as both excuse and expiation for a forgotten area of the west end of Newcastle.

The west end of Newcastle. A land that spawned monsters.

The parents: poverty, bad housing, bad education, neglect. The offspring: crime, incest, hatred, nihilism. Drugs.

The bad magic badlands.

Keenyside stood in the back garden wasteland of a boarded-up and smoke-blackened house. As close to the wall as he could get in a vain attempt to avoid the rain. His overcoat, black and expensive-looking, was buttoned right up to his throat, collar up. Hands thrust deep into pockets.

He was being kept waiting. He didn't like to be kept waiting.

It showed on his face.

From out of the rain, to his right, emerged a figure.

Short, poorly dressed and hurrying across the blasted mini-heath of stunted, skinny trees, sparse yellow grass, weeds, mud and animal shit that bordered the backs of the houses overlooking the Tyne.

Keenyside watched the man approach, fixing him with a baleful, unblinking stare. Eventually the man reached him. Stopped.

He was small, late thirties, aged more than his chronological years. Wearing leaking trainers, jeans and an overlarge overcoat pulled close, he shivered. The rain lent him a pathetic air.

'You're late.' Keenyside's voice was flat, uninflected, yet carried beneath it notes of rage and menace.

'Sorry, Mr Keenyside.' The man swallowed hard, flinched as if expecting a blow. 'I've had to hurry from work . . .'

Keenyside stared at him, eyes boring like lasers.

'Work?' He gave a harsh, unpleasant laugh. 'You work for me. First and foremost. Me. You're only walking the street because I say so. Got that, Mikey?'

Mikey Blackmore dropped his head, nodded.

'Good.'

Keenyside swept the area with his eyes, gave a swift, careful check for spies and eavesdroppers. Found none. Then back to Mikey Blackmore.

'So,' he said, 'what you got for me?'

Mikey dug into his overcoat, hand trembling, brought out a badly wrapped bundle in a Co-op carrier bag. Keenyside gave it a disdainful look.

'Can't you wrap it better than this? Pathetic.'

'It's all there, Mr Keenyside. You can count it.'

'Oh I will, Mikey. Later. For now I'll have to take your word. Because you wouldn't fuck me about, would you?'

His words, his voice, were morgue cold. Mikey looked away.

'No, Mr Keenyside.'

'Good. I know we understand each other.'

Keenyside pocketed the bundle in his overcoat, stared at the rain. Mikey waited, not daring to move until he'd been dismissed.

'So,' said Keenyside eventually, 'what else you got for me? Talk.'

Mikey talked. He knew what Keenyside wanted. Information on the area drugs gangs. When new shipments were expected, how and where they were coming in, what local power struggles were taking place that could be exploited, who was on the way out, who was on the way up.

Mikey finished talking, waited.

Keenyside stood deep in thought. Eventually he nodded his approval.

'Good stuff, Mikey. Very good stuff.'

Mikey couldn't hide his relief. He sighed, noticed for the first time how much his legs were shaking.

Keenyside dug into his overcoat, brought out a bag containing several bundles, much better wrapped than Mikey's had been, handed it over.

'Here,' he said. 'Coke to wash into rocks. Heroin. Make sure you stamp on it well. Some weed and some pills.' He smiled. 'Spread a little happiness. Now go and work your magic. Turn it into money.'

'Thank you, Mr Keenyside.'

'And remember.' Keenyside stared at Mikey again. Hard. 'Next time I want to see you, you'll be on time. You'll remember that it was me got you that job, that set you up in that flat and that allows you to go about your daily business unmolested. Remember.'

'I do, Mr Keenyside.'

He grabbed hold of Mikey in one swift movement, pinned him up against the side of the house. The boards of the window shook with the sudden force. Mikey looked terrified.

'You're well paid. For what you are. So have some fucking respect. And don't be late.'

'I . . . I . . . I . . . won't . . . Mr Keenyside . . .'

Keenyside dropped his hand, loosened his grip, stepped back. Mikey almost collapsed in a heap on the ground.

Keenyside smiled. 'Good. Now fuck off.'

Mikey turned and hurried away, almost running. He was soon lost in the dark maze of streets and shadowed walkways.

Keenyside watched him go, then turned and made his way back to the car. It was where he had left it, beside a row of garages, just off the road. A Jaguar X-type V6 looked out of place next to the old Mondeos, Astras and Peugeots that were parked nearby. It hadn't befallen the same fate as the burned-out Nova next to it. But then it wouldn't. Because people knew whom the car belonged to. And they wouldn't dare touch it.

Because they knew what would happen to them if they did.

He climbed inside, checked he wasn't being watched, opened the bag Mikey had handed him, counted the money. All notes, smoothed out like he had told Mikey to do. Nearly six thousand pounds. Not bad for a couple of days' work. He sighed. But not enough. Never enough.

He placed the package of money in the glove compartment, locked it.

Drove away. Quickly.

He had been born there. But felt no love for it; nothing but contempt. Wanted to put as much distance between himself and his origins as possible.

But not far: only to the top of Westgate Road. Just past the General Hospital. Only a short geographical distance between where he had been and where he was now, but the tree-lined streets and old Edwardian buildings marked a much bigger psychogeographical one.

Black-metal bars over all the Edwardian buildings' windows. Keeping the bad magic badlands at bay.

He indicated, pulled off the main road and into a reserved parking space. He turned the engine off, checked once again that the glove compartment was secured and got out, centrally locking the car and activating the alarm as he did so.

Even though no one would dare break into it here.

Keenyside stopped, looked up at the building he was about to enter. Built in the late 1950s, tall and solid, it imposed itself on the surrounding area. Like a lighthouse, he thought, illuminating everything in its sweep.

Both lengthening and darkening the shadows.

He smiled, went inside. Past the front desk, where he exchanged pleasantries with a uniformed man sitting behind it, keying the number code into the pad by the inner door, gaining access to the building proper.

Then up to fourth, a few cheery hellos and exchanges concerning football and alcohol on the way, then into his office. His workroom. He looked at the open-plan desks, fed on the hum of activity. He made his way to the glass-walled office, throwing out greetings as he went.

Inside, and closed the door.

He took his overcoat off, shook excess water from it, placed it on its hanger, hung it in the cupboard. Sat down at his desk, smoothed his drying hair back, looked around to check he wasn't about to be disturbed, picked up the phone, dialled a mobile number from heart.

He waited. It was answered.

'It's me,' he said. Listened. 'Line tapped? Only by me. Now, what you got for me?'

He listened to the answer. Smiled.

'You've found him? Good. He got any word on our runner?'

He listened again. Was asked a question. Thought long and hard before answering. Thought of the six thousand pounds. How it was never enough. Thought of how much he stood to make. Chewed his lower lip. Smiled again. Decision made.

'Do what you have to do. But do it well. Might just be some scummy fucking rent boy who won't be missed, but I don't want it coming back and biting me on the arse, right?'

He waited for a response, sighed again. 'Yeah, I know how much a thing like that'll cost. Don't worry, you'll get paid.' Thought of how much money he would soon be making. 'But no trail. Right?' He listened. Nodded. 'Good. Now what about the surveillance, anything there?'

The answer came.

He sighed again. 'Good. Keep it up.'

He listened.

'Right. When you've done that, I want you back up here. Time to step things up. Give proceedings a little push.' He listened again. 'Yeah, I know it's difficult, backwards and forwards to Newcastle and London. But you're the best, and that's why I employ you.'

He hoped the flattery worked.

It did. 'Later, then. You know when and where.'

He waited for the response, replaced the receiver. Expelled a breath he hadn't been aware he was holding.

He crossed his feet at the ankles, stretched back in his chair, the black leather creaking against his weight. He was aware of what he had just sanctioned. Aware that another line had been crossed.

He sighed, rubbed his face with his hands.

Had to be done, he told himself, had to be done. The rewards were worth the risks. And the risks would be great.

He smiled. Shook his head, tried to clear it.

Six thousand pounds. Not bad. Even with all the deductions.

All things considered, it had been a good morning's work for Detective Inspector Alan Keenyside.

Si stood outside the door, thinking. He swallowed hard and, mind made up, knocked.

No reply. He knocked again.

'Jack?' he called.

Muffled, unhappy-sounding grumbling came through the door.

'Fuck off,' Jack called. 'I'm asleep.'

Si waited. What he had to say was important, and Jack would want to hear it. But Jack was unpredictable, the line to be crossed changing by the hour. There weren't many people or things Si had respect for, but Jack was one of them.

Respect. And fear. Mainly fear.

Si breathed heavily, knocked again.

'Listen, man, it's Si. I've got somethin' for you.'

No reply.

'It's good. You'll wanna hear this.'

From behind the door came a reluctant rumble of movement, a dragging of mass almost neo-tectonic in its heaviness, accompanied by a low, ominous growl. In contrast to this, the door was flung open so rapidly Si gasped and jumped back.

'I'd fuckin' better.'

Jack's eyes were tiny rage-fuelled dots sunk into his pink, fat face. He looked like an angry pig. Si's heart was beating rapidly.

'Yeah, yeah,' he said. 'You'll wanna hear this.'

'Come in.'

Jack turned, walked back to the bed, sat down.

Si entered. The room was a tip. The detritus of Jack's trade. Si didn't flinch. He'd seen it all before. Been part of it before.

At first as the victim, the crying, snivelling new boy, broken in, broken down. He had been forced to enjoy it. And gradually he had been allowed to play the part of the aggressor. And he much preferred inflicting pain than taking it. Had learned to love it. So he had hung on to that, done everything Father Jack wanted, happy to please him. Because he knew the alternative. That the crying, snivelling boy was just below the surface and Jack could bring him out whenever the fancy took him.

Si tried to ensure the fancy never took Jack.

Jack sat on the bed, looked at him.

'What?' he said flatly. 'This had better be good.'

Si swallowed. There seemed to be a stone lodged there. He spoke.

'It's the new boy, Jamal.'

'What about him?'

'You know I told you I thought he was up to somethin'?'

Jack stared at him by way of an answer. Si continued.

'Well, he is.'

A flicker of interest sparked in Jack's eye.

'Tell me.'

'Well, he kept asking for a charger for his mobile. Said he needed to phone some punter. So I got suspicious, like. Sounded like he was hidin' somethin'.'

'So?'

'So last night he went out again. An' I followed him.'

'Did he see you?'

'No.'

Jack scrutinized him.

'Honest. Had no idea I was there. He looked around a

lot, checkin' no one was followin', but I was better than him.'

Jack scowled. 'Never mind about you. Just tell me what fuckin' happened.'

The harshness of Jack's tone made Si jump.

'Sorry, Jack. So I followed him. An' he went to a phone box an' dialled a number. Asked to speak to someone. I was in the one backin' on to it.'

'A phone box? Why did he want his fuckin' mobile charged, then?'

'I'll come to that,' Si said quickly.

'Well, hurry up. I haven't got all fuckin' day.'

Si said nothing.

'Come on, then. Who was this someone?'

Si pulled a piece of paper from the back pocket of his jeans. He read out the spidery, unformed scrawl.

'Joe Donovan. I came back an' wrote it all down.'

If Si expected a word of praise or encouragement, then it wasn't forthcoming from Jack. Slightly dispirited, he continued.

'So they gave him another number. An' he calls it. An' I heard him say to this Donovan that he had the disc.'

'Disc?'

'Yeah, disc. An' Donovan must've said how much does he want for it an' that, 'cos then Jamal says a million.'

Father Jack's features became less angry, more calculating. 'A million?'

'Yeah, that's what he said. An' then this Donovan must've laughed or somethin', 'cos then Jamal said how much then, an' then he said five thousand. So that's what Donovan must've said.'

'Five thousand? Did he agree?'

'Yeah. But said it was a matter of life an' death. Kept sayin' that. Matter of life an' death.'

A razor smile split Father Jack's piggy face open.

'Sounds like we've got a little blackmailer on our hands. Life and death. Five grand . . . I'm sure it could be worth more than that. I think we'd better have a word with our little friend.'

'Yeah.'

'So what's he doing next? Don't tell me you didn't get that bit.'

'No, no, I got it. They made plans to meet tomorrow night. That's tonight. Down on the quayside. An' then they're goin' back to Donovan's hotel to do the changeover. Money for the disc.'

Father Jack smiled again. It was no less unpleasant.

'Treating this Donovan like a punter in case anyone's listening. Clever boy.'

Si nodded. He hadn't thought about that but it sounded right.

'An' then he gave him his mobile number. To contact him if there was any change.'

'Regular chums.'

Si laughed. 'Yeah.'

Si looked at Father Jack expectantly. Jack was frowning, seemingly thinking hard.

'So what d'you want me to do?'

'Keep an eye on him,' said Jack thoughtfully. 'And before he goes out, we'll have words.'

The tone of Father Jack's voice made Si glad he wasn't the one to be receiving those words.

'Right.'

Father Jack nodded. 'You did good, Si. Very good. You're a grand lad.'

A flush of pride ran through Si.

'Thank you, Father Jack.'

'Good lad.' Jack's tone changed. 'But if you disturb me

again when I'm sleeping, I'll cut your cock off and eat it while you watch.' He rolled back on to the bed. 'Now, fuck off an' leave me alone.'

Si flinched. He didn't doubt it. He got straight up, crossed to the door, out, and closed it behind him. The sub-continental movement of Jack getting comfortable came through the wood.

Si stood on the landing against the wall and sighed. Hard. His legs were trembling, threatening to give way.

Well, he thought, that went quite well.

He shivered.

It could have been a lot worse.

Night fell heavy around King's Cross. Became dark in a way no streetlight could illuminate.

Two worlds side by side, occupying the same physical but not psychic space, the station as interface. Feeding off and into each other. As day fell away, so, too, did its citizens. As night ascended, so, too, did its denizens. Remaining day-dwellers confined their journeys to below ground or the mainline station, only venturing above and beyond if they had to.

Or wanted to.

For this was the land of the hustle where everything was for sale. Sex. Drugs. Bodies. Minds. Hope. Futures.

Razor capitalism. Animalistic consumerism.

Sex and death. However they were packaged.

Attempts at fashionable gentrification had been made, but their success was only short term. Long term, the status quo would reassert, erode the newcomers or consume them, like waves turning stone to sand.

Dean stood in his usual spot. Against the blackened, brick side wall of King's Cross Station on York Way, half in, half out of the streetlight, letting those interested know he was available.

And there was always interest.

He saw the same black Saab, third time now, turn the corner at the lights. Come towards him, slow down, then take off again before Dean could approach. Building up courage, Dean knew. He'd be back. And if he wasn't? Didn't matter. There'd be others.

He felt the side pockets of his jeans. Bulging with notes. He moved his jaw, side to side, up and down. Beginning to ache. No problem. He was used to it.

The buzz from his last rock was tailing off. Didn't last long, anyway. He wanted a spliff, something to fuck with his head in a mellow way, keep the cold away.

He put his hands in his pockets. Lonely without Jamal.

But the cash compensated. And much as he liked Jamal, he knew which he would prefer to have with him.

He looked down the street, waiting for the Saab to come round again, noticed a potential customer. A big, well-muscled man. Shaved head. Bag slung over his shoulder. He drew near, almost level.

And Dean recognized him.

'Aw shit, man,' Dean said. 'What you want now?'

The man stopped walking, put his hands in front of him, palms up, like he was in an old war movie, surrendering.

'It's all right,' he said, 'I'm not here on business. I'm not going to ask you anything.'

'Yeah?' said Dean warily. 'I told you I ain't heard from Jamal. Don't know where he is.'

The man smiled. There was that blue tooth again. The one Dean couldn't take his eyes off. The one that gave him the creeps.

'That's OK,' said the skinhead. 'I'm not looking for him any more.'

'Yeah? Then what d'you want?'

He pulled something out of his trouser pocket. A fifty-pound note.

'I've come to see you.'

Dean smiled, relaxed slightly at the sight of the money. 'Well, that's different, innit? Where d'you wanna go? You gotta car?'

The man shook his head.

'Have to be the hotel, then.' Dean made to walk away. 'Come—'

'Not the hotel.'

'Where, then?'

'I've got somewhere in mind.'

And there was that smile again. That creepy smile. Dean became uneasy. The fifty was waved in his face.

'Here,' Spooky Tooth said. 'That's upfront. There'll be another one afterwards.'

Dean plucked the note, smiled. That went a long way towards calming his fears.

'After you,' he said.

Dean was led up York Way, past old warehouses turned into bars and nightclubs, down a set of narrow concrete steps towards the canal.

'You got a name, then?'

'Alan,' said the man after a moment's thought.

'Alan it is.'

Weeds, cans, needles and other detritus were strewn on the towpath and the embankment. Inner-city flowers. Occasional rusting shopping trolleys and bicycles rose from the water, looking in the darkness like ancient sea serpents, sunken cities. The overhead lights were bulbless, the walls graffitied and tagged. Under the bridge's arch and beyond, shadows consumated furtive lusts. Rats scavenged around them. Dean knew the place, had used it before.

'I know a good spot. Come on.'

He led Dean away from the lights of the main road, the thump of the bars and nightclubs no more than a distant heartbeat. Derelict, half-demolished buildings fronted an even more barren part of the canal. Desolate. Deserted. Even the rats were absent.

Alan led him into one of the old buildings. Dean shivered from more than the cold. The place had a bad atmosphere. Like something horrific had once happened there and the echoes could still be felt.

'I like somewhere with a bit of atmosphere,' he said, fronting, thinking of the other fifty-pound note, wondering what he would have to do for it.

Alan smiled. Said nothing. Undid his belt, began to open his jeans.

'Come on, Dean,' he said. 'You should be doing this. It's what I'm paying you for.'

Dean kneeled down before him, began unbuttoning. He found Alan's already hardening penis, pulled it out. Felt along the shaft. Then stopped, gasping.

'Fuckin' 'ell, what's that?'

Alan smiled. 'You like it? Ten millimetres thick. Three centimetres wide.' Pride in his tone.

Augmented by metal, it felt like some medieval instrument of torture.

'Does that hurt?'

'No,' said Alan, a small note of sadness in his voice. 'Not even when you pull it.' He placed his hands on the back of Dean's head, forced him forward. 'So pull it.'

Dean got to work. It was difficult. He couldn't breathe through his mouth. And it hurt his fillings. Alan was shuffling about, too, which made it hard to concentrate. He was about to stop, say something, when the back of his hair was roughly grabbed, his head forced away.

'What the fuck—'

The words died in Dean's mouth. Alan was before him, one arm restraining his body, the other holding a machete against his throat.

'I was enjoying that,' said Alan, 'so this had better be worthwhile.'

Dean had been threatened before, beaten up, even. But this was much worse. He was too terrified to speak.

'You know I said I wasn't here on business? I lied. Now, if you lie, something horrible will happen to you. Got that?'

Dean felt like he couldn't get enough air into his body. He tried to pull his neck away from the blade. Alan held him too tightly.

'OK?'

Dean nodded, whimpering as he did so.

'Good. Now, where's Jamal?'

Dean said nothing.

'I told you, don't fuck with me.'

Dean felt the blade deepen against his neck. His front began to feel wet.

'Now, I've just broken the skin,' said Alan, his voice calm and low. 'If I keep pushing, I'll sever your windpipe. And if I move it round to the side here . . .' He demonstrated. 'It goes through your vein. Or artery. Whichever. Doesn't matter. You'll die either way.'

Dean sobbed.

'Now, I'll ask again. Where's Jamal?'

'Nuh – nuh – Newcastle . . .'

'Newcastle? What's he doing there?'

'Dunno . . .'

'What's he doing there?'

The blade began to bite again.

'Donovan!' he gasped.

'Donovan?'

'Yeah . . . Said he would be makin' buh-bare money soon

from someone called Donovan . . . Jamal . . . had a plan . . .
he was . . . was excited . . .'

The machete eased away from Dean's throat. Alan relaxed
his grip. Dean began to gasp down air.

'I said it would be all right if you told me the truth.'

Dean was down on his hands and knees. 'Th – thank
you . . . thank you . . .'

'Now empty your pockets.'

Dean looked up, confused. 'What?'

'Empty your pockets. Just the money will do.'

Dean felt anger rising within him but reluctantly handed
the cash over, hands shaking as he did so. Giving up Jamal
was one thing, but losing his money . . .

'Bastard . . .'

Alan turned on him. 'What did you say?'

Dean had spoken without thinking. 'Nothing . . . nothing . . . I'm sorry . . .'

'You little piece of shit. Talking back to me.' His eyes glittered in the dark, lit by a malevolent light, almost beyond
human.

Before Dean could say or do another thing, Alan was on
him, the blade against his throat. Pressing hard.

'Piece of shit.' His eyes dancing to a mad, unheard tune.

The machete was pushed further.

Dean tried to scream.

But had no vocal cords.

Dean tried to think.

But the blood had been cut off from his brain.

Dean tried to breathe.

But his windpipe had been severed.

Dean tried to live.

But he was beyond that now.

The Hammer watched as the body floated for a few seconds

then, weighed down by the breeze blocks and bricks it had been trussed with, began to sink. The last of the surface bubbles popped and there was nothing to indicate a body had ever been there.

He had on a spare set of clothes, his soiled ones in the bag along with the machete.

And his trophy.

He sighed, his body returning to what passed for equilibrium. Back to Newcastle. Again. To step things up. Give proceedings a little push.

This travelling was tiring. He patted the bag, heaved it on to his shoulder. Smiled his blue-toothed smile. But not without its rewards.

A final check to see if he had left anything incriminating. Nothing.

But then, no one would look here anyway.

He gave the bag another pat and set off.

Back to Newcastle.

7

When he closed his eyes, Gary Myers could see their faces. Amanda, his wife. Georgie, eight, and Rosie, five. Could imagine Amanda's body next to him, the kids jumping on the bed, laughing and hugging them both, the Saturday-morning lie-ins that he always treasured when he was home.

He imagined their faces sick with worry, their lives incomplete, and sighed in exasperation as rage, long fermented with fear and helplessness, bubbled within. Embryonic tears tickled and stung the corners of his eyes.

He grabbed his right hand with his left, began to pull. Hard. And again. Grunting, growling as he did so. The chain links held. The pipe remained firmly planted in the wall and floor. The cuff dug into him, dredged deep into badly bruised flesh, rubbed and worked open wounds barely healed from his last attempt.

He ignored the pain, kept pulling. Willed the iron pipe to come away from the wall. Rattled, tugged, groaned, screamed.

And eventually lay, anger spent and new pain piling on old, panting on the floor.

'It's no good . . . you're better off conserving your strength . . .'

Gary opened his eyes. Colin sat at the opposite end of the radiator, slouched against the wall. John McCarthy to his Brian Keenan. Colin didn't look well. Previously dapper, he seemed to have unravelled, given up. Dishevelled and unkempt, his deterioration seemed to be part of a domino effect; once one piece had toppled, everything had gone.

Gary had almost forgotten Colin was there. When they exhausted themselves of each other's forced intimacy, Gary would slip into a neo-fugue state, depart the real world; create an imaginary one in his head where he could go by himself or with his wife and children, get lost anywhere that helped him to cope with the captivity. He imagined that Colin, although he had never said, did something similar.

'I know him,' Colin continued, holding his arm awkwardly against his body, breathing carefully and with difficulty, 'know what he wants. And we can't give him it. So don't fight it.'

Gary closed his eyes, not wanting to see the absence of hope in his companion's eyes.

'I knew he was ruthless,' Colin said dreamily, almost to himself. 'And manipulative. But this . . . this is the act of a madman. Psychotic . . .'

'Well, when we get out, I'll see to it that he's punished. Not only that—' Gary laughed against the pain. '—but we'll write the book together. Big advance, serialization rights, chat-show circuit, the lot. We'll be quids in.'

Colin gave a sad smile, the kind a terminally ill man gives when told that summer is only weeks away.

'It's a nice thought,' he said.

Colin closed his eyes, laid his back against the wall, slid further down.

Gary did likewise.

He didn't know how long he lay like that; minutes, hours, days, even. Time had become a fluid and elastic thing, an untrustworthy and mockingly constant companion.

He heard the first outside lock being turned, the bolt pushed back.

Quickly he grabbed for his hood, started to fumble it on with one hand. The pain from his wrist was sharp and intense. He thought it might be broken.

The door opened. Light flooded the floor, so strong and sudden it seemed almost biblical. Gary squinted. His hood was partway on to his head but not yet over his eyes.

Two figures entered, closed the door behind them. The outside world was abruptly cut off. Miniature starbursts hit Gary's eyes, like he'd been staring into the sun and blinked.

'Hoods won't be necessary, gentlemen,' said one of the captors. Gary didn't know which one; his eyes were still dazzled.

'You letting us go?' asked Gary, hope rising within.

'In a manner of speaking,' said the same man. 'Decisions have been taken. Plans made.'

Gary let the words sink in, the figures come into focus. The one talking was well dressed, a dark overcoat covering his suit and tie. The other one he had seen before. Big, bald and bad. Leather jacket covering a lethally muscled body. Tattooed knuckles.

'Just you.' The well-dressed man pointed at Gary.

And Gary suddenly knew what he meant.

His stomach flipped, his breathing became laboured. He opened his mouth to speak, but no words would come out.

He sat up, tried to pull away. But it was no good.

The bald-headed figure strode purposefully towards him.

'No . . . no . . .'

Heard a weak, whimpering voice, realized it was his own.

Felt a hand grab his shirt, haul him up.

Felt the pain in his wrist, ignored it.

Saw the skinhead's other hand pull back, curl into a fist.

Thought of Amanda's body next to him. Georgie, eight, and Rosie, five, jumping on the bed, laughing and hugging them both. The Saturday lie-ins he'd always treasured when he was home.

Home.

He saw the fist released, coming towards him. Saw the blur of a blue-jewelled shark smile. Saw the word flash quickly before his eyes: LOVE.

Felt pain; sudden, intense, red hot.

Then nothing.

Jamal checked his disc again: still there.

He sat on the edge of the bed, pulled on his trainers. Straightening up, he noticed how short he was of breath. How nervous he felt.

This was it. The first step to a new life. In a few hours he would be five grand richer and hassle free. As soon as that disc disappeared, everything else went with it. The threats on his life. Punters who wanted to touch him. Father Jack and his plans.

He had tried phoning Dean, just to see if he was OK, but kept getting just his voicemail. Probably let the battery run down, Jamal had thought, or off raving. Or lost it. Yeah, that's it. Something like that.

Jamal stood up, pulled on his jacket. Patted the minidisc player in one pocket, mobile in the other. He had checked obsessively to see if there was any message from Donovan. Nothing. Good sign, meant the meet was still on. Nothing from Dean either. But Dean was OK. Yeah, he would be OK.

He gave one last tug at the front of his hair − getting nappy, needed a cut − checked his no-longer-box-white Nikes and made his way out. He was down the stairs with his hand on the door, when he heard his name being called. He turned. Si was standing in the frame of the living room door, smiling, 50 Cent shouting in the background about how drinking Bacardi made him a hard man.

Get Rich or Die Trying.

'Off out?'

Jamal swallowed hard. 'Yeah.'

'Where to?'

'Punter.'

Si's grin got wider. 'Same one?'

Jamal shrugged non-committally.

'Must be fond of you. Want to adopt you, does he? Take you home?'

Jamal turned, made a grab for the front door.

Si got there first. Stuck out a swift arm, kept the door firmly shut.

'Fuck you doin', man?' said Jamal, nerves manifesting themselves as anger. 'Outta my way.'

'Not yet,' said Si. 'Father Jack wants to see you.'

Jamal tried to deaden his eyes. Turn his features to stone. He failed.

'Get out of my way. I'm goin' out.'

Si grabbed the front of Jamal's jacket, pushed him back on to the stairs. Held him down. Faces began to appear from the front room. Si looked towards them.

'Fuck off,' he said, eyes lit by a harsh light. 'Me an' Jamal are talkin'. Private.'

The door was quickly closed, 50 Cent silenced.

'That's better,' said Si. 'Now, get upstairs. Father Jack's waitin' for you.'

Jamal got slowly to his feet, trudged reluctantly upstairs.

'You don't need to knock. He's expectin' you.'

Jamal went in. Father Jack was sitting on the bed, fully dressed in a Hawaiian shirt that looked big enough to cover Hawaii and pair of chinos that a group of boy scouts could have gone camping in for a week. Probably had.

But there was nothing remotely comical about his expression. He looked beyond predatory, beyond wicked. He looked expectant at the prospect of causing pain.

He swallowed hard, tried to will himself to stone.

Failed again.

Si closed the door behind them, stood with his back against it.

'Off out again?' said Father Jack.

Jamal said nothing.

'Off to see this punter again? This boyfriend?'

Jamal gave a strained nod.

Father Jack stood up. The way he moved his bulk was menacing.

'Pays well, I hear. Not the million you wanted, but good enough. For a boy like you.'

Jamal felt the air had been punched from his body. Felt his legs buckle and weaken.

'Five grand, isn't it? Generous, our Mr Donovan.'

Jamal's breath came in laboured gasps. He couldn't think fast enough. How had they found out? He had been so careful. He saw the mental image of five grand disappearing before him.

He made to turn, to run for it, but Si was there. Si grabbed him, twisted his arm up behind his back. Jamal gasped, winced in pain. Jack approached him. Got right in his face. Jamal smelled honey and mint, cologne and soap covering the stink of old sweat and corruption.

'Don't fuck me about now, boy. You do not want to fuck me about.'

Jamal stared; no answer would come.

'Now,' said Father Jack, 'where's this disc?'

Jamal opened his mouth slowly. 'What disc?' he said. His throat felt like sandpaper. 'I don't know nothin' about no—'

Father Jack touched him. Poked his fingers hard into strategic places. Jamal felt pain shoot around the middle of his body, up his spine. His knees gave way; he started to fall. Si gripped his arm tighter, the only thing holding Jamal upright. Counter-pain bled out from that. Jamal twisted and struggled, tried to move away from the pain, find respite, stand – and think – straight.

'You're fucking me about, boy,' Father Jack shouted into his face. 'I told you not to. Now, where's the disc?'

Jamal opened his mouth to speak. No sound would emerge.

More fingers. More strategic poking. More pain.

Jamal felt like he was on the verge of passing out.

'Let him go,' said Father Jack.

Si loosened his grip, stepped back. Father Jack took his fingers away. Jamal collapsed on to the floor, panting hard. He didn't know what to do first, faint or throw up.

He threw up.

'Oh that's disgusting,' said Father Jack. 'You're cleaning that up.'

Jamal said nothing.

Father Jack fixed him with a dispassionate stare. 'The disc. Where is it?'

Jamal slowly inched his hand round to the small of his back. 'Jacket . . .' he said, his voice tiny and fragile.

Si tore the jacket off him. He felt all round until his fingers alighted on the shape of the disc. He tore the lining in two, pulled it out.

'Here it is,' he said, triumph in his voice. He found a lump in the pocket, pulled out the minidisc player.

'And look what we have here,' he said.

Father Jack smiled. 'Very nice.' He kneeled before Jamal, waved a hand theatrically, made a face. 'You stink. Now, what's on this disc that's so important?'

'All sortsa shit,' gasped Jamal. 'This journalist is gonna pay me to get it back. Pay me big time . . .'

Father Jack stood up, took the disc and player from Si, inserted the disc, put the headphones on.

'Get that mess cleaned up,' he said to Jamal, who was beginning to, with difficulty, sit up.

'And you,' Father Jack pointed at Si. 'When he's done that, get him cleaned up.'

'Why?' said Si.

Father Jack didn't like to be questioned. His expression said as much.

Si swallowed hard.

'Sorry,' he said. 'I didn't mean anything. I just meant—'

'Do as you're told,' said Father Jack, ending any argument. 'I want him cleaned up and ready to meet this Donovan bloke.'

Si looked at him. 'You mean he's still gonna—'

'Oh yes,' said Father Jack, 'he certainly is. Now, do as you're told.'

Si did as he was told.

Father Jack sat back on the bed.

Pressed PLAY.

8

'Hey look. Quick, look.'

Amar was standing by the window. Peta came up to join him.

'The newbie's off out. And he's got that Si kid with him. The creepy one.'

Peta looked closely. 'And I'd say newbie didn't look too happy about it.'

'What d'you reckon?' said Amar. 'Should one of us follow?'

Peta smiled sarcastically. 'By one of us, I presume you mean me?'

'Well, I . . .'

'Got a hot date, I know. And you can't keep him waiting.'

Amar gave a relieved smile. 'You're a darling,' he said. 'Be quick, though. This could be interesting.'

'Thanks, mother,' said Peta, loading a small digital camera and tape recorder into a pocket of her three-quarter-length leather jacket and making for the door. 'Any other aspects of the business you'd like to enlighten me on?'

'Yeah. Don't talk to strange men.'

'Says you.'

She closed the door, left.

Amar stood at the window watching her walk up the street. 'Be careful,' he said, but her image was already receding.

Donovan stood leaned on a railing at the quayside, listening to the Tyne slosh along. Killing time; letting it pass, watching it change.

All along the quay on both sides was transformation, gentrification. New flats, bars, restaurants, hotels; the old Tyne
of dockers, mills and warehouses so last century. So pre-
millennium.

The Baltic Centre for Contemporary Art had been a flour
mill in a previous life. Now, queues regularly snaked round the
newly built and christened Baltic Square and often over the
newly built and christened Millennium Bridge to see cutting-
edge modern art. He himself had joined the queue one day,
from curiosity, to see an Antony Gormley exhibition. The
inclusivity of the other queuers had surprised him: in front
had been two bus drivers, necks heavily tattooed, telling each
other how much they had been looking forward to this trip all
throughout their shifts, behind were two Jesmond
Guardianista mothers struggling to control their overenthusi-
astic Jocastas and Henriettas, behind them a retired couple
eager for, as they said, something a bit different.

Donovan had left his cynicism at home that day. Enjoyed
himself.

Next to the Baltic was the Sage Music Centre. A
sparkling concert hall created from concentric silver bands,
it looked like a huge metallic slug caught mid-undulation.
Either that, or the mother ship had landed.

Transformation.

The city of Donovan's childhood, of coal mines, heavy
industry and manual labour, was long gone. In its place was
a city of culture and tourism, of call centres and service
industries. And the largest growth industry in the north-east:
IT and software development. From 'whey aye, man' to
'whey imac'.

He smiled, pleased with that one. Then looked around,
sighed. Wished he had someone to share it with.

He had no close family living in the area any more, no
reason to ever visit. He had left, never looking back.

College, work and life in London had taken him away from it. The city could have been anywhere.

In the cottage he would sometimes talk to David. Sit in David's room, have a conversation. Sometimes David would answer. Or Donovan would imagine he would answer. But mostly David didn't and Donovan became aware that he was just sitting on the floor talking to himself. Like throwing his voice out into the fog. That was when he knew it was time to get out of the house.

And go to Newcastle. Book into a hotel, go drinking, eat out. See life, but not touch it.

All the time he was in the city he was never of it. The people in this city seemed so sure of themselves; indestructible as they planned their jobs, lives, futures. Dreams. Secure in the knowledge they would live them out. He had been like that once. Now, he felt like a citizen of a parallel, invisible city, one with no such self-delusional surety, where there was no point making plans for the future because a roll of some capricious god's dice would upset them, where inhabitants knew that hope and despair were the same thing.

Before he had left he had said goodbye to David. Stood in the centre of the room and whispered:

'I'm going away for a little bit, but I'll be back soon. I'm doing this for you.'

He smiled at the images of his son, tried to quell the rising excitement at being involved with something again, tried to ignore the guilt that excitement provoked.

Donovan turned his back on the railing, looked at the street. The Crown Court building stood before him, bars and restaurants dotted around and filling up. He checked his watch: eight p.m. The boy should be here any time.

Donovan was dressed as he had described himself over the phone: three-quarter-length brown-leather jacket, old Levi's, Timberlands. Hair long, greying. The boy had not offered a description of himself, but he had formed a mental image of what he would look like. He doubted he would be disappointed.

Another check of the watch: nearly five past eight. He put his hands in his pockets, tapped his feet. Despite everything, he wanted to smile. The thrill of being involved again was getting to him.

And then he saw the boy. Or who he assumed was the boy. A teenager, small-looking, wearing baggy jeans, trainers and an Avirex leather jacket embossed with brands and adverts like a Formula One driver. Light-skinned black boy, he stood out against the crowd. Most of the people around him were relaxed, out for a good time. The boy looked like he was calculating the odds, on the make.

In the city but not of it. Another inhabitant from that parallel, invisible city.

He clocked Donovan, who nodded. The boy approached.

Getting close, Donovan looked into the boy's eyes. They were wary and, although the arrogant swagger attempted disguise, scared.

Donovan smiled. 'We meet at last.'

The boy nodded.

'Got the disc?'

The boy's eyes darted quickly around, like swallows trapped in a barn. Scoping the area for backup to rain down on him, Donovan thought.

'Not here, man.'

'What?'

'Not here, man. Back at the hotel.'

Donovan was impressed. He was managing to speak without moving his lips. If there were anyone watching, they wouldn't be able to lip-read.

'The hotel.'

'Yeah, man, like we agreed. Anybody watchin' thinks you just picked me up. You a john.'

'A what?'

'A punter, man. You know.'

'Thanks a lot,' said Donovan. 'Do I look like the kind of person who picks up boys, then?'

'Don't matter what you look like, man. S'what you want. Now, your hotel, yeah?'

The boy shot another glance around. Perhaps it's him being watched, thought Donovan. Not me.

'Come on, then,' he said. 'My hotel.'

Donovan's hotel fronted the river along the Close at the base of the hill up to Forth Street. Along the hill was a series of old stairways leading away from the Tyne and up to the city itself. Some were self-explanatory – Castle Stairs, Tuthill Stairs, Long Stairs – one invited explanation – Dog Leap Stairs – and one was obvious and cautionary – Breakneck Stairs.

Donovan's hotel was directly opposite Breakneck Stairs.

Neither had spoken on the walk back.

The night had moved in, obscuring the moon with heavy clouds. A storm was coming.

'Close the curtains, man.'

Donovan closed the curtains and stepped away from the window. He turned to face the boy, who was standing at the other side of the double bed staring at him, unmoving.

'So,' said Donovan, opening the minibar and uncapping a bottle of chilled beer, 'you got a name?'

'Tony Montana,' said Jamal, lip curling in arrogance.

Donovan smiled. He admired front in people with whom he was dealing. Gave him something to work with.

'How original,' he said. 'If you're going to lie, at least pick a better film.'

Donovan smiled. Jamal almost did, stopped himself.

Donovan took a mouthful of beer, nodded towards the minibar.

'Want anything?' he asked.

'Yeah,' said Jamal, and gestured towards Donovan's beer.

Donovan took out another, uncapped it, passed it across.

'Say hello to your leetle friend,' he said as he did so.

Jamal gave a small but genuine smile, which soon disappeared.

It's a start, thought Donovan, progress. Something to help open negotiations. He sat down on the bed. Jamal remained standing.

'So what's your real name, then?'

Jamal thought for a moment, then, decision made, said: 'Jamal.'

'Jamal,' repeated Donovan, 'You Muslim?'

Jamal looked confused. 'Why?'

'It's a Muslim name,' he said. 'Thought you must be Muslim.'

'Nah, man, it's from my dad. He was some African warrior.'

Donovan sat forward, interested. 'Really? Is he back in Africa now?'

Jamal shrugged. 'Dunno. 'Swhat my mum tole me when I was little.'

Donovan nodded. He was starting to put together a picture of the boy. His mix of street hardness and naivety. A lost boy.

He thought of his own lost boy.

'What you starin' at me like that for, man?' Jamal seemed angry and uncomfortable.

Donovan thought for a moment. 'You're just different from how I imagined you'd look from your voice on the phone.'

'Yeah? Well, so are you, man. I wasn't expectin' no scruffy hippie.'

Donovan caught a look at himself in the mirror. He smiled.

'Yeah, Jamal,' he said. 'You've got a point.'

The two of them regarded each other, drank their beer. Jamal leaned against the side cupboard, tense, ready to dart for the door at any moment.

Donovan knew he should press on, get the disc into his possession, but Jamal intrigued him. He wanted to find out more about him.

'So, Jamal,' he said, 'you're a hustler, that right?'

Jamal shrugged. 'Yeah. S'pose so.'

'How d'you get into that?'

Jamal's mood changed. He began to pace the room, agitatedly.

'What you wanna know for? You some fuckin' social worker?'

'No, I'm not a social worker—'

'Then you get off on it? You a pervert or somethin'?'

'Neither, Jamal. I'm just interested.' Donovan sighed, looked at the angry boy with the scared, hurt eyes. Made a decision he couldn't explain to himself.

'I had a son,' he said, 'and he disappeared. He'd be eight now. And I looked, but I never found him.'

'An' you think I seen him?' Jamal stopped pacing. His voice had a superficial dismissiveness and arrogance, but it was the eyes again. They gave him away. Donovan's admission had affected him. He just didn't know how to react to it.

'No,' said Donovan calmly and quietly. 'I just wondered what it involved. How you survived. How you coped. You know, just in case . . .' He shrugged.

Jamal looked around at the door. Uncomfortable.

'Look, man, let's do the fuckin' business, yeah?' He was waving his beer bottle around, gesturing with it. 'I'm sorry about your son an' that, but let's do the business. Ain't got all night.'

Donovan drained his bottle, stood up. He crossed to the sideboard, powered up his laptop.

'You got the disc?'

'You got the money?'

'That drawer there,' said Donovan pointing.

'Lemme see.'

Donovan opened the drawer. Jamal crossed the room, looked in. Saw bundles of notes, neatly laid out in two piles. He extended his hand. Donovan slammed the drawer shut.

'Disc first,' he said.

'Didn't look that much,' said Jamal. 'That all of it?'

'That's all of it.' He held out his hand. 'Please.'

Jamal took the minidisc from his pocket, handed it over. Donovan placed it on the CD tray, watched it slide back in.

'So how did you come by this?' he asked.

'Found it.' Jamal shrugged. His body shivered.

Donovan looked at him closely. 'Where?'

'London.'

He had further questions to ask, but his media player was asking him to press PLAY. He did so.

'Hope this is worth waiting for,' he said.

A voice came out of the speakers. High-pitched, camp even, but with an ugly, hard edge to it. A voice Donovan had never heard before.

'I doubt this was what you were expecting, was it?' the voice said. 'It's Mr Donovan, isn't it? Well, if you're listening to this it means that Jamal has been a good boy and done as he was told.'

Donovan looked at Jamal, who looked at the carpet. The voice continued.

'There is another disc, and what is on it is very interest-ing to the right person. Are you the right person, Mr Donovan? I think you are. And I think you will want it. Jamal will tell you how. And Mr Donovan? Needless to say, the price has just gone up. Quite a bit. Goodbye, Mr Donovan. I look forward to hearing from you.'

Donovan pressed STOP.

'Sorry, man,' said Jamal. 'They found out. Cut me out, an' . . .' He shrugged, shivered again. 'You gotta do what they say, man. They bad people.'

'Who are "they"?'

Jamal shrugged, shook his head. 'Bad, bad people . . .'

Donovan sighed, angry and impotent suddenly.

Jamal stood staring at him, mouth moving like he wanted to articulate something but couldn't find the words.

'I . . .' he began. 'I'm . . . sorry about your son, man.'

Donovan nodded. He had to do something, take some kind of action. He saw Jamal walk towards the door.

'Wait there, Jamal,' he said. 'Don't go. I want to talk to you.'

Jamal stopped, waited. Donovan picked up his mobile, speed-dialled Maria. She answered.

'It's Donovan. Listen, things have changed.'

Maria gave a bitter laugh. 'You're telling me,' she said. 'Look, I'm on my way up.'

'From London?'

'From the hotel lobby. I'll reach your room in a couple of minutes.'

'What?'

'Everything's changed, Joe. Gary Myers has turned up. Dead.'

She broke the connection.

'Wait there!'

Jamal was trying to slip out of the door.

Donovan threw the mobile on the bed.

There came a crash of thunder.

Rain lashed against the window.

The storm had broken.

PART TWO:
SECRETS AND LIES

9

Jamal stood up. Donovan caught the movement, pointed a finger.

'I said, stay where you are.'

Jamal sat back down on the corner of the bed, warily, his eyes never leaving Donovan. Waiting.

From beyond the door came occasional voices, lift movement, footsteps, doors opening and closing. The other city going about its business. Inside the hotel room, time had ground to a tense halt. The lighting dark and diffuse, the only sounds breathing and the rain pummelling the glass like tracer fire. Now part of the shadow city.

Maria sat on an armchair beneath the window. Donovan stood, his back to the mirror, staring ahead.

'Tell me again,' he said. 'I don't think I took it in first time.'

Maria looked around the room, down at her hastily packed suitcase, back to Donovan.

'He's dead. Gary Myers is dead.' She stopped talking, shook her head, as if speaking the words had made the act itself happen. 'Dead . . .'

'Murdered?' asked Donovan. Trying to quell the shock, letting his long-disused journalistic instincts kick in. Working through his emotions.

She shrugged. 'Don't know. They haven't done the post-mortem yet. They found him in the Pennines. At the bottom of some steep hill. By the gorge at Allen Banks. Off the path.'

'Who found him?'

'Some—' With guilty self-admonishment, Maria stopped herself smiling. 'Some amateur photographers. Naturists, I suppose.'

'In this weather?'

'Specialist interest. The readers' wives brigade.'

Donovan smiled despite himself. 'Doggers?'

Maria reddened. 'Doggers.'

Jamal looked between the pair of them, trying to gauge their reactions. He had heard of the practice of going to some out-of-the-way place, letting strangers watch you have sex, join in even. Didn't know why they were making such a big thing of it, he thought. A lot better than some of the stuff he had been asked to do.

While they were talking, he slowly got to his feet, began to edge his way to the door.

'Stay where you are.' Donovan again.

Jamal sighed, sat down.

'What was he doing there?' said Maria almost to herself.

'What were they doing there?' replied Donovan, then continued, answering himself. 'A secluded spot. Secluded but accessible. You can get up to what you want there. Having sex without being disturbed, or . . .'

'Dump bodies,' said Maria with a shiver. 'Without being disturbed.'

Donovan looked at Maria, who couldn't hold his gaze, looked away.

'I know it's jumping to conclusions,' she said, 'but I . . .' She sighed, shook her head.

'What do the police say?' asked Donovan.

'Nothing firm until they get the preliminary results.' She sighed, her chest and shoulders almost rigid.

No one spoke. No sounds but the outside world, the rain.

Maria explained why she was there and not at the office.

Sharkey's idea, she said. Thought Donovan was on to something that could solve the mystery of Gary Myers' death. Something important.

'And are you?' she asked.

He turned to Jamal. 'Are we?'

Jamal shook his head. 'Oh man,' he said, 'don't do this . . .'

'There are complications.' Donovan played the disc for Maria. As it finished, she sighed, sat back.

'This changes everything,' she said.

'You do realize,' said Donovan to Jamal, 'that it's Gary Myers, the man whose voice you said was on that disc, who's now dead?'

Jamal nodded, wide-eyed.

'Think there's a connection?'

Jamal opened his mouth to reply, saw only the hotel room in King's Cross. The shaven head, the blue-jewelled smile. FEAR, LOVE, muscle and leather. Death's eyes locked on him like laser beams. The chase in cinematic black and white slomo: street noise pushed up, slowed down, like the howls of monsters.

Heard the words on the disc.

He shivered.

'Dunno,' he said, his voice pitifully small.

The other two exchanged glances, waited for him to speak further. He didn't.

Donovan pulled out his mobile, looked at it, sighed, then began to punch in numbers.

'Who are you calling?' asked Maria.

'The police,' he said. 'Out of our hands now. Up to them what happens.' He looked at Jamal. 'I'll get them to come here. Listen to the disc. We just sit tight until then.'

Jamal stood up, looked at Donovan, his hands in front of him as if fending off blows. 'Aw no, man, low it, low it . . .'

'Sorry, Jamal, but there's no sale. You'd better get your story ready for the boys in blue.'

Jamal looked around, his eyes staring, like a scared animal. 'What about the money?'

'Sorry, mate,' said Donovan. 'Police matter now.'

Fear crept into Jamal's features. He thought of going back to Byker empty-handed. Of Father Jack's reaction . . .

'You all right?' Donovan looked at him, genuine concern in his eyes.

Jamal's throat was cold and dry. He swallowed hard. 'What if,' he said slowly, 'what if I tell you about the other man?'

Donovan pressed a key on his phone, cut the call. He glanced at Maria, who frowned. 'What other man?'

'In the—' He almost said room. 'On the disc. If I tell you about him, will you keep the feds off, get me my money, yeah?'

Another exchanged glance. 'Well,' said Maria, 'I'll do my best. I'll have to talk to—'

'Money or no deal. But no feds.'

Donovan and Maria looked at each other.

'Deal?' Jamal was almost shouting.

Donovan sighed, looked at Maria, who shrugged, nodded.

Jamal looked around, as if someone was about to enter the room, drag him away. Without saying another word, he jumped for the door, twisted the handle, and, despite Donovan reaching out to stop him, was out of the room and gone. Donovan looked at a startled Maria, ran through the door and after him.

He saw Jamal disappearing round a corner at the far end of the corridor. Before he did, he turned to Donovan and, without slowing down, held his hand to his face, extending his thumb and little finger in the universally acknowledged sign of the phone.

'Wait!' shouted Donovan.

To no one. Jamal was gone.

Donovan stopped, panting, looked around, tried to pick up a trace. He saw double doors at the far end: the stairs. He made for them, thinking that was the route the boy would have taken. He banged through the double doors and down, trying to find a fast running rhythm that didn't involve him jumping and perhaps falling. Trying to listen for some sign that Jamal was ahead of him.

He heard nothing but his own clumping feet, hard breathing.

Then out through the blond-wood doors on the ground floor, into the lobby. He scoped it: swaths of minimalist corporate fixtures and fittings. More blond wood, both real and laminate. Contrasting raspberry and orange chairs. Airport lounge lighting. People.

But no sign of Jamal.

He checked round corners, walls, drew curious glances from staff and customers, ignored them.

No Jamal.

He sighed and pushed through the double glass doors into the night. A sound behind him, he turned: Maria hurrying from the lift, joining him outside. He looked at her, shook his head.

'Shit,' she said.

Cold and rain hit them, making them immediately shiver. They looked around, saw only the streetlit, windswept northern night. Cars rushed past in blurs of light, like scurrying insects, carapaces slick and shiny with rain.

They ran to the end of the car park, looked up and down the street.

No Jamal.

'What's happening there?' Maria pointed to the other side of the road. By the brick-walled entrance to a darkened set of stone stairs stood a man and a woman. The man, suited and bullish, was gripping the woman's arms, anger rising within him. The woman, blonde, wearing a black-leather jacket and jeans, was trying to pull away.

'Domestic,' said Donovan, eyes still sweeping the street. 'Best not to get involved.'

'Rubbish,' said Maria. 'Come on.'

She pulled him, running, across the road. They walked quickly up to the couple. In his anger, the suited man hadn't noticed their approach.

'Everything all right?' asked Maria.

The man turned, ready to start on hearing another woman's voice. Then he saw Donovan.

'This whore,' said the suited man, voice embittered by alcohol, 'says she's not working.'

'I am not a whore,' shouted the blonde woman, attempting to ready her hands and arms to strike him. 'Now get off me, or I'll—'

'Just trying to give you a bit of business,' said the man, not letting go. 'What's the matter? Putting the price up by playing hard to get?'

Donovan stepped forward, placed his hand on the man's arm. 'I think you'd better go now. Leave the lady alone.'

The suited man turned, looked down at Donovan's hand. His red face, if anything, getting redder. 'Get your hand off me,' he spat. 'What are you, her pimp?' He gestured towards Maria. 'This another one of yours?' He gave a drunken, leering laugh. 'I'll have her as well. How much for them both?'

And that was it for Donovan. The night's events had peaked. Broken.

With both hands he slammed the man up against the wall, winding him, then, while the man was still too surprised to retaliate, pinning him there by his neck. The man gagged and spluttered as he attempted to breathe, arms flailing uselessly.

'Now listen, needledick,' said Donovan. 'I've had a very bad night. And you've just capped it off. Leave the lady alone. And take your stinking, fucking self off somewhere else. Before I change my mind and fucking kill you. Got that?'

Donovan's face was right in the other man's; he was bellowing the words at him. Fear penetrated the man's clouded bloodshot eyes.

'I said, got that?'

The man swallowed hard, nodded.

Donovan didn't loosen his grip.

'Now, before you go, apologize. To my friend and this lady. For calling them whores.'

'I'm . . . I'm sorry . . .' he managed to choke out.

'For?' Donovan pushed harder.

'. . . calling you . . . whores . . .'

'That's better.'

Donovan slackened his grip. The man began gasping for air.

'Now, fuck off. And don't let me see you here again.'

The man stumbled hurriedly off, then, when he had put enough space between himself and Donovan, bent double and retched all over the pavement. He looked back at Donovan, delivered some feeble and inaudible threat, then lurched slowly and unsteadily off. They watched until he was out of sight.

Donovan turned to Maria. 'Welcome to Newcastle,' he said.

'Thank you,' she said, looking into his eyes and trying a tentative smile to ease the tension. 'My hero.'

Donovan wanted to return the look but didn't trust himself. He looked at the blonde woman.

'Are you OK?' he asked.

She nodded. 'I'm fine,' she said. 'Just wet.'

'Can we do anything?' said Maria. 'Call you a cab?'

'I . . . I was waiting for someone,' the blonde woman replied. 'Looks like he's not going to show.'

'Come into the hotel,' said Donovan. 'Out of the cold. We'll call from there.'

'Thanks,' she said. 'Thank you.'

They crossed the road, approached the hotel.

'Oh by the way,' said Donovan. 'I'm Joe and this is Maria.'

'Pleased to meet you. I'm Peta,' said the blonde woman. 'Peta Knight.'

The hotel's automatic glass doors admitted the three and closed silently behind them, shutting out the cold, the rain and the night.

10

Amar stirred his cappuccino slowly, letting the brown sugar dissolve at the bottom without disturbing the thick, foamy cap. Job done, he put his spoon in the saucer, took a sip. Perfect. The best cappuccino outside of Italy. Not that he had ever been to Italy. But certainly the best cappuccino outside of Bar Italia in Soho. And he had been to Soho many times. Particularly Old Compton Street.

The Intermezzo coffee bar fronted the Tyneside Cinema off Pilgrim Street in Newcastle. Once a run-down old Deco newsreel cinema, now restored as the premiere art house cinema in the north-east of England. Glass-fronted and glass-sided, the Intermezzo's décor was modernist 1950s retro, the music mellow and Latin. Amar perched on a high, red-vinyl and chrome window stool watching the people ebb and flow along High Friar Lane, umbrellaed and damp, the Saturday-morning rain hitting the outdoor café tables and chairs. Around him, other drinkers separated sections from their morning broadsheets, read, drank and ate leisurely. He waited for Peta.

Another sip of coffee. His hand was shaking. Noticeably. He needed to stop, slow down, re-evaluate. He knew that. Surveillance with Peta during the day, acting as cameraman for a wealthy gay voyeur at night. Sustained by cocaine and caffeine, sleep snatched in odd moments or deposited and banked, ready to be withdrawn at some often postponed future date. Not a good way to live. He caught his reflection in the glass, tried to pretend the shadows and hollows beneath his eyes and cheekbones were distortions cast by the overhanging clouds, the dark, grey day.

Last night had been intense. He had, not for the first time, become involved. Moved from paid observer to participant. Like nights previous, it had been fun, but the whole thing was starting to take its toll. He was coming down heavily, his body giving him payback for weeks of abuse.

But he wasn't that bad, he told himself. He didn't have that smell coming off him, that speed freak stink from the kidneys and liver not processing fast enough for the rest of the body. And his eyes weren't reduced to pinwheeling pinpricks. He checked the glass again. Not yet, anyway.

'Morning.'

Peta. Standing at the counter with coffee and pastry. Amar pushed his previous thoughts to the back of his mind, smiled, turning up the wattage.

She paid, walked over, sat on the stool next to him. Scrutinized his face, wrinkled her nose.

'You've overdone the aftershave.'

Amar ignored her. 'So how was last night?' he said, voice slightly brittle and shrill.

'How was yours?' she said, still examining his face.

'Never mind that,' he said. 'Tell me.'

She drew her concerned eyes from him, slipped into work mode, told him. About following the newbie and Creepy Si. About the newbie meeting someone.

'Who?' asked Amar. 'A punter?'

'No,' replied Peta. She tore a strip off her croissant. 'You should have some of this. Lovely.'

'No, thanks. No carbs pass my lips. Only protein.'

'I can imagine.'

Amar sighed. 'Keep going.'

She told him about waiting outside the hotel in the rain, the businessman accosting her, mistaking her for a prostitute.

'Why didn't you use some of your Tae Kwon Do on him?'

'I was about to, but then the newbie — whose name is Jamal, by the way — came running out right past me.'

'And you went after him?'

'No, he was straight off. And this guy was still badgering me, wouldn't leave me alone. But then . . .' She smiled. 'My knight in shining armour rode to my rescue.'

'What?'

'Joe Donovan. He's a journalist. From the *Herald*.'

Amar smiled. 'Really? What's he look like?'

'Tall, long hair. Mid-thirties. Leather jacket and boots. Bit like that old cowboy actor from the 1970s. Sam Elliott? Yeah. But without the moustache.' She smiled. 'Not your type, I'm afraid.'

Amar made a face. 'Too rugged. So when are you seeing him again?'

Peta shrugged. 'Very soon, probably. He was the person Jamal went to meet.'

Amar frowned. 'Personally or professionally?'

'Professionally. And he was there with the paper's editor, too. Maria Bennett.'

'So what's Creepy Si got to do with this? Is he selling out the fat man? What's going on?'

'I don't know. I had a drink with them—'

'Non-alcoholic, I hope.'

Peta sighed. 'Yes, mum. Anyway, I tried to get them to talk, but they wouldn't.'

Amar shook his head. 'This is either very good or very bad news.'

'My thoughts exactly.' Peta took a sip of coffee, frowned. 'If someone else is interested in Father Jack's little enterprise and they get there before us, then everything we've done will be for nothing.'

'And bye-bye Knight Security and Investigations.'

Peta sighed. 'Exactly.'

They watched the rain through the glass. Behind them, love was declared in Spanish over a snake-hipped beat. The baristas discussed their Friday-night exploits in discreet/loud voices.

'On the other hand,' said Peta, turning to face Amar, 'this could work to our advantage.'

Amar waited.

'Think about it,' she said. 'They may be interested in the story but they don't have any evidence. We do.'

'So what are you suggesting?'

'We keep an eye on Mr Donovan. We make sure that if and when he makes his move he does it with us.'

'And if he doesn't?'

Peta's gaze hardened. 'I've come too far with this. I'm not having someone else just appear and beat us to it.' She was breathing heavily.

Amar dug into his pocket, pulled out a roll of notes.

'Speaking of which,' he said, not keeping eye contact. He handed them to her. 'Next month's rent. For the office and the surveillance flat. I got paid last night.'

She looked at it like it would soil her hands to touch it.

'Go on, take it.'

Reluctantly, she took it, pocketing it quickly with another sigh. 'I just wish . . .'

'I know. It won't be for much longer.'

'I'm not going to kiss goodbye to my business now, not after all the work we've done. *Herald* journalist or not.'

Amar nodded, tried not to yawn. He could feel his body beginning to grind to a halt. 'Let's have another coffee,' he said.

Peta, eventually, nodded.

Amar went to the counter. Peta stared out of the window.

The rain continued to fall.

Jamal lay on the bed, listening to the rain on the window. Thinking.

He stared at the ceiling, at the brown, bowed, damp patch directly above his bed, imagining it a real place, a desert island. Imagining he was on a plane now, descending towards it. To peace. To safety.

Elsewhere in the house, life, with its madness and masks, went on.

Jamal looked at the windows, the rain bleaching accumulated dirt from them. The bars beyond the glass twisted, scrolled and rusted. But still bars. They extended within him: caging his heart, locking down his emotions.

The sickness built within, washed and crashed over him like a toxic wave on a poisoned beach.

The sickness.

His name for it. For the times when the reality of his life invaded his secret place, buckled and broke through the bars that caged his heart. Made him see things in stark white clarity.

He was a rent boy. A hustler. Making money from letting perverts use his body. But not gay. Not a batty boy. He did it only for money. Money. His other friends in the house in London did it, too. Friends.

The first time in the children's home had hurt. An older boy, Johnson, had forced him to do things. At night. In the dark. When all the other boys had been sleeping. Or pretending to sleep. Afterwards, Jamal had rushed to the bathroom to be sick. Looked in the mirror and saw the scared, snivelling six-year-old again. Then cried until it felt like his heart had burst. A few nights later Johnson was there again. Forcing him to do things he didn't want to do. Again Jamal was sick. Again he looked in the mirror. Again he cried his heart out.

Jamal had no one to turn to, no one to tell. Johnson had said if he did, he would kill him. Jamal believed him.

He hated his life, the children's home. Saw Johnson everywhere, had to give in to his demands all the time. Eventually he scored some tablets, took them. Staff found him, rushed him to hospital, pumped his stomach.

Saved him.

Questioned him. Analysed him.

He wouldn't talk. Couldn't. Not to them. Not to anyone. And still Johnson came. Forcing him to do things.

Jamal would imagine a dungeon in a huge, dark castle. Somewhere he could lock away his true self, hide until the danger was past and he could come out.

But it never worked, he couldn't. He had to stay with it, feel everything.

Johnson kept going. Brought his friends round. Passed Jamal to the other boys.

He felt like a malfunctioning machine, a sci-fi robot with his insides a jumble and tangle of twisted wiring. Head like a radio; tuning randomly round the dial, trying to lock on to a signal, a station, and stay there, but mostly just picking up white noise. Not living life, just grazing; zapping and surfing.

Jamal ran away, stayed out all night, scared to return. Got into trouble. They always found him, brought him back. The social workers wanting to help, but only if Jamal would open up, let them in. Jamal tuned out, heard only white noise again.

Then on one of his escapes he met Les. Les the charmer. Les the one who told Jamal his life was worth something, that he was special. Les would buy him meals, give him blow, take him places. Les wanted Jamal to leave the home, come to live in a house he owned. Les promised him a new life. A happy, rich life. With money for clothes. Sounds.

Drugs. Anything he wanted. Jamal liked Les. Made him feel proud, happy.

Jamal went to live at Les's house. Met Dean. Felt immediately the almost electric charge of a kindred soul. Began to feel like he belonged somewhere.

Then Les stopped being the charmer. Became Les the hard man. Les the bully. Les the pimp. Told him the price to pay for saving his life. Put Jamal to work.

Dean helped him through. Showed him the ropes, the practicalities, how to find a safe place to go inside himself when they started touching you. Jamal was nervous at first, sensed some of the punters getting off on that. Then he began to learn how to handle them. Gain control. Let them not harm him, not hurt him. Not reach him.

In the safe place Dean had shown him.

And he managed. Because he had Dean.

But the sickness would build within him, would take over him, whisper truths in his ear. Control was just a lie. Life was no better here, Dean or no Dean. He had to take measures. Block the voices out.

He did. Drugs. Booze. Raving and speeding. Find a girl and fuck her for hours, just to prove that he could. Whatever it took to make the sickness subside.

And it would. For a while.

And now it was back again. Reminding him of what he did, what he truly was.

Father Jack. Joe Donovan. Si. All crowding in, wresting control away from him, ruining his life, ordering him what to do. And no Dean.

He wanted some rocks and a pipe. Some skunk. To fuck the girl downstairs whose name he couldn't remember. He wanted Father Jack dead. He wanted Donovan's money.

He wanted to escape. To that brown water-stain island. To anywhere.

He had dreaded returning to Father Jack. Telling him what had happened with Donovan. Si had pushed him into Jack's bedroom. Jack had looked at them, lip curling.

'You're dripping on my fucking carpet.'

They had both apologized.

'This had better be worth it.'

Jamal had started to tremble.

'Well?'

He opened his mouth. Father Jack leaned suddenly and sharply forward. Jamal yelped.

'He's . . . the man on the disc . . . he's . . . the one talking, he's . . . dead . . .'

Jamal flinched, expecting the worst from Father Jack, but to his surprise Jack did nothing. Except look curiously at him.

'Dead?' Jack asked. 'How?'

Jamal repeated what he had heard Maria say. Father Jack nodded, mulled it over.

'What about the other one? Is he dead?'

Jamal shook his head vigorously. 'Nuh – no. Well, she never said.'

'Do they know what's on the disc? Do they know about the other man?'

Jamal's head was shaking so fast he was in danger of dislocating it. His eyes were wide, almost wholly circular. 'Not from me, Jack, honest. Not from me.'

'But do they know?' His voice was still, calm, like a humid swamp with an alligator waiting beneath.

'Nuh – no. They don't know.'

Father Jack sat back. That seemed to be the answer he wanted. Jamal relaxed very slightly. Father Jack thought hard. Then spoke.

'We don't want the police here, do we?'

Jamal said nothing.

'Do we?'

Jamal had thought the question rhetorical, didn't realize he was being pressed for an answer. He shook his head again.

'No,' Father Jack continued. 'But they don't know what's on the disc. Or who's involved . . .'

He folded his arms, brought his head back, eyes on the ceiling, sighed.

Jamal said nothing. Just dripped on the carpet.

Jack brought his head back down, swivelled it round. His eyes bored into Jamal, made him feel like he was an assassin's target.

Then Father Jack smiled.

'What would you do?'

Jamal just stared at him. He wasn't sure he had heard correctly.

'Wuh – what?'

Father Jack smiled again. Spoke patiently and slowly. 'What would you do?'

Jamal looked at him, warily. A trick.

Father Jack sighed. 'It's a simple question, Jamal. You're one of my boys now, one of the family.' His voice sounded like honey poured over harsh metallic gears. 'I value my family's input. Like a good father should. So please. What would you do?'

'I'd . . . give Donovan another go. Let him make an offer. An' see.'

Father Jack nodded, still smiling. 'D'you know what, Jamal? I think you're right. We'll give Mr Donovan one more chance. See what he's willing to pay in light of recent developments. If not, well . . .' He shrugged. 'Easy come, easy go.'

A sense of relief flooded through Jamal. He couldn't speak, couldn't move.

'Good boy,' said Father Jack. 'Well done. You can go now.'

Jamal, surprised and wary, backed quickly out of the room. Closed the door behind him.

Knew that wouldn't be an end to it. Knew Jack would be watching him.

Jamal lay on the bed, rode the tide of sickness.

Trapped.

He knew Father Jack had played him. Manipulated him with talk of loyalty. Inclusive talk. At the time, though, he had been convinced. But not when he thought about it afterwards. Just another way of tightening the locks on the cage.

He stared at the bars on the window. He had to find a way to escape. To lose Si. To make a deal with Donovan.

To disappear.

Had to.

He sighed. Stared at the bars, rode the sickness.

There had to be a way of escape.

A real one, not just water-stained imaginary islands.

A real one. Had to.

11

The bar was dark and pleasantly warm, muted, coloured lighting over bare-brick walls and arches giving it a laid-back ambience. Joe Donovan sat on a long, chocolate-leather sofa, took a mouthful of beer from the bottleneck, tried to go with it, relax. Next to him, Maria perched on the edge of the sofa sipping a gin and tonic. She was wearing a black sleeveless dress, front-buttoning, revealing a tantalizing glimpse of cleavage accentuated by jewellery, with heeled, knee-high boots. Her suede jacket draped over the arm of the sofa. Her dark hair clean and shining. Donovan had taken off his brown-leather jacket to reveal a vintage CBGBs T-shirt, blue Levi's and boots. He had done what he could with his hair. Coldplay were playing on the bar's sound system, Chris Martin singing about taking things back to the start.

Gershwins bar and restaurant was at the top of Dean Street in what had once been the city's financial district, buffering the Georgian splendour of old Graingertown and the film noirish sweep of Dean Street down to the Tyne. Old Victorian and Edwardian temples of commerce were now massively imposing bars and restaurants. Gershwins was underground, the vaulted-brick ceiling and walls betraying its earlier incarnation. The walls were a warm red colour, the curved ceilings netted with thousands of fairy lights against a black background; an artificial, starlit night, untouched by the city's light pollution. The main room was long and quite narrow, with a small stage at the far end. Where money and bullion was once stored now sat diners and drinkers. To the right, a set of steps led down to a small bar, all diffused lighting and chunky leather sofas, where Donovan and Maria now sat.

They smiled quick smiles at each other, sipped their drinks.

'So,' Maria said, setting down her drink, 'shoptalk now or later?'

'Nothing to talk about,' said Donovan, 'remember?'

It had been Maria's idea. A Saturday night out. There would be no news on Gary Myers' post-mortem until Monday at the earliest. The next move regarding the disc was in Jamal's hands. There was nothing they could proactively do to move things forward. So why not relax, reintroduce themselves to each other and recharge, all on the *Herald*'s expense account?

Maria nodded, burying whatever she had been about to say, nervous that they had nothing but work between them.

'True,' she said.

After Donovan had agreed to Maria's proposal, he had taken a walk round the city centre. A strange experience; it left him feeling almost engaged with life again. Still, a cursory glance in store windows showed he was well out of touch with what was going on. He toyed with the idea of having his hair cut, perhaps buying a suit, fitting in, but decided against it. He wasn't ready for that yet. He had gone back to the hotel, showered, dug something clean from his bag, changed. Surprised himself by checking the mirror, by wanting to look his best. He smiled; like a semi-retired rock star on a comeback tour, the rhythm rusty but the songs still inside him.

The gun was still in his bag. Not near the top, but not buried either.

'Relax, recharge, all that,' he said, draining his bottle,

aware that neither of them seemed particularly relaxed. 'Let's have another drink.'

The waitress chose that moment to inform them that their table was ready. They moved up the small staircase, took their seats beneath the artificial night sky. The music changed; something sax-heavy and bebop – Miles Davis, Donovan reckoned. Whatever, it fitted, began working on him like an aural massage, helped, along with the alcohol, to loosen him up.

They ordered. Stilton dumplings followed by lamb for Donovan, seafood thermidor and pigeon breast for Maria. Another gin and tonic, another beer and a Merlot between them. New World.

The drinks arrived. Donovan held up his glass, looked at Maria.

'Here's to?'

'The future,' she said without hesitation.

'Because it can't be any worse than the past,' Donovan said.

'And second chances,' she said, eyes anywhere but on his.

Glasses chinked. Stars twinkled. They caught each other's gaze now, smiled.

'You look good tonight,' said Donovan.

Maria set her glass down, eyes on the table as she did so. Picked up her gin and tonic. 'Thank you.' She smiled, then sighed.

'What's up?' he asked.

'Oh . . . I don't know.' She shook her head. 'This could just be paranoia, but . . . I think I'm being set up.'

'What?'

'I think there's a fall coming and I'm the one expected to take it.'

Donovan took a mouthful of beer, set down his bottle. 'Explain.'

'Well . . . I feel I've been manipulated into coming up here. By Sharkey. He played on the fact that John Greene wanted to be in charge of the paper again and that the dep. wants my job and got them to send me up here. Out of the loop.' She sighed again. 'Oh I don't know. I'm the editor, for God's sake. I'm in charge. I shouldn't be this paranoid.'

'Perhaps,' said Donovan, looking for words of comfort that also contained truth, 'Sharkey, much as I can't stand the man, and John Greene think this is an important enough story for you to be here. They can hold the fort. Let you do what you're best at.'

Maria took a long time to reply.

'I wanted to come up here,' she said. 'They just agreed a little too quickly, that's all.'

'That's hardly the basis for a conspiracy theory, is it?'

'No, but . . .' She took another mouthful of gin and tonic, realized her glass was empty, started on the wine. 'It's hard to explain. Journalism's changing. It's not the boys' club it used to be, but there's still some way to go. It may sound like a cliché, but it is so much harder for a woman to take a top job in this business. And keep it.'

Before Donovan could reply, she began telling him, her voice breathless and rushed, about other female editors who had tried to take the men on at their own game and ended up either defeated by the system or more testosterone-fuelled than their male counterparts. He let her talk until her paranoid fantasies and war stories crossbred, multiplied and eventually ran out. She took another mouthful of wine.

'Sorry,' she said. She looked hot, flustered. She shook her head. 'Don't usually talk that way. Must be the booze, gone straight to my head.'

Donovan smiled. 'Best place for it.'

She sighed again. Donovan had been nervous about this

night out. Wondering what to say, how to behave. It was a difficult situation for him. He had never thought Maria might be feeling the same way.

She sat, eyes downcast. Something in her stirred something deep within him, something he hadn't allowed himself to feel in years. Almost without thinking, he reached across the table, placed his hand on top of hers.

She looked up, eyes wide, as if she had just received an electric shock.

They caught each other's eyes, locked, held on. And in that moment Donovan knew, and suspected Maria knew also, that a line, no matter how small, had been crossed.

And there could be no going back.

The food arrived. They ate. Made appreciative noises, swapped small portions for tasting. The starter dishes were cleared away. They emptied the wine bottle, ordered another. The waitress brought it, departed, and they were left with only each other.

'So,' said Donovan after taking a hefty mouthful of Merlot, 'you seeing anyone? Thought you'd be married by now.'

His voice aimed for lightness, but the words came out tight, strangulated.

Maria sounded equally forced in her reply.

'Married?' she said, voice straining to laugh. 'No, I'm a successful, independent woman. Most men have a problem with that. You know, good for a shag, if you've fantasies about dominance, but not wife and mother material.'

'Not unless you marry another journalist.'

'Who'd have to be the same level or higher. I know what you inky cowboys are like.'

Donovan smiled. 'Inky cowboys? You still have a facility for the apt phrase.'

Maria smiled, almost blushed. 'Thank you. It's a gift.

But you know what I mean. Terrible egos.' She took another sip, continued talking. 'But I am seeing someone, yes.' Her eyes dropped to the tablecloth as she spoke. She buttered a piece of bread from the basket, gave her hands something to do.

'Serious?' asked Donovan, eyes on her hands.

She hesitated before speaking, as if reaching a conclusion within herself. 'Not . . . really.' She smiled, as if in surprise at her words. 'There. I've said it now. Made it real.'

Donovan frowned. 'This something you've been thinking about a long time?'

'Well . . .' She cut her bread in half, looked at it. Then quartered it. 'He's very good to me and we enjoy each other's company, but . . .'

'But what?'

'Well, he's got his work, I've got mine. Like two separate lives that occasionally collide.'

'So what does he do?'

Maria began moving quarters of bread round her side plate with her knife.

'A dentist,' she said.

Donovan gave a little laugh. 'A dentist?'

'You sound surprised.'

'You sound defensive.'

'I'm not,' she said defensively. 'What's wrong with that?'

'Nothing,' said Donovan, smiling. 'I just expected you to say lawyer or, I don't know, media big knob. Something like that.'

It was Maria's turn to smile. 'Media big knob? Nice to see your gift for the apt phrase hasn't deserted you.'

Donovan reddened slightly. 'Touché,' he said, looking at her quartered bread.

She put the knife down, left the bread alone.

'I know what you mean,' she said. 'But it took me a lot of

hard work to get where I am now. A lot of sacrifices. A marriage either wouldn't have lasted or would have just turned into something of convenience. So I've got Greg. He's divorced, sees his kids every other weekend and when I'm not working we get together. There you go. Not perfect, but then life isn't.'

'And in the meantime you've become the *Daily Mail*'s worst nightmare. The all-powerful career woman who doesn't know her place.'

Maria smiled. 'It's worth it for that.'

'How are your parents?'

On the occasions he had met them, Donovan had liked her parents. Her mother had worked in Poundstretcher, her father for the council. They had scrimped and saved to get Maria to university; consequently Donovan felt she had always worked twice as hard to prove herself.

'Fine. Mum's retired now. Dad's still going strong. Down the pub, Old Trafford, shouting at the telly. You know.'

Donovan nodded.

'I'm sure they wished I'd given them grandchildren, but there you go. Can't have everything.'

'There's still time.'

Maria made a face, drank. 'How are yours?'

Donovan explained that his father was dead and his mother was living in Eastbourne, his brother in Indonesia. 'Running a sweatshop or something, I don't know. We were never a close family.'

Donovan had never felt he had anything in common with his family. He was the second son and all of his parents' expectations seemed to have been poured into the first one. Consequently he was free to do what he wanted. He had wanted to get away, make a name for himself. On his own terms.

They had started at the *Herald* at the same time. They

were the only ones on the staff, apart from the cleaners and caterers, who were northern and working class. They took every opportunity to mention it. Compared matching shoulder chips. When she was stressed, North London would drop away and her Salford vowels would come to the fore. He had never bothered to lose his Geordie accent.

Donovan noticed that another button had become undone at the top of her dress, exposing the curve of a white breast, the shadow of a lace-edged bra. He tried not to stare. Too much.

'Anyway,' Maria said, 'what about you? You seeing anyone?'

'No,' he said quietly.

'No strapping milkmaid from some nearby farm?' Maria smiled as she spoke.

Donovan smiled, shook his head, laughed slightly. Maria laughed also.

'Must get lonely up there. Just you and your—'

She froze as she spoke the words.

Donovan's eyes were on the table. His earlier good mood was gone, like a thin sheet that had been yanked away to expose a never-ending pain.

'I'm sorry . . .' Maria said. The words seemed small. 'I just thought you'd have started to . . .'

Something rose within him. Something heated and poisonous that needed to get out. He wanted to say it to Maria, punish her for reminding him of his pain, for allowing him to think he could ever forget, for her happy life, imperfections and all.

'Put my life back together? No. But it does get lonely up there. So you know what I do?' He began to feel hot as he talked. 'I come down here, to Newcastle, pick up a girl, take her back to the hotel. It's not too difficult. 'Sometimes . . .'

The heat was rising inside him. 'Sometimes I'll even pay for her.' He waited, making sure the words had sunk in, breathing hard. 'Does that shock you?'

Maria looked nervously at him, not quite meeting his gaze. 'No . . . no . . .'

Donovan nodded, taking a perverse thrill in the fact that his words were hurting both of them. The poison spreading. 'Yeah, Maria, that's how far I've fallen. I didn't want love or involvement. Half the time I didn't even want to fuck.'

'Then what did you want?'

Donovan looked at Maria, saw the fear in her face, felt shame that he was the one who had instilled it. His pain wasn't her fault. He shook his head, looked up, saw the artificial stars. His own eyes began to glitter. The heat, the poison started leaching out of his body.

'Release,' he said tiredly. 'A way to let the demons out. Or keep them away for another night.' He sighed and continued, his voice small. 'Just something I could take back with me. Help me cope.'

Their main courses arrived. They fell on them gratefully and silently, occasionally making appreciative noises, offering portions for tasting, but mainly spending the time in their own heads. Thinking.

They finished. Dishes were cleared, pudding menus offered and refused. They drank coffee.

'I'm sorry,' Maria said eventually.

'No,' said Donovan. 'It's my fault. You're the first person I've . . . spoken to . . . really spoken to, for years.' He shook his head, sighed. A world of words passed through his head. None would come out of his mouth. 'I'm sorry. We used to be . . . friends.'

Maria looked at him. 'We still are.'

They sat in silence. John Coltrane played. 'A Love Supreme' to 'The Damned Don't Cry'.

The bill arrived; Maria put it on the company credit card. They rose from their seats. Donovan placed a hand on her arm. She jumped slightly.

'D'you want to go for a walk?'

The rain had ceased during the afternoon, leaving the city exhausted but cleansed.

The night was still, and the air promised winter. The sky was cloudless; real stars above the city. Donovan and Maria walked along the quayside; Saturday-night revellers moved round them. They walked by the Tyne, the river making oily, feathery slaps alongside them. They were side by side. Occasionally they would touch accidentally. Neither pulled away when this happened. They had hardly spoken since the restaurant.

The river not the only thing with undercurrents.

Away from the hotel, past the sights Donovan had seen the previous night. The Gateshead Hilton. The Sage. The Baltic. The Millennium Bridge. All beautifully lit with cinematic drama and clarity.

Past the Crown Court. The Pitcher and Piano. Malmaison. Running into Byker. Running out of space.

'I bet this place has changed for you,' said Maria.

'Hardly recognize it from when I was a kid,' Donovan replied. 'Like coming back to a different city. Who'd have thought a flour mill could become a modern art gallery? Or that an old warehouse would become a Malmaison hotel? Everything changes. Nothing stays the same.'

They stopped walking, looked across the Tyne, the lights catching their eyes. Donovan sneaked a glance at Maria.

'All the industy has changed, too,' he said. 'It used to be all heavy stuff, mining and shipyards. Now, it's all call centres and culture. And the biggest growth industry of them all up here is technology. IT and creative software companies. Even in Northumberland.' He sighed, smiled. 'It's gone from "whey aye, man" to "whey imac".'

Maria laughed. 'Good one. You been working on that?'

Donovan kept a straight face. 'Just thought of it. Honest.'

Maria smiled, shook her head. Donovan was still looking across the river.

'Listen,' she said, eyes on whatever she thought he was looking at, 'about before. In the restaurant. It was . . . I shouldn't—'

Donovan turned her towards him. 'Let's try and forget it.'

They looked at each other. Their eyes locked.

'Everything changes,' he said.

'Nothing stays the same,' Maria replied.

They kissed.

The Tyne made oily, feathery slaps alongside them. The stars above them were real.

12

Sunday morning and the rain had held off. No matter: Alan Keenyside would have still had to go out.

He pulled up in the Ponteland golf club car park, Blaupunkt blaring.

Amy Winehouse: 'Fuck Me Pumps'. Say the word, darling.

Got out of the Jag, saw it lined up next to the Mercs and Beamers, gave an appreciative nod at the way it fitted in, locked it, took his clubs from the boot. Titanium, leather bagged. The best. Unsnapped the wheels and trolleyed them over to the course.

The air was cold; he was glad of his fleece. The rest of his clothes were designer-bright golf chic; both practical and, even though he thought so himself, stylish. All the right labels. Labels were important.

He looked up at the sky, saw heavy clouds. His mood changed as he felt the equivalent creep into himself. He sighed. Couldn't put it off any longer. Pulling his trolley, he set off for the fairway.

Water squelched around his feet, leaving mud on his shoes, damp in his socks. He cursed inwardly.

As a young man with ambitions and aspirations beyond the housing estate in the West End of Newcastle he had grown up on, he imagined golf to be a symbol of contentment. A sense that he had succeeded in reaching, and now belonged to, a higher level of society. He now looked on his increasingly occasional forays on to the green with dread.

Think of it as tax, he thought. Just paying your taxes. Well, if that was the case, it was time for a new fucking accountant.

He saw them on the third tee. They hadn't waited for him. Stride unconsciously slowing, he walked towards them. They saw him coming. Didn't acknowledge him. He reached them.

'Started without me,' said Keenyside, attempting to affect a cheeriness he didn't feel.

'Didn't think you'd mind.' The man who spoke was slightly older than Keenyside, early forties. Hair greying but trimmed short, clothes well fitting, more understated than Keenyside's, accentuating the fact that he was in good shape.

Chief Superintendent Palmer. Keenyside's boss.

He was about to take a swing. He demanded, and got, concentration and silence. He hit the ball; a straight arc down the fairway.

'Good one,' said the other man.

'Yes, well done,' echoed Keenyside.

Palmer acknowledged the other man's response, ignored Keenyside's.

The other man: larger, steel-wool hair cropped close to his skull. Older than Palmer and heavier, like a boxer whose muscle had been coated with a layer of fat. Keenyside knew who he was. Most of the police in Newcastle knew who he was. Keenyside also knew that his lucrative sideline could only continue to flourish because of this man's magnanimousness. And because of what Keenyside told him about his business rivals.

The other man teed up, swung. Not as good a shot as Palmer's. No one dared mention the fact.

Keenyside teed up. The other two, not impatiently, waited for him to strike the ball. He did. They began to walk.

'Business good?' asked Palmer.

Keenyside didn't know how to answer. If he said yes his contributions would be increased. If he said no he would be made to work harder. 'Not bad,' he said.

'Good,' Palmer said, eyes ahead. 'Got anything for me, then?'

Without stopping and barely slowing, Keenyside lifted a plastic-wrapped bundle from the top of his bag and placed it in Palmer's. He did the same with the other man.

'Anything else?' asked the other man, voice rough and rasping, like an industrial file on a stubborn lump of hard-wood.

'Yeah,' said Keenyside. He passed on the information Mikey Blackmore, and his other informers, had told him. The big man listened impassively, nodded.

'Good. Good work.'

The other two gave their attention back to the game in hand, ignoring Keenyside once more. They waited, again not impatiently, while he took his shot, then set off again, not waiting for him to catch them up.

He hated this. Hated it all the more because he knew Palmer did it deliberately. Invited him along, took his money, his information; tolerating but patronizing him. Reminding him of his place.

So far, no further.

He looked around. Palmer and his companion had moved on without waiting for him.

Not even bothering to remove a club from his bag and take his shot, he trudged after them.

Keenyside drove home, up into Northumberland.

He rotated the CDs in the player, found an album he wasn't familiar with, something his wife must have left there.

Elton John. The song: 'Border Lines'.

He sighed.

Borders. Lines. The story of his life. Lines to cross, borders to obstruct him.

Palmer taking every opportunity to remind him that he wasn't one of them and never would be.

He had grown up in the West End of Newcastle. And hated it. He remembered as a child being desperate for escape. The only options open to him were the police or the army. He didn't like the idea of the army, so he settled for the police. And worked hard to get in. Crossed several lines to become a policeman.

Once on the force, he worked even harder. Proving himself. Made detective inspector in record time. Then: transferred to the West End of Newcastle. His patch, it was argued, his old home area. One of their own; they would respect and respond to that.

Work was work: he did it. But wanted nothing to do with them, felt nothing but revulsion for his former neighbours. They represented a barrier he had broken free from. He wouldn't be going back. He married. A woman the opposite to the ones on the estate and in his family. Suzanne was socially ambitious. Almost sociopathically so. She complemented him well. They were on the way.

Then Suzanne fell pregnant. It wasn't planned. It wasn't wanted. But as a Catholic, Suzanne couldn't bring herself to terminate the pregnancy, no matter how much she wanted to. She went full term. Gave birth to twins.

Now the lifestyle the Keenysides aspired to was unattainable on his salary, even with overtime. Something had to change. Suzanne couldn't work because of the children. Keenyside thought of night school; get a qualification, advance his career to maybe a solicitor or something. But that took so long. Instead, he hit on a better idea.

It meant another line to cross. It meant he would have to become something other than that which he had prided himself in. But he had to do it. The twins were approaching school age. He didn't want them to go to school in the West End. Mix with the offspring of the children he'd had to mix with, the scum he dealt with every day. And Suzanne was demanding certain things for their lives. He didn't begrudge her them; he wanted them, too.

He would catch dealers on the estate and give them a choice. Surrender their supply and dealing network to him, or face arrest. They always chose the former.

The idea was a success. So much so that he needed help. Well-chosen colleagues were approached. Sympathetic allies found within his team. Soon, they were all at it. And it was very lucrative. He had no compunction about exploiting his old neighbours, friends and family, even, on the estates he had left behind. Those that were stupid or thick enough to stay, he reasoned, deserved all they got.

Another line had to be crossed. On the strength of his sideline, Keenyside had soon moved his family out of the West End of Newcastle, to a place more commensurate with his increasing earnings. A private community of new executive dwellings (he loved that word) in Wansbeck Moor, Northumberland. The car, the private schooling, had followed. He was stretched to the limit, but he knew the money would continue to come in, the lifestyle to improve.

And then Palmer found out about his scheme. Keenyside was terrified that his empire would come crashing down. But instead of turning him in, he surprised Keenyside by demanding a cut in exchange for silence. A big cut.

Keenyside had no choice but to, reluctantly, comply.

That would have been bearable had not other players then become involved. Local gang lords demanding tributes in exchange for allowing him to operate. Demanding information on their rivals. Suddenly everyone wanted a cut. And Keenyside had to do it.

And he was stretched again. Desperately stretched. But determined not to give in. Despite the pressures.

He found ways of relieving those pressures. Other lines to cross.

His release: forcing transgression. Indulging the urge to subjugate.

A pleasurable diversion, but nothing that would allow his focus to diminish, his goal to be compromised.

He thought of his old housing estate. There was no way he was going back to something like that. No way. He would do whatever it took to keep moving forward.

Whatever it took.

Rain started to fall. Hard. He turned on the wipers, pushed the volume on the CD higher to drown out the sound. Shuffled the discs.

Van Morrison: *Greatest Hits*. 'Bright Side of the Road'.

Turned it off. Last thing he wanted to hear.

Thought about his scheme. His big money scheme. Soon he would have more money than Palmer and his friend put together.

It had involved crossing several more lines. But he had done it. And would cross more, if needs be. The end result justified it.

Justified anything.

He banished Palmer to the back of his mind, focused on the task in hand.

Turned the CD back on.

The music didn't seem so incongruous, after all.

Monday morning. Caroline woke.

Eyes wide, startled by the radio. Chris Moyles spilling out fat bile, begging through the ether for complicity in his self-loathing. With travel updates and news. The jarring noise emptied Caroline's mind, gave her a blank, morning slate.

But only for a second or two, until the rest of her consciousness caught up with her.

Then she remembered.

And closed her eyes, tried to will it all away. Will everything back to how it used to be.

But it didn't happen.

She opened her eyes again. The room — everything — was as it had been the previous night. Sunday had been the hardest day to make it through. A dead day, made worse through the lack of news, of developments.

She lay still, contemplated staying in bed all day. Pulling the duvet up, pushing the world out. But she knew she wouldn't. Because that would be giving in. And she had already told herself she wouldn't give in.

She threw the duvet back, swung her legs to the floor, stood up, walked to the bathroom.

Everything was lead.

She heard the newspaper fall through the letterbox. She left the bathroom, grabbed it quickly, opened it on the dining table. Scrutinized it, page by page.

Nothing.

She knew there wouldn't have been. Knew the police had said they would keep her informed, tell her first. She checked the phones. Landline: dial tone. Mobile: fully charged, ready to receive.

It had become her new routine, a thing born of quiet desperation, a way to keep order, to keep the screams internal.

The TV was next; waiting until suited inanities had stopped babbling, linked up to local news. Sometimes the TV got there first, turned events into stories before the police had a chance to inform the family. She had read that somewhere, heard stories.

But not this time. Not today.

She turned the TV off, knew the next half-hourly broad-cast would be word for word.

She sighed, looked out of the window.

The car was absent.

It had been parked there, on and off, since her father dis-appeared. At first she had been worried, thinking she was being watched by some unmoving figure behind the wheel, but had mentally slapped herself around for being paranoid. It was probably a policeman watching the flat in case her father returned. Or a journalist wanting to be first on the scene. Or someone entirely unconnected with her. Anyway, it wasn't there this morning.

She turned away from the window, looked around the flat. She loved this flat. Not only was it the only bit of the planet she could call her own, but it reminded Caroline of her father. He had helped her with the money, the removals, the decorating. But not in an overbearing way; he had known when to stand back, let her fly on her own.

Had. Past tense.

She shook her head. Wouldn't allow herself to think that way.

She saw the photo by the TV. Mum. Dad. Her. Happier times. Seemed like another lifetime.

She sighed again, picked up the phone. Dialled a number she knew off by heart. A number she had used a lot lately.

She wouldn't be in. No, no news. Yes, yes, it was. Then thanks. Replaced the receiver.

She sat on the sofa, looked at her watch, waiting for the next news bulletin. She felt her hair. Long and greasy. Uncared for. Her teeth needed brushing, too. And she should eat some-thing. She didn't feel like doing anything about anything.

Caroline looked at the phone again. Maybe she should call the police. See if they had heard anything. But they had told her they would contact her if they had. She didn't want to be a nuisance, one of those comical members of the public she had seen in cop shows, always pestering the detectives, getting them angry, causing them to make up private jokes about her.

She would have to wait.

Wait.

She sighed again, flicked on the TV. Flicked it off again.

She stood up. She had to do something. Anything. Try to take her mind off it.

She would go for a run. Down the dene, over the moor, maybe. Just do something. Take her mind off things.

Then come back, have a shower. Eat.

See if there was any news.

She went back to the bedroom to change. Find her running shoes. Change her routine; make this day different from the last few. Make this the day things happened on.

The day things changed for her.

Grey's Monument, Newcastle city centre. The old Georgian heart of Graingertown. Donovan sat on the stone perimeter of the statue, waited.

Tried to make sense of the last few days.

Their Saturday-night kissing had intensified to the point where they had to race back to the hotel. In Donovan's room they hurriedly undressed, fell on each other with real hunger. Their lovemaking was passionate, furious, yet also anonymous; barely making eye contact. When their eyes did accidentally glance off each other's they quickly focused their gaze somewhere else.

Afterwards they lay side by side, spent. Not touching. Eventually Maria rolled over to Donovan, faced him. Smiled. 'OK?' she said, sensing he wasn't.

Donovan sighed, eyes fluttering over hers, managed a smile. 'Yeah.'

She stroked his chest. 'Sure?'

Donovan sighed again, placed his hand over hers. 'It's . . . I don't know. Took me by surprise. All those years . . . Wasn't ready, I suppose.'

'Are we ever?'

Donovan couldn't explain. It wasn't so much the memory of his estranged wife. He felt like his son had been watching him, judging his actions. He had tried to shake it off, give in to an animalistic lust, but now, post-coitally, it had returned. He felt like he had failed David in some way.

She looked at him, waiting for, but not demanding, answers. Donovan couldn't meet her eyes.

'Don't worry,' she said, removing her hand, 'we don't have to do it again. We'll pretend it never happened.'

She began to get out of the bed.

'Don't go.'

She stopped. Turned at Donovan's voice.

'Don't go.'

She sat down on the bed, looked at him.

He tried to return her gaze. 'I have had sex since I split with Annie.'

'You mentioned it earlier.'

'But that was just release. I don't . . . It's . . .' He sighed, looked away. 'It's hard to talk about this.'

Maria lay down next to him again. 'Then don't.'

He looked at Maria, at her naked body, as if seeing her properly for the first time since they had entered the room. In that moment he felt something more than lust. Something that would diminish the guilt.

'You're beautiful,' he said, looking at her face.

She smiled, stroked his cheek. 'So are you.'

Their eyes met. Locked this time.

They kissed again. Entwined. Hesitant at first, building up slowly, tenderly.

Communicating: looks and smiles. No words.

Their nakedness became deeper than flesh. Donovan felt his guilt diminishing, being replaced by an intimacy at once beautiful and terrible.

His son's eyes no longer on him.

He looked down, saw Maria; eyes closed, head back, small sighs of inexpressible joy escaping from her lips. Her eyes opened caught his. She smiled, whispered.

'You're crying.'

Donovan returned the smile, buried his face in her neck and hair.

And in that moment no longer felt alone. A warmth, both erotically and intimately charged, built within him. He sighed. Came.

Later they lay, bodies loosely entwined, fingers idly stroking each other, massaging still-tingling, post-coital skin.

In the dark, faces, bodies, indiscernible shades of grey. Talked nightspeak. Lovers' talk.

'Well,' said Donovan, 'that was a long time in coming.'

'Everyone always thought we were shagging back in the old days. Said we were too close to be just friends.' Maria smiled. 'We'll have to tell them they were right.'

Donovan smiled. 'We flirted like mad, didn't we?'

'I remember it as being the only way we ever communicated.'

It had been their way of bonding. Great things had been expected of them at the *Herald*. They had become friends at the outset. And remained friends until Donovan had cut himself off.

Maria held him harder. 'Did you ever want to sleep with me?'

'Yeah. But I wasn't about to do it. Because I thought that if we did sleep together we would never be friends again.'

'I know. Fancied you something rotten. But it wouldn't have been right. For one thing, you were so happy with Annie.'

Donovan didn't reply. Maria felt his body stiffen beneath her hand.

'Sorry,' she said.

'It's all right.'

They lay in silence for a while.

'Do you ever see her?' asked Maria eventually.

Donovan looked around before answering, checking for ghosts. He could see none. Hiding, he thought. Hiding in the shadows.

'No,' he said. 'Not for ages.'

'Maybe you should.' Maria spoke quietly.

Donovan sighed. 'It would be difficult. I remember after . . . after it happened . . . I couldn't . . . She used to try and get me to open up. Talk. Pull me towards her, trying . . . I . . . sometimes I would find myself staring at her. And find her looking at me in return. It was like we wanted to come together, but something always . . . stopped us. Came between us. And in the end I had to . . . get away. For both of us.'

Maria was staring straight ahead, knowing what it was costing him to speak, not looking at him in case it broke the spell. 'What about Abigail?'

'Nearly a teenager now.' He sighed. 'She hates me.'

'I doubt that.'

'Oh she does. Thinks I care more for him than for her. Because . . .' He shook his head. 'But I couldn't give it up, that hope . . . I couldn't make her understand. She said it was like there were still four of us in that house. And one was a ghost, haunting us. So I had to go. Exorcism.'

He sighed.

'Two years. You can fall a long way in two years.'

Silence again.

'We're a right pair, aren't we?' said Maria.

Donovan smiled, held her tighter. 'Yeah,' he said. 'We're a right pair.'

They made love again. Lay still, content. Waiting for morning.

'They never . . .' Maria began, enfolded in Donovan's arms, 'they never found him, then? Any trace?'

'None.' Donovan's eyes were on the ceiling.

'Oh that must be . . .' Maria couldn't finish.

'When I was a kid,' said Donovan, 'I used to read comics. Loved comics, superhero ones, had a huge collection. Well, there was one series I used to really love. The Doom Patrol, they were called. They were these misfits, outsiders. The lead guy was Robotman.'

He felt a shaking against his chest.

'Don't laugh. Robotman. He used to be human but now he was a robot with a human brain and human emotions. Superstrong and superhard on the outside, superemotional on the inside.'

Maria stopped laughing, said nothing. Listened.

'Well, of course, they had these enemies whom they fought. And one of them, I forget his name, had all the superpowers you couldn't think of. So as soon as you thought of one it disappeared, stopped being real. That's how you defeated him.'

Donovan kept staring at the ceiling. Movies unspooling, running, movies only he could see.

'And that's how I think about David,' he said, voice beginning to tremble. 'Tried to imagine everything that . . . that could have happened to him. The darkest, most . . . most evil . . . depraved thing I could imagine.'

He stopped talking, swallowing hard, taking hard, steady breaths. Waited until he was calm again before speaking.

'Everything,' he said. 'Because if I could think of something, it stopped . . . stopped being real. And if, if it stopped
being real . . . that meant it couldn't . . . it hadn't . . . it
could only . . .'

Maria held him in her arms.

Morning still felt a long way off.

Later they talked again until sleep took them. Talked carefully; avoided making promises that would fade with the
dawn. But hoping to carry something more than memories
with them into the day.

Sunday morning came.

For Donovan, no Annie, no Abigail, no David in the
room now. Only himself and Maria.

The ghosts resting.

They spent the day together. In bed for most of it.
Relaxed.

Taking time to touch and explore each other, kiss and
lick, caress and impress. Show each other what they enjoyed,
find out what the other liked done.

Rediscovering who they had been. Finding out who they
were now. Near to happy. Donovan not daring to acknowledge the word hope, knowing it was too closely allied to the
word despair. But feeling it inside him anyway.

Then the call from Jamal. Ready to deal. Monday. Grey's
Monument.

'Oi!'

The boy turned, saw him. Came towards him.

'What you smilin' for, man?' Jamal asked, getting level.

'Just pleased to see you, Jamal.'

Jamal shook his head, laughed. 'You're weird, man. Come
out with some weird shit.'

Donovan nodded, dropped the smile. Business. 'So,' he
said, 'We ready to deal?'

Jamal's smile flicked off, his eyes became haunted. He shrugged: a monosyllabic response.

'OK.' Donovan remembered the strategy he and Maria had agreed in handling Jamal. Befriend him. Court him. Win his trust. Listen to him. No matter what he had done, what he was involved with, he was just a boy.

'Listen,' said Donovan, his voice calm, reasonable. 'We can't talk here.' He looked around. 'Why don't we go to lunch? I'll buy.'

Jamal nodded. 'McDonald's?'

Donovan smiled. 'There's more to life than McDonald's, Jamal. And I don't mean KFC either. Come on.'

Pani's was a small, relaxed Italian restaurant down High Bridge, a narrow, cobbled backstreet between the Georgian splendour of Grey Street and the mostly boarded-up Pilgrim Street. With blond-wood floors, faux Umbrian décor and model-grade waiting staff, it hardly ever seemed to be empty.

The lunchtime rush was just beginning. They found a table, studied the menu.

'What is this shit? Don't they do proper food? Burgers an' fries?'

Donovan agreed to order for both of them. He asked the black-clad waitress for two Italian sausage sandwiches in ciabatta, a coke, a cappuccino and extra chips for Jamal. She repeated the order back in Italian-accented Geordie then sashayed away, treating the diners to a view of her languidly swinging, perfectly rounded backside.

Donovan studied Jamal. The boy was looking around, taking in his unfamiliar surroundings, trying to front up the situation even though behind the mask he was scared. Donovan wondered about the boy's life, what had led him to the place he was at now. What kind of future he would have.

'You're doin' that look again, man.'

Donovan, startled, looked up. 'What?'

Jamal smiled, shook his head. 'Well fucked up . . .'

The waitress arrived with the drinks. Jamal tried hard to pretend he wasn't looking down her blouse.

'Fit bird,' he said as she moved off.

Donovan smiled. 'No chance.'

'Why not? I'm a player.'

'You're a teenager.'

Jamal's face reddened. 'Yeah? Well, at least I'm not some old Grizzly Adams-lookin' dude.'

'Just drink your drink, sonny.'

Jamal put his head down to his drink, tried to hide his smile. Time to move on, thought Donovan reluctantly.

'Right,' Donovan said. 'We'd better talk business.'

'Yeah,' said Jamal. He looked up, reluctantly, from his drink. Like a death-row inmate who had momentarily forgotten their fate.

'Here's the proposal,' said Donovan, leaning forward and steepling his fingers. 'It seems to me that there are two things happening here. There's what you know. And what's on the disc.'

Jamal listened. Donovan continued, his voice calm, reasonable.

'I've spoken to Maria—'

'The lady from the newspaper.'

'Right. And she says that if you can tell us everything, let us tape you, everything you know, and it all checks out, then we'll pay you.'

'How much?'

'A grand.'

'A grand? You were gonna pay me five.'

'For the disc. Which you don't have. This is just for the sweet sound of your own voice.'

Jamal shook his head, laughed. 'A grand? Shit, man, I want more for what I've got in my head. It's worth bare cash. A grand? I can make that in a week. No, a day.'

'Then don't let me stop you.'

Jamal looked puzzled. 'What?'

'There's the door. Off you go. Go and make more than that in a week. If that's what you really want.'

Jamal looked at the door, trying to hide the hurt expression on his face. Donovan felt sorry for the kid, wished he could have thought of another way to play this.

'What about the disc?' asked Jamal.

'That's a separate issue. D'you know what's on it?'

Jamal nodded, fronting again. 'Yeah. Pretty much.'

'Then we may not need it. If this turns out to be a murder and the police get involved, you'll have to tell me where the disc is. You might have to get involved with them, tell them what you tell us, though.'

'But I still get the money to keep, yeah?'

'Assuming you agree to the deal.'

'And I just have to talk?'

Donovan nodded.

Jamal stuck out his hand to shake. 'Safe, Joe.'

Donovan shook. The food arrived. Jamal ate his with relish.

'Better than McDonald's?'

'Yeah,' said Jamal, cramming more chips into his mouth. 'Wicked.'

Jamal kept eating. Donovan kept watching.

'So where you from?' asked Donovan.

Jamal looked up, instantly suspicious. 'What you wanna know for?'

Donovan shrugged. 'No reason. Just interested.'

'Streatham.'

Donovan nodded. 'I know it.'

Jamal's head was down, looking at his plate. 'Then foster homes. Children's homes. Not for long, though.'

'Why not?'

'Kept runnin' away. Tryin' to go see my mum.'

'And what happened?'

Jamal's eyes became veiled. He looked down, became interested in his sandwich, tearing strips of bread from it. 'Got problems, man.' He pointed to his head. 'Couldn't cope. Sent me back.' His eyes found something in the shredded bread that Donovan couldn't see. 'Ran away for good in the end.'

Donovan nodded.

They finished their meal in silence.

'So what happens next?' asked Jamal.

'I need to know who's got the disc. That way—'

Jamal's face had turned ashen. 'Naw, naw, man, low it, low it. Can't do that.'

'Why not?'

'If I didn't make a deal,' said Jamal, his voice small, unsteady, 'then I would be in trouble.'

'But you have made a deal. You've just left him out of it.'

Jamal shook his head. 'You don't get it . . .' Jamal couldn't keep the pain from his voice, his face.

Donovan looked at Jamal. 'What d'you mean? Hurt you?'

Jamal lowered his eyes, didn't answer.

Donovan's sympathetic, angry heart went out to the lost boy. In that moment he came to a decision he hadn't been consciously aware he was thinking about.

'Listen, Jamal. I'll get you put up at the hotel, the paper to pay for it. Yeah?'

Jamal looked at him, hope rising in his features.

'And when this is all over, I'll get you help with finding somewhere to live permanently. Help get you sorted out.'

Suspicion crept back into Jamal's eyes. 'Why?'

Donovan shrugged. 'You prefer things the way they are?'

'People don't do something for nothing.'

Donovan shook his head. There, then gone. 'Some people do.'

'But I don't have to see Father Jack again. Right?'

'Is that his name? Father Jack?'

Jamal was looking around, quickly. Donovan thought he was about to bolt.

Donovan felt anger rising within him. 'Why are you so scared of him?'

'You don't know him. He'll hurt me, man, hurt me good . . .'

'He's not going to hurt you anymore, Jamal.' Donovan's anger became a galvanizing, charging thing. 'Or anyone else. I'll see to that. Just show me where he is and I'll take it from there.'

Jamal shook his head.

'We'll get a cab. You don't have to come in.'

'What you gonna do?'

'Well, I should just find out where he lives. Leave it at that. Turn the information over. But I'm not going to. He's a bully. He might get away with hurting children. Let's see what happens when he picks on someone his own size.'

Jamal looked Donovan up and down. 'That would be difficult,' he said.

Donovan threw some notes down on the table, stood up. 'Come on. Let's go.'

They left the restaurant. The waitress click-clacked over, picked up the money. Smiled.

If only everyone left tips of nearly fifteen pounds, she thought.

She walked back up the aisle of the restaurant, an extra bounce in her buttocks.

13

Hammer pulled up outside the girl's flat. Usual space. Usual time. He knew her name but preferred to think of her as the girl. His target. Objectified her more.

He settled down to wait, holdall on the back seat, Slipknot on the CD player. Easy listening. He hated stake-outs, hated waiting.

Almost immediately there was a tap on the window. Hammer jumped. He hadn't been expecting it. He looked: Keenyside.

Keenyside opened the door, sat in the passenger seat. About to speak, he stopped, wrinkled his nose.

'What's that smell?'

Hammer ignored him. Keenyside, realizing he wasn't about to receive an answer, remembered why he was there.

'So what you got for me? And it better be good, because I'm very disappointed.'

Hammer's eyes became hot coals. He stared ahead, his face frozen. Body so taut he was almost vibrating. He gripped hard on the wheel, felt it begin to buckle under his grip.

'Disappointed.' His voice was barely above a whisper. 'In what?'

'Gary Myers. The body's been found.'

'I heard.'

'And you're not bothered? This could be very serious.'

'For you. Should have done it my way. Bury him. There are proper ways of doing things. I'm not an amateur.' Emphasis on the I'm.

'Hammer,' said Keenyside eventually. Then stopped. 'Can you turn that down a bit? Can't hear myself think in here.'

Hammer ignored him. Keenyside, unnerved, continued. His tone more placatory. 'Look, I've said this before. We need to think long term. His body shouldn't have been found for months. Years. Should have decayed, made the death look accidental. You can't do that if he's been buried.' A pause. 'Now, what else you got?'

Hammer turned to him for the first time, told him. About Dean, headless and weighted at the bottom of the Regent's Canal. About who Jamal had been trying to contact. The *Herald*. Joe Donovan.

Keenyside gave a small laugh. 'Joe Donovan? There's a blast from the past. Don't think we need worry about him, though. Broken man. Still, I'll keep an ear out. What about the boy? Still in Newcastle?'

Hammer nodded. 'Far as we know.'

'Good.' Keenyside paused, thinking. 'I'll look out for the boy. Don't worry, we'll find him. Toerag like that can't stay hidden for long.'

'And in the meantime?'

'Keep watching the flat.' Hammer didn't respond. 'You're doing a good job. The best.'

Hammer looked again at Keenyside. 'I know.'

'It'll be worth it. It will.'

Hammer said nothing.

'Right, well . . .' Keenyside got out of the car. 'The best,' he said, closing the door, and was off.

Hammer watched him go. The policeman had seemed nervous, less sure of himself, more driven than usual. On the verge of desperate, even.

Hammer put Keenyside out of his mind. Listened to the music, watched the flat.

He hated stakeouts. Hated waiting.

He was grateful for what Keenyside had done for him, but even that had its limits.

Hammer had been a gangster's enforcer. A gangster Keenyside had fitted up. He made a deal with Hammer: do me some favours and I'll keep you out of prison. Hammer saw the sense in that. Now he paid him. Not the going rate, but he wasn't in prison. And Hammer freelanced. Sometimes even for other coppers.

He rotated his neck, heard it click.

He hated stakeouts. Hated waiting.

He thought of the holdall on the back seat. What was inside it.

Felt better.

Felt pleasure spread within him, knew the thought of it would sustain him while he sat.

The minicab pulled up outside the house, the driver having followed Jamal's idiosyncratic directions. Once paid, he sped off.

'I thought I was going to wait in the car,' said Jamal, fear in his voice.

'Don't worry,' said Donovan. 'You're with me. Wait out here if you want to.'

Jamal said nothing, just trembled slightly, eyes saucer wide.

Donovan hadn't spoken much on the journey, nurturing his anger, priming it for release on a deserving subject. Seeing the state of Jamal, he realized he had found one.

'Why don't you open the door,' said Donovan, 'then step back and let me in.'

Jamal nodded, looking down at the pavement. Played join the dots with blackened chewing gum and dogshit. He walked up the path like a condemned man, opened the door with his key.

Donovan stepped past him into the hall. It was unexceptional, banal. Dirty walls with peeling paper, unvacuumed carpet. The smell of fried food and overripe rubbish. There was a door off to his left. From behind it came the testosterone sounds of Hollywood mayhem. He cracked it open slightly, looked in. Three teenagers – two boys, one girl – pale and acned, sat on the sofa staring at the source of the noise. A half-eaten pizza and its box, Archers bottles and overflowing ashtrays littered the floor. One of the boys had his hand down the girl's top, was idly playing with her nipple. Donovan saw their eyes and they chilled him. Completely passive, letting the violent images play on their eyeballs before washing over them.

Dismemberment followed by a leaden one-liner. The children smiled slightly, laughed; whether at the carnage or the joke, Donovan couldn't tell. Their faces soon returned to their earlier passivity. Like automatons, waiting for activation. No spark of inner life.

Donovan thought of Jamal living here.

Of David.

He turned to Jamal. 'Where is he?'

Jamal, shaking, replied, 'I'll find out.'

'You don't have to.'

Jamal shrugged, averted his eyes.

'Go on then,' said Donovan. 'Tell him I'm here to deal. Then let me in and you get out quickly.'

Jamal nodded. He looked terrified. 'You gonna hurt him?'

'Maybe.'

'Hope so. Wanna be there when it happens, you get me?'

Anger at what an adult could do to a child flowed through Donovan like ammonia in his veins. It had to come out. It would poison him otherwise. 'I get you.'

Jamal opened the living room door, walked in. Donovan

flattened himself against the wall. He heard Jamal asking where Father Jack was, a couple of non-committal replies. Then a high voice, the one from the disc, called his name, told him to step into the kitchen.

Donovan waited. Wished he hadn't let Jamal go in on his own. Listened.

An angry voice made itself heard above the noise of the film. Accompanied by the unmistakable sound of flesh striking flesh. Again. And again.

Donovan ran through the living room, to the door at the far end. He tried to push it open. Something was blocking it. He heard sobbing, pushed harder. The door opened. Jamal had been blocking the door. He lay on the floor curled, trying not to cry. At the other side of the kitchen, half-completed sandwich before him, was one of the fattest men Donovan had ever seen. Donovan stopped dead. The fat man used Donovan's inaction to take control of the situation.

'Who the fuck are you and why are you assaulting me in my own kitchen?'

The man was angry rather than scared. A thread of danger ran through his voice that it would have been unwise to ignore. Donovan didn't hear it. Could barely hear anything over the film in the next room, the pounding of blood in his head.

'Who the fuck am I? Who the fuck am I? I'll tell you. I'm Joe Donovan. And your child abusing days are over, you fat bastard.'

Father Jack spat out a laugh. 'Don't I have something you want?'

Donovan was breathing like a bull about to charge. 'This is more important.'

'Then I'd better phone the police.'

'Go ahead. I'm sure they'd love to know what goes on here.'

'This is a refuge for runaway children. They know that.'

'Do they?'

'Why?' said Father Jack, stepping closer, his tone playful. 'Have you heard otherwise?'

'Don't fuck with me.'

'You think I sell them? That it?' He gestured to Jamal. 'Take that one lying over there. If you want him. And who wouldn't? Firm little body. Not very tight, though. Well, he wouldn't be, would he? All the cocks he's had—'

Father Jack didn't get to finish his sentence. Donovan swung his left fist straight into his face. He was rusty from lack of practice, and the blow sent shock waves up his arm, jarring his shoulder, but it felt good. Righteous.

Father Jack staggered back, fingers caging his face, blood seeping through.

'Hurt, did it?' said Donovan. 'I fucking hope so.'

Donovan moved in for another shot, but Jack was expecting him. As Donovan raised his arm, Jack slipped his hand round Donovan's back, leaving a greasy trail of blood along the leather, knotted his knuckles and dug them into the small of Donovan's back.

'Those are your kidneys,' said Jack, blood spraying with his words. 'Very tender.'

Jack ground in further. Donovan tried to pull away but Jack clamped his other arm round him, holding him in a ferocious bear hug. Donovan struggled, gasped in pain.

'You're going to do what to me, eh? What to me?' Jack breathed in his ear as he ground in further. 'Had enough yet, eh?'

Donovan felt like he wanted to throw up, black out. He feebly grasped at air with his right hand, the only part of him that could move, desperately trying to find something that would help him.

Nothing.

His arm hit the worktop, upsetting the sandwich Father Jack had been preparing. His hand hit somnething solid.

A kitchen knife. Small but sharp.

He scrambled for the handle, picked it up.

Black clouds gathered before his eyes. Jack clung on, dug in harder. He had only one chance before he blacked out completely. Breathing heavily, gathering together what last remaining strength he had, he stuck the knife into Jack's groin.

The result was instantaneous. Jack stopped hurting Donovan and tried to pull away. But Donovan clung on hard, pushing the blade in as far as it would go.

Jack screamed. Blood seeped through Father Jack's pale-coloured chinos. Donovan held on.

Jack kept screaming.

Eventually Donovan could hold on no longer and dropped to his knees, his grip loosening. Jack was too pre-occupied to keep hurting him. Donovan reached for the sink, used it to pull himself slowly into a standing position. His head spun like an Alton Towers near-death ride.

Father Jack was on the floor, backed up against the cupboards. Wailing, hands hovering over the handle, undecided as to which was best: pull it out or leave it in.

'That hurt?' gasped Donovan, clinging to the sink. 'Good. Now you and me—'

But Father Jack wasn't listening. His eyes had drifted behind Donovan.

'Si! Si!' he shouted, his voice near-castrato.

Donovan turned. The youths he had seen in the front room were standing in the doorway. Along with a tall, blond haired boy who was undoubtedly their leader. He made a rallying gesture and they all rushed forward.

Donovan tried to pull himself to his feet but failed. He tried to hold his hands out, ward them off, but it was no good. They were on him.

Practising what they had learned from watching the film.

He kept thinking: They're only children. I can't hurt children.

But they had no childhood left in them. Only a gleeful, feral rage.

Fists rained down on him, kicks connected with him. The girl, no match for the others physically, scratched and gouged at his skin.

He curled his hands over his head, tried to roll away.

'Get him . . . get him out of here . . .'

Father Jack's command was obeyed. Donovan was dragged along the floor, legs making useless attempts to right themselves, through the front room. He caught Jamal's eye; the boy, still prone on the floor, looked away.

Donovan was pulled, pushed and kicked into the hall. He had given up trying to fight back, just wanted the ordeal to end.

He was aware of the front door opening through the change in the air and was soon out on the street. He lay there, eyes closed, breathing deeply, anticipating the next blow.

It never came.

Donovan closed his eyes. Angry voices buzzed in his head. Then a gradual silence. Slowly, he opened his eyes, saw a face he didn't recognize. Closed them again.

Felt nothing.

14

Donovan opened his eyes. Blinked, waited for blows. They didn't come.

His eyes roved, tried to focus on his surroundings. He had no idea where he was. He was still on his back, on a camp-bed, but indoors; a bare bulb above him made him squint. He tried to move, get up. Ached down both sides. He flopped backwards, emitting a sound that was part groan, part sigh.

Saw movement from the corner of his eyes. Someone crossed towards him.

He tried to get up, get away. Felt the pain again. The figure spoke.

'How you feeling?'

'Hurt . . .'

The figure smiled. 'Just lie there. You'll be OK.'

He breathed deeply, did as he was told. The speaker was a young Asian man Donovan had never seen before. Hair neatly trimmed, black T-shirt discreetly bearing a designer label, immaculately faded and distressed jeans, box-white trainers. Well groomed, trailing an expensive yet subtle scent, his clothes proudly displaying a gym-worked physique. Donovan didn't want to jump to conclusions, but first impressions made him assume the man was gay.

He looked around the room. The furnishings were rudi-mentary: a table, two chairs, bare walls. Cardboard coffee cups and old sandwich wrappers on the table. By the window, pointing outwards, were two tripods, one holding a top-of-the-range digital camcorder, the other a telephotoed Nikon.

A surveillance setup.

The Asian man looked down at Donovan. 'Examined you as much as I could. They gave you a going-over, but I don't think there's any lasting damage. Nothing broken.'

'Did I pass out?'

'More like fell asleep. Thought it best not to wake you.' His voice was flat and calm, like still lake water trailing undercurrents of Geordie dialect and cultural origin.

Donovan pulled himself on to his elbows. 'How did I . . .?'

'Get here?' He told him. He had heard the commotion, ran to the street and stepped in. 'Don't think they fancied mixing it, so they went away. I'm Amar, by the way.'

'Joe Donovan.'

Amar smiled. 'I know.'

Donovan tried to stand up from the camp-bed. His head spun. 'What?'

The door opened. He looked at the new entrant. A blonde woman. He knew her from somewhere . . .

'How are you feeling, Mr Donovan?'

He continued to stare.

'We met outside the hotel on Friday.'

'Yeah . . .' He climbed off the camp-bed, rose unsteadily to his feet. 'But . . . What . . .'

'I think we need to talk, don't you?'

She talked. Donovan listened.

Amar handed round mugs of tea.

'Peta Knight. Knight Security and Investigations.'

'Please, no jokes about private dicks,' said Amar in his campest voice. He sat on the camp-bed, Donovan and Peta on the chairs. Donovan didn't feel as bad as he thought he would have done. He felt disorientated but nothing broken, just badly bruised, scratched. Like he'd been spinning in a washing machine with a couple of pairs of paratroopers' boots.

Peta ignored Amar, continued. 'We've been watching Father Jack's house for quite a while now. It's supposed to be a safe house for teenage runaways.' Bitterness entered her voice. 'But, of course, we know better.'

Father Jack. Real name Daniel Jackson. Started out in social work, playing an active part in running several children's homes. Eventually, with the aid of private finance and charitable donations, set up the home he has now. However, this is all a front. His real business is trading in teenage flesh.

'He does the usual thing,' said Peta. 'You know, picking up the stragglers, befriending, empowering, then hitting them with the bill. Hiring them out on the network.'

Donovan nodded. 'Bet he was abused as a child.'

'My heart bleeds,' said Peta, eyes like stone. 'It's the predatory bastard that he is now we have to deal with, though.'

His business is run under the protection of certain local councillors and police officials who 'have first-hand experience of what's going on there and take a cut of the profits. Very lucrative.' Consequently the regional media has never been interested in taking him on. He has a gift for self-promotion; the first whiff of trouble and he was out sound-biting up his good works.

'And stonewalling,' added Amar.

'No,' said Peta. 'His protectors do that for him. Along with delivering threats.'

With no one challenging him, Peta had decided, proactively, to investigate Father Jack. They had tried to hack into his financial affairs but got nowhere. They had tried to gain entry, have Amar pose as a customer and plant cameras and mikes, but that proved impossible, too.

'Vetting,' said Amar, all trace of earlier campness gone from his voice. 'Invite only.'

So Knight S&I had adopted twenty-four-hour surveillance, logged every coming and going. Amassing a whole dossier of evidence.

'Then we'll go public with it,' said Peta. 'Nationally. TV, broadsheets, tabloids, whatever. As long as it breaks big. Destroy the operation, take everyone down with it.'

'And what do you get out of it?' asked Donovan.

'Knight S&I, my company, is going under.' Peta took a sip of her tea, swallowed hard. It was cold in her mouth. She placed the cup on the table, left it alone. 'Just me and Amar at the moment.'

'Why's the company in trouble?' asked Donovan.

Peta smiled. No humour in it, only sadness. 'No natural client base. Apparently, so I've been told, private detectives are all seedy, middle-aged blokes employed by other seedy, middle-aged blokes. To spy on their wives, usually. Or their business partners. Well—' she shrugged. '—those people don't trust me. They think I'll side with the wife in divorce work and don't think I'm intelligent enough to handle their business partners.'

'Why?'

'Because not only am I a woman, but I'm a blonde woman. The fact that I'm an ex-copper and a black belt in tae kwon do apparently count for nothing. We had some great operatives. For security, too. Really good.' She sighed. 'But not any more. Because if you haven't got half a dozen fat-necked, steroid-pumped skinheads with fifty-six-inch chests on hand, or geeks in twonky-looking uniforms itching to go postal, you're not giving value for money. Honestly. Stuff like that you can pick up from any JobCentre.'

'Employing a gay Asian doesn't earn you many brownie points either,' said Amar.

'Despite the fact that you're the best surveillance expert I've ever worked with.'

Donovan shook his head. 'Hasn't the twenty-first century hit the north-east?'

'To hear them, Newcastle is a flagship city for Britain's future. But the cloth cap is still there,' she said. 'It's just worn on the inside now.'

Donovan nodded. 'Ex-copper?' he said. 'Was it the cloth-cap mentality made you leave?'

Peta nodded, her eyes clouded, face masked. 'Something like that.'

'Glass ceiling,' said Amar quickly. 'You know what it's like for women in those kinds of institutions.'

A look passed between Peta and him. He said no more.

'So . . .' Donovan gestured round the room to the cameras. 'All this . . . you want the big payday?'

'We *need* the big payday. Otherwise we go bust.'

'And we thought we were nearly there,' said Amar. 'But then you turned up. Joe Donovan, *Herald* journalist.'

'And you thought,' said Donovan, standing up, grimacing, 'that I was just going to walk in, steal your thunder and walk off with the story.'

Peta leaned forward, threat implicit in her words. 'That did cross our minds, yes.'

Donovan walked to the window, looked across at the house. All was silent.

'Well, I'm not,' he said, turning back into the room. 'That's not why I'm here.'

'Why, then?' asked Amar.

'I'll tell you,' said Donovan. 'But could I have another cup of tea first?'

Amar moved towards the kitchen.

'A drinkable one, this time.'

Amar scowled at him. 'Want me to finish off what the kids over there started?'

Donovan shook his head, smiling.

'Thought not.'

Amar sashayed into the kitchen, a look of mock petty triumph on his face.

He talked, Peta listened.

Amar handed round mugs of tea.

Donovan told them about Jamal. Gary Myers. The minidisc.

The rest he left out.

His tea, for all Amar's complaining, was much better than the last one.

He finished talking, sat back. Peta and Amar looked between themselves, then at Donovan.

'Different but parallel interests,' said Peta.

'But mutually beneficial,' said Amar. 'We should team up. Your paper publishes our story and in return you get surveillance and strong-arm. It makes sense.'

Donovan looked between the two of them. Before he could speak, his mobile rang. He answered it. Maria.

'I've got the result of Gary Myers' post-mortem,' she said without any preamble. Her Salford vowels had returned. 'You'd better take a look. Come back to the hotel.'

'OK,' he said. He looked around the room. Liked what he saw, made a decision. 'But I'll be bringing a couple of friends with me.'

He ended the call, looked at the two of them. Smiled.

'Grab your coats, partners,' he said. 'You've pulled.'

The kids had returned from their gleeful attack on Donovan still hyped up. A couple had tried to trash the living room before being smacked around by Si. Music had been played loud, jumped around to, violent DVDs viewed. Another couple had been so charged they had started having sex.

Father Jack had been placed on the kitchen table, knife protruding from his blood-soaked groin.

'Get it out! Get it out!'

Si pulled the blade free, used a tea towel that could have been an al-Qaeda testing ground for biological weapons to stanch the flow. The others crowded round to watch, Jamal, ignored, at the back.

Behind them the TV blared, unwatched, bodycount building.

Si's emergency procedures continued.

'You should go to a hospital, Jack,' he said. 'I'll call an ambulance.'

'I'm . . . not going . . . to a fucking . . . hospital . . .' Jack gasped, grimacing from the pain, body making involuntary contractions as he spoke. 'I'm going . . . to get . . . the bastard that . . . did this . . .'

Si had Father Jack's clothes pulled apart, was trying to locate the wound.

'First-aid kit . . . cupboard . . . bandages . . .'

Father Jack pointed to the cupboard under the sink. Si was immediately down there on his hands and knees, throwing cans, bottles and never-used cloths aside until he pulled out the green-plastic box.

'Gimme it . . .'

Father Jack snatched it off him, attempted to haul himself up into a sitting position. Blood pooled in the creases of his stomach, the tops of his legs. He pulled out a bottle of Dettol, found the point of entry with his fingers, poured it on.

Liquid hit open wound. Father Jack howled again.

'Towel . . . towel . . .'

Si handed him the tea towel, now a sodden crimson. Jack held it against himself, ordered Si to make up a dressing from cotton wool, gauze and tape. Si did so. Father Jack turned to his onlookers.

'Did anybody see . . . where he went?'

They all looked at him, at each other.

'Did anyone see where that cunt went?' The words spat, a command.

'With that—' one of the boys began, '—that Paki.'

Nods, assent.

'Them flats opposite . . .'

'Over the road . . .'

'That Paki, aye . . .'

'We'll get that Paki . . .'

'Aye, Paki bastard . . .'

Father Jack spoke over them, silencing them.

'Get the phone,' he said to the nearest boy, 'I'm going to call in some favours. Dr Blake. And someone to get that bastard. Now . . .'

The phone was brought. Si continued to apply the dressing. When they saw nothing more was going to happen, when all the thrill had been leached from the scene, the children drifted away.

Jamal drifted away first, not wanting to be singled out by Father Jack, reminded that he was the one who had brought Donovan into the house. He tried to read the other children's reactions. Some looked concerned on seeing Father Jack in distress; some had smiled, registered pleasure, but tried to keep it to themselves. Jamal understood. There was no such thing as pure, unmixed emotion when your benefactor was also your abuser.

The TV was still playing. The film finished, back to terrestrial channels. A local news broadcast. That same photo – the half-familiar middle-aged man, features dancing on the edge of Jamal's memory. He heard the soundtrack to the image:

'. . . as to the whereabouts of the missing chemist, Colin Huntley. Last seen leaving his home in the Northumberland village of Wansbeck Moor a week last Tuesday . . .'

Tuesday, thought Jamal. The day he came to Newcastle.
Tuesday.

And then it clicked. With a lurch in his stomach that left
him feeling faint, legs trembling, he remembered where he
had seen that face before.

Not some half-anonymous punter.

'Look, Mr Myers —'

'Call me Gary. If it makes it any easier for you.'

A sigh, then: 'All right. Gary . . .'

King's Cross. The hotel room.

Life and death. Life and fucking death.

He slumped to the sofa, almost hyperventilating.

The disc. Never mind just talking, he had to get the disc.
And then get out of there.

He looked around, checked the kitchen. Si was still
fussing over Father Jack. Neither looked like they would be
going anywhere any time soon. He scoped the living
room. The kids were regrouping, sitting round, already
mythologizing their own actions. No one paying him any
attention.

He stood up, moved to the door. Into the hall and up the
stairs as quietly as possible, two at a time. He stood on the
landing, holding his breath. No one about.

He extended his arm slowly, as if the very act of doing
that would attract unwanted attention. He slowly pushed
open the door to Father Jack's room, let it swing wide, then
stepped inside, closing it silently behind him.

Jamal scoped the room. It looked as he had last seen it.

He was sure the disc was in this room. He began pulling
videos and DVDs off the shelves; slowly at first, then with
more abandon. Careful to check that the contents matched
the sleeves. Nothing.

He tried cupboards, pulled out sex toys, lubricants, con-
doms. Nothing.

He lay flat on the floor, looked under the bed. Nothing but dust, used condom wrappers, soiled underwear.

In the wardrobe, checking the pockets of Jack's tent-like clothes, upending and shaking his neatly arrayed rows of comfortable, slip-on shoes.

Nothing.

He did find Jack's wallet, left hanging in a jacket pocket. He helped himself to the large wad of notes in it, put the wallet back.

Another look around. Where was left?

The bedside cabinet.

Kneeling before it, he tried the door. Locked.

'Fuck.' His voice whispery fast.

He needed something to prise the door with. Something long, heavy, sharp . . .

His eyes darted round the room. Came to rest on a restraining bar among the pile of sex toys. A chromed, heavy-metal bar with ankle manacles at either end. Perfect.

Fitting.

He hefted it in his left hand, placed the edge of the bar against the edge of the door, put his weight behind it, pushed.

It slid off, clattering to the floor, hurting his hands and leaving a gouged trail through the wood of the cabinet.

'Bastard . . .'

He picked it up, tried again.

Pushed down hard, found purchase.

The door began to give slightly.

Heartened, Jamal, grimacing, pushed harder . . .

Heard the sound of wood reluctantly splintering round the lock.

Harder . . . One more push and it would spring open . . .

'What the fuck d'you think you're doin'?'

Startled, Jamal dropped the bar, turned round.

Si stood in the doorway, staring down at him. Jamal quickly stood up. Si advanced into the room.

'I said, what the fuck d'you think you're doin'?'

'Look, man,' said Jamal, hands before him, palms out, 'I don't want no trouble. I just want what's mine, yeah? Then I'll blow.'

'You mean that disc?' Si sneered. 'You've kissed goodbye to that.'

Jamal's heart was beating so hard he felt it would smash open his ribcage and escape. He needed to do something, take some positive action. Get out of there and away.

'Look, man, please.' He heard a voice whining, begging. Was surprised to find it was his own. But not surprised enough to care, to stop. 'Please. Just gimme that disc an' I'll be gone. An' this whole world a' trouble with it.'

Si laughed. 'I'll give you something.'

Jamal saw the blow coming, managed to sidestep. Instead of his face, Si's fist connected with his shoulder. Only slightly, but it still hurt.

'Bastard . . .'

Si lunged again. Jamal lost his balance, fell on to the bed. Si tried to jump on top of him, hands aiming for his throat. Jamal scurried out of the way. He scrambled on to the floor, tried to pull himself to his feet, ended up half kneeling, half standing.

'No more trouble, yeah? I'll go, yeah?'

His words had no effect. Si kneeled on the bed consumed by anger, driven by rage, looking for an outlet. His face spilled into a snarl. Told Jamal he had found his outlet.

Jamal knew the blond boy was ready to attack, beyond listening to anything he could say. He needed a weapon. His eyes landed on the discarded restraint bar. Jamal quickly picked it up as Si came for him.

He swung the bar hard, putting all his strength behind it.

It connected with the side of Si's forehead, above his left eyebrow. Si stopped moving. Stared at him.

Jamal, arms shaking, hands sweating, looked at the blond boy. He didn't know what to do. For good measure he swung the bar again, connecting in the same place.

Si went down like a detonated chimney.

And then the blood started to pump.

'Fuck . . .'

Jamal looked around, looked down at Si.

He was unmoving.

'Oh fuck . . .'

Jamal threw the bar into the pile of sex toys and looked down at the bedside cabinet.

No time for that. He had to get out of there.

He ran down the stairs and out of the door.

As fast as he could go.

'So,' said Maria, looking around the crowded hotel room. 'Short version or long?'

'Short,' said Donovan. 'Layman's terms. Pretend you're a tabloid editor.'

She gave him a smile that wanted to contain hope. 'Might not even end up with that.'

Introductions had been made, explanations provided. Maria had shown concern over Donovan's appearance; he was starting to bruise over, seize up. She had insisted he take a shower, change clothes.

'I should take a look at your injuries,' she said, eyes tracing the scratchmarks on his skin.

Donovan smiled. 'Later,' he said, and took his shower.

'OK, then,' Maria said, picking up several A4 sheets. 'This is top secret. Even the police haven't got this yet.'

Peta looked at Donovan, frowned. Donovan shrugged.

'Journalists,' he said.

Gary Myers, the report said, died from asphyxiation and a broken neck. 'But the asphyxiation . . .' She read through the pages, head down.

'What?' said Donovan.

Maria looked up. 'They've speculated here, but it's not possible. It says the asphyxiation was caused by a massive blow to the neck which crushed his windpipe. Probably unbalanced him, sent him over the cliff.' She read on. 'Here's where they've speculated. They say the blow—' she looked up '—was caused by a fist.'

'Fuck me,' said Amar.

'Kind offer, but you're not my type,' said Donovan. 'A fist? There must have been some force behind that.'

'And anger,' said Peta.

'There's more.' Maria moved her finger down. 'Broken left clavicle . . .' She flicked over the page. '. . . compacted pelvis, left side . . . left ankle . . . all broken. All consistent with the fall and the landing. All left side. But this is interesting. Broken right wrist. Done, they reckon, at least twenty-four hours earlier. Also . . .' She shook her head. '. . . they say the break was made pulling away from something. Other marks round the wrist back this up.'

Peta frowned. 'Tied up?'

Maria looked down the pages, then back to Peta. 'Chained.'

'That's cold,' said Amar.

'Shit,' said Donovan.

Maria nodded, put the pages down. 'That's about it. Forensics and toxicology are still ongoing. Hopefully we should know more then.'

Silence fell.

'So it seems like . . .' said Donovan, thinking aloud, 'Gary Myers was forcibly abducted, held captive somewhere—'

'Chained,' said Peta.

'Chained,' repeated Donovan. 'Tried to escape . . .'

'Then taken somewhere remote to be disposed of,' said Maria, 'somewhere—'

Donovan clapped his hands together. 'Somewhere his body wouldn't be discovered until it had decayed so much there would be no way of telling which injuries were accidental, which inflicted and which—'

'The provenance of woodland creatures?' said Amar.

'Wrapping it up nicely,' said Maria. 'Death by . . . misadventure? Accidental?'

'In a couple of years time,' Donovan nodded, 'forgotten about. End of story. Talk about forward planning. Someone's confident.' He gave a grim smile. 'Thank God for doggers. Or not, depending whose side you're on.'

'Of course,' said Peta, 'if we've reached this conclusion, chances are the police will, too.'

'So what happens next?' asked Donovan.

'I've phoned Sharkey. He's on his way up.'

'Joy,' said Donovan.

'We need our arses covering,' said Maria. 'And we need Jamal. And the disc, preferably.'

Donovan sighed. 'Tried his mobile. No reply.'

'Keep trying.'

'My fault,' said Donovan. 'I should have brought him straight back here. Got him sorted out, instead of . . .' He sighed. 'We've got to get him out of there. I wouldn't like to say what's happening to him.'

'I know,' said Maria. She sat on the edge of the bed, sighed again. Donovan noticed the minibar had been seriously raided. 'This isn't just a story any more,' she said. 'One of my colleagues . . . someone I know has been murdered . . . Now this boy . . .'

She seemed to crumple before their eyes. Donovan sat

down next to her. Put his arm round her. Peta and Amar looked uncomfortable.

Maria stood up. 'Come on,' she said, sniffing. 'We've got jobs to do. Get the boy, get the disc. Find out who did this.'

She looked at the other three, face a mask of professionalism once again, North London back in her voice.

'Any ideas?'

15

Mikey's hands were shaking. He could barely build his roll-up.

Flakes and strands sprinkled the pub table; the scarred wood looked like diseased skin shot through with old, broken veins.

He put down the rolling paper with its small hill of tobacco inside, took a dark, bitter mouthful of his pint. Replaced it. Spilled beer soaked through the Rizla, rendering it useless. He scraped the abortive fag into his palm, dropped it in an ashtray. Cursed the waste.

Started again.

Another sigh. Atlas-huge.

The pub was a housing estate local in a particularly run-down area of Scotswood. All low-level, flat-roofed 1970s style, all concrete panelling and wood cladding. All thwarted optimism. The clientele matched their surroundings.

The jukebox seemingly not updated since before he went inside.

Queen: 'I Want to Break Free'.

You and me both, pal.

Early afternoon in the pub and already it seemed as dark as night.

He took another mouthful. No less bitter.

'Bit of a stomach bug,' he had said earlier that morning. His mobile was incoming calls only, supplied by Keenyside. He had used a phone box, miraculously unvandalized but stinking of piss and other bodily secretions. 'Don't think I'll be in today.'

Not far from the truth. He felt like throwing up.

The voice on the other end all solicitous concern, calling him mate. That fake prole accent. Those immaculately flattened vowels.

He really felt like throwing up.

'Twenty-four-hour thing, back in the morning probably.' Hung up on the get well soons.

He did some dealing for Keenyside, a few regulars; small stuff, but it just increased his anger, mixed it with his depression, a lethal lager/cider snakebite.

As soon as the Magpie had opened, he had been there.

The Queen song ended. Was replaced by Bryan Adams: 'Everything I Do, I Do It For You'.

Mikey shook his head, took another drink.

This wasn't what he had wanted. What he had dreamed of all those years.

What he had planned for, worked so hard for.

His dreams had been in colour. Blue sky, green grass. Brown trees with green leaves. Flowers of every shade and hue. He had looked through books at the prison library. Done sketches and watercolours in the art class. Became so involved with his dreams he could smell the scents of the flowers, of cut grass, hear a breeze gently crinkle the leaves, feel the sun on the back of his neck.

It was what had nourished him, sustained him. Given him something to aim for, helped him get an early release.

Transferred to an open prison; countryside all round him, joking, laughing with the officers, relaxed there. Planning a life beyond. Building up hope.

Leaving with hope. And dreams.

Then this. The reality. A brutal truth.

No colour but grey. Different shades, but grey. The estate where they had housed him. The dead patches of grass. The stunted trees. The sky. All grey.

And his dreams: dried up and hardened like the concrete of the estate.

Like prison.

No time to fear, though, no time to worry about acclimatizing. They found him a job. In a multi-storey car park. Re-creating a false criminal past.

Get Carter.

And his bosses on the *Get Carter* tour: middle-class posh boys playing at working-class hard men. Wearing artfully distressed expensive jeans and T-shirts. Drinking overpriced weak beer from the bottle. Seeing who could out-quote each other as Pacino from *Scarface.*

Looking like students. Mikey hated students.

Loving Mikey because he 'conferred authenticity'. Because he'd 'been there an' done it'. Because he was 'the genuine article'. Because he was 'the man'.

Tagging him along with them like he was their mascot. Patronizing him, exhibiting him like he was some circus freak.

Always trying to get him to perform, to live up to what they wanted him to be.

'Tell us about what you got up to.'

'Yeah, y'know, back in the day.'

Which day?

'About the gangsters, yeah? The criminals. You must have known them.'

The gangsters. The criminals. Had he known them? Of course he had. Everyone who grew up on those same streets in Benwell knew gangsters and criminals.

They made their grand gestures, their giving money to children's charities, their ostentation to hospitals. Their perceived kindnesses to local people. Their looking after their own.

But all that came later.

Because there was no glamour, no action about them. Just a hardness, a meanness. A hunger to escape their social boundaries, a willingness to stamp on, humiliate, injure or even kill those from the same streets, in their same class, to do it. Once they had done that, then they could act the benefactor.

But what they were actually paying for was respect.

Through fear.

The communities bought and paid for, acting as eyes and ears, a functioning early-warning system marking out predators or encroachment.

That was how they operated, thrived.

And Mikey wanted no part of that. Of them.

And none of them quoted Pacino from *Scarface*.

'You should branch out, Mikey.'

'Give gangland tours of Newcastle.'

'We'll help you do that, set it up.'

'We've got contacts.'

Fingers jabbing, beer bottles pointed at him. Grins belonging to people who think they've got the world sussed, but in reality know nothing.

'Get your memoirs ghosted.'

'Do talks, the chat-show circuit.'

'We'll help you do that, set it up.'

'We've got contacts.'

All the things Mikey had tried to put behind him, to escape from, thrust back in his face on a daily basis.

Two things he had never been: a gangster and a criminal.

Two things he had been: angry and unlucky.

He didn't know which had come first. Which had given birth to the other.

But they had both led, ultimately, to murder.

His mother, all he had, all he loved in the world, died. The painful, messy, lingering kind. And Mikey, devoted, didn't know what to do.

Mikey as a teenager: bookish, shy, interested in space and science, happier kicking round an idea in his head than a football off the garage doors with the other kids.

Mikey at seventeen: technically an adult, emotionally a child.

With all the cares in the world and no one to care for.

No one to talk to, to come home to. Cast adrift by the services: social, educational, familial.

He began drinking. Gave him somewhere to go, something to do.

He began walking. Anywhere, everywhere. Day and night. Time meant nothing.

Then came the attack.

A bench in Leazes Park. At God knows what time in the morning. Mikey's bed for that night. His dad's old overcoat wrapped round him, the remains of his giro, bottle and burning liquid in his pocket. Alco-anaesthetized dreams. Lost in space.

Two college kids on their way home from a club. Decide to have some fun with a tramp. Steal whatever money he's got. Humiliate him. Give him a good kicking. Set fire to him, maybe.

Mikey was wrenched back to reality from space to find the two of them roughly hauling him upright, swearing at him, slapping him around.

Angry and unlucky.

He reached inside his pocket, fear and self-preservation guiding his hand, found the near-empty sherry bottle. He pulled it out and, hand gripping the neck, smacked it against the side of the nearest youth's head. It didn't break.

This was real life, not a film.

The student looked up at him, surprised. Then the pain hit him.

'Fuck you do that for?'

The other one behind him, confused now.

The first one getting angry. 'Bastard . . . fucking bastard tramp . . .'

Mikey, scared, hit him again with the bottle, then dropped it, letting it smash over the tarmac. The student was bent double, cradling his head in pain and shock. He looked at the other student.

Who turned and ran.

Mikey looked at the first one. His good haircut. His casual but expensive clothes. His confidence. His lack of a fear of failure.

Angry and unlucky.

Mikey pushed him away. The student stumbled backwards, hitting the concrete post of the bench with his head in the same place the bottle had connected.

Hard.

Light went out in the student's eyes. His body hit the ground. A darkening stain spread from beneath his head, like a pillow against the grass.

Mikey ran.

They found him the next day. Fingerprints on the bottleneck. A clear nineteen pointer. A match for the ones previously on file for a dismissed D&D.

The other student told the police Mikey had started it. Had attacked them on their way home. It was the story he stuck to, reiterated by his expensive solicitor and barrister all the way through the trial.

Mikey told the truth. His legal aid solicitor was too distracted, harassed or exhausted to do much with the argument. His inexperienced barrister likewise.

The verdict: murder. The sentence: life.

For Mikey: frustration and impotence during the trial. Rage and resentment afterwards.

And then prison. Which wasn't as bad as he was

expecting it to be. The regime suited him. Gave structure to his life.

But the lack of colour. Grey everywhere. That was when he made the promise to himself. When he got out he would go somewhere green. With blue sky. Somewhere he was unknown.

He came back to Newcastle. To Scotswood. The terms of his licence dictated it. His heart sank.

Chance, his probation officer and the JobCentre intervened. And he became a *Get Carter* tour guide.

And then came Keenyside. Mikey hadn't known who he was.

'Your fairy godfather,' Keenyside had said, setting down a pint of bitter in front of him.

The Magpie pub. Same seat, just about.

'I need someone to be my eyes and ears. I can't be everywhere.'

It had been only months, but it seemed like a lifetime away. And now he was part of his life. Like a malignant cancer that couldn't be cut out.

'Why me?' Mikey had asked.

Keenyside shrugged. 'Because I can trust you. Because you'll do it.'

'Will I?' An impotent rage rising in Mikey. 'Why?'

Another shrug. 'Because I'll send you back to prison if you don't.'

Mikey felt like he had been punched in the stomach. 'For what?'

Keenyside smiled. No humour. Only the joy of control. 'I'll think of something.'

No choice.

'Oh,' said Keenyside. 'There's one more thing I want you to do for me . . .'

Mikey had started his second job. Hated everything about

it. Being an informer was bad enough, but the drugs . . .
Hated them. Everything about them. The effect they had on
people. The effect they had on him. In prison he had
avoided drug dealers. Thought they were scum, on a level
with child abusers.

And here he was. One of them.

People on the estate looked at him, treated him, differently. They either wanted him there, or didn't want him
there, depending on their needs. They served him in the pub
here but kept their distance. They knew what he did, and,
more important, who he did it for.

Because Keenyside was a very clever man.

The dirtiest copper Mikey had ever met. He knew who
to target, who to ignore. Who to lean on and pick on and
who to encourage and allow to flourish. He made arrests,
got results. Made convictions stick. But only for those he
wanted out of the way.

No one would speak out against him. No one dared.

Because whatever else he was, he was a copper. And he
could still bring the full weight of the law down to bear.

Keenyside ruled the west side of Newcastle with a quiet
restraint no gangster could match. And without a single
children's charitable donation.

No respect.

'And Mikey,' he had said, 'you're over the proverbial barrel.'

Mikey finished building his roll-up. It looked dreadful.
He tried to light it, smoke it. It fell apart in his hands.

Angry and unlucky.

That familiar impotent rage began to build and bubble.
He remembered the words of the Ed. Psych. in prison: don't
get angry at events, only causes. Trace it down to the roots
and deal with it accordingly and calmly.

He traced. It wasn't his ability to build a roll-up. It wasn't
even the grinning, gormless *Get Carter* boys.

No. It was Keenyside.

He had traced it. Keenyside. Now he could deal with it accordingly and calmly.

Rage was still building inside him. Hard and strong.

He took out his tobacco pouch, began to build another roll-up.

The rage became focused. His hands steady.

The roll-up successfully built, he put it between his lips, lit it, inhaled.

Rage: hard, strong and perfect.

Deal with it accordingly.

Keenyside.

Mikey exhaled.

Perfect.

Mikey stood by the entrance to the car park, watching.

Waiting.

His fingers curled round the kitchen knife in his overcoat pocket.

He had tried to get into the car park, inside the grounds of the police station, but it had proved impossible. Gated security and CCTV told him not even to bother. He had tried entering from the rear, working his way down the side of the bowling alley next door and over the wall, but that was too risky. It was bad enough just carrying a knife. That was enough to get him sent straight back to prison.

So standing by the entrance it would have to be.

It was getting dark. The security man on the gate would become suspicious if Mikey didn't leave soon. He tried to pretend, roll-up on his lips, that he was wating for someone. That he was a copper's nark.

It wasn't a million miles from the truth.

Then: chucking-out time.

He clocked all the faces as they came and went, searching.

Mikey had no plan. Was he going to scratch Keenyside's car? Stab him? He didn't know. So he watched, waited, hoped an idea would emerge.

More people left the building, came past him, ignored him. Civilian staff on their way home, mostly. Mikey began to feel foolish. What was he going to do? What could he do? He was about to give up, go home, when he came out.

Keenyside.

Mikey took a drag, dropped his butt, ground it out under his heel. Swallowed hard. His throat dry, like ash and embers.

His hand went to the knife again, fingered the handle. His heart was beating fast. He didn't know whether to approach or watch. However, events soon dictated he would be a spectator.

Keenyside swept from the building, arrogance worn like a kevlar vest; bullets would bounce off him. But there was something else. Something unusually set and determined about his features. Keenyside made for his car, the only Jaguar on the lot. But didn't reach it.

A woman burst from the building after him. Mid- to late twenties, Mikey reckoned, although he was no good at those sorts of things, dark-haired, thin. Could have been attractive if she had made the effort. But she hadn't. All her effort seemed to have been used up just to function. She was dark-eyed, haunted-looking. Hair unwashed, clothes plain and tired. Face devoid of make-up.

'Alan,' she called to him, ran across.

Keenyside sighed in tired exasperation, turned to her.

Mikey struggled to hear what was being said, picking up only occasional words:

'Promised, Alan . . .'

'. . . go on, Janine. It's finished . . .'

'. . . don't know . . . feels . . . left me like . . .'

And body language.

Janine: imploring, almost begging, barely restrained hysteria bubbling beneath the surface. Eyes fixed on him like a drowning woman to a life raft.

Keenyside: arms folded, defensive. Unmoving, not letting her in. Eyes looking anywhere but at her.

After a final speech that left her in no uncertain terms where she stood, Keenyside got into his car and backed out. Janine had to jump out of the way as he manoeuvred past her. He made for the gate; it lifted and he was off, speeding up the West Road, not once looking back.

Janine ran alongside the car and out into the street. She watched it recede, shoulders slumped, like her final hope had just disappeared.

She didn't move.

'Excuse me . . .' Mikey had walked up slowly behind her.

She jumped, turned. Mikey could tell instantly from the look she greeted him with that she found him frightening, repulsive or at the very least unpleasant.

'Please,' he said, raising his hands, 'I'm not . . . not goin' to . . . hurt you . . .'

She backed away, unconvinced.

'No,' he said quickly. 'It's Keenyside. Alan Keenyside.'

Her mood changed at the mention of his name. Still cautious, she became curious. 'What about him?'

'Well,' he said, 'I know him as well. And I think you like him as much as I do.'

She kept staring at him. 'So?'

Mikey scratched his head. Sighed. 'I came here today to . . . to do him some harm. I don't know what. And then you came out. And then . . .' Mikey shrugged.

'What's he done to you, then?' she asked.

'Taken my life away.' Anger accompanied his words.

Janine nodded. Recognition in her eyes.

'Listen,' said Mikey. He felt awkward. 'Maybe we should . . . get . . . together . . .'

She looked like he'd just made an improper suggestion.

'No, no, not like that . . .' He was conscious of his waving arms, his red face. 'No, I mean . . . talk. He's done us both wrong, from the sounds of it.' He shrugged. 'Y'know. Problem shared, an' that. Two heads . . . Find a way to . . . I don't know. Deal with him.'

Janine stared hard. She made up her mind.

'OK,' she said. 'But I'm phonin' a friend, tellin' them where I'll be.'

'That's all right.'

'Just so you know.'

'That's all right.'

She checked her watch. 'Listen, my shift's nearly finished. Wait here and we'll go to a pub when I come out.'

She went back inside.

Mikey watched her go, lit another roll-up, began working his way down it.

For the first time in ages, he smiled.

Keenyside loved the summer. But the summer was gone. Instead, he sat and stared at the autumn rain.

He closed his eyes, tried to will the season back. Apart from his villa in Lanzarote, his mock-Georgian executive home in Wansbeck Moor, Northumberland, was the place he most enjoyed spending those summer months in. The warm air, sweet from honeysuckle and lobelia in nearby gardens, the pastel-pink and blue sunsets. He would come home with the other commuters, shed his work clothes, take up tools of leisure; hedges would be trimmed, lawns would be mowed. Later, he would cook meat on his gas-fired barbecue and, along with his wife and children, dine al fresco on the decking-wood patio, drink bottled beer and sip Australian Chardonnay.

They would talk, laugh, smile. Be content in each others' company. He was a good husband. A good father. His two children were helped with their homework, praised for their schoolwork, allowed out to play with their friends.

He sighed. Opened his eyes. That had never happened. Only in his idealized fantasies. The house was a money hole, the mortgage a monthly struggle. The car on the drive; its payments unmade for the previous month. From beyond his study door came the over-raucous sounds of the twins, their voices shrill and overeducated, even at their early age. Like strangers to him. And his wife in their bedroom, trying on her latest must-have designer creation that his near-maxed-out credit card had taken a hammering for. And the villa would have to go.

He breathed in, exhaled, hoping all the stress and tension would leave his body too. It didn't. He took a large mouthful from the glass of malt in his hands, hoping that would help. It didn't.

The house was meant to be his refuge, a retreat from the job; the mindless violence, the filth and squalor of the lives he had to come into contact with, the scum on scum killings. Human garbage, and he was the one who had to cart it away. A retreat from his past. A way of escape.

He sighed. No good. No escape. He thought of Palmer's face that afternoon.

'Investigated?' Keenyside had said.

The chief super could barely contain a smile. 'Only rumours, little ones. Ripples.'

'Yeah, before a tidal wave,' Keenyside said. 'I know.' He looked around the room. Back at Palmer. 'What can I do?'

Palmer looked surprised. Shrugged. 'Not my place to say. Just thought you ought to know.'

Keenyside felt something well within him. Panic. Fear. 'Can't you . . . say something? Put in a good word? Stall it? I mean, you'll be dragged along too.'

Palmer's gaze became hard and cold. 'Don't know what you're taking about.'

Keenyside stared at him. Couldn't speak.

'In feudal Japan,' said Palmer, gaze unwavering, 'disgraced samurai fell on their swords.' He sat back, fingers steepled. 'Think on it.'

Keenyside couldn't think. Heard only his heart pounding, his blood rushing in his ears.

'I have a meeting to attend. So . . .'

And that had been that.

His glass was empty. He couldn't remember drinking it. He refilled it.

He sighed. Autumn. The season of death and dying. Leading to winter, the prison season. Lockdown.

Rain lashed the windows. Stormy Northumberland weather.

Walking through the station he had felt eyes on him, mouths moving behind hands, words coming in whispers, heads nodding. He tried to ascribe it to paranoia, but could feel it.

Marked.

But by who?

Names had gone round and round in his head all day since Palmer told him, until it had spun. None of his team had grassed. He was sure of it. They were on the books with him. Had nearly as much to lose as him.

Then who?

Janine had been off with him. But that was only to be expected. Like the others, she was following the pattern. And he loved it. The power. The complicity of corruption.

But she wouldn't have had the nerve. Not the way he had left her.

So who?

He looked around his house again, seeing it as nothing more than an expensive prison, his family as grinning jailers. He wanted to stand up, take hold of something heavy and smash everything. The wide-screen TV. The DVD player. The hi-fi system. His wife's crystal collection. No one but him could wreck everything. Break it all up.

Break free.

He felt himself hyperventilating, beginning a panic attack. Forced himself to calm down.

He looked at his watch. He had to speed things along.

Stop pissing about, being lenient. Patient. Put his plan into action.

Move that payday closer.

The escape. Really escape.

Not to Wansbeck Moor or Lanzarote.

To a land further away, where it was summer all year round.

16

The street was dark when the Saab convertible pulled up outside the block of flats. Donovan, body still aching but unimpaired, exited the passenger side first. Amar uncurled himself from the cramped back seat, bemoaning convertibles for the lack of space in the rear. Peta got out of the driver's side, centrally locked the car.

No more taxis. No more subterfuge.

No more hiding.

'My pride and joy, this car,' Peta had told Donovan when they had gone to pick it up from the car park it had been left in.

'Taking a risk, parking it in Byker.'

She laughed. 'Anybody touches this is taking a risk.'

Their plan. Peta and Amar, along with Donovan, return to the flat. Maintain surveillance but let Father Jack know they are on to him. Make him force his hand.

Maria stay at the hotel. Wait for Sharkey, try to reach Jamal on his mobile.

In through the communal entrance smelling of stale air and vinyl flooring and up to the flat. Peta put the key in the lock, opened the door. They stepped inside. Donovan closed the door behind them. Peta hit the light switch.

And stopped dead.

Sitting by the window, before the cameras, was Father Jack.

'This belong to anyone?' He held up the minidisc.

Four figures holding baseball bats detached themselves from the shadows and ringed the three. Faces twisted, bodies cranked up for violence. Waiting for their corpulent master's Pavlovian command.

The cameras had been wrecked.

Donovan looked at Jack. The fat man didn't look well. He had changed clothes into a looser Hawaiian shirt and bigger chinos. His stomach was distended even further, pushed out by the wadded dressing covering his injury. His skin looked sickly; he was sweating. He smelled bad. The hand that held the disc shook.

He looked haunted, a ghost that didn't know it was dead.

'Called in some favours . . .' Father Jack gestured to the bat-wielders. 'Gym candy and a bad attitude. Perfect for me . . . bad for you.'

Father Jack held the disc up.

'You're going to . . . suffer for what you've done to me . . .' Anger broke through his pain. 'So this is your last chance.'

The three of them looked at each other, expectant.

'Ready to make a deal?'

The Gate. Short strips of franchised bars and fast-food restaurants topped off by a multi-screen cinema. Blockbusters churning in perpetual rotation. The décor, all metal and neon, dated as soon as the last screwdriver was packed away.

Maria stood on the top level of the high glass-fronted building, looked down on the city, her feet tingling with vertigo, watched ordinary lives being played out: people driving cars, buses, leaving just-closing shops, entering bars, restaurants, going home. Ordinary lives. The other city.

'Man, this feels like you're standin' on air, an' shit. Man could fall an' keep fallin'.'

She turned round. Jamal had materialized at her left, was staring down at the street, eyes avoiding hers. Dressed identically to the last time she had seen him; but his emblematic urban armour of Avirex and box-white trainers had lost their shine and lustre. He hopped from foot to foot. She caught his eyes. He looked more than agitated. Scared.

Tread carefully. 'Thought you wouldn't come.'

Jamal shrugged, aimed for casual, his tension giving him away. 'Said I would, didn't I?' Shaking slightly as he spoke.

He had said a lot more than that. Maria had left a message on his mobile voicemail, reminding him who she was, asking him to get in touch so they could go ahead with what he had agreed with Donovan. His response had been surprisingly swift.

He told her he had to meet her. Had something big to tell her. Like, major big. And to bring her handbag 'cause it was going to cost her. He had arranged the place and time, hung up.

'So,' said Maria, smiling unthreateningly, like he was a wild animal she didn't want to spook, 'what have you got to tell me?'

'You got the money?'

'If what you've got to say turns out to be the truth, then—'

'No. Now. I gotta split.' There was pleading in his eyes, his voice. 'I need it now.'

Maria sighed. 'I'll have to hear what you've got to say first.'

Jamal weighed his options. Nodded.

Maria waited.

Jamal's eyes darted around, as if the half-deserted level was full of eavesdroppers.

He shook his head. 'Not here.'

'Well . . .' Maria looked around, saw the restaurants. 'You hungry?'

Jamal shrugged again. And again his eyes gave him away.

Ravenous, she thought.

'Come on, then.' She walked towards the escalator. 'I'm buying.'

Jamal pretended nonchalance, but almost ran to get there.

Nando's was quite empty. It took them hardly any time at all to get their food.

As with other branches of the franchise, the restaurant was all exposed dark beams, flagged terracotta floors and rough adobe walls. Was it just her, thought Maria, or was the idea of being sold a fake sense of history along with her meal unsettling? Especially in a steel and glass edifice like the Gate.

She filed the thought away for future reference. Saturday colour supp. piece, perhaps.

Jamal had wolfed down his peri-peri chicken and fries and corn on the cob in record time. So much so that she had ended up giving him part of hers.

Jamal drained his glass of coke, sat back satiated.

'Enjoy that?'

He smiled. 'Yeah.'

'Good. Now, business. What have you got to tell me?'

The smile disappeared. He began speaking but ended up stammering, tongue-tied.

'Just take your time,' she said, trying to calm him. 'There's no hurry.'

Jamal looked grave. 'There is. I gotta go.'

He took a deep breath, continued before she could say anything else.

'The disc, yeah? It's two guys. Talkin'.'

Maria nodded, interested, encouraging.

'One of them is that reporter guy. The one who turned up dead.'

Maria felt her heart quicken. She struggled to stay seated. 'Go on.'

'The other guy—'

'Look, Mr Myers . . .'

'The other guy . . .'

He told her. Slowly and carefully. The man from the TV. The newspapers. The missing man.

Him.

Jamal finished speaking. Maria sat there stunned, her heart smashing furiously like a John Bonham drum solo. She wanted to jump up, run from the restaurant, start screaming orders into her mobile, get the staff moving. If this was true, it was going to be one of the major stories of the year.

If it was true.

'Can you prove this?'

'Yeah. If I had that disc you could hear for yourself.'

'Where is the disc now?'

A shadow crossed Jamal's features. 'Father Jack,' he mumbled.

Maria took the mobile from her bag. 'I'll phone Joe.'

'Don't bother.' The words were said quietly; she didn't hear.

'No reply,' she said, putting the phone down and looking at Jamal. 'What's the matter?'

Si.

He was unmoving . . .

'Listen,' said Jamal, pleading desperately. 'I've told you what you want to know. I need that money. Now.'

'Why?'

'I just . . .' He looked as if he would bolt, scream or burst into tears. 'I need it . . .'

Maria sighed. 'Right,' she said. 'I can authorize a thousand pounds. But I have to wait and see if your story checks out.'

Jamal almost pounded the table in frustration. 'I gotta have it, like I gotta disappear, man . . .'

That was the last thing Maria wanted. 'Wait a minute,' she said. 'I just need to make a couple of phone calls. Go get another cola or something.'

Jamal sighed, then, when he knew she would say no more, made his way to the drinks dispenser.

'Right,' said Maria, folding up her phone and replacing it in her bag. Her notebook, open before her, was filled with copious notes.

She had spoken to several journalists on her own paper, trying to piece together the facts behind Colin Huntley's disappearance.

He had vanished the previous Tuesday, telling his cleaner that he would be back late or stay overnight. He lived alone following the death of his wife. His only daughter lived in Newcastle. He lived in a village in Northumberland. Wansbeck Moor.

His work colleagues talked of him as being anxious, distracted in the days before his disappearance. 'Like he was building up to doing something he wasn't looking forward to,' one fellow worker had said.

The day had been booked off work, so no one had thought anything of it. But when he failed to make a pre-arranged dinner appointment with his daughter on the Wednesday night, the police were called. And an official investigation started.

'Apparently CCTV footage has him getting on a King's Cross-bound train in Newcastle on the Tuesday,' Maria told Jamal. 'And a similar one in London shows him getting off. So that would appear to back up your story.'

'Can I have my money?'

'Let's just get this straight.'

There had been no contact between Colin Huntley and his daughter. Other friends and family had been questioned and eliminated. Publicly, the investigation was ongoing, but unless there was a break soon, Maria's sources had told her, it would start to be wound down.

'You'll have to talk to the police, you know,' Maria said. 'You're a witness.'

The colour drained from his face. He began to shake. 'No way. Joe said that. I gave you this so I wouldn't have to. I just want my money.'

Maria sighed. She couldn't just let him go. He was, at present, the only source for a potentially huge story. She had to have his credibility verified, have him protected from her competitors. Even get a sympathetic plod to talk to him when the time was right.

She looked at her watch. Sharkey would be here soon. He could throw some kind of legal blanket over the whole thing, buy her some time. Until then, she had to hang on to Jamal, not let him out of her sight.

She smiled at him, putting pen and notebook back in her bag. He didn't return the smile. Looked only anxious.

'Listen. Mr Sharkey, the man with the money, won't be here until later on tonight. I've got to do some work before then. Why don't you come with me?'

'Doin' what?' He sounded suspicious.

'Colin Huntley has a daughter. And she lives just up the road. Now, I need to talk to her about all this, so why don't you come along? You don't have to say anything. I'll tell her you're a trainee or my assistant or something.'

Jamal shrugged, although there was a hint of pride somewhere in his features. "K.'

Maria smiled with what she hoped was encouragement. 'What harm can it do, eh?'

They left the restaurant, the crowd flowing against them, eager for the latest slice of Hollywood comic-book escapism, and headed for the cab rank outside.

17

Donovan stared hard at Father Jack. Tried not to let the lethal goons on either side intimidate him.

Failed.

Donovan tried to keep his voice calm and even. 'What's the deal, then?'

Father Jack looked at the disc.

'This,' he said, clearly enjoying the moment despite his all-too-obvious pain, 'in return for — let's not be greedy — fifty thousand pounds. And that half-caste boy.'

The last few words spat out, Jack's brows twisting with fury.

'Good try, Jack,' said Donovan, 'but the price is too high. And last time I saw Jamal, he was with you.' He smiled despite the situation. 'How's your injury, by the way? Is that a nappy you're wearing? Didn't know they made them so big.'

A fresh wave of sweat broke over Father Jack. His breathing became heavier, his gaze darker.

'Mock all you want,' he said, 'but what's about to happen is going to hurt you more than you hurt me. I take consolation from that.'

'Take your pleasure where you can,' said Peta, angry and unafraid, 'because your nasty little operation is finished.'

Father Jack attempted another smile. 'Don't be . . . so melodramatic. Your cameras . . . are destroyed . . .'

'Think we didn't back things up?' said Amar.

'Think we didn't expect something like this?' Peta said, hands on hips.

Donovan was impressed by how cool she was being. He was still terrified.

Jack waved his hand in a dismissive gesture. 'I have friends . . .'

Peta continued: 'It's all been passed on to a national paper. There's enough hard evidence to convict you. And you won't be able to rely on your tame councillors or police. They're part of our package. Get ready, Jack. You're going to be famous.'

Father Jack was wheezing hard now, red-faced, as if he was sitting in a pressure cooker. He looked about to explode. When he spoke, his voice had a forced quality to it.

'This disc . . .' he said, '. . . you still need this disc. Trade. Pass over what you've got. And you walk out of . . . here . . . unharmed.'

'Bollocks,' said Donovan, with a fearlessness he wished he felt. 'Like we believe you.'

'And it's too late,' said Amar, seemingly as unperturbed as Peta. 'We've passed it on. Finito.'

Father Jack looked like he had reached the foothills of a major heart attack.

'Mark . . .'

One of his soldiers stepped forward, helped him to his feet. Once there, Jack seemed unsteady, swaying as if about to faint. He passed the disc to Mark, nodded.

Mark placed the disc on the table, brought his baseball bat down on it. Again. And again. Until there was nothing lift but silvered shards.

Jack locked eyes with Donovan, his face a mask of pain and hatred.

'Nobody wins now.' His voice was a fetid whisper.

He gestured. Mark helped him to the door. He turned, spoke to him.

'Wait till I'm gone, then . . . have some fun with them.'

Father Jack closed the door behind him. In the silence that followed, he could be heard making his laboured way down the stairs.

Silence returned to the room.

'Sorry, folks,' said Mark, smiling. 'Nothing personal.'

The men laughed.

Peta didn't.

She kicked out sharply, hitting the nearest one with a blow to the groin. He doubled over, air leaving his body in a painful huff of surprise. His grip on the bat loosened. Bringing both hands up, she disarmed him, dislocating his thumb and several of his fingers in the process.

'Joe!'

She threw the bat to Donovan. He clumsily caught it, put the right end in the palm of his hand.

The thug dropped to his knees.

Her actions had bought them precious seconds, the thug crew too surprised to respond. Now they did.

They attacked, one on one, anger driving their movements. They didn't like being bested, especially not by a woman.

Adrenalin kicked in to Donovan; he felt no tiredness, no ache, just the desire to survive.

'Bastard!'

A bat was bearing down on him held by Mark. He turned, dodged just in time. The blow landed against the wall. Trusting to his survival instinct, he quickly brought his own bat down on Mark's side. The man cried out, crumpled. Donovan was sure he heard ribs crack.

He swung again, catching Mark on the shoulder. Nothing broke this time, but Donovan felt the reverberation of the blow the length of his arm.

The thug grunted in pain. He turned, swung his bat wildly, pain pushing up his anger, losing his grip on it.

It hit Donovan in the stomach. He bent over as the air was knocked out of him.

Mark leaped at Donovan. He connected, hard, knocking him back into the table, pulling him painfully to the floor, Donovan dropping his bat in the process. Mark kneeled on him, one hand round Donovan's throat.

Donovan saw the anger and hatred the man held for him, a man he had never met before. The thought momentarily confused him. He was brought back in to focus when he saw Mark pull back his other arm, make his hand a fist.

It was the arm that Donovan had hit, but he was sure it could still do some damage. There was no way Donovan could fight back on his attacker's terms, meet like with like. He needed to use his own strengths.

Donovan brought his hands up, pushed back into Mark's twisted face. He forced the heel of his left hand on to his top lip, pushing lip and nose back as far and as hard as he could. Mark dropped his arm, let it join the other, pushing hard round Donovan's neck.

With his other hand Donovan scratched round the man's face, trying to get a grip of something he could use. He tried Mark's neck, but it was too fat and gym-pumped to get a grip. He tried his cheeks. No good.

He found Mark's eyes, tried to claw at them.

Mark guessed what he was doing, tried to rotate his head away, kept the pressure on Donovan's neck.

Donovan brought his other hand up, found the other eye. Clawed, raked, tried to get a grip.

Mark kept squeezing Donovan's neck.

Donovan felt the air being choked from his body, a final constricting gurgle. He felt his strength ebbing away. Black holes, like openings to a universe beyond, began to appear in his vision. He knew he had enough left in him for only one last, desperate chance.

Donovan put his thumbs over Mark's eyes.

Pushed.

Hard as he could.

Mark screamed. He tried to pull his head back while still maintaining pressure on Donovan's neck.

Donovan held on, hands like rigored claws.

Mark gave up, pulled away. He rolled off Donovan, lay curled on his side, left arm trailing limply, right covering his face.

'You've blinded me . . . You've fuckin' blinded me . . .' Whimpering.

Gasping and coughing for air, Donovan struggled to his feet, reached for the baseball bat. He swung it into Mark's kidneys. Once. Twice.

He pulled his arm back for a third swing, found his strength had deserted him. He slumped, back against the upended table, bat cradled in his hands, looked around the rest of the room.

The other three crew members had been similarly disarmed. Amar was kneeling over one of them, arm locked round the man's throat. The man clawed ineffectually at the hold. Amar's muscles no longer looked like those of a gymnarcissist. They, and the look on his face, meant business.

The other two lay groaning on the floor.

Peta kneeled down before the captured man. She looked lit up by the violence, truly alive.

'Listen,' she said to her captive, 'I know you're just the hired help. Get up and leave now and that's the end of it. But keep going and so will we.'

She looked around. Smiled.

'And we'll finish it.'

The man, seeing he had no option, nodded.

Amar tentatively loosened his grip. The man rose warily to his feet.

The others joined him. Donovan's assailant held his hands over his face, was helped out by one of the others.

'You nearly fuckin' blinded him!' said the man Amar had just released.

'And I'll do the same to you,' said Peta. 'Get out.'

The man stared at her. She returned his gaze, unblinking. Eventually he broke the look, left.

'And tell everyone you were beaten by a blonde girl and a Paki poof,' shouted Amar.

She and Amar looked at each other, exchanged high fives.

They noticed Donovan. Crossed to him. Peta kneeled down.

'You OK?'

Donovan managed a weak smile. 'Should have seen the other feller.'

'I did.' She laughed. 'And you made a right mess of him. Well done.'

Donovan looked at her and Amar. They were buzzing. The violence had energized them. It had just tired him out.

'Room's a mess . . .' said Donovan.

'Think we'll get our deposit back?' asked Amar.

They laughed, cleansing the flat of tension.

Donovan sighed. 'Well,' he said, 'suppose we should go give Father Jack the good news.'

Hammer was bored.

He sat behind the wheel of his car, his anonymous Vauxhall Vectra, watching the girl's flat. It felt like he had been there for weeks. It felt like he had been there for ever.

Since leaving Keenyside at the station house he had come back to the same spot. Now it was dark and there had been no movement.

Usually on jobs like this he would fall into a near-fugue state while waiting. Pass the time by playing back all the

injustices ever done to him throughout his life. He would
imagine them as short stories. With the holdall on the seat
next to him, unzipped, its contents face up, as an audience.
The stories had new endings. Ones where his tormentors
were terrified by his strength, where he tortured and humil-
iated them before forcing fearful repentance from their
shattered bodies, ultimately finding peace by killing them,
even eating their bodies, symbolically taking their souls.

Failing that, there was his iPod, death metal on heavy
rotation.

But nothing worked for him today. He knew why. The
last few days had fired him up. Regent's Canal, the
Pennines . . . that was his true calling. His real work. Not
this. This bored him.

And when he became bored, he became angry.

And when he got angry, someone had to pay.

'Let something happen!' he shouted, pounding the steering wheel.

Soon after that, something did.

He blinked, thought he was seeing things.

He wasn't.

It was the rent boy. Jamal. Walking up to the block of flats
with a woman beside him. He didn't recognize her, but she
wasn't important. The boy was the important one.

His first thought: phone Keenyside.

The boy and the woman walked up to the block of flats.
Rang a bell.

Her bell.

Keenyside's mobile rang and rang. No answer. Must still
be at his house in the countryside. No reception there.
Hammer hung up before voicemail kicked in, not risking
leaving a message.

He looked around, wondered what to do.

The woman was talking into the entryphone, talking

quite a bit. Eventually the door buzzed open and the two of them were admitted inside.

Hammer rubbed his face. Needed to think.

Make a decision. Use his initiative.

He looked at his mobile one last time, as if the very act of doing that would will a call through from Keenyside.

Nothing.

Hammer gave an angry sigh, zipped up the holdall, opened the car door, swung his body out. He locked the door behind him, pulled his woollen hat down over his ears, scoped the street to see if he was being watched.

He wasn't.

Turning his collar up to hide his face, he crossed the street to the flats, approached the front door.

Ready to ring the bell.

18

Donovan saw that the door of the house was unlocked, turned to both Peta and Amar, who shrugged. Exhausted and badly shaken, but not giving up yet, he pushed it open.

The children were gone. A cursory look around downstairs confirmed that. And quickly, too: like looters had ransacked the place, taken CDs, DVDs, anything saleable.

A noise from upstairs: a creak of the floorboards.

Donovan motioned to the other two, pointed at the stairs, began silently to ascend. Peta and Amar nodded, did likewise.

On the landing Donovan paused, looked around. All the rooms were empty, evacuated in the same haste as downstairs. Single items of clothing lay scattered, discarded; hands not quick enough to stuff them into holdalls before running. But a thoroughness amid the mess; these children were used to running.

Donovan stopped before Father Jack's room. The only door closed. Noises coming from behind it. He touched the handle, pushed it open, stepped into the room.

All round was carnage. Drawers and cupboards pulled out, contents spilled and strewn over every surface. Father Jack's inner life exposed; like dangerous, guilty secrets confessed aloud.

Blood everywhere. The white furnishings accentuating it. Jackson Pollock gone postal.

On the bed, half lying, half sitting, was Father Jack. The eye of a sickening storm. Cradled in his arms the broken, unmoving body of Si.

Father Jack was sobbing.

The three watched, not knowing how to proceed. Father Jack, eventually registering their presences, looked up. He realized who it was and panic spread across his features. He made a move to run, but something inside him signalled the futility of that. He sighed, nodded.

Donovan almost found pity in the man's plight.

Almost.

'We're calling the police, Jack,' said Donovan.

'Well, make sure they get the half-caste,' said Father Jack, his voice watery and blubbery. 'Make sure that little cunt pays for what he did to my boy.'

The paedophile looked at Si's face. Spreading purple bruises and whitening of skin. Began tenderly to wipe the blood away from the boy's eyes, sobs sending flubbery oscillations through his body.

'Yeah,' said Donovan, 'blame Jamal. Blame us. Blame your childhood. Blame fucking *Coronation Street*, if you must. Blame anyone but yourself.'

A howl ripped itself free of Father Jack's throat.

'He did it, you cunt! With this! With this!' He held up the heavy-metal separator and restraint. 'He hit him with this! He hit . . .'

His voice trailed away, obscured by sobs.

Donovan was unmoved. 'Maybe so. But your prints are on it now. Your DNA. A violent child abuser or a phantom boy. Who's a court more likely to believe? You're fucked, Jack.' He gave a mirthless laugh. 'And not in a good way.'

The sobs continued unabated.

Donovan turned to Peta and Amar. 'You got enough?'

Peta nodded. 'I think so.'

'Let's call the police,' he said. 'Then Maria. Get it sorted out.'

He reached inside his jacket pocket for his mobile. His hand stopped halfway. He looked at Peta.

'Could you do it?' he said. 'I'm just too tired to deal with anything.'

Donovan walked out of the room, down the stairs and out of the house. He sat on the pavement outside, sighed. He closed his eyes.

Tried to feel nothing.

'Caroline Huntley?' Maria spoke through the metal grille of the entryphone.

'Yes?' A weary voice, but expectant with a tiny dash of desperate hope.

'My name's Maria Bennett. I'm the editor of the *Herald*. Could I come in and talk to you, please?'

The voice on the other side of the grille sighed, as if suddenly tired beyond hope. 'I'm not talking to journalists. Please go away.'

'I understand that, Ms Huntley,' Maria said quickly before the woman could hang up, walk away. 'I don't want anything from you. I might have some information for you. About your father.'

The desperate hope returned to the voice. 'What sort of information? Is he alive? Have the police found him? Is he all right?'

'Could I come in and talk to you, please?'

Silence.

Maria knew she was thinking it over, wondering if the words were just a ruse to gain entry. The next thing she said, she knew from experience, would be the thing that either opened the door or locked her out for good.

'Ms Huntley,' Maria said, 'I'm not from one of the tabloids. I'm from the *Herald*. The editor of the *Herald*. If you wanted to check me out, I could give you a number to call. But I do need to talk to you. And you must hear what I've got to say.'

Silence.

Maria looked at Jamal, crossed her fingers. Jamal shrugged.

Then: a sigh through the grille. 'OK. Third floor. Number eight.'

The door buzzed. Maria opened it, ushered Jamal inside, waited for it to close behind her, lock solidly. Then began to climb the stairs.

Maria had to admit it felt good to be back in the field. She had been a desk jockey too long.

On the third floor, Caroline Huntley was waiting for them, the door to her flat open.

Maria held out her hand to shake, Caroline accepted it. Maria gave what she hoped was a friendly, reassuring smile.

'Maria Bennett.'

'Caroline Huntley.'

Caroline was blonde, late twenties, Maria reckoned, tall and attractive if her features hadn't been ravaged by lack of sleep and excess worry.

'Could we come in, please?' said Maria. 'It's easier to talk inside.'

Caroline noticed Jamal. 'Who's this?' she said, fear and doubt creeping into her voice as if she had been duped. 'He's not a journalist.'

'This is Jamal. And he's the reason we're here talking to you.' She pointed to the door. 'Could we?'

Caroline nodded, stepped aside. Maria smiled, thanked her and entered. Jamal nodded shyly, followed.

Caroline closed the door behind them.

Maria looked around. 'Lovely flat,' she said.

'Not at its best,' said Caroline, sitting down in an armchair. 'But then neither am I.'

Maria nodded sympathetically. She noticed that Caroline's sweatshirt and sweatpants were stained, her hair unbrushed.

Caroline shrugged. 'So?'

Maria and Jamal sat down next to each other on the sofa. At Maria's instigation, Jamal told Caroline what he had already told her. The facts were the same but his manner more deferential than with Maria: he didn't want to upset Caroline.

'OK,' he said, shrugging as if embarrassed when he had finished, 'that's that.'

The silence in the room seemed to have taken on an almost physical presence. Jamal looked at Maria, seeking reassurance that he had said the right thing. She smiled, gave him a small nod.

'I'm sorry, Caroline . . .' said Maria.

Caroline began to cry. Hugging herself, head down, shoulders shaking.

'I'll, er . . .' said Maria, 'I'll get you a drink of water.'

Caroline nodded, not really hearing.

Maria stood up, looked for the kitchen. The action was more to give Caroline a chance to take in the news alone. She motioned for Jamal to stand up, come and join her. Jamal frowned, confused.

Then the doorbell rang.

'D'you want me to get that?' asked Maria.

Again, Caroline nodded absently.

Maria crossed to the door, lifted the phone.

'Yes?'

'Interflora,' said a male voice. 'Delivery for . . .' The sound of paper rustling. 'Huntley? Miss Caroline Huntley.'

'Interflora? You're working late.'

'Traffic,' said the voice. 'Last one of the night. Then I can go home.'

Maria put her hand over the mouthpiece, turned to Caroline. 'Interflora,' she said. 'Should I say yes?'

Caroline waved her hand absently, blew her nose. 'Whatever,' she said.

Maria pressed the buzzer. 'Third floor, flat eight,' she said and replaced the handset. She then went into the kitchen to find a glass, fill it with water.

Soon there was a knock at the door.

'He was quick,' said Maria to herself. She raised her voice. 'Can you get that, Jamal? Save Caroline getting up.'

Jamal made his way to the door, opened it.

He didn't recognize the man at first: the hat threw him. But that cruel smile on seeing Jamal, that darkly glittering sapphire, left him in no doubt.

Fear rooted Jamal to the spot. He felt his body turn to water, then dust. He opened his mouth to scream. But had trouble finding the words.

'Ma – Ma – Maria! Maria!'

Terror was making Jamal hysterical. He tried to back away, stumbled. Hammer entered the flat, advanced towards him.

Then stopped.

Maria was standing before him, glass of water in hand.

Hammer looked between them, smiled. The luxury of choice.

Jamal took that moment to recover his wits, dodged round Hammer and was out of the door and away before Hammer even made an attempt to grab him.

'Jamal!' Maria's shout had no effect.

Hammer looked at the retreating boy, about to run after him.

Maria spoke angrily. 'You're not from Interflora,' she said, standing in front of the intruder, squaring up to him. 'Who the hell are you? What d'you want?'

Hammer smiled at her.

The tooth. The blue-jewel tooth.

Jamal's description of his pursuer at King's Cross came back to her. A shiver of dread ran through her body. And she knew who he was.

She looked to the doorway, the living room and back to the glass in her hand. Not knowing what else to do, she threw the water in his face.

Hammer, as an automatic reaction, punched her. His fist connected with the glass, shattering it, driving it into the front of Maria's neck. The force of the blow carried her body back; her shoulders and head smashed against the hallway with a dull thud, the glass cutting into Maria's flesh.

Maria went rigid, her body impaled on an icy stalactite of shock. She raised her hands to her neck, brought them away covered in blood. The jagged edges had severed arteries and veins. Blood pumped from her, fountaining against the walls and ceiling, the flat no longer warm and earthy.

Maria slid down the wall, dropped to her knees, fingers grasping uselessly at air. She couldn't believe what was happening to her. She tried to breathe, heard only a ragged, wet, sucking sound from her throat.

She scrabbled frantically at her neck, trying to stem the flow.

She tried to scream; nothing came out.

She fell over on her side, prayers flying through her mind like express trains to heaven. Her body was shaking. Twitching uncontrollably.

The stalactite shattered; icy cold all over her.

Her vision began to contract; darkness blurred the edges, crept slowly towards the centre.

She saw Caroline Huntley, face a mask of terror. She saw the intruder knock her to the floor with a single swipe. She saw him look around, find something to wrap Caroline's body in. She saw him walk towards the door, step over her.

She tried to cry out, ask him to call an ambulance.

The words screamed, but only in her head.

Her body began to stop twitching, shaking.

The ice had penetrated her bones now.

Her vision darkened, as if she had closed her eyelids while her eyes were open.

The prayers still ran round her head, the voice becoming fainter.

Felt coldness spread to every part of her.

Felt nothing.

PART THREE

SECRET HISTORIES

19

The room was small, barely big enough for the chairs and table. The windowless walls were covered with acoustic tiles, the door heavy and grey. One single overhead strip, quietly fizzing like a dying fly, threw out shallow, flat light. The room was oppressive, thick with the ghosts of useless lies, of desperate deals, of dead-ending self-revelations. It was hard to breathe; air, like hope, sucked from within the four walls.

Peta stared at the wall, wished she still smoked.

Not that she missed the burn of nicotine in her mouth or the feel of tar in her lungs. Smoking was a coping tool, a crutch. Something to do with her hands while she talked. Or waited. Something she drew false courage from. Like alcohol.

But she no longer used either of those things.

She sighed. Her heart fluttered. On the other side of the table. Not a good feeling for an ex-copper.

She looked at the surface, traced names both written and carved, read protestations of innocence and sometimes love, noted experiences of the police in general and certain individuals in particular, anonymous attempts to grass up members of their community.

No names she recognized. Turnover this side of the table was higher than at McDonald's. And with fewer vacancies.

She sighed again, looked at her watch. Coming up for seven o'clock. She replayed the events of the previous night in her mind.

Donovan had been sitting on the pavement outside

Father Jack's house. He looked exhausted. She sat down next to him.

'They're all gone,' he said. 'All the children . . . gone . . .'

Peta sighed, nodded. 'We can't do everything, Joe. We've stopped a vicious abuser. But we can't save everyone.'

Donovan shook his head. 'But one . . . just one . . .'

She had stood up. Decided it best to leave him alone.

She had phoned the police then, told them the score. On their arrival, Amar, Donovan and herself had been asked to make out separate statements. They had agreed, while waiting, on their selective version of the truth, one that was deliberately vague over why Donovan was looking for Jamal in the first place.

Father Jack had been escorted out into a waiting car. He barely acknowledged them, looked completely broken.

'What'll happen to him?' Donovan had asked. 'Something nasty, I hope.'

'The police force doesn't operate like that any more, sir,' replied the detective inspector, his expression leaving the words 'more's the pity' hanging in the air but unsaid.

Si's blanket-covered body was wheeled out, put in a waiting ambulance. Driven off.

Arc lights and white-suited SOCOs made it appear unreal, like a film set.

After nearly three hours of cross-questioning, having their statements checked for mistakes, contradictions or outright lies, the detectives seemed satisfied. The fact that Peta was ex-police helped add weight. They were free to go.

Around them news crews, print journalists, attracted by the lights, were beginning to gather.

'If you want your story to be told properly,' said Donovan to Peta, 'you'd better beat this lot to it. Do it now.'

He phoned Maria, received no reply. Frowning, he put the phone away.

'Not there,' he said. 'Must be asleep.'

'Listen,' said Peta, 'I know a journalist, head of a freelance agency in Newcastle, Dave Bolland. Know him?'

'Heard the name,' said Donovan.

'I could call him. He could get things going. Sort out an exclusive with the *Herald.*'

Donovan yawned. He looked beyond tired, Peta thought, down from his adrenalin high. Drained.

She probably looked the same.

'OK,' said Donovan. 'Whatever. We'll sort it out in the morning.'

They went their separate ways. As she was getting into her car, Peta was stopped by a uniformed constable.

He wanted her to come with him. Down to the station. 'What for?'

'Detectives would like to ask you a few more questions, miss.'

She had tried arguing but knew it would be futile. She had allowed herself to be driven to the Market Street police station.

And there she sat, still waiting.

The door opened behind her. She turned round.

'Sorry about the delay.' The voice was cheerful and familiar. Heart-skip-a-beat familiar.

'Hello, Paul,' she said, her throat suddenly dry. She swallowed hard.

Detective Sergeant Paul Turnbull smiled. Too professionally for Peta to read anything into it.

'Thought it was you,' he said. He closed the door behind him, crossed the room, sat down opposite her.

His dark hair was turning grey, adding to his monochromatic appearance, his face slightly heavier, but other than that he looked the same as the last time she had seen him. Still monochromatic. An outward manifestation of his belief in life's absolutes. Peta knew what bollocks that was. From first-hand experience of him.

He looked at her, smiled again. 'You're looking well.'

'It's the middle of the night, I've had a shit day, I'm exhausted and I look awful.' The words wrapped themselves defensively round her like armour. Then, with exaggerated grace, 'But thank you.'

Turnbull's face was a blank mask. 'How's—' he shrugged '—everything?'

'Fine,' she replied, giving nothing away. 'Good.'

'Good.' He stared at her again.

Peta shifted uncomfortably in her chair. 'So you've had a good look. Can I go now?'

Turnbull's mask reddened slightly. 'Just a couple of things . . .'

Peta folded her arms. She hadn't been aware of how hard her heart was beating.

Turnbull picked up a sheet of paper, looked at it. 'Just need you to . . . to go over your statement again. Confirm a few things . . .'

Peta sighed, started again. Yes, Father Jack's house had been under surveillance. Yes, the photos and tapes would be made available to the police. Yes, including the one of a high-ranking police officer and a well-known local council-lor frequenting the establishment on more than one occasion. Yes, there were also copies lodged with a national newspaper. Father Jack's house was already open; they didn't force their way in. Jack had heard about the operation, sent someone to wreck their equipment, them in the process. And, yes, they found Father Jack cradling the body of a dead teenager with what they assumed was the murder weapon in his hand.

Peta leaned back in her chair. 'So can I go now?'

Turnbull studied the paper before him, looked back at

Peta. 'I know that—' he checked himself '—Asian worked for you. What about this Joe Donovan? Where does he fit in?'

'He's the journalist, helping us write the story.'

'Works for the *Herald*? Or used to?'

Peta nodded.

'Working on anything else at the moment?'

'You'd have to ask him that.'

Turnbull's eyes were caught by a strange light. He looked down, scanned his notes. 'Odd choice. Not done anything for a few years, it says here. Not since—' his fingers traced a path down the page '—not since his son disappeared. Sent him off the rails. A breakdown. Son never turned up. Alive or dead.'

'What?'

Turnbull looked up. Saw concern on her face. 'Didn't you know?' he said. 'Didn't he tell you any of this?'

'No . . .' Peta shook her head slowly. 'Oh my God . . .'

Turnbull gave a small smile. Triumph leaked from the sides. 'This upset you, has it?' He leaned forward. 'Fond of this Donovan bloke, are you?'

Peta felt her cheeks redden. She realized her hands were clenched into fists.

'Fuck you, Paul. Fuck you.'

Turnbull laughed. 'Any time, pet.'

Peta's anger increased. 'Not if you were the last man on earth.'

'That's not what you used to say.'

She stared at him, hard. Composed herself. 'How's the wife, Paul? How are the kids?'

A shadow passed over his features. He didn't answer.

'Does she believe in a statute of limitations, Paul? Or does she think that things that happened in the past stay in the past? Maybe she doesn't know what happened. Should I tell her? Maybe things are still going on with my replacement.'

Turnbull said nothing, just stared at her.

'Bitch.'

Peta smiled. Cold and mirthless. 'I'm not the naive idiot I was when I first met you. I'm not the booze-dependent wreck I was when you'd finished with me either. Bitch? I could be, Paul.'

He stared at her. She returned it. He broke away first, fear flash-illuminating his features like forked lightning.

'So is that it?' Peta said. 'You saw my name on the sheet so you thought you'd haul me in. Have a look. Curiosity, old times' sake, whatever.'

He stared at her.

'So can I go now?'

'There's the door.' He smiled. 'I'm sure we'll be seeing each other again soon.'

She stared at him, not able to disguise her hatred. 'I doubt it.'

He waved goodbye to her. She rose, turned and stalked out, slamming the door behind her.

Turnbull sat unmoving, staring at the space she had occupied.

He hadn't told her what case he was really working on. And why he imagined he would be seeing her again. Very soon.

He smiled.

Unaware that he was grinding his teeth, balling his fists.

Donovan lay in his hotel room bath, water as hot as his body could take it, bubbles up to his chin.

He luxuriated. Felt the best he had in months, if not years.

His concerns over the missing children had receded. Peta was right. They had handed a murderous child abuser over to the police. And that, once he had passed through his barrier of tiredness, had given him a high he didn't think he would ever come down from. But nearly three hours of giving his statement had convinced him otherwise.

He had wanted to contact Maria, share the news with her. Fall asleep in her arms, wake up next to her. But she probably wouldn't have taken kindly to being disturbed. So he would let her sleep, tell her in the morning. There would be other nights. He knew there would.

He had slept as soon as he crawled on to the bed. A deep, dreamless sleep. Peaceful. Other troubles would take care of themselves.

Tomorrow.

He had woken, felt the night's ache settled in to his body, decided to run a bath, ease it out.

Phone room service for breakfast.

Get Maria to share it.

There was knock at the door.

Donovan brought up his submerged head, blew trapped water from his nose and mouth, pushed his hair back off his face.

'Just leave it outside,' he called. 'I'll get it in a minute.'

A pause, then another knock.

Donovan sighed. 'Oh for fuck's sake.'

He pulled himself out of the bath, grabbed a white towelling robe and, dripping, made his way to the door. He pulled it open.

'I said just leave—'

And stopped.

He knew they were coppers, even without the warrant cards thrust in his face. One was female, mid-thirties, short blondish hair and plain-looking from features to suit. The other was slightly younger; monochromatic from hair to suit to tie. The woman spoke.

'DI Nattrass.' She gestured to her male companion. 'DS Turnbull. May we come in, please?'

'I gave a statement last night,' said Donovan. 'What more d'you want?'

'Could we come in, please.' Nattrass' voice was flat, impassive.

Donovan stood aside to let them in, closed the door behind them, looked at them.

Turnbull was scanning the room, making swift value judgements on its inhabitant. Not positive judgements, if the sneer on his lip and the cold cast to his eye were any indication. Nattrass was standing in the room by the mirror, waiting for Donovan to join them.

'May we sit down?'

Donovan cleared old clothes from the bed, pulled the duvet up.

'Thank you,' Nattrass said, and sat. Turnbull did likewise.

It was clear that Nattrass wasn't going to speak until Donovan had sat also, so he obliged, taking the chair in the corner.

'Mr Donovan,' Nattrass began, her voice low and calm, 'I'm afraid we've got some bad news for you.'

Donovan opened his mouth to make a weary quip, but the expression on Nattrass' face stopped him. Her eyes were professionally void. He began to feel uneasy.

'It's . . . Maria Bennett. I'm afraid she's dead.'

Donovan felt his heart lurch in his chest.

'Dead . . .'

He looked between the two police, faces both stone flat.

'But . . . dead . . .'

His head, his heart, couldn't accept, process, the information. He felt like his body was spiralling into a steep, dark vortex while his head was being stretched in the opposite direction. Both snapped back together. He felt suddenly nauseous.

He shook his head to clear it. Felt worse.

'She . . . she was . . .' He pointed numbly towards the door. Shook his head. 'No . . .'

The two police looked at each other, waited.

'How did . . . how did . . . it . . . happen?'

'She was murdered,' said Turnbull bluntly.

Donovan looked at him as if not seeing clearly. 'Murdered . . . who by?'

'That's what we were hoping you would tell us, Mr Donovan.'

Turnbull's attitude brought Donovan sharply back into focus. 'What d'you mean?' asked Donovan sharply.

'What DS Turnbull means,' said Nattrass, throwing a look of admonishment towards her junior colleague, 'is that we have found a body answering Ms Bennett's description and carrying her documentation.'

'And you need me to make an identification of the body.' Donovan's voice was hollow.

'I'm sorry to ask you this,' said Nattrass.

Donovan rubbed his face. 'Oh God . . .'

Nattrass stood up, followed by Turnbull. She turned to him, eye to eye.

'We really are very sorry.'

Donovan nodded.

They left, promising to wait for him downstairs. Donovan sat back down on the chair, stared straight ahead.

Thoughts tumbled through his head like slo-mo acrobats; emotions ran through his heart like runaway trains.

It felt like the world he had been constructing for himself on waking had disappeared. A fragile world of hope and straw, blown away by a dark, truthful wind.

He felt alone again. Bereft.

He felt . . .

Like he had done when David disappeared.

He sat there.

Room service came. Knocked. Knocked. Left.

He sat there.

Eventually he remembered the two police waiting for him in the lobby. He stood up, made his way into the bathroom. Looked in the mirror.

It was only when he saw how wet his face was that he realized he had been crying.

'I suppose I should tell you that Maria and I . . .' Donovan paused, sighed, 'are lovers.' Another sigh. '*Were* lovers.'

Nattrass nodded, as if his words confirmed something she had known or expected.

'I'm sure that must make it doubly difficult,' she said.

Donovan hunched forward, elbows on knees, cat's-cradled his fingers into ineffectual, insubstantial patterns. He sighed. Words, inadequate forms for articulating his emotions, had deserted him.

They sat next to each other on moulded-plastic chairs in a strip-lighted, anonymous corridor that seemed to be purgatorially unending; Donovan in his own world, Nattrass waiting for permission to enter.

The Royal Victoria Infirmary. Mortuary.

Donovan had been guided through doors and down corridors, the arteries of the building, heat steadily falling away until the final set of double doors swished slowly and steadily shut behind him, leaving him sealed in the chill heart of the mortuary.

Before him was a series of stainless-steel tables, edged and inset with drainage gullies. On the table lay a covered body. Turnbull crossed to a blue-suited lab technician, pointed back at Donovan. The technician moved forward, folded back the sheet.

Donovan was shaking, head down, staring at the floor. He had rehearsed this moment over and over in his mind:

the sheet pulled back, a look at the body, the question asked, confirmed.

'Yes,' he would say, 'that's my son. That's David.'

Then the pain would build, find release and with that release would come a sense of hideous calm and the foundations of a kind of closure.

But this wasn't David.

It was Maria. Eyes closed, dark hair splayed out behind her head. Her finely featured face peaceful, like the night before when he had watched her sleep.

The ragged gash on her neck, already purpling, reminded him she was beyond sleep. Beyond everything.

'Yes,' he said, nodding, 'it's her.'

And turned away, tried to wipe that image from his memory. Knew it would be there for ever.

Another loss.

Another ghost to haunt him.

'Do you have any idea who could have done this, Mr Donovan?' Nattrass again.

Donovan shook his head.

'Anyone connected with a story you were working on?'

Jamal, Donovan thought, then dismissed it. Shook his head.

'What was that, Mr Donovan?'

'No, I don't know.'

'What story were you working on? What were you both doing here?'

Donovan looked up, his eyes red-rimmed. 'Please . . . look, I know you've got your job to do, and I want her killer caught as well, but . . . I can't . . .' He shook his head.

Nattrass nodded, sat silently back but didn't rest.

Turnbull chose that moment to return, walking up the corridor with two plastic cups. He handed one to Donovan, who looked at the contents wonderingly.

'It's tea,' said Turnbull.

Donovan gave a vague nod of thanks, placed the cup on the floor, his shaking hands creating a microcosm of ripples, whirlpools and tidal waves on the surface. They quickly vanished and all was calm. Donovan sighed.

Turnbull sat at the other side of him. Donovan looked up.

'Where was she found?'

A look passed between the two police: Nattrass nodded, Turnbull spoke.

'At the flat of Caroline Huntley.'

Donovan frowned. 'Who?'

'Caroline Huntley,' said Nattrass. 'Daughter of Colin Huntley.'

Something small and electric – a weak signal, a last spark – snapped across Donovan's memory, then disappeared.

'Colin Huntley?' he said.

'The missing scientist,' said Turnbull, scrutinizing Donovan's reactions.

'You must have heard of him,' said Nattrass. 'It's been all over the media. Lot of coverage, lot of bodies out hunting.'

'Lot of overtime,' said Turnbull. Nattrass ignored him.

'I've been out of circulation,' said Donovan.

Nattrass explained about Colin Huntley's disappearance. Donovan listened, nodding.

That must be where he had heard the name, he thought. The papers. TV. But something persisted, niggling and fizzing at the back of his mind . . .

He looked up. Nattrass had asked him something.

'Sorry? What?'

'Her notebook, Mr Donovan,' she said. 'Ms Bennett had a full account of the disappearance of Colin Huntley in her notebook. We've checked with the *Herald*, and they've confirmed the time she phoned for information.'

'When you were in Byker,' added Turnbull.

'She then went up to Jesmond to see Caroline Huntley. A neighbour phoned 999 at roughly ten thirty last night to say there was what sounded like a fight taking place in the upstairs flat.'

'Caroline Huntley's flat,' said Turnbull.

'And what does Caroline Huntley say?' asked Donovan.

'Nothing,' said Nattrass. 'She's disappeared.'

Donovan looked between the two of them. 'What?'

Turnbull took out his notebook. 'At approximately ten forty-five,' he said, 'this same neighbour saw a lone figure carrying what looked like a heavy carpet, leave the flats, deposit this item in the boot of his car, a Vauxhall Vectra, and drive away.'

'Licence number?' asked Donovan.

'Didn't get it,' said Turnbull. 'Didn't think it important at the time.'

'We checked Caroline Huntley's flat,' said Nattrass. 'It would appear that a large rug is missing from the living room.'

'So that was her,' said Donovan.

'We think so,' said Nattrass. 'We're trying to get the neighbour to come up with an e-fit of the man she saw. It could be a major breakthrough. And the car, too, although we're less hopeful about that. Vectras are very common. But we think that this is the man who took her father. Why, we don't know.'

Turnbull turned, looking Donovan square in the face. His features had a default neutral setting, but his eyes were intense.

'So,' he said, 'any ideas?'

Donovan matched his stare. 'No,' he said, 'I don't.'

'Would you go and get Mr Donovan another drink, please, Paul?'

'I just got—'

'I don't think Mr Donovan cares for it. Now, please.'

The look Nattrass gave him was designed to brook no argument. It worked. Turnbull rose reluctantly to his feet, stomped off. Nattrass watched him go, then turned to Donovan, a sympathetic smile in place.

'I must apologize for my colleague's attitude, Mr Donovan. In his zeal to see justice done he can sometimes be . . . confrontational.'

Donovan nodded, said nothing.

'Mr Donovan,' she said, 'I realize this may not be the best time to talk.' She produced a card, handed it to him. 'There's my number. If you think of anything, anything at all, please get in touch. I'm sure you want to see the murderer caught just as much as we do.'

Donovan pocketed the card, nodded.

'I'm going to be frank with you. I'm not one of those detectives who believe the press and police should be at each other's throats. We've both got our jobs to do, and sometimes those jobs can work out mutually beneficial to the other.'

Donovan narrowed his eyes. 'How d'you mean?'

Nattrass allowed herself a small smile. 'I think you know what I mean. You help me on this, and I'll help you.'

Donovan nodded. That old game. Journalists and their sources.

'OK,' he said. 'Deal.'

Nattrass smiled. 'Good.' Then her eyes hardened. 'But no playing cowboy. That won't help anyone. Least of all you. Clear?'

'Crystal.'

Turnbull returned with a cup and a scowl.

Nattrass stood up. 'Thank you, Paul, but I'm afraid we're going now.'

Turnbull, scowling at Donovan, upended the cup into a nearby bin.

'Can we drop you anywhere, Mr Donovan?' asked Nattrass. 'Your hotel, perhaps?'

'No, thanks,' said Donovan. 'I think I'll walk.'

They saw him to the door, went their separate ways.

'We'll talk soon,' said Nattrass.

Outside, another day was in full swing. The sky electric Edward Hopper blue, nearby Leazes Park a riot of autumnal red and gold. The sun was shining, life was going on. The kind of day that would make most people glad to be alive.

Donovan walked away, tried to ignore it.

The walk failed to sort anything out. He eventually reached the hotel.

'Oh shit,' he said out loud and stopped.

Cameramen were camped out in front, a TV news crew. All waiting to talk to the other journalist, no doubt. All waiting for him.

Before they could see him he ducked round the side of the building, looking for another entrance. He went right round the hotel, coming out by the back door to the restaurant's kitchen. He nipped inside. A chef looked up quizzically at him.

'Environmental Health,' said Donovan. 'Better get tidying up if I were you.'

No one else challenged him.

He walked right through to the foyer, tried to creep into the lift, but the receptionist saw him.

'Mr Donovan, Mr Donovan . . .'

Sighing, he went reluctantly across, keeping out of sight of the main door. She held up a stack of paper big enough to reforest Cumbria.

'I've got some messages for you . . .'

He knew they'd be from journalists asking him to talk to them. He'd done it often enough himself.

'Bin them,' he said, 'the lot.'

'And Mr Sharkey has arrived. He said he has to see you urgently.'

'He can fuck off as well,' said Donovan.

'Excuse me?' said the receptionist, eyes saucer-wide.

Donovan smiled apologetically. 'I'm sorry,' he said. 'You didn't deserve to hear that. Thinking out loud.'

She nodded, apology accepted.

He made his way up to his room, called the *Herald*.

Asked for all the information they had on Colin Huntley.

Colin Huntley could no longer tell if it was day or night.

His time was measured not in hours or minutes but in more basic, yet abstract, forms. The length of time between food deliveries. Between ingestion and bowel movements. Drinking and urinating. The number of rats seen in any one time.

A single bare bulb illuminated the place, an artificial, per-manent sun, throwing out more shadows than light. Since Gary Myers' enforced departure, along with a few old stink-ing blankets to keep out the bitter cold, Colin had been given a few old paperbacks to read. Jeffrey Archer. John Grisham. Tom Clancy. Colin suspected this was part of the torture.

The pain in his arm was still there. Another constant. And he didn't feel at all well.

He wondered if he was going mad. Mephisto was trying to break him, he knew that. He could hear his voice even when he wasn't there.

'Make the call,' the voice said, more insistent now. 'Once you've done that you'll be able to go free. And be rich.'

He couldn't make the call. He wished he could. Because once he had, he would never be free . . .

The chains rattled, the padlock was released, the key turned in the lock. The door opened.

Colin squinted against the light. He no longer bothered reaching for the hood. He knew who his captors were, and his body was too weary to be pushed through the motions. With Gary Myers gone, there was no need for pretence.

It was Hammer.

'Brought something to keep you company,' he said.

Keeping the inset door open, he went back outside, dragged in what looked like a rolled-up rug. He pulled it across the floor, laid it next to Colin, began unwrapping it.

Colin, still chained to the radiator, pulled himself forward, tried to see. Something about it looked familiar. What was inside even more so.

'Caroline!'

Hammer turned, swatted him with the back of his hand, sent him sprawling backwards against the wall. His arm hurt even more.

'Keep your voice down, cunt,' said Hammer. 'Or I'll take her away again. Piece by piece.'

'Suh – sorry . . .'

Colin pulled himself upright again, rubbed his injured face with his hand. He was bleeding. He didn't care. Caroline was here. His daughter.

His new world.

Hammer finished unwrapping Caroline, left her lying on the spread rug. Her wrists and ankles had been bound, her mouth sealed with a strip of gaffer tape. Her eyes darted all around the room. Even the sight of her father couldn't wipe the terror from her features.

Hammer ripped the tape from her mouth, slit the bonds on her wrists and ankles. The cuff that had held Gary Myers was still attached to the radiator. Hammer yanked Caroline's arm across, ignoring her yelp of pain, roughly closed it round her wrist. He stood up.

'There,' he said. 'Happy families.'

He left, locking the door firmly behind him.

Father and daughter looked at each other, emotions rollercoastering around inside them. Then fell into each other's arms. Or as far as they could manage, the cuffs clanking against pipes, chafing against skin, pulling them in opposite directions.

Huge waves of emotion built inside them, came crashing down as cascading tears, enormous, jerking sobs. Desperately clinging to each other, not wanting to let go for fear the other would be borne away again.

Eventually the tears washed themselves out. They pulled apart, looked at each other. Checking the other was real.

'Caroline . . .' Colin's voice was like old, untreated leather, cracked and stiff from disuse. 'Caroline . . . what . . . have they hurt you?'

Caroline shook her head. 'No . . .' She grabbed him again. 'Oh Dad . . . I thought you were dead . . .'

'No, no, I'm still here . . .'

She pulled back, studied him again. More closely this time.

'Oh my God . . . Look at you . . . What have they done to you?'

Colin involuntarily cradled his arm. 'It's . . . all right . . . I'm all right . . .'

They hugged again. Tears and sobs broke, subsided.

She looked at him again. Quizzical now.

'What's going on? Why are you here?'

Colin sighed, slid back against the wall.

'Oh Caroline,' he said, 'I've done a terrible thing . . .'

20

'That was brilliant, mate.'

'Yeah, Mikey, best you've ever done.'

'Had them right there, mate, right there.'

Mikey was walking over the High Level Bridge back to Gateshead, his mockney employers alongside him. He smiled, nodded.

'Thanks,' Mikey said. 'Felt good.'

The blackened metal frame of the High Level was all-encompassing, the nuts, bolts, girders and uprights of the Victorian construction keeping the sunshine out. But Mikey didn't care. He could see a way out, light at the end of the tunnel.

Because he had an ally.

Janine had walked in to the Prince of Wales twenty minutes after their encounter in front of the police station. He saw her stand inside the doorway, look around uncertainly. He waved, she acknowledged. Made her way warily towards him.

He tried to see himself from her point of view: scruffy, unshaven, cheaply dressed. Clinging to the fashions of ten, fifteen years ago. Carrying prison around with him.

Mikey could well understand her wariness.

She sat down opposite him, began going through her handbag.

'I didn't . . .' Mikey cleared his throat, tried again. 'I'll get you a drink. Didn't know what you . . . what you wanted.'

He made to rise.

'I'm fine,' she said.

She pulled out her mobile, punched in numbers. Her hands, Mikey noticed, were shaking.

'Hello, Mam,' she said into the phone. 'I'm just havin' a drink wth a friend after work.' A pause, listening. 'The Prince of Wales. No, I won't be long. I'll call you when I'm leavin'.'

Mikey drank his pint.

Janine replaced the phone in her bag, sat back on the chair, looked at him.

'So,' she said, 'what were you gonna do to Alan Keenyside?'

Mikey licked his lips. Despite his pint his mouth felt dry.

'Do his car,' he said. 'Hurt him. I dunno.' He tried to make the next words sound light. Jokey. 'Kill him, even.'

'That's what he deserves.' Janine nodded, her gaze fixed on Mikey's pint. Intense. Impassive.

Mikey sighed. Felt unburdening himself was now an imperative. 'He's ruinin' my life. I just wanted to . . . strike back at him.'

Janine gave a hollow laugh. 'You'll have to try harder than that.' She dug into her bag again, brought out a packet of Silk Cut and a lighter. Shook a cigarette from the pack, placed it between her lips and tried, hands trembling, to light it.

'Here,' Mikey said, leaning across the table, 'let me.'

He held her lighter. She recoiled from his touch. He pulled away.

'Sorry,' he said.

'No,' she said quickly. 'It's me. I'm just . . . Never mind.'

She had another go. Managed to get it lit. Took a drag, held it, exhaled. And with the smoke went some of her tension. 'He's a bastard,' she said. 'And you couldn't hurt him enough. Even if you killed him it wouldn't be enough.' She took another drag. 'So what did he do to you?'

Mikey thought the best way to prove he meant her no harm was to tell her the truth. Or as much as he could. He didn't want to tell her about prison. At least not yet. She might run. 'He made me a drug dealer.'

Janine just stared at him.

'He said I would be one of his paid informants. I mean, I didn't even want to do that,' he said. 'But he made me. An' then he made me a dealer.'

'How?'

'He gets his informants to tell him about local dealers. Where they are, when their next shipment is comin' in, that kind of thing. Then him an' his squad arrest them. Then skim off them. Take their stuff. Then give the stuff to his paid informants to peddle it.'

'Why d'you do it?'

Mikey sighed. 'Because if I didn't he'd have me in prison.'

'Could he do that?'

Mikey tried to smile. 'What d'you think?'

Another drag. Another release of tension. Janine nodded. 'Alan Keenyside enjoys ruinin' people's lives. Doesn't even have to make money out of it. He'll just do it for fun.'

'What about you?'

She looked at her cigarette, as if weighing up what to tell him. Decision made, she began. 'Him an' me started seein' each other. I knew he was married, but I thought it was only a bit o' fun.' She shook her head. 'By God, I grew up fast.'

Another drag. Mikey said nothing.

'I was flattered, you know? This big detective askin' out one of the filin' clerks. A civilian. An' he was very persuasive. Chased an' chased . . .' She shook her head, almost smiled. 'Knew what to say to make you feel special, you know?'

Although he didn't, Mikey nodded.

She sucked the last ember of life out of her cigarette, stubbed the butt out hard in the ashtray. 'Bastard.' She sighed. Stared off somewhere Mikey couldn't see. Then delved back into her bag, produced another Silk Cut, lit up again. Her hand didn't shake as much this time.

'It was romantic.' She leaned forward, into her story now. 'Dinners in flash restaurants. Drinks in posh cocktail bars. An' dresses to wear in them. Nights out. Weekends away. It was fun, darin'.'

Another sigh, another drag.

Mikey was surprised by how much Janine was telling him. She must really need to talk, he thought, really need to get Keenyside out of her system. And who better to confide in than someone who's not only a stranger but hates the man as much as she does?

'Then things began to change.' A shadow fell on her features. 'He started to . . . make me do things. Force me.' Her eyes dropped back to the cigarette, became focused on the burning tip. The slightest breeze inflaming it, quickening its deterioration to ash and smoke.

'Physical things,' she said to the cigarette, 'sexual things. Unpleasant things.'

Mikey felt uncomfortable. This was the first time a woman had spoken to him about sex. He felt himself blush.

She put the cigarette to her lips, drew down hard.

Burning the tip. Ash and smoke.

'He liked the control,' she said. 'He got off on that. Got his kicks.'

Mikey shook his head. 'Bastard . . .'

'I had a friend once,' Janine said, 'who lived with a bloke who used to beat her up. I'd say, "How can you live with 'im? Get away." An' she would say, "But I love 'im. 'E'll change."' She sighed. 'I used to think she was soft. But I don't now. Because I know it can happen to anyone. It happened to me.'

The shadow across her features darkened. She gave a bitter laugh. 'Then it got worse. Drugs.'

She stubbed her cigarette out, thought about it, decided to light another. Hands steadier all the time.

'I've done drugs before,' she said. 'Y'know, down the Bigg Market or the Quay or out clubbin'. Coke an' ecstasy. Bit o' blow. I mean, who hasn't?'

Mikey nodded, said nothing.

'Enjoyed them. Nothin' against them. But Alan wanted me to do heroin. Crack. Well, not want me to do it, make me do it. He forced me. An' then . . . an' then . . .' She shook her head, averted her eyes. 'He . . . did things to me. Made me do things. Horrible things . . .'

She shivered, eyes seeing something Mikey couldn't, didn't want to see.

'I was a real mess.' Her voice sounded small, like a child lost in a big world. Mikey sat forward, strained to listen.

'A real mess . . . An' I didn't know what to do. Who to . . . talk to. Anythin'.'

She shook her head, lost in her story now.

'I mean, me mam was good. She was great.'

Mikey nodded.

'She really helped. Gave us the strength I needed to pull away from him.' She gave a small, sad smile. Then a little laugh. 'Me dad wanted to do him in. I couldn't let 'im. Didn't tell 'im who he was or what he did.' Her voice darkened. 'An' I couldn't tell either of them what he'd done to me.'

Mikey noticed that his glass was empty. Decided to forgo a refill until Janine had finished her story.

'But they gave us the strength to get help. Seek treatment. Work was good an' all. I told them I was really ill. Couldn't tell them about him, of course. But they let me have sick leave to sort meself out.' She sighed. 'An' it was goin' well.' She sat up straight in her seat. 'Really well. I was back at

work, avoidin' 'im an' seekin' a new job as well. I kept me
distance, kept meself strong.'

Another sigh. And the shadow fell again.

'But then he came back. All apologetic, y'know. Sorry
about before, one last chance, not like that any more, promise things'll be different . . .' She shook her head.

'But you told him to get lost.'

She dropped her head. Shook it slowly and sadly. When
she spoke, her voice had shrunk again.

'I had . . . sex with him.'

Mikey said nothing.

'Not only that,' she said, eyes still downcast, voice a
tremulous, fragile thing, 'I found out I was pregnant.'

'What?'

She nodded again. Struggled to control her voice, her
body. 'I told him, confronted him. He just laughed. Told me
to go an' have an abortion.'

She sighed, looked at her cigarettes, decided against one.
Forgot there was one already smouldering in the ashtray.

'If it had just been that, though . . . it was the abuse as
well. It was a mongrel, he said.' She spat the word out. 'A
mongrel . . . Have it cut out, thrown away . . . stamp on
it . . . stamp on it . . .'

Her hand went to her face, covered her nose and mouth.
She screwed her eyes tight shut, but the long-dammed,
long-threatened tears forced their way out.

Mikey didn't know what to do, what to say. He wanted
to comfort her, hold her, tell her she had a friend, that
things would be all right. But he didn't know how to touch
her, find the words that would make her stop crying. So he
sat still, waiting for this particular wave of sadness to ride
itself out of her.

Eventually her tears subsided. She dug in to her handbag,
brought out a tissue. Dabbed her eyes, her cheeks. Blew her

nose. Noticed that her ashtray–berthed cigarette had burned itself out. She lit up another.

The shakes had returned.

'Sorry,' she said, her voice cracked and scratchy, like an old record.

'Not you that has to apologize,' said Mikey.

She nodded, dragged deep.

'So what did you do about . . .' Mikey's voice barely registering, unobtrusive.

'Got rid of it,' she said. 'That's what I was telling tonight. When I saw you. But he didn't want to know. Had more important things on his mind, he said.' Another deep drag. 'But I saw that look in his eyes . . . that triumph . . . he couldn't hide it . . .'

She shook her head.

'That's what turns him on,' she said. 'He finds people's weaknesses an' exploits them. Like he did with me.' Her voice took on a harsh, angry edge. 'He gets off on corruptin' folks. Twistin' them all out of shape, emptyin' them until there's nothin' left.'

'He uses your fear against you,' said Mikey. 'He knows I don't want to go back to prison. That's his threat.'

Janine looked at him. 'Back to prison? What d'you mean? What were you in prison for?'

Mikey stopped dead, mouth open. He didn't know what to say. Decided on the truth. Because she had been straight with him.

'Murder,' he said as simply as possible.

Immediately her expression changed. Her eyes widened with fear. She clutched her handbag as if about to run.

Her reaction saddened Mikey, even though he had been expecting it. He tried to smile, hoped it looked reassuring.

'Don't worry,' he said. 'It was a long time ago. And these things are never black and white.'

Janine didn't look reassured.

'You're quite safe with me. You really are.'

She said nothing.

'Look,' said Mikey, 'Keenyside's the dangerous one. Not me.'

She looked at her watch. 'I'd better go now.' She made to stand up.

'Wait.' Mikey stood also, reached across the table and placed his hand on her arm. She looked at it but made no attempt to remove it.

'Listen,' he said. 'Thank you for talking to me. I thought I was the only one he . . .' Mikey sighed. 'Thank you.'

Her features softened. She smiled.

'At least I know I'm not alone,' she said and patted his hand.

'Thank you,' said Mikey.

'I'd better go.'

Mikey nodded. 'We'll get him. Don't worry.'

She sketched a smile, left the pub. Mikey made his way to the bar, ordered another pint. Thought about what Janine had told him. Her experiences, horrific though they had been, had helped him. They legitimized the thoughts he had been having about Keenyside. Morally vindicated his dark, vengeful fantasies.

He took his pint back to the table, sat down. Looked at the dead butts in the ashtray. Thought of Janine.

Smiled.

Began to plan.

The shift finished, *Get Carter* groupies off home happy.

Mikey gathered his things together, prepared to leave. The mockneys approached him.

'Hey, great show, Mikey.'

'Yeah, good one, mate. Really real.'

'Felt it, yeah.'

Mikey smiled. 'Thanks, lads.'

He looked at the three of them. He didn't mind them, really. They weren't bad lads. Just the way they were. Some people couldn't do anything about the way they were.

And some could.

'Comin' for a beer, Mikey?'

'Yeah, hittin' the town, meetin' some mates.'

'What you say, mate? Love to have you along.'

'It's a kind offer, lads, but no thanks. I've got plans.'

He made his goodbyes, left. The mockneys watched him go.

'Mikey seemed in a well good mood.'

'Yeah, like he's found, like, I dunno, like a new purpose in life. Or somethin'.'

'Yeah.'

'An' 'e was good today an' all. Played a blinder.'

'Knockout. Best 'e's done. You know what? For the first time I really believed he could murder someone.'

'Yeah . . .'

They put that thought behind them, headed off to a bar.

'Idiot. You fucking, fucking idiot.'

Keenyside was screaming down the phone. Hammer sat on a bench on the Town Moor, listened impassively. His face betrayed no emotion. But his eyes burned like a medieval hell.

The sound of Keenyside's heavy breathing subsided in his ear.

'What happened?' the policeman said eventually.

Hammer told him again. As simply and monosyllabically as possible. Keenyside listened.

'No one saw anything,' said Hammer as a way of finishing.

'Really?' asked Keenyside. 'Then why are they trying to get an eyewitness to work up an e-fit of you? Why are they looking for Vauxhall Vectras? Why are they doing all this if no one saw anything?'

Hammer's heart came close to skipping a beat. 'Tell me who this eyewitness is,' he said. 'I'll make sure they can't—'

'No,' said Keenyside firmly. 'Not this time. The best thing you can do is take a few days off. Get some R and R. Make yourself scarce for a while. I'll cope with things at this end.'

'Whatever. You're paying me.'

'Yes, I am. And I don't want any more fuck-ups. We need him to make that call soon. We've got to get this over with. I'm being investigated at work, that rent boy's still missing, apparently Joe Donovan was sharing a bed with that journalist you killed—'

'Donovan? Coincidence.'

'Yes. And I don't believe in coincidences.' Keenyside sighed. 'Leave it to me. I'll handle things here. I'll call you when I need you. Let's hope you haven't fucked up big time.'

He cut the connection.

Hammer replaced the phone in his pocket. He didn't mind taking a few days off. He could go and have some fun. Then come back, take care of business.

And Keenyside. He was starting to annoy him.

Hammer walked to the car, drove away.

Jamal woke up, stretched.

He had nodded off. Not surprising, the amount of crack he had smoked.

He was back in the car again, had gone there straight after running away from Caroline's flat. He had nowhere else to go. Joe Donovan had been trying to contact him, but it wasn't safe enough to call him back. He was also scared that the police could be after him for Si's murder. So the car had presented the best option.

He felt rough. Knew he must look dreadful. The short, fast high from the rocks long gone, just the long, empty down to replace it. The depression. As if he didn't have enough. Nearly all the money he had taken from Father Jack was gone. Up in smoke some of it, the rest to a gang of kids who had sold him the rocks, then held him down and gone through his pockets, punching him all the time, calling him Paki. They had taken the money and run. Jamal had been confused more than anything else. Even the car wasn't safe now.

He stood up, stretched again.

Down from more than the rocks.

He needed money. It would be so easy to call Joe Donovan, let him sort it out, make him keep his promises. But he couldn't. It was too risky. So instead he would have to go back to work. Earn it.

Sighing, he pulled his now-battered jacket about him and set out for the bridge. Walking over to the city, heart heavy, body weary, ready to find the places where he would be wanted.

21

Donovan knew it was a dream. But that didn't make it any more bearable.

He was back in the department store. With David. Sea of humanity all round him. Everything monochrome.

He knew what was going to happen.

The same dream, back again. He couldn't stop it, couldn't change it.

There, then gone.

There, then gone.

The crowd slowed down, changed from fluid sea to dense, immovable mass. Donovan's legs wouldn't work. Body wouldn't move.

Then the dream changed.

The air became colder, Donovan's breath coming out in plumes of steam. Monochrome turned silver and grey. Stark, shivery hues. The crowd parted. And there stood Maria. Draped in the sheet she was covered with in the mortuary, skin pallid, drained, throat a livid, black mess.

'Maria . . .' Donovan heard his own voice.

She stared at him, eyes devoid of emotion, of life.

'Please,' he heard himself say, 'come back. I want you back . . .'

Then David was at her side. Standing close like mother and son. Same pale skin, blank eyes.

Donovan shook his head. 'No . . .'

Maria spoke. 'The future.'

Donovan tried to cross to them but couldn't move

quickly enough. David lifted his arm and, with dream logic, the scene changed again.

Father Jack's house. The crowd behind Maria and David turned, stared at Donovan. Hatred, the threat of violence in their eyes. David pointed a finger at Donovan.

'He let the children go . . . Get him . . .'

And they were on him. Donovan couldn't move, couldn't find the will to defend himself, to run. The mass of bodies fell on him; pummelling, ripping, scratching, screaming.

They pushed Donovan to the floor.

Like the world was crushing him.

Donovan didn't fight back.

Just let it happen.

Donovan woke, fighting for breath.

Coughing, like he was swallowing his tongue.

He lay back on the bed, breathing deeply. His body filmed with a slick of sweat, he threw the covers back. Opened his eyes.

Behind the heavy curtains, dawn threatened. Thin beams of light crept into the hotel room, deepened the shadows for his ghosts to hide in. He lay there, unmoving. The day brightened, the light strengthened. The ghosts retreated. Back into the shadows.

Back inside him.

He pulled himself out of bed and into the bathroom, wearily abluted. His body, his head, ached. Longed for a rest that sleep couldn't give him.

He stepped into the shower, turned it up high; water hit his skin in hot needles.

His mind ran back over the events of the previous day. He steeled himself for what he had to do next.

★   ★   ★

The *Herald* promised to e-mail him with all the information they had on Colin Huntley. His laptop was on the desk, plugged into the hotel's broadband connection.

He looked around, waiting. Sighed. He couldn't stand being in the room. He couldn't sit down, couldn't concentrate on anything.

His CBGBs T-shirt was on the floor next to his holdall. Where he had thrown it in his haste to be naked with Maria on Saturday night.

Emotions welled inside him: sadness, anger, loneliness. He picked up the T-shirt, screwed it into as small a lump as possible. Threw it as hard as he could against the wall. It landed with a sound too soft to be a slap, slid slowly down the wall, came to rest on the unmade bed in a crumpled heap.

Donovan, drained by the throw, crumpled next to it. He picked it up, put it to his nose. Her scent still clung faintly to it. He breathed in, trying to give it artificial respiration, will her back to life.

He smelled her perfume . . . felt her skin . . .

Another breath . . .

Sensed the air from her mouth blow softly on his skin . . .

Another breath . . .

Her fingers trace their way . . .

He stopped. Opened his eyes.

Felt nothing but alone.

Pushing the T-shirt into his face to catch the tears.

Sat there, silent but for sobs, immobile but for deep, shuddering breaths.

Rode the wave out. He stood up.

His head spinning, all mist and fog. His stomach writhed like a snake pit.

He glanced at his holdall. The barrel of the revolver was sticking out, catching the light, winking at him.

Tempting him.

He could just walk over, pick it up, spin it and . . .

No. That wasn't the way.

His mobile rang.

He sighed, annoyed yet grateful for the interruption. He answered it. Peta.

'Listen, Joe . . .' She was struggling with her words. 'I just heard from Dave Bolland. About Maria . . .'

'Yeah,' said Donovan, sighing. 'Yeah. She's dead.'

He couldn't believe what he was saying was real. Only increasing repetition of the words confirmed it for him.

He nodded. 'Dead . . .'

The tears came again. Peta waited, the silence on the line electric.

'Look,' she said eventually. 'If there's anything I can do. Anything Amar or I can do. Please, just . . . anything.'

He broke the connection. Sighed. Looked again at the gun.

It no longer winked at him, tempted him.

He threw his CBGBs T-shirt at it, hiding it.

He switched his mobile off. The only person he wanted to hear from was Jamal. Donovan had left messages but the boy wasn't answering. It worried him, but there was nothing he could do about it. He would turn it on later, try again. The rest – police, Sharkey – could wait.

He checked his laptop. He had mail. He settled himself down before it. Sighed to shake the fog from his head.

Began to read.

Dr Colin Huntley was a biochemist working for NorTec, a chemical company with its main British base in Northumberland. Most of their work was in the commercial and industrial sector, creating, testing and supplying various solvents and detergents. Boring stuff, it seemed to Donovan, although a full client list revealed that beyond the usual household name-owning multi-nationals there nestled the MoD.

He tried not to let his imagination run away with him, read on.

The plant had suffered what looked like an attempted break-in three months previously. It was quite a low-level thing, the reports said, the wire-mesh fence cut, CCTV cameras put out of action, but the building's security didn't seem to have been breached and nothing apparently was taken. The conclusion the police had reached at the time was that it was some kind of eco protest that had broken down, perhaps the perpetrators losing their nerve. The police had looked into it again in the light of Colin Huntley's disappearance but had concluded there was nothing to link the two events.

He read on.

Colin Huntley lived in Wansbeck Moor.

Donovan sat back, thinking.

Wansbeck Moor. The place seemed familiar to him for some reason. He read on, hoping that reason would come to him.

Wansbeck Moor was an exclusive upscale enclave in one of the most picturesque, yet accessible, areas of Northumberland. An entirely artificial community of executive houses built round a sculpted village green and containing shops, a school, a golf course and a village pub. It was one step away from being a gated community, although the price of the houses alone ensured exclusivity. Any outsiders would have been quickly noted.

And dealt with, thought Donovan. He remembered the place now. He scrolled down.

And there it was.

A group of Irish travellers had set up camp in a field just

by the main body of houses. The newly created village had been the target for travellers several times in the past, so much so that the residents had formed a consortium in order to buy the surrounding land from the farmers who owned it in an attempt to deter any more travellers from setting up camp there. The field they had chosen was one that the consortium owned.

The villagers, thinking they had, legally, the upper hand, weren't too concerned. However, when the travellers delivered a retrospective planning application on a Friday night, knowing that the local council offices were closed, then spent the weekend installing drainage and sewerage, hooking up generators and creating a flat, tarmacked surface for the caravans to rest on, the villagers' position changed.

Donovan remembered the story. He had decided to cover it for the *Herald*. It wasn't his usual type of story; they usually involved cover-ups, corruption or social injustice. He remembered that this represented, for him, the shrivelled, Daily Hate Mail heart of middle England getting its come-uppance. And that, he had thought, was worth gaining as wide an audience for as possible. Holding values he found hypocritical and hateful up to public ridicule. If they had been asylum seekers as well as travellers it would have been even better. Suburbia's own pathetic War on Terror.

He folded his arms, stared at the screen.

Two years ago. Something there . . . He had been working on the story when . . .

When David disappeared.

He shook his head, read on.

But there was nothing else. It simply stated that legal proceedings had been started but not allowed to progress. The travellers had moved on.

Something there . . .

There had been a reason he had gone to Wansbeck

Moor, a deeper reason beyond the one he remembered. Something that tied the story in with his usual type. Cover-up. Corruption. Social injustice.

He thought. But couldn't remember. All his memories from round that time were inaccessible. It was self-preservation: like a corrupted section of a computer hard drive memory, cordoned off so the rest of the machine could still function.

Donovan frowned.

There was a knock at the door.

Sharkey, he thought. He crossed the room to answer it, invective at the ready. Pulled the door open.

'Hello, Mr Donovan. Sorry to disturb you again so soon.'

The curses died on his lips. DI Nattrass and DS Turnbull.

'Could we come in, please?'

Donovan stood aside, let them in. 'Make yourselves at home,' he said.

He gave a quick glance at his holdall. The revolver was still hidden beneath the T-shirt.

Nattrass sat on the edge of the bed. Turnbull stood, looking around. Donovan sat on the bed also. Looked at Nattrass.

'Have you got someone?' asked Donovan. 'For Maria?'

'Not yet,' said Nattrass, 'but we will. Got another couple of questions for you, though.'

Donovan said nothing, waited. He was aware, through his peripheral vision, of Turnbull prowling the room. His actions irritated Donovan. He was coming to really dislike the man.

'As we said earlier,' said Nattrass, 'Maria Bennett's notebook contained details of Colin Huntley.'

'As does your laptop.'

Donovan turned. Turnbull was standing by the desk, scrolling up and down the screen. He looked at Donovan, vindication and triumph in his eyes.

Nattrass threw him a questioning glance.

'You mentioned it yourself,' said Donovan. 'Said Maria had been looking into it. So I did, too. Wouldn't be doing my job properly if I didn't.'

'And we wouldn't be doing ours properly if we didn't question you on it,' said Nattrass. 'Did you find anything?'

Donovan flattened his eyes, looked at Nattrass. 'I'd just started looking.'

Nattrass' flat, poker eyes never left his. She nodded.

'We've had a look at Ms Bennett's mobile phone records. The *Herald* supplied them to us. Most of the calls we can trace. But there's one we can't. An unregistered number. She called it approximately six hours before her death. They then returned the call.' She read the number out.

'Ring any bells?' said Turnbull, pleased with himself.

Nattrass glanced at him, unable to hide her irritation with her junior colleague. She turned back to Donovan, poker-faced once more.

Donovan recognised Jamal's number. Shook his head slowly. Said nothing.

'We've got an eyewitness saying that when Ms Bennett approached Caroline Huntley's flat she was accompanied by, and I quote, "A coloured lad. Looked like one of them rappers."' She shrugged, gave him the poker face. 'Anything?'

Donovan tried to return the poker face.

'No,' he said. He resisted the urge to swallow. Or look away. Or blink.

Nattrass didn't drop her gaze.

'Mr Donovan, we want to find Maria's killers as much as you do. What were you working on when she died?'

Donovan felt Turnbull circling behind him. Making him feel uneasy.

'Does that matter?' asked Donovan.

Nattrass sighed.

'Look,' said Turnbull, standing directly in front of Donovan, legs apart, hands on hips, 'it'll be better in the long term if you cooperate. Better for you, I mean.'

Donovan looked up. Eyes the same level as Turnbull's crotch.

'Or what?' he said. 'You'll give me a lap dance?'

Nattrass looked away. Donovan caught the ghost of a smile on her lips. Turnbull reddened.

'Right . . .' he said.

Nattrass intervened.

'We've spoken to her newspaper,' she said, 'and they've told us she was up here working on a story with you. They couldn't tell us what. Told us to speak to either yourself or Francis Sharkey.'

'And you are.'

All three turned to the door. There stood Sharkey, unable to stop grinning at the dramatic impact of his arrival.

'The door was open, so . . .' He shrugged.

Sharkey entered the room, handed his card to Turnbull. 'Francis Sharkey. I represent good ship *Herald* and all who sail in her. Even those—' he looked at Donovan '—who just get caught in her slipstream.'

Donovan frowned, opened his mouth to speak. Sharkey ignored him.

'Now,' said Sharkey, voice polite yet commanding, 'since I've introduced myself, would you be so kind as to supply me with your names?'

Nattrass told him, handed him her card. Indicated Turnbull.

Sharkey nodded. 'Good. Well, now that introductions have been made, I believe you had questions to ask both myself and my client.'

Sharkey looked between the two of them. Turnbull wanted to go ahead, but Nattrass indicated they should leave.

Turnbull, begrudgingly and silently, did so. Nattrass turned to Donovan.

'Remember our earlier conversation, Mr Donovan,' she said, voice hushed.

'Which?' said Donovan. 'The one about exchanging information or about me not playing cowboy?'

'Both,' she said.

Donovan nodded.

'You've got my card.' Nattrass stood up, nodded at Sharkey and left the room, closing the door behind her.

Sharkey smiled at Donovan, pleased with himself. 'If I hadn't been a newspaper lawyer they'd have had us down the station by now,' he said. 'Trying to sweat the truth out of us in a tiny little room.'

Donovan just stared at him. Sharkey's jocular mask disappeared. He became sombre, serious.

'May I just express my sincerest condolences,' he said. 'I'm sure you—'

'Fuck off, Sharkey,' said Donovan. He stood up. 'You've kept them off my back. Good. Now get out of my sight.'

Sharkey remained where he was. Looked at Donovan, his expression businesslike.

'I need to talk to you, Joe,' he said. 'Personal differences aside, there are a couple of things we need to discuss. Newcastle's crawling with media right now, all wanting Maria's story. I've tried to keep them off you, but I think the best thing you can do is talk to one of the *Herald*'s journos. Get your side of the story—'

'Fuck off, Sharkey. I'm not talking to anyone.'

'But—'

Donovan crossed to the lawyer. Sharkey took an involuntary step back.

'I came here to do a specific job. With a specific person, for a specific reason. Unfortunately that person isn't here any more. But the job is. And I'm going to see it through.' He stepped up close to Sharkey, went face to face. 'And that specific reason had better be there at the end. Or the person who promised it will be in very specific trouble. Got that?'

Sharkey swallowed hard.

'Listen,' he said. He looked trepidacious. 'We still need to talk . . .'

'No, we don't. Now get out.'

Donovan, still eyeball to eyeball, began to walk Sharkey towards the door.

'I . . . I can see this isn't a good time for you . . . We'll talk later, when you're feeling more . . . receptive . . . I'm, I'm afraid I have a funeral to organize . . .'

His words took him over the threshold and out of the door.

Donovan sat back on the bed, spent. He rubbed his face with his hands, sighed. He looked at the laptop, crossed to it, sat before it. Read, from start to finish again, all the information on Colin Huntley. Twice.

Thirty-five minutes later, he sat back rubbing his eyes.

He knew what to do next.

He switched the shower off, body tingling, and began to towel himself dry.

Remembered the phone call he had made the previous day to Peta. Asking for her and Amar to help find Jamal.

'Will you be coming along, too?' she had asked.

'No,' said Donovan.

'Why not?'

Donovan sighed.

'Because I've got to go home.'

22

Donovan lurched forward, opened his eyes. He had been asleep again.

'Good, you're back,' said a voice next to him. 'You can keep an eye out for coppers.'

Donovan looked around, momentarily confused. Then he remembered. Peta's car, Peta driving. Headed towards London. He checked the speedometer: touching a hundred on the outside lane of the M1.

The previous day's phone call: Peta had persuaded him to allow her to accompany him while he went to London to get his old laptop, go through his old notes. Visit his old home. Where his wife and daughter still lived.

She had weighed and chosen her words carefully. She could drive Donovan, be a sounding board for anything that came up. That kind of thing. Her interviews had been done, everything taken care of. Amar was more than capable of running the business, fielding any new offers of work. Finding Jamal, even.

She had put forward a very persuasive argument.

Donovan felt she was keeping something back or not telling him something. But he didn't feel this extended to a hidden or separate agenda, so he had agreed. Glad of the company but not wanting to admit it.

'OK,' he said. 'But you've got to emphasize to Amar that when he finds Jamal he's got to make him feel safe. Safe. Right?'

'Right.'

'That's the only way we can get him to stay in one place and be settled long enough to talk to us with any degree of recall about what's on that disc. What was on that disc.'

If Jamal's still there, thought Donovan. If he can be found.

'OK.'

Decided.

A car in the middle lane gave a small, vague signal, began to drift to the outside lane. Peta pressed the horn, flashed her lights. The car moved swiftly back, as if jolted awake from a lilting dream. The Saab cannonballed past.

'Testosterone levels high today?' asked Donovan.

'Are cars just for boys, then?' Peta replied, eyes staying ahead of her.

Donovan said nothing.

'I'd hate to be thought of as a girlie girl.'

'Heaven forbid.'

Peta looked briefly at him, smiled. Pushed down harder on the accelerator.

Donovan had always had an ambivalent relationship with cars, taking public transport whenever possible and viewing them only as a necessary evil. Donovan would never have driven like Peta was doing; he was too fearful of crashing. Peta handled the Saab with the skill of a rally driver: a speed junkie but in complete control.

Smoothly guiding the car like a heat-seeking missile.

Donovan shook his head. Resumed his lookout for police.

They reached Crouch End by early dusk.

The flat, wide sterility of the M1 had given way to the choked, claustrophobic North Circular. The road encircled Inner London like a too-tight elastic band round a wrist, keeping it held together but throbbing painfully.

Tree-lined streets and premium-priced flats of unremarkable design gave way to characterless retail parks, floodlit billboards and urban blight. Cars were driven in neo-grid-locked, selfish desperation; traffic moved like one huge, Darwinistic, carbon monoxide-pumping snake.

Even Peta seemed cowed.

'Don't know how anyone could live here,' she said.

'It's the place to be,' said Donovan.

'You really believe that?'

Donovan looked out of the window. Everything seemed squashed together, crushed down, crowded both in and out. Aggression behind every encounter, easily escalating: accidental pavement collision becoming territorial threat becoming call for retaliation becoming nasty, bloody fight.

Urban paranoia.

London living.

'Not any more,' he said.

He directed her off the North Circular, away from urban survivalism through more affluent, leafy areas. Although the houses became bigger, the streets wider, Donovan couldn't shake the feeling of paranoia, of threat.

Maybe it's just being out of the city so long, missing its rhythm, its beat, he thought. Maybe it's me.

Maybe it's who I'm going to visit.

They drove into the Broadway, the heart of Crouch End. Independent bookshops, exotic restaurants and cafés, gastropubs and expensive, exclusive furniture shops. All well-preserved Edwardian and Victorian architecture, huge, mature trees dotted along the streets.

'This is quite pleasant,' said Peta.

'I used to think so.'

And he did. As they drove, his mind slipped back a few years and he could almost glimpse his younger, more confident and idealistic self walking along the pavement. The working-class northern kid with the glittering, award-winning media career ahead of him, the beautiful Scottish wife who directed TV news and current affairs programmes at his side, the young family. A man with no concept of failure, only success.

'Which way now?'

Donovan blinked. His younger self was gone, dissipated to mist and shadows like a CGI ghost. Never real in the first place, only an artful construct.

'Next right,' he said.

Peta followed his instructions.

'Pull up here,' he said.

The car stopped on Weston Park. He looked around. Took it all in. At the top of the street he could see his old flat. Just as he had left it. He felt strange; like déjà vu, or re-entering a dream.

It was becoming harder to breathe. His body gave out a difficult sigh.

'Right,' he said. 'I doubt we'll get back to Newcastle tonight. D'you want to ring round, find a hotel for the night?'

'Sure you don't want me to come inside with you?'

'I think it's better if it's just me.'

Peta nodded.

Another sharp intake of breath. 'Right. I'll go and see if anyone's in.'

Peta looked at him. 'Didn't you phone ahead? Tell your wife you were coming?'

Donovan was pleased his features were obscured by shadow. He shook his head.

'Why not?'

Donovan looked out of the window. Found himself staring at a brick wall.

'Thought if she knew I was coming she might not be here.'

Peta sighed. 'Give her a call. Now. It'll be an even bigger shock if you just turn up.'

Donovan kept staring at the wall. 'Look, Peta,' he said. 'It's . . . there's something I should tell you.'

Peta placed a hand on his arm. Her voice was soft. 'I know, Joe. About what happened. Give her a call.'

Donovan looked at her. So this was what she was keeping back, not telling him. He nodded.

'OK.'

He got out of the car. His legs were less than steady. He closed the door, took out his mobile, dialled a number he had never forgotten.

It took him three attempts, his fingers shook so much.

It rang. He couldn't breathe. Was answered.

And there was that voice again. The one he used to think he would hear every day for the rest of his life.

Annie. His wife.

'Hi,' he said in response to her greeting. 'It's me.' And then, just in case she had forgotten, 'Joe.'

He heard a gasp at the other end of the line as if she had just taken a physical blow to the stomach.

Then silence.

Donovan heard static. His own breathing.

'Joe . . .'

'Yeah.'

'What d'you . . . this is . . .'

'I know,' he said, his voice sounding strange, disembodied. The conversation unreal. He took another deep, difficult breath. 'Look . . . I need to . . . to come to the house. Get something. See you.'

'When?'

'Now. I'm standing on the street. Down from the flat.'

He heard footsteps on the line, saw the front bay window curtain twitch.

'Well . . .' Annie sighed. 'You'd . . . you'd better come in.'

Donovan sighed, relieved. 'Thanks.'

He broke the connection. Stood looking at the phone. Then bent down to the car window. Peta lowered it.

'She's in,' he said.

'Good luck.'

Donovan nodded, already looking at the flat. The front door had opened. He could see a figure standing there, back-lit by the interior glow.

Donovan walked towards that glow.

He felt her eyes on him as he approached. Unwavering. Unflinching. A human CCTV camera. With added judgement.

He reached the gate, faltered. Placed his hand on the bricks to steady himself. His breathing laboured again.

Annie watched him, unmoving.

The path was authentic Edwardian tile, black and white in a repeating pattern. Donovan could remember having it restored. He walked slowly up it.

Reached the door.

And Annie.

She stepped aside, allowed him entry. Didn't meet his eyes.

He stood inside the hallway, looked around. Everything was familiar, almost as he recalled it, but not quite. Little things: new pictures on the wall, different phone. Newer coats hanging on the rack. Furniture slightly moved. Subtle differences. Like a remembered dream dragged through to daylight.

Annie closed the door behind them. Donovan gave a small jump at the noise.

'Go through,' she said. 'You know where everything is.'

He walked into the living room. The same sensation. Sofa and chairs the same only older, books, CDs and DVDs on the shelves newer. The rug covering the stripped boards unfamiliar. New.

The warmth of the house was still there. Donovan felt it

tugging at him, drawing him back. It tempted him with the promise of a comfortable chair, soothing music, a relaxing room. Tempted him to forget. Ignore. Keep the rest of the world beyond the front door, become enwombed.

But he couldn't. Because what lay beyond the front door had invaded his home. Broken through the illusion of safety. Now he was offered only comfort's cold shadow. And that knowledge forbade him to ever go home again.

'Sit down,' Annie said from behind him. 'Make yourself at home.'

Donovan couldn't tell from her flat intonation whether she had intended irony or not. He sat automatically in what used to be his favourite chair and immediately felt like a presumptuous intruder. Annie sat opposite him on the sofa.

Donovan looked at her. Properly, for the first time since he had been there. He felt she was doing the same to him.

Her hair was a different shade from when he had last seen her, red rather than brown. It had been cut and styled differently, too. Her clothes were new to him, her body not. Her face looked the same, eyes perhaps edged by a few more lines.

Then their eyes locked. And in that moment the superficial changes and differences dropped away as a deeper connection was re-established. Donovan felt something long repressed stir within. Like some ancient, clanking, Victorian turbine found to be still working, still capable of producing a spark.

But that spark soon flared and died as he realized that the thing that still emotionally bound them also separated them. Joined their hearts yet broke them.

He sensed Annie felt it, too. Neither could hold on to the other's gaze. Both looked away.

They sat in uncomfortable silence. The space between them wider than merely physical.

'So how are you?' she said, looking at her hands.

Donovan nodded. 'Fine,' he said, not altogether convinc-
ingly.

'You're working again?'

Donovan nodded again. 'Yeah.'

'Good.' Annie nodded. Sat with her feet together, arms
hugging herself.

'How are you?' Donovan sat forward, back bent, forearms
on thighs, fingers, thumbs and palms clasped together
between his knees.

Annie gave a slight bob of her head. 'Good,' she said.
'Well.'

'Working?'

She nodded. 'Freelance.'

'Good. And Abigail?'

A hesitation: mouth open to speak, right words not formed
in it. 'Good,' she said again. She unfurled her arms, clasped
her hands together. 'Coping. She's over at a friend's house.'

Donovan nodded.

More silence. More space between them.

'So,' said Annie, body remaining still, only her thumbs
moving. 'What d'you want?'

'Some old work stuff,' said Donovan, relieved to be back
on relatively sure ground. 'Files I kept. Notebooks. My old
laptop if it's still here.'

Annie's posture softened slightly; her body moved mar-
ginally forward. 'What are you working on?'

'You've probably seen it on the news,' he said and told her
about Colin Huntley's disappearance.

'I know,' she said. 'His daughter's gone now, too. And . . .'
Annie's hand went to her mouth as if in shock. 'My God.
Maria Bennett,' she said quickly, eyes wide. 'Did you hear
about what happened to her?'

Donovan nodded, eyes on the rug. 'I was there. Working
with her.'

'Oh my God . . .'

'I think there's a connection between her death and Colin Huntley's disappearance.' He shrugged. 'Maybe even a connection with an old story of mine.'

Annie stared at him. 'And the *Herald* want you to look into it?'

Donovan gave a small smile. 'Back on the payroll. For one night only.'

'And they're paying you?'

'More like bribing me.'

'With what?'

Donovan realized he had said too much. Annie wouldn't understand. But he had never lied to her. Ever. He had to tell her.

'Brace yourself,' he said, aiming for a smile and missing. 'With . . . resources. At my disposal.' He looked at the rug again. Used to be a kelim. Now something abstract and swirly. Ikea. The Pier, perhaps. 'To find David.'

Annie stiffened. Her face froze. Eyes clouded over. Thunderclouds. She sat still, breathing hard as if struggling to control herself.

Eventually she found her voice.

'Your old things are in the spare bedroom,' she said, her voice tight, contained. 'You know where that is.'

Without another word she stood up, left the room. He heard her walk down the hall, heard the kitchen door slam.

Donovan rubbed his face with his hands. Sighed.

He rose slowly to his feet. Made his hesitant way upstairs.

He stood on the landing, looked around. Saw his old bedroom. Couldn't resist. A quick check for movement from the stairs, then in.

The walls had been painted, the furniture the same. The bed linen was new, the bed unmade. Donovan smiled. Annie was always up after him and she hated making the bed.

Called it a waste of energy. He looked again. Stopped smiling. Both pillows bore head imprints.

Something sank in his stomach. It could be Abigail wanting a morning cuddle. Yeah. That was it.

He left the bedroom, closed the door behind him. Abigail's bedroom was next, the door firmly closed. Donovan didn't open it. Didn't want to have his suspicions confirmed or denied.

He went into the spare bedroom. Piled high with cardboard boxes and bulging black bin bags. Donovan didn't have a clue where to start. He grabbed the nearest box, pulled it open.

Action Man. Pokemon cards. Diggers and trucks.

David's things.

He felt like the air had been punched out of him.

Donovan sat down on the floor with a sigh.

He went through virtually every box. Steeled himself. Pulling back every cardboard flap was like pulling the trigger on his Russian roulette revolver; which memory could rip into him hardest, do the most damage.

David's toys and clothes. Books and keepsakes. Mementos meant to chart his boy's life, record and celebrate milestones. Left behind, waiting to be resumed, no matter how long the hiatus.

Annie's hope, he thought, buried and boxed away but not completely discarded.

His own stuff there, too: work files, books, CDs, clothes. Like the detritus of a previous life, not needed any more but nearly impossible to get rid of.

He wondered whether Annie's boxed hope extended to him.

He found what he was looking for. His box of files and notebooks, his laptop. He looked through the other stuff, too, picked up a couple of CDs, dropped them into the box. Songs listened to by another person in a previous life.

But his eyes kept being drawn back to David's things. And, like picking at a wound, stopping it healing, he kept looking through those boxes, triggers firing bullets at point-blank range.

'I miss him too, you know.'

Donovan jumped, turned. He didn't know how long Annie had been standing there. Didn't know how long he had been sitting there. Lost in time.

Annie's posture had changed. At first glance Donovan thought she seemed to have relaxed. But looking closer he realized she was just resigned. He stood up.

'I miss you, too,' she said quietly. 'You did your best, Don. You tried to find him, bring him back. You did what anyone would.'

She placed her hand on his forearm. Donovan sighed, looked into her eyes for the second time that day. He could feel her breath on his skin.

'It's time to move on,' she said. 'Don't forget him, maybe keep a little flame of hope alive somewhere inside you. A little candle lit . . .' She sighed. 'But get moving again. You can't bring him back, Don.'

Donovan shook his head, sighed. 'No,' he said. 'This job . . . it's giving me a chance. Us. All of us. He might be out there. He might need me.' He dropped his eyes. 'I've got to try.'

Annie's hand fell away from his arm. Her body posture became defensive again, arms wrapped round her torso, shielding her body.

'Come with me,' she said and walked out of the room.

Donovan followed.

She led him to her bedroom, stood in the doorway looking in. Donovan joined her.

'See that?' Annie said, pointing to the bed. 'We used to share that. See those sheets? Tangled and rumpled like they are? That should be from our bodies, yours and mine.'

She turned to him. Eyes hard and glittering, like semi-liquid diamonds.

'But you're dead to me,' she said, her voice rough and uneven, like it was catching on an old rusty nail, tearing. 'Dead. And I've had to go on living. Find someone else. Who's living.'

'Who.'

Annie sighed. 'His name's Michael. And he's very good to me. And Abigail. He cares for another man's daughter.'

Donovan said nothing.

'David's gone,' she said, staring at the bed, her voice still catching. 'Gone. From the land of the living. He needed you? Right. So did your wife. So did your daughter.'

She crossed to a bedside table, picked up a framed photo. Thrust it in front of Donovan's eyes.

'Recognize her?' asked Annie. 'That's Abigail. Your daughter. Take a good, long look.'

Donovan looked at the photo. A pretty brunette with fiercly intelligent eyes. 'She looks beautiful.'

'She is,' said Annie. 'She's a very brave, very strong kid. And I'm very proud of her. So should you be.'

Donovan nodded.

'Although God knows what she thinks of her father.'

Annie replaced the photo. Looked at Donovan as if expecting him to say something.

But out of all the things he wanted to say, there was nothing he could articulate. Annie sensed this, sighed.

'You'd better go,' she said. 'If you've got what you came for, go.'

Donovan nodded, picked up the box, put the laptop on it. Made his way downstairs to the door.

Annie stopped him.

'Where are you staying tonight?'

'Hotel.'

Annie nodded.

Donovan sighed. 'Give my love to Abigail. I'm sorry I missed her.'

'I don't think I'll tell her you've been here.'

She opened the door. What lay beyond it swiftly invaded. The cold night air began to bite immediately. Donovan stepped outside, turned back.

'When this is all over,' he said, 'I'll call you.'

Annie closed the door without replying. Donovan saw her bottom lip begin to tremble as she did so.

Donovan walked down the street back to the car.

He wanted to look back, see if Annie was watching him.

But didn't dare.

He put the box and the laptop in the boot, got in the car.

'How did it go?' asked Peta.

Donovan rubbed his face, sighed. 'I got what I went for.'

She nodded. 'Come on, then. Let's go to the hotel.'

Peta drove away.

Donovan looked out of the window.

A song off one of the CDs he had found and taken came into his head. The album had been one of his and Annie's favourites when they had met. Shawn Colvin: 'A Few Small Repairs'.

Colvin had sung about all the happy couples only renting time and space to fill up their dreams, and that dreams are all that would be left when they have gone.

The same lines, round and round in his head, like a continuous loop.

He stared out of the window. Said nothing.

23

Amar woke with blood on the pillow.

He sat up quickly, looked around. And wished he hadn't: his head was pounding, swirling, his stomach tight and knotted like he had swallowed a tree trunk. Difficult to breathe.

He lay back. Felt his face. His left nostril caked and dried. Checked his fingers. Blood. He sighed.

It had been building for months but this was the worst yet. Highs getting shorter, comedowns longer and harder.

'Hurricane Charlie has been and gone,' he declaimed aloud, 'leaving behind nothing but a trail of devastation . . .'

He threw back the duvet, rose cautiously to his feet. Made his way to the shower, fixed the water hot enough to cleanse and purify. Wash the toxins out. Finished, he towelled off, padded into the kitchen area, got a drink of water from the bottle in the fridge. Sipped it slowly, like liquid ice seeping into his body.

Some of the aches were beginning to clear, but his head, his heart, was heavy in a way the comedown couldn't touch.

He had told his stories, banked his cheque and was fielding offers of work for Knight Security. A forty-eight-hour circumstantial changearound.

Father Jack. The disappeared children. Maria's death.

There was an ongoing effort being made to find the children who had lived at Father Jack's but so far no progress had been made. They had just vanished back into the shadows. Whatever sense of victory he had felt with the successful culmination of their work was heavily tempered by Maria's death. He knew the police were looking into it and Donovan and Peta were off doing something about it but it still hurt.

He had gone out the previous night to celebrate but it had turned into a sorrow-drowning exercise. At least he hadn't picked anyone up, brought them back just to have a body to wake up to. A small mercy.

He dressed, tried to lift his spirits, concentrate on the job in hand.

Timecheck: eleven fifteen. Perfect. The people he needed to talk to would be just getting up.

He looked out of the window. The day looked cold and cloudy. Yesterday's sun gone. He pulled on his black parka, cleared his mind for the final time and left the flat, focused on the task before him.

He had a missing rent boy to find.

Keenyside was being kept waiting. And he wasn't happy about it.

Usual meeting place on the estate, usual time. No Mikey. As if things weren't bad enough. At least Mikey would have an excuse. He would be too scared not to.

What with the anti-corruption squad rumours and murder of that journalist, it was all Keenyside could do not to lash out, take some drastic action. But he had held it together, kept his head. Focused on the goal. Once Huntley did his part, he would be walking down Easy Street and all this would be long behind him.

The things that kept him sane:

His packed emergency holdall. His new identity passport. His plane ticket.

One way.

His new life.

He would miss his wife and kids, but they could join him later. When he was settled.

Maybe.

But in the meantime he had to wait.

He checked his watch again, angry now. Looked up. Saw Mikey Blackmore sauntering down the walkway towards him, looking like he had all the time in the world.

Keenyside couldn't believe it. Mikey in no hurry. His anger threatened to overspill. He wanted to rush over to Mikey, punch him, hurt him, rip his head from his shoulders . . .

But he didn't. He tamped it down, kept his rage internalized. There should he need it.

Mikey reached him, stopped.

'Where the fuck have you been? You're late.'

Mikey flinched at the first words but held his ground. 'Couldn't get away from work.' He shrugged. 'Long way from here to Gateshead.'

Keenyside felt his face reddening. 'Don't you fucking answer me back. I tell you when to be here and you fucking well make sure you are here.'

Mikey said nothing.

'Got that?'

Mikey smiled.

'Something funny?'

'No.'

Keenyside was breathing hard. Something wasn't right. Then he realized.

Mikey Blackmore wasn't afraid of him.

Keenyside grabbed him by the lapels of his overcoat, swung him round, pushed him hard against the brick wall.

'You taking the piss out of me, eh? That it?'

Mikey shook his head. He was breathing hard, winded. 'No . . .'

'You sure?' Keenyside pushed him against the wall, hard. Mikey's eyes flickered with fear.

'That's better . . .'

He punched him in the stomach. Mikey hit the ground, stayed down.

Keenyside looked at the prone figure, felt his earlier tamped-down rage begin to well, threaten to overspill. He kicked Mikey in the ribs.

'You frightened of me now?'

Mikey groaned.

Another kick. 'You respect me now?'

Another groan.

Another kick. 'Eh? Can't hear you . . .'

'Yes . . .' Mikey could barely choke the word out. 'Yes . . .'

Keenyside stood, looked down at him. Breathing heavily, he leaned against the wall, fighting to regain his breath.

His control.

'Good . . .' he said. 'Good. That's better . . .' The moment was passing, the adrenalin subsiding.

Mikey was attempting to sit up, clutching his ribs, face screwed up in pain.

'So,' said Keenyside, 'what you got for me?'

Mikey, his hand shaking, reached slowly into his pocket, pulled out a creased brown envelope, passed it over. Keenyside opened it, counted the notes inside.

'What's this?' he said, anger swelling within him once more. 'There's hardly anything here.'

Mikey said nothing, breathed heavily.

'Where's the rest?'

'That's it . . .'

Keenyside took a step back, tried to calm himself. He forced a harsh laugh through clenched teeth.

'Right,' he said, 'that's it. You've had your chance. I'm phoning your probation officer this afternoon.'

Mikey didn't move. 'Do it, then.'

Keenyside recoiled as if he had been punched. 'What?'

'Do it,' he said again, through ragged breaths. 'I don't care any more. I'll even tell him what you're up to.'

Keenyside gave another laugh. 'Yeah? He won't believe you. They hear stories like that all the time.'

Mikey gripped the wall, slowly managed to pull himself to his feet. He gave Keenyside a look of pure hate.

'Maybe they do,' said Mikey, tears in his eyes, 'but I don't care. Do what you like.'

He turned, began moving painfully away. 'I'll tell 'im what you do . . . what else you've been up to . . .'

He walked off.

Keenyside stared after him, too stunned to move. What had he said? What else you've been up to? What did he mean? Huntley? The break-in? The death of the journalist?

He wanted to run after Mikey, smash his face on the concrete until there was nothing left of him.

He wanted to scream.

He wanted to stick his fingers into his own flesh, pull away the skin, work his way down through to muscle and bone. Rip himself apart.

He tried to breathe deep. Calm down.

Don't overreact. He was probably bluffing. He knew nothing.

He couldn't.

Keenyside concentrated on his packed emergency holdall. His new identity passport. His plane ticket.

Held on to that thought as a drowning man to a life belt, held on to it all the way back to his office.

There was, thought Amar, nothing less glamorous than a nightclub in the harsh light of day.

Even one that described itself as a bar until dark.

Daylight showed up torn furniture, worn, stained carpet, tatty, trashy décor. Every imperfection that darkness and gaudy lighting concealed was exposed. Chairs and tables were dotted about. A raised stage and runway was crammed in at the far end. Unlit and unoccupied, it looked depressing; more a place of execution than a site of entertainment. It smelled, too: stale alcohol, stale smoke, stale sweat and stale hope and desperation.

The bar seemed hungover. It matched Amar's mood perfectly.

The Hole in the Wall was one of a number of gay bars and clubs in the area between Westgate Road and Railway Street. The pink triangle, as it was commonly called.

Amar stood at the bar. Looked around. There were several besuited punters sipping halves and eating sandwiches, hoping for a quick, surreptitious lunchtime fumble before they planted their bodies back at the office and one or both feet back in the closet. Amar himself had been given the eye several times. He had ignored it. He was working.

The barman eventually sauntered over to serve him. Graham was an ex-actor who had started working there between jobs. He had been working there for as long as Amar had been drinking there. He was an old queen, but not too bitter with it. Paunchy and cardiganed; like the bar, he looked better in the night-time.

And he knew the scene better than anyone else.

He smiled as he approached. 'Hello, film star. Bit early for you, isn't it?'

'Damn right,' said Amar, stifling a yawn.

Graham put his hands on the counter. 'Saw you in the papers. And on the news. Regular James Bond.'

Amar blushed. 'Thank you.'

'Or rather Jane Bond. More coverage than I ever got. What can I get you?'

'A sparkling mineral water,' he said, 'and a bit of help.'

Graham put his hand theatrically to his chest, turned his

eyes heavenwards. 'He wants me at last. After all these years . . .'

Amar smiled. 'Just get me my drink.'

He did so, returned to the bar. 'What kind of help?'

Amar looked around, made sure no one was listening. 'I'm looking for a rent boy.'

A smile widened on Graham's features. 'Didn't know you liked them young.'

'Not like that,' said Amar. 'I'm working. Missing persons thing.'

Graham said nothing. Just stared.

Amar sighed, dug into his pocket. Glad he'd stopped off at the cashpoint on the way. Folded a tenner, passed it across. It disappeared.

'Not really my thing. Prefer men to boys. Don't have a lot of time for the chickenhawks. Gives us poofs a bad name.' Graham nodded, making sure he had been understood. 'And I won't have any truck with that kind of thing in this bar. Nothing underage.'

'I know that.'

'Not worth the hassle.'

'I know you won't know personally, but I'm sure you know a man who does.'

Graham looked around, checked for eavesdroppers. None. 'What's the one you're after look like?'

Amar told him. Graham nodded. Thought a moment.

'All right,' he said, voice dropping. 'You're in luck. There was a guy in last night. Name's Ralphie. Bit of a semi-reg. Overheard him boasting to one of the other regs about this little black kid he'd had. Only reason I remembered was because he's black. And we don't get many of them round here.' A theatrical sigh. 'More's the pity. Anyway, he said how he'd enjoyed it so much he was going back for some more.'

'Did he say where?'

Graham shook his head.

'Will he be in here tonight?'

Graham shrugged. 'Might be. If not here, somewhere else along the strip. We are but a small community.'

'How would I recognize him?'

Graham frowned. 'Big guy. Fat but muscly, y'know? Always wears check shirts and jeans. Like a trucker. Hair cut short. Oh, and a silver earring. Cannabis leaf.'

Amar smiled. Slipped him another tenner. 'Thanks, Graham.'

The note disappeared, the smile was returned. 'Any time. And I mean anytime.'

Amar turned to go.

'Oh by the way,' said Graham. 'You still in the movie business? Got a bit more work I can put your way.'

Amar thought. 'Not at the moment,' he said. 'But thanks anyway.'

He left the bar.

Amar looked at his watch. Eight thirty p.m.

He had bar and café hopped all afternoon. He had met people he knew, chatted, drunk soft drinks and coffee. Looked for someone answering the description of Ralphie. Looked for Jamal.

Nothing.

He had been offered meals out, dates, sex, camera work. Offered drugs and booze.

He had turned them all down. He was working.

Amar stood in the Courtyard, nursing a bottle of J2O. In the playground watching the best game in town. And he couldn't join in.

'Stop looking so miserable, man,' said the barman. 'I bet I could cheer you up.'

Amar told him he couldn't. Not at the moment.

His mobile rang. He couldn't answer it quick enough. Graham.

'Hi, gorgeous. Guess who just walked in?'

'I'm on my way.'

Graham chuckled. 'You've got some big IOUs to make good on.'

Amar finished the call, winked at the barman, left the bar. Better than he had felt all day.

As soon as Mikey saw the look on Janine's face, he knew he had her.

'What happened?'

He was sitting in the Prince of Wales, waiting for her. He had tried to hide the damage Keenyside had inflicted on him, but the bruises were starting to flower.

'Guess who.'

'Not Alan . . .'

Mikey nodded. The effort hurt him. Janine sat down opposite him.

She looked lovely, he thought. Then wondered how an animal like Keenyside could do what he had done to her. Anger began to swell within him. He tried to stifle it, looked at Janine.

'Got you a present . . .' He reached painfully into his pocket, didn't see the look of trepidation in her eyes, handed it over. Janine unwrapped it, looked at it.

'Thanks,' she said. 'What is it?'

'It's a ring tree,' he said. 'Porcelain, I think. You hang your rings there, your bracelets on there when you, you know, get home. Got it from a pound shop in the Green Market. D'you like it?'

She smiled. 'It's lovely.'

Thinking afterwards, her smile could have been bigger, more joyful. But at the time it had seemed all right.

She put it straight into her bag. 'Does it hurt?'

Mikey nodded. 'A bit. But never mind him. I've got a plan that'll get rid of him for good.'

Mikey bent painfully, conspiratorially, forward. Kept the anger and rage in check, stuck to the facts. Told her.

Janine listened, nodded. Asked questions that he answered.

Finished, he sat back. Looked pleased with himself.

'What d'you think?'

She had taken a little more persuading. Asked questions that Mikey patiently answered. Hummed and hawed. Mikey had kept on. The bruises helped.

Eventually agreed. She would help him.

Mikey smiled. Felt the pain dissolve.

Amar stood on the corner of Waterloo Street and Westmorland Road, backlit by the fluorescent tubes and blue-neon fly killers of a kebab shop. It was starting to rain. He pressed himself back against the glass, waited.

Watched.

Ralphie had left the Hole in the Wall in no particular hurry to go home. He had walked the streets, taking his time. He would stop a while, look around, then head slowly off in the direction he had come from. Amar following at a discreet distance.

Obvious what he was looking for. And with who.

Ralphie was on the move again. Down Westmorland Road, then right down Westmorland Lane. Amar put his hood up, followed. Open wasteland behind the main road of Blenheim Street. Lots of dereliction. Lots of redevelopment.

Lots of shadows.

Ralphie walked slowly, focused on his goal. Alert to any impediments to that goal, legal or otherwise. Amar had heard him boasting in the bar about the boy he had had, was so good he was going back for a second night.

Ralphie stopped walking. Amar did, too, sliding back into the shadow of a doorway, watching. Ralphie looked around, head on one side. listening. Amar pushed himself back, remained still, hardly breathing. Heard only distant traffic, rain and wind.

Ralphie – slowly, cautiously – resumed his walk.

He turned right again, down Derland Street. More derelict, empty buildings. Empty shells. At the corner with Waterloo Street was a building site. Dating from the 1930s, the building had started life as commercial premises and had, at various times, been a straight bar with a club licence and strippers, two gay clubs complete with fetish rooms and, most bizarrely, a Teutonic-style beer cellar. Now it was in the process of being gutted and turned into luxury urbanite flats. Scaffolding on all sides; the ground floor and basement that had once housed the gay club were now open, walls and windows gone, only structural supports, rubble.

And shadows.

It was from out of these shadows that a figure emerged. A middle-aged man with greying hair, wearing an anorak, jeans and a nondescript air. The kind of person who looked unthreatening, who wouldn't remain too long in the memory, who used that as a shield.

The kind of person who got away with abusing children.

The man walked up the steps, looked furtively about, then walked away, back into the night.

Back to his family, thought Amar.

Ralphie hadn't moved. He stood against the window of an abandoned second-hand record shop as if waiting for a signal.

A second figure emerged from the basement of the building. Amar recognized him straight away. Small, light-skinned black boy. Avirex jacket.

Jamal.

Ralphie, on seeing him, crossed the road. Jamal saw him approach, waited. As Amar watched, the two looked around, made furtive conversation, then walked down the concrete steps together.

Amar counted slowly to thirty, then crossed the road.

He reached the steps, tried to squeeze noiselessly between the great metal mesh screens that had been erected to keep out trespassers, walk down the steps. At the bottom he blinked, allowed his eyes to become accustomed to the gloom, looked around.

Rubble, trestles, the odd bucket, length of wood. Movement on the periphery of his vision: rats.

Amar ignored them, kept himself in shadow, listened.

Wind and rain, whistling and spattering.

Beyond that, sounds were coming from the back of the building. Sounds he recognized. Slowly, looking out for debris and other obstacles, he made his way towards them.

Although gutted and unrecognizable from its previous incarnation, the layout hadn't yet been altered. Amar tried to remember it, overlay that with what was before him now, minimize impediments, pinpoint the source of the sounds.

They were coming from the shell of a room to the right and back, what he presumed must have been a storage area behind the bar. As he approached, he realized he was right; the bar was still there. He walked up to it.

Dimly lit by the diffused, ground-level streetlighting seeping in through an overhead grate, he saw them. The bulk of Ralphie taking up most of the space, Jamal kneeling before him.

Amar hadn't planned for this moment, how he would actually approach Jamal, because he didn't know how he would find him. He needed to do two things: stop Ralphie, make Jamal feel safe.

He looked around. Saw a thick, square baton of wood. About a metre long, four centimetres thick.

Perfect.

He carefully picked it up, watched rats scurry away at his approach, then crossed the room until he stood at the corner of the bar, behind Ralphie. There wasn't much space in the room; his first shot would be his only one.

He gripped the wood with both hands, centred himself. Headache, nausea, chest pains all gone. He focused, brought the stick back . . .

'Ralphie!'

And let it go.

Ralphie stopped dead on hearing his name. As he was turning his head to the source, the bar hit, connecting with the side of his head: his ear, his cheekbone. He recoiled from the blow, lost his footing, stumbled against the wall. His hands went to his face, he began to wail in agony. His erection rapidly diminished.

'Shut up,' said Amar as sternly as he couldn manage, 'or you'll get another.'

Amar held on to the stick. He looked at Jamal. The boy was struggling to his feet. Even in the dark, Amar could see how wide his eyes were. He was preparing to run.

'Jamal, wait.'

The boy stopped, surprised to hear his own name used.

Amar pressed forward his advantage. 'Jamal, listen to me. I'm not police. I'm not here to hurt you. I'm here to help you.'

Jamal still looked fear-stricken, ready to bolt.

'Joe Donovan sent me,' said Amar. 'I'm a friend of Joe Donovan.'

The name had an impact on the boy; his posture changed. He became slightly less fearful, more inquisitive. Amar kept talking.

'Joe Donovan. I'm a friend of his. I'm here to take care of you. To get you somewhere safe.'

Ralphie groaned loudly again, tried to get to his feet, hand on his face. 'I think I've broken something . . . You bastard. What you do that for? What've I ever done to you?'

'You fuck children and boast about it,' said Amar.

'I'll fuckin' 'ave you,' said Ralphie unsteadily, painfully, on his feet now. 'Get the law on to you.'

'No, you won't,' said Amar. 'Law won't touch a child abuser. And, anyway, you've got to get past me first.'

Ralphie stared at Amar.

Amar hefted the bar. 'Ready?'

Ralphie looked at the wood, at Amar. Looked right in his eyes.

Made his mind up.

'But I paid for him,' Ralphie said, attempting to regain his dignity. 'I want my money back.'

'The boy's not for sale,' said Amar. 'No refunds. And tuck yourself in.'

Ralphie fumbled with his zipper, tried to hold eye contact. Failed. Knowing he was defeated, he rubbed his ear and grimaced, turned and left the building.

Amar waited until he was sure the man had gone, then turned back to Jamal. The boy had his back pressed against the furthest wall. Amar realized he was still holding the wood, dropped it.

'It's OK, Jamal,' he said. 'You're safe now.'

Jamal kept staring at him. 'Yeah? I trusted Joe Donovan an' nearly got me killed. Why should I trust you?'

Amar sighed. Felt suddenly tired. It had been a long day.

'I don't know why you should trust me, Jamal,' he said, his voice weary. 'No idea. But Joe Donovan asked me to look for you, and I've spent all day doing it. I'm not here to hurt you or use you or anything like that. I'm here to take you home, yeah? Make you feel safe.'

'Where is Joe Donovan?'

'He had to go away for a few days. But I can give you a bed for the night. No hassle.'

Jamal stared at him.

Amar rubbed his face, held his hands out, palms upwards. 'What more can I say? It's up to you.'

Jamal thought. Amar didn't move. Eventually Jamal nodded.

'OK,' he said.

Amar smiled. 'Good. Come on, then.'

They picked their way through the debris and up on to street level. Amar allowed Jamal to lead.

'Right,' said Amar, once there, 'let's get a taxi.'

Jamal seemed reluctant to move.

'What?'

Jamal looked around. 'Lemme get somethin' to eat first, yeah?'

Amar nodded. He felt hungry, too; first time in days.

'OK,' he said. 'I think I'll join you. What d'you fancy? Indian? Chinese?'

Jamal looked around. 'Ain't that a kebab place on the corner?'

Amar smiled. 'Kebab it is.'

They went to get their food.

Falling into step together.

24

Donovan couldn't sleep.

In his bed in a room in a chain hotel in Swiss Cottage; the hotel full of American or European tourists or middle-management business travellers.

Files and notebooks thrown all over the floor, old laptop plugged in on the desk, raided minibar evidence on all available surfaces. He had tried to lose himself.

Failed.

They had driven straight there after leaving Crouch End, Donovan monosyllabic and introspective all the way. Only speaking to insist the cost be put on the *Herald*'s credit card. Once in the hotel, Peta, thinking it not her place to extend unsolicited advice and that he would want some time on his own, had taken off to the pool. Donovan to the minibar.

They had regrouped, eaten dinner in the hotel – Donovan only picking – and, at Peta's suggestion, started work in his room.

Going through old notes, old compuer files, Peta helping him.

'What am I looking for?' she asked.

'Wansbeck Moor, travellers . . .'

He had tried to throw himself into it. He brought her up to speed, told her about Wansbeck Moor, its traveller problem and the steps they had taken as a community to get rid of it.

'Can see their point,' she said. 'I'm sure I'd be pissed off, too.'

Donovan was too tired to argue with her. He sighed. Flopped back on the bed.

'Look,' Peta said, 'd'you want to talk? Will it help?'

Donovan sighed. 'Probably not.'

Peta opened her mouth, about to say something more, but Donovan sat suddenly upright.

'Tosher . . .' he said. 'That was his name, Tosher . . .'

Peta looked at him, confused.

'Tosher . . .' He repeated the name like a ruminative mantra. 'He was one of the travellers. Contacted me, wanted to tell me what he'd seen. The truth about what was going on, he said. Something more.'

Donovan got off the bed, crossed to the laptop, began looking through files.

'And did he?'

Donovan didn't look up. 'Never got the chance. You know what happened to me then.'

Peta said nothing. Looked at him. He was looking at the computer screen but not seeing it. Seeing something much further away, something she didn't want to share in.

She kept looking through the piles of paper and notebooks on the floor.

They worked quietly for some time. The night noises of the city intruded faintly into the room, the desk lamp and bedside lamps throwing out concentrated pools of light.

Donovan forcing himself to concentrate.

'Here's our boy,' said Donovan eventually. 'Tosher. Real name Anthony Langrish.'

'So what's this got to do with Colin Huntley?' asked Peta.

'No idea,' said Donovan. 'At least not yet. Perhaps there is a connection. Perhaps Tosher, a.k.a. Anthony Langrish, can help us.'

'And how do we find Tosher, a.k.a. Anthony Langrish?'

Donovan took out his new laptop, plugged it in to the hotel's broadband socket.

'We hope luck is on our side,' he said.

It was. Trawls through various electoral rolls and sub-scription-only Internet directories had given an address for him in Essex. They consulted the atlas, decided that would be the next day's activity. Then it was time for bed. Peta checked he was OK, then made her way to her own room.

But he wasn't OK. Sleep, he had thought, would come heavily and quickly. But it hadn't. Whatever respite he had found in work had been only temporary.

Every time he had tried to sleep, the dreams had returned. And with them the ghosts. All jumbled up; all pressing down on him.

All blaming him.

David living Jamal's rent boy life.

Annie making him wait outside their bedroom while she was inside with another man.

Abigail screaming at him from the picture frame.

Maria, shrouded and bloodied, telling him she would be alive if not for him.

All pressing down on him.

He rolled from the bed, eyes screwed tight, knuckles pushing into his temples.

He made his way to the minibar, raided it again.

But there was nothing left. Everything in miniature, too small to be effective. He curled up on the floor, making a noise he couldn't classify, trying to force it from his body. Tears fell, unnoticed.

Trying to clear his head, he stuck one of the CDs he had taken from his old home into the laptop. Johnny Cash: *Solitary Man*.

He flicked through the tracks, rejecting them in turn. 'I Won't Back Down'. 'Solitary Man'. 'I See A Darkness'.

'The Mercy Seat'. Too tired to reject it, he let it play.

Nick Cave's covered murder ballad; a death-row con dying on the electric chair. Refusing to confront his actions or consequences until death finally forces one last confession from him.

Then that noise again.

Johnny sang in his Old Testament prophet growl that the mercy seat was waiting . . .

The JCB tearing up his brain.

Johnny sang that he felt his head was burning . . .

His heart.

His soul.

David . . .

Annie . . .

Abigail . . .

Maria . . .

Johnny sang that he was yearning to be done . . .

The JCB . . . tearing . . .

To be done . . .

Tearing . . .

Something to take away the pain . . . anything . . .

He had something.

And anyway, Johnny sang, he told the truth . . .

Donovan crawled on his knees to the holdall, brought it crashing to the floor, contents spilling out. He rummaged through, throwing his belongings everywhere, not caring where they landed, pain blotting out everything else.

He found what he was looking for.

An eye for an eye, Johnny sang, a tooth for a tooth . . .

His revolver.

And he wasn't afraid to die . . .

His heart beat wildly, his chest heaved.

The pain . . . JCB . . .

He spun the chamber.

Placed the barrel to his forehead.

Began to squeeze the trigger.

Smiling, almost in relief.

A knock at the door.

'Joe? You OK?'

Peta's voice.

Donovan opened his eyes. Looked around as if waking from a dream. His heart was beating wildly, his chest heaving. He looked at his hand. The gun.

Johnny Cash now singing 'Would You Lay with Me in a Field of Stone?'.

'Joe?'

Donovan tried to speak, found his throat hard and dry, like sun-baked clay.

'Ye – yeah?'

'The music's very loud and I heard you shouting. Are you OK?'

'Just . . . just a minute . . .'

He stuck the gun under the pillow. Moved towards the door, stopped when he saw his reflection in the mirror. In CBGBs T-shirt and boxers, his eyes red-rimmed, his face wet and tear-tracked. He wiped it on his shirt.

Opened the door.

Peta couldn't hide her shock at his appearance.

'Joe . . .'

Donovan said nothing.

'Can I come in?'

'It's . . . erm . . .'

'I think I'd better,' she said and walked in. Then stopped, looked around.

'What . . . what d'you want?' Donovan couldn't face her.

She turned to him. 'I've just heard from Amar. He's found Jamal. He's safe. I thought you'd want to know.'

'Yes. I do. Thank you.' He sighed.

Peta shook her head. Looked at him. There was warmth and compassion in that gaze. More than that, understanding.

'Don't take this the wrong way,' she said, 'but I don't think you should be left alone tonight.'

Donovan said nothing.

'I'll get my duvet. Be back in a minute.' Peta left the room.

Donovan looked around, sighed.

Johnny now singing that he was just a wayfaring stranger, that there was no sickness, toil or danger in the bright land he was heading to, only his loved ones who had gone on.

Donovan was suddenly weary beyond tears.

25

Caroline slept. Colin watched her.

She was curled up on her side near the radiator, a couple of old, stinking blankets wrapped round her to keep out the cold. She slept long, deep and often, Colin had noticed, her body shutting down, protecting itself.

Colin sat back against the wall, cradling his injured arm. It had been strapped up; a field dressing, nothing more. It still hurt, needed proper medical attention. No chance of that.

Caroline's face. Peaceful in repose.

But he couldn't tell what she was thinking, dreaming. What she now thought of him.

'What's going on?' she had said. 'Why are you here?'

Colin had sighed, sat back against the wall.

'Oh Caroline,' he said, 'I've done a terrible thing . . .'

And he told her.

'It started with your mother's death,' he said. 'Everything . . . everything started then.'

Caroline looked at him, confused, patiently waiting for him to continue.

'It was a . . .' He sighed. 'A bad time. A difficult time. The cancer had . . . well, I don't need to tell you, you know. You hadn't moved out, then. It was hard. To come to terms with. And then there were the travellers.'

Caroline tutted, shook her head. 'I don't know why you let them get to you so much.'

'You know why.' His voice, snappy and sharp, made Caroline jump. She stared at him. He looked away.

Silence stretched, became almost a presence in the room.

He continued. 'Every year they came . . . with their mess, and their fires, their washing strung out, their rubbish thrown all over the place.' He gestured, his chain rattling against the pipe. 'And the children . . . running round naked, filthy . . . feral. The noise, the revving engines at all hours, lorries coming and going, loading and unloading God knows what in the middle of the night . . . and all that shouting, swearing, rolling home drunk . . .'

Caroline nodded absently. 'I know, Dad.'

'We knew they'd be back. So we thought we'd outsmart them. That's why we bought that land. Worth it, too, we thought. Even if that farmer did charge us over three times what it was worth.'

Caroline said nothing. She had heard it all before.

'Yes, well . . . They outsmarted us, didn't they? Good and proper. Remember? The drainage? The tarmac?' He shook his head, lips curled in angry remembrance.

'I remember.'

'And there they were . . . all round the houses, sneering at us, taunting us to challenge them . . . selling furniture out of the back of vans, trying to scare us into having our houses reroofed, our drives done . . . thieving from us . . .'

Caroline laughed in exasperation. 'No they didn't. They weren't like that at all.'

There were small points of fire in Colin's eyes. 'Well, you would say that, wouldn't you? They showed a different side to you. But I saw them as they really were . . .' He sighed.

Caroline looked at him confused. This wasn't the father she knew talking. He caught the look, cast his eyes down.

'Sorry,' he said. 'That was unfair.'

She nodded.

Colin continued, his voice smaller. 'It was awful, it really was. Awful. Hell. I was trying to come to terms with Helen's death, with your mother's death, to mourn . . . and all I could see and hear were them . . . They terrorized us . . .'

He shook his head as if to dislodge the memory. Risked a look at his daughter.

'And then you got friendly with them.'

Caroline rolled her eyes. 'Oh Dad . . .'

'Well, you did. That biker.'

'Tosher? So what?' Caroline attempted a shrug. 'He was a nice guy.' She leaned forward. 'If you'd taken the time to get to know him, you'd have realized he wasn't the monster you thought he was.'

Colin shook his head. 'I just remember thinking . . . I'm glad your mother wasn't there to see her daughter with . . .' He sighed. 'Oh I don't know . . .' He shook his head again. 'I was being driven mad. Helen was gone, you were with that . . . that biker . . . I wanted them to go. And I wasn't the only one.'

'What d'you mean?'

Colin took a deep breath as if steeling himself.

'Alan Keenyside invited me round.'

'Alan Keenyside? The policeman? What for?'

Colin looked away.

'He had a proposal . . .'

And Alan Keenyside's house was before him again. And there was Keenyside himself in polo shirt and chinos; weekend leisurewear as much a uniform as his weekday suits. Coming towards him, all affable smile and miss nothing eyes.

'Drink, Colin?' The light catching his eyes, sparkling like diamond in dark, subterranean graphite.

'Ah . . . no, no.'

'Go on . . . one won't hurt you . . .' Those eyes again.

Colin caved in. 'Just the one.'

Keenyside nodded. The right answer. He turned, disappeared.

Colin stood in the hall of Keenyside's house, not sure whether he was supposed to follow or not. He stayed where he was. Looked around.

The house was new, one of the larger ones in the development. Decorated by Keenyside's wife, Suzanne, with money if not taste. All laminate and leopardskin, glass furniture and 'artistic' wall hangings. Bright and shiny. Jamie Cullen making good songs unlistenable on a CD from somewhere in the house.

Keenyside reappeared bearing two drinks, led Colin to his study, closed the door behind them. This room had none of the brightness of the rest of the house; all dark walls, heavy, reproduction wooden furniture, blood-burgundy-leather chairs and settee. Keenyside handed Colin a tumbler of whisky, sat in his studded-leather desk chair, swivelled to look at Colin, who sat on the chesterfield. The room was manly, businesslike. Books of military history on the shelves. Keenyside sat higher than Colin. Colin felt like a supplicant visiting a feudal lord. The effect was deliberate.

'So,' said Keenyside, sipping his malt and smacking his lips, 'what you got for me?'

Colin leaned forward, hands clasped. 'It's about what you were saying the other day, remember?'

Keenyside gave an imperceptible nod.

'You remember?'

'I want to hear you say it, Colin. You tell me.'

Colin found his lips suddenly dry. He quickly licked them.

'The travellers. I don't know what to do, they're . . .' His fingers became rigid; he made involuntary strangling gestures. 'They're driving me insane . . .'

It all tumbled out of him then. The anguish at Helen's

death, the subsequent pain and madness, the impotent rage he felt at the way the travellers had outsmarted the village, 'And then there's Caroline. She's got . . . involved . . . with one of them. A biker. Tosher, she said his name was.' He shook his head. 'I've lost Helen. What if I lose Caroline?' He held his hands out, imploring. 'What if she just . . . rides off one day? And I never see her again?' He sighed. 'Something has to be done.'

Keenyside watched him, sipped his whisky. 'There's the legal challenge,' he said.

Colin nodded.

'Might be costly. But it'll probably come out in your favour.'

'That's just it,' said Colin. 'Might. It might not, too. We might be stuck with them.' He sighed, ran his hands through his hair. His face was contorted with pain. 'They won't go away . . . and if they do, they might take Caroline with them . . .'

Keenyside swirled his glass, watched the ice turn to water, release the oils in the malt.

'So,' he said, voice quiet, controlled, 'what d'you want me to do about it?'

Colin looked up. 'I don't know.' His voice was choked with desperation. 'But you're a policeman. Isn't there . . . something you can do? Some way to, I don't know . . . move them on?'

Keenyside studied his glass, smiled. Spoke slowly.

'Back in the old days, it wouldn't have been a problem. They'd pitch themselves up somewhere, piss the locals off and a squad in body armour would turn up at night and forcibly evict them. Burn them out if needs be.' He shrugged. 'So I'm told, anyway.'

He looked directly at Colin, that subterranean jewelled glitter back in his eyes.

'That the kind of thing you've got in mind?'

Colin swallowed hard. He felt hot all of a sudden.

'We're just speaking hypothetically here, Colin.'

Colin nodded. His voice became shaky, untrustworthy.

'Yuh – yuh – yes . . . yes . . .'

Keenyside took a sip of his drink. Frowned. 'Asking a lot, you know. You'd have to put together a crew, shall we say, of like-minded members of the force, get them working off the clock, give them a bit of a cash incentive . . . Could come to quite a bit . . .'

He took another sip. Continued talking, his voice as smooth as the malt.

'And then there's the risk involved. An illegal operation like that, if something went wrong . . .' He shook his head.

Colin said nothing. His head was beginning to ache.

Keenyside sat back. Light picked out the spines of books behind him. Anthony Beevor: *Stalingrad. Berlin.* Andy McNab's novels in hardback.

'Hypothetically,' he began, 'this could be dangerous for the person in charge. Say me, for instance. In that case it would be only fair that the person who wanted this thing to take place, namely you, should shoulder some of the risk himself.'

'Wuh – wuh – what d'you mean?'

Keenyside looked thoughtful. 'You do a lot of research at your lab, don't you?'

'Well, yes. I mean, not me personally—'

'MoD stuff? Top secret?'

'Look, I . . .'

Keenyside was warming to his subject. 'Biological warfare? Viruses that could be weaponized? Should imagine there's a big demand for that kind of thing. War on terror and all that. How much would something like that go for on the open market? To the highest bidder?'

'I . . . I wouldn't know.'

'Oh don't be coy, Colin. I bet you get approached.'

'Well, yes, sometimes, but . . .'

'Millions, are we talking?'

'Look.' Colin was almost shouting. His head was aching. 'What has this got to do with the travellers?'

Keenyside sat back, a look of shock on his face. 'Just . . .' He gave a small shrug. 'Talking hypothetically, Colin. Risk assessment. Once you commit yourself to something like this, you're in it all the way.'

Colin said nothing. Stared at the floor. His untouched drink. The ice melting. He sighed. Keenyside pressed on.

'Anyway, that's one hypothetical solution. Another would involve you.'

'Me?'

'What we would need,' he began ruminatively, 'would be something from your labs. Something that could dissolve in water, be colourless, odourless. Untraceable in the human system.'

'A poison?'

'Yes, a poison. I'm sure you've got loads of stuff like that lying around up there. What we do is introduce it to the water supply they've just installed, then watch them fall over one by one. Blame it on some kind of bug. Impurity in the system they set up. Or use a traceable poison. Make it seem like a suicide pact. Make them out to be some kind of death cult.' Keenyside gave a small laugh. 'Exciting, isn't it? Like working for the CIA.'

Colin shook his head. The pain increased. 'No . . . no . . . That's awful . . .'

'Drastic times, Colin, drastic measures needed.' He gestured towards the door. 'You can always go home, Colin. Back to the noise, the smell. Back to your new neighbours.'

Colin shook his head. The ache had become a pain.

'Ever heard of Chechnya?' asked Keenyside.

Colin nodded.

'Lots of stuff gone on there you never hear of over here. They have a way of dealing with undesirables. Want to hear it?'

Colin said nothing, just sat, shoulders slumped.

Keenyside told him. How the Russian army treated their prisoners. Made an example of them to the rest.

Told him about the gas masks. The mustard gas.

The torture and interrogation.

The broken prisoner returned, a human warning to the others.

Told him how it could be applied to their problem.

'All we would need would be one person,' Keenyside said. 'Just one. And when they see what's happened to him, they won't want to stay around in case the same happens to them. Just one. To make an example of. Can you think of one you'd like that to happen to?'

Colin said nothing. He looked in pain.

'I can,' said Keenyside.

Colin shook his head.

He locked eyes with Colin. 'D'you want rid of them, Colin? Really want rid of them?'

Colin sighed. The inside of his head felt like it was being chipped away at by hundreds of tiny pickaxes. He couldn't think.

'I want . . . peace . . .'

Keenyside kept his eyes locked.

'Peace costs,' he said. 'Real, long-lasting peace.'

'How much?' His throat felt parched.

'Financially? Nothing. Only your complicity.'

Colin stared wildly around, pained and lost.

'That or nothing,' Keenyside said.

Colin looked at the floor. Picked up his untouched whisky. Downed it in one. Nodded.

'I'll pay.'

Keenyside smiled. 'Good man.' He sat back.

Colin felt exhausted. Dirty. Sweat ran and danced all over his body. He was shaking.

But his headache seemed to be receding.

'I feel like Faust . . . with Mephistopheles . . .'

Keenyside kept smiling, his eyes glittering.

'Whatever,' he said. He pointed a finger at the other man. 'Your glass is empty, Colin. Another?'

Colin nodded.

Caroline stared at him. Like she was unable to reconcile the father she had known all her life with the things he was telling her.

'Tosher . . . what happened to him?'

'I . . . I don't know . . .' He looked away from her, hid his eyes. Tried not to look in the centre of the room. At the stains on the floor. 'I just appropriated their compound for them. I don't know.'

'Appropriated . . . You let them . . .' She shook her head, incredulous. 'What about the rest of the travellers? What happened to them?'

He saw flames dance before his eyes. Heard screams and cries of pain.

'I said I don't know,' he snapped. 'I don't know . . .what they did . . .' He sighed, shook his head. 'Look, I had to do something. I'd lost Helen. I could have lost you.' He sighed. 'I had to do something . . .'

The words had sunk in. Anger was beginning to rise within Caroline now. 'What d'you mean you had to do something? It was never going to last between me and Tosher. You knew that. It was just a bit of fun. God knows

I needed it after all we'd been through. He and I just went out a few times. Rode on his bike with him. That's all. I was never going to go away with him. You knew that.' She shook her head. 'My God . . .'

'That's not how it seemed to me at the time . . .' He was close to tears. 'Look, I knew what I'd done was bad. I tried to make it up to you with the flat. Helping you move, decorating, helping you pay . . .'

Caroline stared at him, eyes cold. 'I just . . . I don't know what to say to you . . .'

He reached out his hand to her.

'Don't touch me. Just don't touch me.'

Colin said nothing. Stared at the chain that bound him to the radiator. By extension, to his daughter. He gave another sad, slow shake of his head.

The silence stretched out. Eventually Caroline spoke.

'And all this—' she gestured with her hand, rattling the chain as she did so '—Keenyside, the whole thing, is because of what you did to Tosher?'

'Kind of,' said Colin in a small voice. 'An extension of that, you might say. A consequence. Let me explain.'

'No,' she said quickly. She looked at him as if seeing him for the first time. 'I don't think I know you. I don't think I want to know you . . .'

The silence stretched out indefinitely.

And now she lay there sleeping. And he watched her.

Not knowing what she was thinking about.

What she thought of him.

What he thought of himself.

26

Donovan had always found seaside towns out of season depressing. He imagined this one just as depressing in season.

Jaywick Sands just beside Clacton. A flat stretch of Essex sliding into the North Sea. Perhaps it had once been a thriving, pleasant resort – although Donovan doubted it – but was now in terminal decline.

Peta drove, Donovan map-read. Out of London, up the A12 to Essex, superstores, retail parks and industrial estates proliferating, then receding, replaced by flat, functional countryside, neatly divided into utilitarian strips and squares.

Donovan had woken up in the hotel room entangled in his sheet and duvet, his hair lank and sweat-plastered to his head, mouth crusted, body stinking of sweat and guilt.

He lay back and groaned, let the past night's jigsaw fit itself together.

The music, the booze.

The ghosts, the gun . . .

Then nothing.

He looked to the side of the bed, confused to see, amid all the strewn papers, a duvet and pillow there. Then remembered.

Peta.

And groaned again.

On the pillow a note, hoping he managed to get some rest and a time to meet her in the restaurant for breakfast.

He looked at his watch, slowly pulled himself from his bed, forced his way into the bathroom, head spinning, stomach churning. His hangover, he knew, wouldn't shift. It would hang around all day, resurfacing like a guilty secret, reminding him of its presence.

He showered, trying to shove the previous night to the back of his mind, made his way down to breakfast wearing an old Batman T-shirt and olive-green combats. He was wary about meeting Peta; he couldn't remember what he had told her. He found her sitting, pink-cheeked, perky and radiant from her morning swim, eating a toasted bagel and fresh fruit, drinking Earl Grey tea. She looked up at his approach.

'How are you?' Real concern in her eyes.

Donovan shrugged. Peta nodded.

'You OK for today?'

Donovan nodded.

'Good,' she said. Went back to her bagel.

Donovan stared at her. 'Look,' he began uncomfortably. 'Last night. I might have said some things that . . . I don't know, I'm . . .'

She smiled. And Donovan felt like he had a friend. 'It's all right,' she said. 'Honestly.'

He nodded. 'Thanks. Sorry for being a . . .'

'Nothing to be ashamed of. We've all been there. Or somewhere similar. Part of being human.'

Donovan looked at her, wanting to ask more, not daring.

She shrugged. 'You've had a rough few days. Let's forget it. Get some food inside you. You'll feel better.'

He did as he was told, ordered himself a full English. If he couldn't stop his heart with a gun, he thought wryly, he would find another way.

It arrived. A piled mass of oil-fried comfort food. He stared at the egg, saw his spoon-faced reflection in its bulbous yellow eye. He looked sick.

Started eating.

'Right,' said Peta, businesslike, 'Today. Jaywick. Is that right?'

Donovan nodded. 'Yeah,' he said through a mouthful of bacon, 'Jaywick. In Essex.'

'And that's where this Tosher now lives?'

Donovan nodded. 'He was kind of a spokesman for the travellers back then. Self-elected, of course.'

'What's he like?'

'Dark, long-haired, good-looking biker.'

Peta smiled. 'Nice.'

'And an arrogant, cocky bastard. The type who goes through life knowing he's going to get away with whatever he wants to do.' The smile still hadn't faded from Peta's face. 'Obnoxious. Mouthy. Just in case you're getting any ideas.'

Peta ignored him. 'What's he doing in Jaywick?'

'Settled down, apparently. Regular citizen, now. That's how I found him so quickly.'

'Born to be mild.'

Donovan smiled. 'Very good.'

Peta pointed to his plate. It was empty.

'You needed that.'

He looked at her, sketched a brief, fragile smile.

'Yeah,' he said, 'I needed that.'

The Broadway, an uneven, potholed strip of tarmac, was Jaywick's main street. Peta drove, Donovan looked out of the window.

Most buildings one storey, the odd one two. Nothing looked inviting or well-maintained. Jaywick had a poverty more than financial; it seeped into the architecture, lacked spirit and hope. A flat, front-boarded façade described itself as Wonderland: Slots of Fun. Next to it a bookie. A dowdy hair salon and a run-down Chinese takeaway. A Shop 'n' Save. The pub: the Never Say Die.

'Looks like last rites have been given,' said Donovan.

Past a boarded-up, weed-choked shell that had once proclaimed itself a casino. A social club that looked anything but social. A cut-price food shop discounting sell-by skirters and stale stuff. A derelict pub ringed by wire mesh and DANGER: KEEP OUT signs. A café with a warped frontage of paint-flaked wood and hanging baskets of dead flowers stood detached from the rest of the strip.

'Hungry?' asked Peta.

'Not enough,' replied Donovan.

All round were expanses of weeds and rubble dotted with empty, derelict buildings. The dull sky clamped the Earth down, flattening it out, stretching it away for miles, keeping it depressed like a thick iron-grey blanket.

'Where are we headed?' Peta asked.

'The Broadlands Estate,' said Donovan. 'Shouldn't be far now.'

They arrived.

'Jesus,' said Peta. 'Munchkin town.'

Originally single-storey summer-holiday chalets from over half a century ago, the houses were now virtually all permanently occupied. Cars dotted round. The further in they went, the less functional the cars became. Eventually they became rusting, burned out husks, scavenger-picked for anything of use, left to rot in the potholed, rubble and rubbish-strewn broken streets.

The houses became less well maintained and ultimately derelict. In among these were barely habitable, but occupied, homes.

Peta shook her head. 'City of God,' she said.

'But without the sun,' said Donovan.

They drove, slowly for fear of damaging the car from a chunk of stone or an unseen hole, until they found the address they were looking for. Pulled up in front of it.

It was pebbledash and chipped, its windows grimy, the net curtains filthy. Weeds choked it. The roof tiles were old and mossed. An abstract sculpture of rubbish and waste fronted the small wall. The door had once been green.

'This the one?' asked Peta, not bothering to hide her distaste.

'This is the one.'

Donovan took a deep breath, walked up the uneven path to the front door, knocked on it.

And waited.

A dog barked within. Donovan and Peta looked at each other.

Eventually they heard the sound of someone moving laboriously towards the door. The noises stopped.

'Who is it?'

The voice was broken, rasping and ripping, like bleeding skin dragged over shattered, sharpened glass.

Peta looked at Donovan, alarmed. He looked wary.

'Tosher?' said Donovan. 'Don't know if you can remember me. Joe Donovan. Used to be a reporter.'

'Yeah.' The word was dredged up from ruined lungs. Followed by a sound that may have been a laugh or a death rattle. 'I remember yer. Now fuck off.'

Donovan and Peta exchanged glances. The dog kept barking. Donovan tried again.

'I appreciate that you might not want to talk to me, Tosher, but if I could just have five or ten minutes . . .'

No reply. Just the barking dog.

Donovan looked to Peta, shrugged. 'I'll pay you.'

A pause, then: 'How much?'

'Five hundred pounds.'

Another laugh/death rattle. 'A thousand.'

'Five hundred's all I've got, Tosher. Take it or leave it.'

Another ruined rumble, a door slamming. The dog's

barking became more distant, muffled. Then the sound of chains being removed, bolts being undone. The door opened.

And there stood Tosher.

Donovan tried not to let the shock appear on his face. The good–looking, dark–maned arrogant biker was gone. In his place stood the physical embodiment of the voice they had heard. His black hair was now predominantly grey, still long but sparse; pink scalp could be glimpsed through it. His face was lined, crinkled, like the life had been sucked out of it. His body too: cheap T-shirt and jeans hung off his emaciated frame. Although still the same height, he looked shorter, like his body had never uncurled from a blow it had received.

But it was the eyes. They looked dead, closed down after witnessing, experiencing, too much.

'Yeah,' said Tosher. He knew why Donovan was staring. 'Two years is a long time.'

Without another word, Tosher turned and walked back into the house, a painful, shuffling limp. Taking that as their cue, Donovan and Peta followed, closing the door behind them.

Tosher led them into the living room, where he slowly lowered himself down into an old, worn velour armchair. Stained and threadbare, it was matched by the sofa Donovan and Peta sat themselves down on.

Somewhere in the house the dog barked and scratched.

The room was a tip. An old TV in one corner, standing on an upturned crate. Motorbike parts lying around. Old beer cans. An overflowing pub ashtray. Other assorted debris and detritus of a broken life.

Donovan shuddered. With recognition.

This would be the next step if he stayed on the road he was on.

He thought of the previous night. Felt delayed nausea well within him. Ignored it.

He had work to do.

'Suddup, Zoltan,' Tosher half growled, half shouted. Then was seized by a bout of racking coughs. The dog kept barking.

Tosher pointed at Peta. 'Who's this?'

'Peta Knight. A work colleague.'

Tosher nodded at her, and Donovan saw in his eyes a glimpse of the man he used to be. Just briefly; it was soon obscured by a cloud of self-loathing.

'You took your time,' Tosher said.

Donovan frowned.

'I thought you'd come eventually,' he rasped and gasped. 'Or somebody like you . . . I saw the news. Huntley and his . . . daughter . . .'

'What happened, Tosher? What d'you know?'

Tosher almost smiled. 'You got me money?'

'In my pocket.'

'Let's see it.'

Donovan took out his wallet, counted out ten fifties he had drawn on the *Herald*'s credit card. Tosher took them, counted them, pocketed them. Hunger in his eyes; need, not greed.

'What happened, Tosher?' asked Donovan. 'Why did you think someone would come to see you? Why now?'

'Because of this.' Tosher stuck out his hands, palms upwards.

They bent forward, looked.

Even in the sick, dim light they could see the damage. The newer skin in the centre of each palm. The left one eaten away, deformed. Tosher lifted it up.

'Got an infection in that one. Lucky they saved it in time. Lucky I didn't have to get it amputated.' He gave a harsh snort that may have been a laugh. 'Lucky.'

'You were tortured?' asked Peta, appalled.

Tosher's laboured breathing sounded like air pumping from a sucking wound. His lip curled. 'You think . . . I always sounded like this?'

Donovan and Peta said nothing.

'An' they did a lot more, an' all. Stuff you . . . can't see.' His eyes dropped to the floor. 'Stuff I'm not goin' to show you.' He looked up. 'I'm not goin' to . . . tell you, though. Because then I'd relive it.' He shuddered, eyes out of focus. 'An' I don't . . . wanna go back there again. Just . . . take my word for it.'

Donovan and Peta exchanged a look. Said nothing. Tosher looked between the two of them.

'I told you,' he said, a twisted vindication in his eyes, 'told you they . . . were plannin' somethin'. But you never came back.'

Donovan swallowed hard. 'I'm sorry,' he said. 'But I had . . . things to deal with.'

'You lost your boy, didn't you?'

Donovan nodded, said nothing.

'Bad, that,' said Tosher. His eyes were lit by the conflicting lights of self-loathing and vindication. They combined to give his face a cruel, twisted expression. 'But not as bad . . . as what happened to me.'

Donovan opened his mouth to reply. Tosher stopped him.

'Think about it, Joe Donovan, which of us . . . would you rather be?'

Donovan said nothing. Allowed Tosher his tiny triumph.

'Who did it, Tosher?' asked Peta. 'Who did this to you?'

Tosher swivelled his gaze to her. He almost smiled.

'Long time since I've had a woman . . . interested in what I said . . .'

Peta said nothing, kept her eyes on him.

Tosher frowned. 'You a copper?'

'Used to be,' she said.

Tosher nodded. 'Used to be . . . It's still in you . . . still on you . . . always will be.' He looked at Donovan. 'Ashamed at you, Joe, hangin' round with the filth.'

Donovan didn't rise to his words, kept going. 'Tosher,' he said, 'why did this happen?'

Tosher gave a dismissive look at Peta, full attention to Donovan. 'It was supposed to be a warnin',' he said slowly. 'They wanted us . . . out. They told us what they'd do if we didn't go . . . Burn us out . . .'

'They can't do that,' said Donovan.

'That's what we thought. We had . . . the law on our side. An' they knew that.' He paused, gasped down air, continued. 'So they took me. Made an . . . example, they said, of me. Did this. Said they'd do it to all of us if we didn't shift.'

'And you went?'

'Fuckin' right, we did. Straight off.'

Peta leaned forward. 'Why didn't you go to the police about this?'

Tosher's throat gave out another harsh, guttural sound. 'Who d'you think done this?'

Peta and Donovan looked at each other. 'The police?' said Donovan.

Tosher nodded. 'Yeah . . . who'd you fuckin' think? We got straight out. Packed up an' . . . off.' Another harsh approximation of a laugh. 'An' they all came out to cheer . . . all those bastards . . . supposed to be respectable, with their posh cars an' their . . . posh houses . . . cheered . . . an' shouted . . . an' threw stuff . . . called us scum . . . bastards . . .'

He stopped talking, gasping for breath again. Face flushed with anger.

'But they were waitin' for us . . . the filth . . . riot gear . . . forced us off the road, into a lay-by . . . got the sticks out . . .'

'That's illegal,' said Peta, clearly shocked.

Tosher just shook his head. 'Where were you stationed at? Fuckin' Toytown?'

Peta reddened.

'They were waitin' . . . Bashed shit out of us . . . even the kids . . .' Tosher's eyes began to glisten with tears. 'Round an' round us like fuckin' Red Indians circlin' the wagons . . . then the petrol . . .' He shook his head, wheezing. 'The screamin' . . . An' they stood there, fuckin' laughin' . . .'

No one spoke. No sound in the house but the slight scratching of the dog.

'Came 'ere eventually.' Tosher's voice was small, as broken as he looked. 'Cousin 'ad a place nearby. An' 'ere I stayed. Fuckin' sick money . . . Fuckin' cripple . . .' He stared at the floor, self-loathing building up again. 'An' 'ere I will stay . . .'

'The police did this?' said Donovan quietly.

Tosher nodded. 'Copper called Keenyside. He was behind it. Had this mad bastard who did the work . . . Hammer, they called 'im.' Tosher shuddered. Fear flickered across his face. 'You don't wanna . . . meet 'im, I'm tellin' you . . . Evil . . . real evil . . .'

'Keenyside . . .' repeated Donovan.

'They had names . . . nicknames,' Tosher said. 'Faust an' Mephisto. But I knew it was them . . .'

'Mephisto was . . . Keenyside,' said Donovan, 'and Hammer was Faust?'

Tosher smiled. A rumble began to build in his chest. 'Hammer was Hammer,' he said.

'Then who was Faust?' asked Peta.

The rumbling sound grew, like an avalanche beginning to roll, leaving destruction in its wake. 'Faust?' he said. 'That spineless little . . . shit . . . Colin Huntley. Him . . .'

Donovan and Peta looked at each other, shocked.

'Colin Huntley?' asked Donovan. 'Why?'

'Because I was fuckin' his daughter . . . He was behind the whole thing . . .' A look of twisted triumph appeared in his eyes. 'He just couldn't stand the thought . . . of his precious daughter . . . fuckin' me . . .'

The laugh came free, the avalanche broke. It carried through Tosher's body until he was beset by racking coughs. Tears streamed down his cheeks.

The dog resumed its barking, throwing itself at the locked door.

Donovan stood up. Peta likewise.

'Thanks, Tosher,' he said. 'I know that must have cost you.'

Tosher sniffed, breathed in deep, wheezing gasps. 'Cost you five hundred quid. Hope it was worth it . . .'

Donovan and Peta left the house. From the street they heard the trapped dog still howling, still fighting inside.

The iron-grey sky was depositing rusty drizzle on the blighted shantytown streets.

Donovan had never been so grateful for fresh air in his life.

27

'I know what you're up to.'

Keenyside almost dropped his coffee. He chose that particular machine because it was the most inaccessible,
underused one in the whole station. He should have been
alone. He turned round. Janine was standing behind him.
She looked different. She was smiling. He glanced around
quickly: no one else about.

'What d'you mean, you know what I'm up to?'

'Just that,' she said, the smile deepening.

Another quick look round: no one about. He wanted to
grab hold of her, throw her against the wall, slap her stupid,
irritating mouth shut. Instead he tried his old charm. He put
on a smile of his own.

'So what am I up to, then?'

'Drugs, for a start.'

'Drugs? I don't—'

'I know how you rip off dealers. Do deals with suppliers.
Blackmail your informants into sellin' the stuff, beat them
up . . .' She shrugged. 'Shall I keep goin'?'

'Anything else?'

Another smile. 'That'd be tellin'.'

Keenyside thought straight away of Huntley. The upcoming deal. Swallowed hard. He looked at Janine properly.
There was a self-assurance about her that had previously
been absent. It unnerved him.

'What d'you want?' His voice was small, dry.

'Lots of things,' she said. 'My own back on you, mainly. But I'll accept money. To keep me quiet.'

His discomfort must have shown on his face. She laughed at him. He felt himself reddening, his hands beginning to shake. His self-control was slipping.

'How much?'

'Fifty thousand.'

He sneered. 'Fuck off.'

'Fifty thousand,' she repeated. She moved closer to him; her face took on a harder aspect. 'You owe me a lot more than that.'

Keenyside recoiled. Coffee spilled over the sides of the plastic cup he was holding. He had burned his fingers.

'All right,' he said, trying to breathe calmly. He needed time to think, time to plan. 'Fifty thousand. How d'you—'

'I'll let you know where and when,' she said. 'But it'll be soon.'

He stared at her. She looked fitter and healthier than she had for a long time. The last traces of his influence were gone. She was beyond his control.

He didn't like that.

He tried the charm again, reached out his hand to her.

'Look, Janine . . .'

She stepped back.

'No, Alan,' she said, fire dancing in her eyes, 'you never touch me again. Ever. Not even one finger.' She sighed, smoothed down the front of her blouse. Smiled at him.

'Well,' she said, 'I'd better be gettin' back. I'll be in touch.'

She turned, went through the doorway, back into the office and walked off. Keenyside watched the confident swing of her hips.

Others did too.

Keenyside felt rage build within him, impotent anger that events were slipping beyond his control.

His hands were shaking. He clenched the plastic cup tight, the liquid vibrating.

He threw the cup at the wall, watched the coffee explode in angry arcs, dribble away.

He turned, stormed off.

Trying to find a way to bring things back under his control.

Jamal opened his eyes. And smiled.

Another morning in that comfortable bed. Another night of the best sleep he had ever had.

He threw back the covers, grabbed the towelling dressing gown off the end of the bed. It was too big but that was good; he wrapped himself up in it, felt luxuriously cocooned with the feel and smell of the freshly laundered fabric against his skin.

Safe.

He went into the bathroom, the trace of a smile still on his lips.

At first he had been wary. Amar appearing the way he did, smashing the john's face in and announcing Joe Donovan had sent him . . . it wasn't what he was expecting.

He told him so while they ate their kebab together. Amar had just laughed.

Jamal looked serious. 'You ain't Five-0, are you?'

Amar shook his head. 'Do I look like it?'

'Nah, man, but you ain't takin' me to them, are you?'

'Why would I do that?'

Jamal's face darkened. 'You know, man. 'Cause of that thing at Father Jack's.'

'All in the past,' said Amar. 'He's in custody now. Going to be charged with lots of stuff. Even murder.'

'Murder? Who'd he kill?'

'His boy. Si.'

Jamal's face changed again. He nearly said something to Amar, something he may have regretted later.

Jamal asked how Si had been killed. Amar told him he had been beaten to death with a metal bar. Jamal's face became pale.

'You OK?' asked Amar.

'Yeah . . . yeah . . . They sure it was him? Jack?'

Amar looked straight at him. 'I was there. I saw.'

Jamal searched his face, his eyes, for the truth. Found no lie in what Amar had said.

'You sure?'

'Yes. Father Jack killed Si.'

Jamal saw it: a flinch. Only briefly, there then gone. But he saw it.

And chose to ignore it. Amar too.

'You batty, yeah?' Jamal asked, his mouth full of meat and bread.

'Yeah,' said Amar. 'You OK with that?'

'Fine, man. No problem. Batty men only like other batty men. Not boys. Never had no trouble with batty men.'

Amar laughed.

Then back to Amar's flat. Which was stunning. High up, with a view of the quayside. Amar started to tell him how he had got it, something to do with favours, working for free and a little leverage in the right places, but Jamal wasn't listening. He was admiring the view through the plate-glass window. He sat on the sofa, admiring the décor, then fell asleep.

He woke up in bed. Amar must have carried him. He checked the time. He had slept for nearly twelve hours.

Jamal asked if he could go out, to which Amar replied, whenever he wanted. He'd give him a key. He wasn't a prisoner. Jamal looked around. Decided he would rather stay in.

Amar seemed uneasy around Jamal, like he wasn't used to

coping with children, didn't know how to deal with him. However, as soon as Jamal set eyes on the PS2 and challenged Amar to a game of Grand Theft Auto: San Andreas, they realized they were going to get along just fine.

The sickness was kept at bay.

Jamal had just stepped out of the shower and walked into the living room when he heard the front door opening, slamming shut.

He stiffened with fear.

'I'm not a great cook,' came a voice from the hall, 'but I can do a fry-up. Fancy that?'

Jamal sighed in relief, said that he did.

Amar entered the room, bag-laden. Stopped when he saw Jamal's face. 'What's the matter with you? Look like you've seen a ghost.'

Jamal assured him it was nothing, even offered him a little smile. Amar didn't probe, went to the kitchen area, put the bags down.

'You can eat bacon, yeah?' he asked. 'You're not Muslim?'

'Nah, man. You?'

'Oh, I eat anything,' said Amar. 'Well, within reason. Why don't you give me a hand?'

Jamal did. They ate. Enjoyed it. Afterwards, Jamal looked around the flat again, sat back. Smiled.

'You're OK, man,' he said. 'Food, PS2 . . . like stayin' at a big brov's flat, you get me?'

Amar smiled.

'I'm ready to talk about that disc now,' Jamal said.

'I'll go and get some recording gear.' Amar left the kitchen, trying not to look too excited.

'Yeah,' said Jamal to himself. He sat back.

Safe.

Keenyside paused, looked around. Made sure no one was

hiding in the darkness, watching him. He began undoing the lock. Once he'd opened the door he gave another look around, then entered, locking the door firmly behind him.

Things were moving too fast. He had to take charge, regain control.

He kept repeating those words like a mantra.

Janine. *Beat them up.* The words had given her away. He followed her out of work. To the Prince of Wales. And there they were together.

Janine and Mikey Blackmore. Then thinking they'd blackmail him to keep them quiet.

Pathetic.

Nothing but minor irritations, but ones that still had to be dealt with. Stick them in the mercy seat. No. Recall Hammer from wherever he was, get him to take care of them. He couldn't have something as irrelevant as them spoiling things now. Brutal but necessary. The amount of money at stake justified it.

It justified everything.

But he didn't need Hammer for what he was about to do.

He waited until his eyes acclimatized to the inner gloom then moved forward. He saw his breath as steam, felt the cold in the building immediately. He looked over at the radiator. Saw Colin and Caroline Huntley huddled into their own blankets.

Unmoving.

His steps quickened. Was it that cold?

He reached them. Caroline stirred. He gave a sigh of relief. She looked up, saw it was him, looked away again.

'Hello, Caroline,' he said.

She didn't reply.

'You should be huddled up together,' he said; 'keep warm that way.'

'Fuck off, Alan,' she said, her voice almost a groan of

pain. 'I wouldn't go near him or you. Not after what you've done.'

Keenyside ignored her. He had more important things to think about than hurt feelings. He looked at Colin Huntley. Even in the weak light of the lockup he didn't look well. His skin was pale, almost opaque. He was still cradling his injured arm. Shunted up against the wall, his position almost foetal. Despite the cold there was sweat on his brow.

Don't die, thought Keenyside. At least don't die before you've done what I want you to do.

'Colin.'

Colin Huntley opened his eyes. His vision looked glassy and vague.

'Are you ready to do it, Colin?'

Colin just stared at him.

Keenyside's voice became quiet, his breathing controlled. His hands were shaking. 'Because if you're not, something horrible's going to happen to Caroline. And I'm going to make you watch.'

No response.

'I've tried to be reasonable,' Keenyside continued, 'but you won't cooperate. I don't want to hurt your daughter, but you're leaving me no option.'

He reached into his overcoat pocket, brought out a hunting knife and a roll of gaffer tape.

Caroline tried to pull away. The chain stopped her.

'This is more in sorrow than anger, Colin.' He pulled out a length of tape, cut it off with his teeth. 'Whatever happens from now on is on your head.'

Keenyside slipped the knife back into his pocket and turned to Caroline. She put her hands before her face, ready to fight back. Keenyside swiftly kicked her in the ribs. She keeled over, gasping. He pulled her head back by the hair, stuck the length of tape over her mouth.

Face contorted with pain, she tried to pull it off. Keenyside pulled her up, wrist straining at the cuff, and punched her. She fell down again.

He pulled her hands together behind her, painfully twisting her as he went, and bound them with tape. She was half slumped, half propped against the radiator.

She began to cry.

Keenyside looked at Colin. 'Say the word and this all stops.'

Colin said nothing.

Keenyside pulled out the knife, grabbed Caroline by the hair until she had lost her balance, placed the tip of the blade beneath her eyes.

'Ready to make that call yet, Colin? Ready for this to be over?'

Colin just stared, his face a mask of pain.

'This is your daughter here.'

He pushed the knife closer to her skin. A teardrop of blood appeared below her eye, ran down the blade.

'Look, Colin, she's crying. She wants you to help her. Won't Daddy help his daughter?'

Caroline's body was heaving with sobs. Colin looked about to start himself.

'One call, Colin, and it's all over.' He moved the knife under her eye. Blood trickled out and down.

'Come on, Colin. You know I'll do it.'

Colin began to shake.

'I'll fucking do it, Colin. You know I will!'

Colin jumped as if he had been slapped. He sighed. Gave a slow nod of his head.

Keenyside smiled. Breathed a huge sigh of relief. Back in full control again. 'That's the spirit.'

Keenyside pocketed the knife, let Caroline drop. He took out from his coat a re-chipped, untraceable mobile that he had liberated from a dealer. From another pocket he produced a piece of paper on which was written a number. He began to key in the number.

'You know,' he said as he did so, 'all this could have been avoided. It's all your fault, Colin. All of it. You had to go down to London, talk to that journalist. I don't think you realized how serious I was about this. The lengths I would go to, to make sure this deal would go through. I bet you do now.' He gave a little laugh. 'Oh yes.'

He finished dialling, put the phone to his ear.

'It's ringing.'

Trying to quell the excitement rising within, Keenyside kneeled down, placed the phone against Colin's ear. The injured man's breath was rank with decay.

He heard the line click as it was answered. Locked eyes with Colin, nodded at him to proceed.

'This is Colin Huntley.'

His voice sounded as broken and weary as his body looked.

'We're ready to deal.'

Keenyside smiled.

It was finally happening.

The Barn at the Biscuit Factory. And Francis Sharkey was trying to bloat out his expense account as much as possible. He was surprised to find somewhere like this in Newcastle, although he had to admit this trip to the north-east had actively challenged his prejudices. In a positive way.

The Biscuit Factory was an original art store housed over two floors in a converted factory in the Shieldfield area of Newcastle. Although Sharkey didn't know much about art, he knew a lot about investment and was sufficiently impressed to consider making a return journey accompanied by someone who would be able to guide him wisely, not only on what to buy but how to make it tax deductible or a claimable expense.

The Barn restaurant on the ground floor he found very acceptable. Chunky wooden furniture, bare walls and muted lighting attempted to re-create a kind of Mid-western atmosphere. He was happy to go along with it, especially since his starter of wild mushroom risotto had gone down well and the Chilean Merlot was proving most pleasant. He sipped, waiting for his main course of roast lamb.

His mobile rang.

He drained his glass, replaced it on the table, put his phone to his ear.

'Francis Sharkey.'

The waiter came to replenish the glass. He nodded his thanks.

'This is Colin Huntley.'

Sharkey froze. His heart skipped a beat.

'We're ready to deal.'

His dinner was placed before him. It looked wonderful and smelled delicious but he didn't want it any more. He had suddenly lost his appetite.

He leaned forward as if shielding his conversation from the other diners.

'I'm listening,' he said.

Mikey Blackmore opened the door of his flat, fish and chips under one arm, entered.

For once he didn't notice the poverty and squalor, feel the sense of failure that usually assailed him on returning. He was too excited.

Janine had set the plan in motion. She would give Keenyside a time and place. Mikey would be there.

'What are you goin' to do?' she had asked him.

'Make him pay,' Mikey had replied.

A look of fear crossed her face.

'Not like that,' Mikey said quickly. 'I mean, make him pay. Give us money.'

'Oh.' Janine looked much more relieved.

Reassured.

He went into the bedroom, kneeled down with some difficulty, his ribs still hurting, felt under the bed.

Pulled out what he wanted.

Smiled to himself.

'Don't worry, Janine,' he said out loud. 'I won't hurt Alan Keenyside.'

He pointed the gun at his reflection in the mirror. Saw his battered face. Thought of Janine and her pain. Remembered who was responsible for both. Mimed pulling the trigger.

Laughed.

'I won't hurt him,' he said. 'I'll kill him.'

Mikey felt the happiest he had been in years.

PART FOUR

IN SECRET LOVE WE DROWN

28

The bar was heaving, standing room only. Air a thick cocktail of fag and spliff smoke, sweat, aged leather and unwashed denim. Old, scarred wooden surfaces of bar and tables were wet with spilled alcohol. Lights cast sporadic, dim illumination. Doom-laden riffs and chest-hammering bass spewed from the wall-mounted speakers like the earth violently giving up its dead. Heads nodded along, some mouthed lyrics.

Cradle of Filth: 'The Principle of Evil Made Flesh'.

The barroom shook; a jubilant jig of rejected assumptions and values, the thump of a sick and angry heart.

Hammer stood at the end of the bar nursing his mineral water and watching, smiling. He had chosen carefully: the right pub in the right-sized town with the right clientele. He took in the atmosphere; it only increased his appetite.

He flexed his knuckles, admired the designs. Drew sustenance from the words.

He had divided the clientele into four main tribes: hardcore, way-of-life metallers proudly displaying their piercings and tattoos, bikers carrying their predisposition to violence as comfortably as they wore their chapter-patched leathers, a smattering of teenaged student goths, either pale and slim-wristed or shapeless and bulky, taking the Rice/Brite tourist route on their way to eventual, comfortable lives, and real headcases. All, by circumstance or design, outcasts, wearing that description like a badge or a brand. But they were nothing as compared with him. But no one had been cast out further than him. He was their king, their superior in every way, if they did but know it.

The principle of evil made flesh.

This wasn't work, this was pleasure.

He waited, knowing his target would appear soon.

The song ended, another one took its place: Slipknot: 'Me Inside'.

Heads bobbed harder. The pub picked up the vibe of the song, made the atmosphere angrier. Voices sang/snarled in Corey Taylor imitation. He picked up on it, nodded along in time, even mouthed the words: 'You can't kill me, coz I'm already inside you . . .'

Then that familiar tingle, that lurch in the pit of his stomach.

The victim. Standing at the bar, brandishing a ten-pound note.

Late twenties, tall, stocky and stacked. The sides of his head shaved but stubbled, greasy hair pulled back and tied at his neck in a long mohican. Muscled arms decorated with biker tattoos bulged from the sleeves of his ancient, faded Motorhead T-shirt. Old, ripped, dark-matter-encrusted jeans almost stood by themselves, biker boots – real, worn working ones – protruded from the ends and covered his feet. Fat strained and spread over his belt like a splitting bin bag full of rotting food. His bearing, his features a mask of arrogance and danger: seemingly unafraid of anyone or anything in the world.

The others in the pub were avoiding the biker; he emanated waves of violence like the blast range of a nuclear bomb. He inspired fear and that fear bought him respect.

Perfect.

He felt the biker look towards him. His gaze flinched slightly, showed a slight unfamiliar tremor of unease, and Hammer knew he had him.

Hammer smiled. The biker curled his lip. Hammer winked. The biker shook his head dismissively and turned away, carrying the drinks back to his chapter clustered round a small table. He could see them talking, knew that the furtive glances were being directed at him. They all began nodding and exchanging cruel, unpleasant smiles. He knew what they were planning. Bring it on. It was what he was there for.

He finished his drink, slapped the glass down on the bar and made his way unsteadily towards the back door. On the way he gave a lurch towards the seated biker, elbowing him in the back, causing him to spill his drink as it made its way to his mouth. The mohicaned biker turned round, anger blazing in his eyes.

'Sorry,' said Hammer in his weakest, most victim-like voice. 'Bit pissed. No harm done, eh?'

The biker turned round, pleased to have the excuse he was looking for.

'What's your game, eh? Eh?'

Hammer gave a wide-eyed, drunk-innocent look. 'No game. No problem. Specially for big, tough lads like you. Could quite go for a man in a leather jacket.' He squeezed the biker on the shoulder in an affectionate gesture and smiled. 'Goin' home now. Nighty night.'

And lurched towards the back door.

Outside, the air was cold, the sky scraped black. The alleyway at the side of the pub was dotted with overspilled drinkers. Hammer walked past them to the end of the alleyway, as if making his drunken way across the exposed, empty, gravelled wasteland that doubled as car and bike park and local fly-tipping area, and waited.

But not for long. The door was flung open and the biker, followed by his cronies, emerged. They were fired up, tooled up with pickaxe handles, baseball bats and lengths of chain, fight-ready. They saw him. The biker made his way towards him, turned him by the shoulder. He pretended to be surprised.

'Don't know what you're fuckin' playin' at,' snarled the biker, 'winkin' an' laughin' at me, if you're queer or not, but it doesn't matter. I think you need to be taught a lesson.'

He could smell beer and dead flesh in the man's mouth. He tried to look scared.

'What? Wh . . . what have I done?'

'Takin' the piss,' he said. 'You must have a death wish.'

The other bikers grabbed him from behind. He allowed himself to be caught, gave what he considered the requisite amount of struggling without actually getting away.

'Hold him, lads.'

The biker made a fist of his right hand, punched him in the stomach with it. He doubled over in apparent pain. The others laughed. The biker hit him again.

Hammer looked up, breathing heavily. He had tensed, expecting the blows, and tried to absorb them as much as he could. But they hadn't hurt him. He wouldn't allow himself to be hurt.

The biker reached into his jacket, pulled out a small axe. The chipped, stained blade glinted dully from the light of the distant streetlamp. He held it up and pulled it back, made to strike. Hammer flinched. The bikers laughed.

'Scared, are you?' The biker gave a mirthless laugh. 'You'll be fuckin' terrified by the time I'm finished with you.'

His chapter laughed, whooping and calling, smacking wood against palm, rattling chains, goading him on. The biker smiled, enjoying himself, playing to his captive audience.

'Let him go,' said the biker. 'Let's have a bit of a chase.'

The bikers released Hammer, who fell to the ground on his knees.

'Get up, you cunt,' snarled the biker. 'Take it like a man.'

Kicks and punches, jeers and spitting. The bikers circled the two men, one prone; the prey brought to ground, the other the hunter, triumphant. He curled into a ball, covered his head with his arms. They gave exploratory prods with their bats and handles, building themselves up for the signal to let them loose.

'Up.'

Hammer felt himself being hauled to his feet. The biker leered in his face.

'You picked the wrong man to mess with.'

The bikers laughed.

The other man smiled. Straightened his back to full height. No trace of his earlier faux fear or smiling clumsiness now, only that trembling feeling he experienced inside when he knew his hunger was about to be assuaged. 'So did you,' he said.

Before the biker could attack, Hammer head-butted him. The biker's head flipped backwards, blood squirting from the sudden wound, but he didn't go down.

The others were too stunned to react. It cost them. Hammer whirled round, disarming a biker of his pickaxe handle as he went. In the same fluid movement, he swung the handle at the nearest biker, connecting with the side of the man's skull. So much force was behind the blow that the man's head crumpled, like a punched paper bag. He fell to his knees, blood pumping down over his ears. The other bikers seemed locked in time, not knowing whether to fight or fly. Hammer gave them no choice.

He held the handle like a kendo stick, swinging it to and fro, his grip loose, never once losing eye contact. The bikers' realized positions had been reversed. They were now the prey. One of the chapter, fat, gruff and bearded, fumbled inside his pocket for a blade, found it, lunged forward.

Hammer whirled out of the way with near-balletic skill. Dodged left. Then right. Then right again. The biker was becoming increasingly desperate, his strikes having less precision. Hammer smiled.

'That the best you can do?' he said. 'This is getting boring.'

He flicked his foot towards the other's wrist, sending the knife spinning into the night. He followed up with a smash to the mouth from the stick. Teeth and blood flew on impact. The biker fell, hands clutching his ruined mouth.

Hammer heard a sound behind him, turned. Too late. The first biker was bringing the axe down on to his back. Hammer pivoted to one side, the blade catching his left shoulder as it did so. It ripped through his T-shirt, breaking skin and drawing blood.

'Bastard!' he shouted. 'Now you've got me fucking angry!'

He turned and brought the handle down on the biker's wrist, disarming him and breaking his wrist in one movement. It cracked loudly. He cried out in pain.

'You've just got me started,' roared Hammer.

He chopped the biker with the stick, once, twice. He fell. Hammer continued smashing at the fallen man, driving him on to his back. Rage built up within his body, channelled down his arms, transferred into the handle, was released on the prone body.

Blood and bodily tissue sprayed out. He ignored it.

Pure rage-nourishment was drawn into his body. He felt himself growing, his body expanding and with it his power, his strength.

Time stood still. All that existed was Hammer, his weapon, his hunger and the lump of meat before him.

He didn't know how long he stood there, but eventually he was too exhausted to continue. Satiated and sighing, his arms trembling with exertion, his chest burning with effort, he looked down. There were no recognizable features left. The body had ruptured and split, like it had been dropped from a great height then danced over. He smiled. He felt tired happiness at seeing the body like that, a post-prandial contentment.

Hammer looked around. The bikers had retreated. A crowd of wary drinkers were standing well back, horrified by what they had witnessed.

Hammer turned, walked away. The crowd too traumatized by what they had seen to move, too scared to call 999, to do anything.

He felt eyes on him as he walked, blood and matter from the body. And something else.

Fear. And respect.

He smiled.

He had destroyed the biker's body. He had eaten the man's soul.

Respect.

He felt ten feet tall. A gargantuan, beautiful superhero. A blood-stain'd king, an emperor among peasants.

They feared him.

They loved him.

Music from the pub jukebox travelled faintly over the night, trailed behind him. He smiled at the irony. 'The Hammer' by Motorhead.

He wasn't worried about being caught. He chose his locations carefully. Made sure he had a similar relationship with at least one local copper as he had with Keenyside. Made sure he knew where the bodies were buried.

He walked away, flexing his arms, back to the Vectra.

As he reached the car his phone rang. He pulled it out, smearing it with blood, placed it to his ear.

'Get up here quick.' Keenyside. 'You're needed.'

'OK.'

'Where are you?'

'East Midlands. Leicester, I think. Took your advice. Had some time off. Bit of R and R. Good workout.'

He heard sirens behind him, travelling in the opposite direction. They wouldn't look at him. The car was too non-descript.

'Right. Well, straight back. I need you. It's on.'

Hammer cut the connection, threw the phone on the seat.

Smiled.

'Ah well,' he said out loud, 'back to work.'

He slipped a Cannibal Corpse CD into the player, headed off to Newcastle.

29

Caroline lay on her side. Feigning sleep; eyes open. Unable to stop touching the wound beneath her eye. Unable to believe it was all real.

She looked at her father. Studied him. Wondered who this stranger was that had unburdened his secret life before her. Craved her understanding. Begged her forgiveness.

Caroline hadn't responded. She was still struggling to process the events of the last few weeks. More than understanding and forgiveness, she wanted the clock turned back. Wanted safety and comfort. Her old life again, the one she had thought was real.

But that was gone. Like a blown cover in a cheesy spy movie. Gone. Never to return.

Her father was backed up against the wall as far as he could go. He looked ill, broken. She felt for him. On a basic human level. Whatever else, he was still her father.

And he had told her more. Everything, he said.

'Look,' he had said, 'you don't know how bad I felt about Tosher. The other travellers.'

'I'm sure that's a great comfort to them.' Caroline's voice as cold as the air they were forced to breathe.

Colin sighed, wiped his forehead against his arm. He was hot. Feverish. He carried on talking.

'You have to listen,' he said. 'You have to understand.' He sighed again. Searched for the right words, the right tone.

'What I did was wrong,' he said, 'very wrong. All of it. I saw Alan Keenyside almost every day.' He shook his head.

'He seemed to be flourishing . . . big cars, holiday home . . . while I had nothing. But guilt. And seeing you . . . It was eating me, killing me like the cancer that took your mother. I had to square it. Atone for it.'

Caroline let him talk. His face was twisted by pain. Reliving it over again.

'I tried to contact Tosher.' He stole a glance at her, gauging her reaction.

'Why?' she said.

'To see if he was all right. I don't know . . . to see if there was some way I might help him.'

Caroline shook her head. 'In the hope he'd forgive you.'

'Well, I had to do something.' His voice rose. He calmed himself, continued. 'But I didn't know how. I thought of hiring a private detective or something, but that didn't feel right. Then I remembered this journalist. Joe Donovan from the *Herald*. He'd been around at the time. I tried to contact him, hoping he could put me in touch.' He sighed. 'But he'd left the paper. They gave me another journalist, Gary Myers, to talk to. By this time I was at my wits' end. I'd had enough. So I thought, what the hell. Told him I had a story for him.'

Another look towards Caroline. She was still, waiting for him to fill the void between them with more words.

'We arranged a meeting. Secret. Neutral ground,' Colin continued. 'Away from home. Gary Myers used this place in King's Cross. London. A hotel where prostitutes and rent boys went.' Colin gave a small laugh. 'If anyone saw us, he said, we'd just be mistaken for customers.'

Caroline put her head back. 'Jesus . . .'

Colin noted her reaction. 'Anyway,' he continued, slightly embarrassed, 'I talked to him. Told him everything. A calculated risk, but if I was going to get any peace I thought it was worth it.'

Colin attempted to lean forward, into his story now. 'And he listened. It was the first time I'd spoken it aloud. To anyone. It felt like a . . . like an unburdening of the soul.'

'A confession,' said Caroline. 'Like you'd give to a Catholic priest.'

Colin's features became animated. 'Exactly right.'

'Or a policeman.'

Colin's face fell. Connection lost. He sighed. 'Gary didn't think it a good idea to contact Tosher. But he came up with a better one.'

Caroline waited.

'A sting.'

She frowned. 'A what?'

'A sting,' he repeated. 'A good old-fashioned, Fleet Street-style sting, Gary said.'

'To do what?'

'Entrap Alan Keenyside.'

Caroline just stared at him.

Colin continued. 'It would get the story into the open. Alan Keenyside would be punished for his actions. The whole world would see it.'

'And it would sell papers.'

'Yes,' said Colin, a light gleaming in his eyes. 'But more important it would give me peace. You don't know how much . . . how much I needed that to happen. There was a chance I could have gone to prison for my part. I knew that. But it was a chance I was willing to take. I had to. We came up with a plan. One that played on Alan Keenyside's weaknesses.'

Gesturing with his shackled, damaged hands, he was now lost in his story.

'He was always asking me about NorTec. What we were working on, any industrial secrets he could pass on, that kind of thing. And the biggie: had I been approached by a buyer offering big money for some secret formula.' He shook his head. 'He kept on at me. On and on. You must get approached all the time, what are you working on now that you can sell, I know how to deal with these people, I'll sell it for you . . . On and on . . .'

Colin sighed. 'Now, industrial spying is very big business. And I get approached more often than you think. But in reality it's, I don't know, a rival company wanting to be first with a new . . . washing-up liquid. Which there is a lot of money in. A lot. But Keenyside was thinking al-Qaeda, international terrorists. James Bond. He was a fantasist. So we came up with a scenario. One that used his fantasy of being some kind of international dealer against them.'

Colin paused for breath, continued. 'I told him I was working on a special project. The experimental development of a genetically engineered compound for use in the treatment of cancer. Something that when introduced into the body would be programmed only to destroy cancer cells.' He smiled. 'Sounds plausible, doesn't it?'

'I wish we'd had it a couple of years ago,' said Caroline.

'So do I,' said Colin sadly. 'In fact, I wished it really existed. But it doesn't. But Alan Keenyside thought it did. Especially when I told him how lucrative the field of cancer research is. Like looking for the Holy Grail. And the one who finds it and patents it is made for life. And if that wasn't enough for him, I told him this compound also had a wide-open market application. It could be changed, reprogrammed, to attack any kind of cell in the human body. Weaponized, even.'

'And I suppose you told him you had a secret buyer for this compound.'

'I did.'

'And he believed you.'

'Jumped at it. I told him I couldn't do it on my own.

Needed someone to be the front man. Almost bit my hand off. Even when I said he'd have to break in to NorTec.'

Caroline almost choked in disbelief. 'What? The one that was on the news?'

He nodded.

'I asked you about it.' She frowned. 'That was you?'

'Keenyside, actually.' Colin couldn't keep the pride from his voice. 'I just coordinated.'

'They said it was eco-terrorists or environmentalists who had lost their nerve. Nothing was stolen, you said.'

'Nothing was stolen. There was nothing to steal. I showed Keenyside where to get into the grounds. Gave him a time. Met him, handed him a case containing what he thought was a sample of the compound. Told him I'd take the written formula out myself.'

Caroline shook her head.

'I wanted Keenyside's complicity.' Colin's eyes danced with electricity. 'Photographic evidence of him breaking into NorTec and committing a criminal act. And thanks to Gary Myers, I got it.'

Caroline rubbed her forehead, her eyes. 'I don't believe I'm hearing this . . .'

'Caroline . . .' He stretched out a hand.

'Don't fucking Caroline me!' She tried to stand up, pull away from him. The cuffs reminded her she couldn't. 'You've had an ex-boyfriend of mine seriously hurt, destroyed innocent people's lives, and now you're telling me you're some kind of cross between a criminal mastermind and James fucking Bond!'

'Please don't swear, Caroline. You know I don't like it when you swear.'

That sounded more like her father. Or one aspect of him: the picky, pedantic paternalist she tolerated until the warm, friendly one returned. Hearing that, she now didn't know which aspect represented her real father. The one she loved. Perhaps all of them.

Perhaps none.

Caroline tried to speak. The words were exasperatedly choked off in her throat. She fought for control. Regained it.

'So what happened next? A car chase through the streets of Ponteland? A giant death ray aimed at Morpeth? What?'

Colin sighed. 'I realize it must sound ridiculous . . .'

Caroline snorted.

'But it's true. Things like this happen all the time and we never get to hear about them. Secrets and lies. The way of the world. Real life isn't what we see every day. Real life is what happens under the surface.'

'I think I'm well aware of that now.'

Silence fell again. The lockup seemed especially cold.

'So,' said Caroline eventually, 'where did it all go wrong?'

'Well, Keenyside may be a fantasist, but he's a dangerous one.' Colin gave a sad little laugh. Looked around the lockup. 'I didn't realize how desperately he wanted to believe in it.' Locked eyes with Caroline. 'I misjudged him.' He dropped his gaze. 'Sorry.'

Caroline said nothing. They sat in silence for a while.

The light faded in Colin's eyes. He began to resemble a sick old man once more. His voice was tired now.

'Well, things came to a head. Gary Myers and I met regularly in the King's Cross hotel room. Gary ran everything by the *Herald*'s lawyer, Francis Sharkey, to get a legal standpoint. He liked the sound of it. So much so that he wanted in. It made sense. Extra bit of security, avoiding entrapment. Gary and him would pose as buyers, have the meeting. Sharkey also wanted a full first-hand record of the plan. So I told the whole thing to Gary and he committed it to minidisc.' Colin sighed. 'Unfortunately, he never had a chance to do anything with it, poor bugger.'

'What d'you mean?'

'Keenyside was having me followed. Obviously didn't want to lose his investment. Well, you've met Hammer. His barely house-trained psychopath.'

Caroline shivered from something more than cold.

Colin continued, his features in shadow. 'Hammer . . . found me. Brought Gary and me here. We made a deal with each other. Don't tell them about the sting. Make out I had an attack of conscience and talked to a journalist.'

He shook his head. 'But then there was the disc . . . what Keenyside would do when he heard it.' He sighed. 'But that didn't happen. The minidisc player with the disc inside it went missing from the hotel room.'

'How?'

'No idea. But it never turned up. If it had, I doubt we'd be alive.'

Caroline looked at her father. She wanted to tell him he was being melodramatic, but seeing his sad, old, tired eyes she knew he was telling her the truth. She looked away.

'I was needed to make the call,' said Colin. 'And you were needed to make me make the call.'

Caroline's voice was quiet. 'But now you've done that.'

Colin nodded.

Silence, cold and hard, filled the room up to bursting.

'And it was answered,' said Colin, his voice lifting lightly. 'I never expected that.' He looked at his daughter, a faint glimmer of hope dancing behind his eyes. 'If the call was answered, it means the meeting is set to go ahead. It means there's a chance we'll get out of this alive.'

Caroline sighed. 'Our only chance.'

She drew her knees up to her body, wrapped her free arm

round them, lowered her forehead. Eventually there came the sounds of muffled sobbing.

Colin watched. Unable to approach her, unable to comfort her.

He turned away, looked at the floor, sighed.

Said nothing.

The bus pulled up to the stop, disgorged its passengers. Westerhope on the westernmost fringes of Newcastle. Late-autumn early-evening darkness. The threat of winter in the air.

Janine walked her usual route home. Over the pedestrian crossing, turning left off the main road, going further down, then left along the hedge-lined alleyway running by the side of the church. She always worried about that path. It was well lit but lonely, the hedges casting deep shadows into the churchyard.

But tonight she would walk it. Because she was feeling good. She was about to come into money.

She had to admit, she had taken some convincing. But Mikey had managed.

Mikey. She smiled.

Janine had found him creepy at first, the kind of person your parents tell you to avoid when you're younger. But he wasn't like that when you got to know him. He was a sad little man, really. Even sweet in his own kind of way.

But not that sweet. Not sweet enough.

Footsteps behind her. She took a sharp intake of breath, turned, quickly.

No one.

She breathed out. Berated herself for panicking.

Her recent experiences with Alan Keenyside had left her shaky. Another deep breath. She rationalized. Other people used this footpath. Plenty of them. It was just a normal commuter short cut.

Just in case, she quickened her step.

Heard footsteps behind her again.

Probably no one. Not a monster, at any rate. Just someone on their way home from work. Or Mikey.

She sighed. Sad though he was, she suspected he could become a nuisance. She would have to be firm with him. Tell him that she wasn't interested in him. Perhaps they could be friends, but . . .

The footsteps got louder, came closer.

It would be Mikey. She knew it now.

She turned, ready to show him her irritation, hear what pretext he had followed her home on, see his morose little face drop further when she told him to go away.

But it wasn't Mikey.

He was big, shaven-headed. Powerfully built. Violence emanated from him.

Her eyes showed fear. He smiled. Streetlight caught the blue-jewelled tooth in his mouth.

Her legs felt as if they had been set in concrete.

She screamed, but no sound came out.

He advanced, raised his hands. FEAR and LOVE.

Coming towards her at an unavoidable speed.

Those words the last thing she saw before darkness brutally, forcefully, claimed her.

30

Donovan stared at Sharkey. Sharkey looked around the room, saw Peta, Jamal and Amar staring at him, too. None of them smiled.

'Well?' said Donovan.

Sharkey ostentatiously cleared his throat. Pulled his silk dressing gown about him. 'I tried to tell you . . .' The words sounded weak.

Donovan said nothing. Remained unblinking.

Sharkey shifted uncomfortably on the hotel chair, as if his buttocks were hot. 'You wouldn't listen . . .' Even weaker.

Sharkey's hotel room. Nearly midnight.

Donovan had phoned Amar on the way back from Jaywick, told him to come to his room at the hotel, bring Jamal. An information-sharing session. Urgent.

Donovan was pleased to see Jamal. Surprised, in fact, at how pleased. Judging from the smile Jamal had given him, the feeling was evidently mutual. The boy looked relaxed, thought Donovan. Happy, even.

Then quickly down to business.

Peta and Donovan told of their meeting with Tosher. Amar went one better, played the recording of Jamal explaining what had been on the minidisc.

A sullen silence had followed. Broken when Donovan strode out of the room and down the hall. Banged frantically on Sharkey's door, shouted his name.

Sharkey had let them in, complaining about the noise but shutting up when he saw Donovan's expression. Donovan pushed him back into the room, straight on to a chair, told him what he had just learned. The others followed.

Donovan stood over the sitting lawyer, crossed his arms. Sharkey flinched at the movement. Donovan said nothing, stared, allowed his brain to process the information he had just absorbed.

Outside, the final Metro train of the night crossed the bridge. Inside was silence.

'Maria,' said Donovan eventually, his voice controlled, 'was sent to Newcastle by you because that's where the story was. Or rather, was going to be.'

Sharkey raised his hands, tried to protest. 'Ah. Now that's not fair. I was—'

Donovan talked over him. 'But you couldn't tell her what was happening, could you? You wouldn't even give her that respect, that decency.'

Sharkey tried again. Donovan ignored him.

'You couldn't. Because she might have called the whole thing off. Or gone to the police, spoken to someone.' Donovan was breathing heavily. 'And if she'd done that, she'd still be alive. And this little sting of yours wouldn't have gone massively out of control.'

'And why you, anyway?' Donovan's teeth were clenched tight. 'Why were you so bothered about all this?'

'Because,' Sharkey said, 'in my profession I've met a sickening amount of bent, amoral, even murderous coppers, and to have the opportunity to personally dispose of one was too good to miss.'

'And grab the glory.'

Sharkey looked affronted. 'I have more morality than you think.'

Donovan turned away from him, shaking with anger. And in that rage came another epiphany. He turned back to face Sharkey.

'You never had any information for me, did you? Nothing that would lead me to David. Nothing that would help me find my son . . .'

Sharkey stood up, hands before him as if preparing to ward off blows. 'Ah,' he said, scrabbling for his courtroom identity. 'In mitigation, I never said I did. If you remember, I quite distinctly said that we would give you access to as many resources and files as possible, plus the means to follow up any leads or sightings. My words were very specific.'

Donovan, breathing harder than an enraged bull: 'Course they fucking were . . .' He grabbed him by the front of his dressing gown, slamming him against the wall.

'Bastard!' shouted Donovan. 'You fucking bastard!'

'Look,' gasped Sharkey, winded, 'we needed you for this.'

'We?'

'All right, me. When Myers went missing and your name was reintroduced, I thought you'd be perfect for taking care of things instead, if needs be. When Gary turned up dead, I knew you had to be.'

'What d'you mean?'

Sharkey sighed. 'It had to be someone unknown to Keenyside but someone with comparable skills and talents to Gary Myers. Someone who knew the background. You were perfect.'

Donovan stared at him, eyes blazing. Too angry to speak.

'Unfortunately,' Sharkey continued, 'you weren't in quite the right frame of mind for the job. I needed something to sharpen you up.' His voice dropped. 'That's why I made you the offer.'

Donovan stared at him, eyes aflame, teeth bared.

'Look,' said Sharkey, exasperation overtaking his voice, 'I needed you to have your wits about you when the call came in.' He risked a smile. 'And it's come. Colin Huntley is alive and the deal is still on. All it needs is for you to front it.'

Sharkey raised his eyebrows: a question.

Donovan could no longer look at the man. He spun him round, threw him to the floor. Began kicking him.

'Bastard! Was it worth it . . . was it . . . you fucking bastard . . .'

Sharkey rolled round, tried to avoid the kicks, stop them from doing too much damage. Donovan kept going, all his pent-up anger channelled into the attack.

Peta and Amar were on him. One on each side, dragging him back, forcing him to the far corner of the room, holding him against the wall until his anger had dissipated.

Jamal covered his face with his hands. 'Oh my days . . .'

Sharkey lay still, tried to regain his breath. Slowly, he began to pull himself up. Pain lanced through his ribcage. He managed to prop himself up on his elbow, used the bed as leverage to reach his feet. Once upright, he felt his sides. They hurt.

He looked at Donovan; malevolent death beams lasered from his eyes.

'So,' said Sharkey, straightening his dressing gown, smoothing down his hair, 'do I take that as a yes?'

It took three attempts, but Mikey finally got the key in the lock.

He pushed the door, lost it to his fingers, heard it slam back against the wall. A dog began barking further down the block. Mikey ignored it. Didn't matter. He would be out of this place soon enough.

He closed the door, lurched down the hall.

Not drunk, he told himself, just merry.

A night in the pub. By himself. Mobile switched off. Planning. Plotting.

Keenyside's death. Then his subsequent romance with a grateful and free Janine.

He had imagined his plans in exquisite detail, the situations so real, the other players so tangible they had been there with him, talking to him. Perhaps a little too loudly, if the looks from the bar staff and other drinkers were anything to go by.

At kicking-out time he had gone willingly. Basking in the warm glow of an imaginary happy future.

Now, a round of toast, a cup of tea and a good night's sleep to top off a satisfactory evening.

He opened the living room door.

And froze.

In his old, threadbare armchair, head on one side, still. Already changing colour.

Janine.

Arm tied off, vein plumped up. Works on the floor beside her.

He sobered up immediately.

His heart was pounding fast, reaching bursting point. His chest felt like it was sucking air in through an eiderdown. His arms, legs, began to shake. Emotions flew at him fast, hit him hard like runaway trains.

He felt trapped, like he was back in prison.

'Keenyside . . .' He didn't realize he had spoken. 'You fucker . . .'

His bones gave way. He sank to his knees, flopped on the floor like a dying fish. Tears began welling behind his eyes.

Then he heard the sirens.

Faint, in the distance, but becoming louder, getting nearer.

Coming, he knew, for him.

They would never dare venture on to the estate under normal circumstances. Only if they were riding a dead cert.

And when they came down, they came down hard. Well tooled up. Riot gear. Dogs, even.

Mikey got slowly to his feet. Shook his head.

He had to get a grip. Had to get out.

He ran into the bedroom, felt under the bed. Found it. His gun. He slipped it into his overcoat pocket, felt round even further. His old tin box containing what money he had. He slipped that into his other pocket.

Then he was out of the door and off, adrenalin pushing his legs faster than he had ever used them. The fear of prison an effective deterrent.

The sirens became louder. Dogs started barking again.

Mikey set off round the darkened alleyways of the estate, hoped his knowledge of the shadow-overhung thoroughfares would be to his advantage.

Hoped he could get as far away as possible from the police.

Hoped he could be free.

Mikey ran for his life.

31

Intermezzo coffee bar. Nine thirty the following day. Friday morning.

TFI. But little sense of relaxation.

Donovan sat with his back to the red-padded wall of a booth sipping his large cappuccino. Peta next to him doing likewise. Opposite on stools were Nattrass and Turnbull, neither drinking, wearing work clothes and expressions of extreme annoyance.

Turnbull, Donovan noticed, was very ill at ease. He kept turning round, eyeballing the *Guardian/New Statesman*/European-novel-reading clientele, providing himself with a sub-audible running commentary of sneers and grunts on eavesdropped conversations. Despising anyone who wasn't part of his buttoned-down world.

Peta, he also noticed, seemed to be enjoying Turnbull's discomfort. She also seemed to be sitting very close to Donovan. Thigh against thigh. He affected not to notice.

Nattrass' focus was on the table. Purely business.

On the sound system: a compilation of the best of the Pixies. 'Debaser'. Worth it, thought Donovan, just to see Turnbull's face.

Donovan swallowed his coffee, replaced his cup on the saucer. Sat forward.

'Before I tell you anything,' he said, locking eyes with each of them in turn, 'I want certain assurances.'

Turnbull snorted. 'You got anything to tell me, you tell

me. Otherwise I'll do you for withholding information in a murder enquiry. At the very least.'

Donovan turned to Nattrass. 'Told you this meeting should have just been you and me.'

Nattrass didn't blink. 'What sort of assurances?' No questioning inflection. Just hard and flat.

'Ones that say this information was given free and willingly. And that none of the charges your judicially zealous colleague here was about to list can be used against the bringers of this information.'

Turnbull bristled, was about to argue; Nattrass silenced him with a look.

'Define "bringers",' she said.

'Myself, Peta here, Amar Miah and a boy named Jamal Jenkins.'

Nattrass kept those unblinking eyes on him. 'Anyone else?'

He thought of Sharkey. 'No.'

Nattrass looked between the two of them, weighing it up. 'All right,' she said eventually. 'Deal.'

Turnbull shook his head. Peta favoured him with a cloyingly sweet smile. This, Donovan noted, seemed to upset him more than the deal, the *Guardian* readers and the Pixies put together.

Donovan took another mouthful of coffee. Started to talk.

He told them everything. From his point of view, using the chronology of the facts he himself had experienced. He kept nothing out, held nothing back. No truth concealed, no opinion or supposition hidden. He no longer possessed the luxury of selectivity. Events had moved beyond that now.

Peta confirmed events, clarified situations. Supplemented Donovan's account.

Nattrass and Turnbull listened. Sometimes in amazement,

sometimes in anger, sometimes in awe. Never non-committally. They made notes. Asked for clarifications, repetitions.

They took everything in.

Finished, Donovan picked up his coffee, sat back, put it to his lips. Replaced it on the saucer. 'Cold,' he said. He looked between the two police. 'Well?'

Turnbull spoke first. 'I think we should bring this Sharkey character in. Throw the book at him.' His face twisted with disdain. 'Or does he qualify for your protection?'

'Do what you like with him,' said Donovan. 'He's a cunt.'

Peta and Nattrass both stared at him.

'Excuse me?' said Nattrass.

Donovan shrugged. 'Well, he is.'

Nattrass shook her head, studied her notes. 'This meeting,' she said. 'When's it taking place?'

'Today.'

'What?' Anger turned her face an immediate purple.

'Today. Six o'clock tonight. In the café bar on the ground floor of the Baltic. The big one with the glass front.'

Nattrass and Turnbull stared at him.

'We need more warning than that,' said Nattrass.

'Well, I'm sorry,' said Donovan, 'but there's nothing I can do about it. I just found out myself a few hours ago.'

Nattrass shook her head. 'This is almost too much to take in.'

'D'you know Alan Keenyside?' asked Peta.

'Not much. Met him once or twice,' said Turnbull. 'West was his patch. Seemed OK to me. Decent bloke.' He shook his head. 'Hard to believe all this . . .'

'I know a DCI works out of that station,' said Nattrass, 'since we're sharing information. Says the dirty squad are after him.'

'What for?' asked Peta.

'You name it,' Nattrass said. 'Bent as they come, if the rumours are true. Drugs, mainly. Fit-ups, ripping off dealers, setting up his own network. Been after him for years, apparently. Finally got someone in his squad to turn.'

Donovan nodded. 'So he'll be desperate for this deal to go through.'

'Thinks the cash will enable him to put a bit of blue sky between himself and the investigation,' said Nattrass. 'He's not going to be a happy bunny, is he?'

'You heard about that filing clerk worked out of that station?' said Turnbull. He went on to tell them about Janine's death. 'OD'd in some dealer's flat in Scotswood last night. Apparently her mother said she'd had trouble with drugs for a while. Some secret bloke got her hooked.'

'Not so secret now,' said Peta.

'Wonder if Keenyside was behind that too?' said Donovan.

Nods, murmurs of assent.

'What did you say his name was? His henchman? Hammer?' said Nattrass.

Donovan nodded.

'I remember him. Yeah. Maria Bennett . . . Caroline Huntley . . . Yes. That would fit.'

'So?' said Donovan.

'Well, if memory serves correctly, he used to be a leg-breaker for the Spalding family.'

'Chief leg-breaker, I think,' said Turnbull.

Nattrass nodded. 'They've got ranks. How nice. Now what was his name?' She closed her eyes, tipped her head back. 'Henderson. That was it. Craig? Christopher?' She opened her eyes again, head forward. 'Christopher Henderson. A mad bastard, even by gangster standards. Real fuck-up. Had this party piece. Could hammer a nail through just about anything with his bare hands. How he got the nickname.'

'So how did he end up working for Keenyside?' asked Donovan.

'Good question. When the Spaldings were put out of business, he disappeared. Really disappeared. Like into thin air. We tried to trace him, but . . .' She shrugged. 'Nothing.'

Donovan smiled grimly. 'Check your records. I'll bet Keenyside was on the arrest team for the Spaldings. I'll bet there's been a few misfiled reports over the years. A few favours done in return.'

Nattrass shook her head.

'Why don't we just arrest him now?' asked Turnbull.

'Because we've got no proof,' replied Nattrass.

'Question is,' said Donovan, 'what are you going to do to get it?'

Nearly thirty-five minutes and another round of coffees later, Nattrass and Turnbull partaking this time, they had the outline of a plan.

The Pixies had given way to American Music Club. Turnbull was ignoring it completely. They all were. The world beyond their table had ceased to exist.

They discussed options, worked through scenarios. Came up with plausible obstacles, talked through strategies to cope with them. Conscious of time, budget, legality. Of organization and requisitioning. Conscious of needing to get a clear result.

Donovan, they decided, would still front the meet.

'This is against my better judgement,' said Nattrass, 'and I still have to clear it with my Super, but I can't see any other way at such short notice. I can only ask you to do it. I can't force you.'

'I know,' said Donovan.

'I wish we could use one of our own. But it's too risky.

He might recognize them. And we don't have time to bring in someone from another force. Get them briefed. So it looks like it's you.'

'Yep,' Donovan said, 'looks like it's me.'

'Usually, we'd have an undercover specialist who's trained for this kind of work. They know, legally, what they can and can't say to get the deal to go through.'

'Avoid entrapment,' added Turnbull.

'Still,' said Nattrass, 'you'll have this lawyer with you.' She said the word as if handling it with tongs. 'Hopefully he should be able to guide you.'

Nattrass insisted that both of them be wired for sound. 'I can't risk placing men round the place. He's a copper; he'll know what to look for. So we'll track you through CCTV. Give you earpieces that fit right inside the ear. You won't know you're wearing them. More important, neither will Keenyside.'

Nattrass would try to requisition a firearms team. A calculated risk in a public building. 'But he's a dangerous man.'

'Not to mention Hammer,' added Peta.

They discussed a signal to move in, a verbal code: 'What an absolute pleasure it has been to make you a millionaire, Mr Keenyside.'

'No problem,' said Donovan.

'Why a place like the Baltic?' said Turnbull.

'Because it's somewhere educated, cultured. Somewhere an undercover cop would stand out a mile,' said Peta, giving Turnbull another cloying smile. 'No offence.'

He stared at her, hard. 'None taken.'

They talked some more. Planned some more. Got everything straight. When they started re-treading, Nattrass stood up. Held out her hand. 'Good luck.'

Donovan took it. 'Thank you.'

They agreed time and place to meet. Speed was of the

essence. Turnbull and Nattrass had a lot of coordinating to do in a very short space of time. They left.

'I'd better get going too,' said Donovan. 'Lots to do.'

Peta frowned. 'Like what?'

Donovan smiled. 'Like buying a suit. Coming?'

She smiled in return. 'I think I'd better.'

They left Intermezzo. Jim White: 'A Perfect Day to Chase Tornadoes' fading out behind them.

Mikey had spent the night in Leazes Park. He hadn't felt like going home.

Getting out of the estate and away had been difficult but not impossible. Down alleys, over fences, through gardens. He wasn't worried about being shopped by a resident – none of them talked to the police – but he didn't want to leave a trail that could be followed, cause any damage, or disturb a tenant who wouldn't take kindly to having their garden invaded. Or, worst of all, invade the territory of a dog. They bred them fierce round there.

Leaving the estate and crossing the road, he had managed to board a city-centre-bound bus. Out of breath, shaking and mad-eyed with fear, he was surprised the driver let him on. He sat well away from the other passengers, looking out of the window and avoiding eye contact. When he saw Leazes Park ahead, he got off.

The night was cold and hard. He had stayed in the shadows, well away from the gays and the gay bashers, with only the rats, the darkness and the inside of his head for company.

He huddled under a tree. Couldn't sleep. Tried to remain still, not to attract attention to himself. Curl away from life.

As soon as he felt morning arrive he was up and off. He raided the tin money box, found, to his surprise, nearly sixty pounds in it. He pocketed the cash, threw the box away.

Looked for a café to take on food and warmth.

Sitting there drinking tea, came a revelation. The police would never find him if he stayed like this. Kept beneath the radar. A non-person.

And a wave of emotion engulfed him. Both pity and self-pity intermingled.

He thought of Janine. Dead. He a non-person. Neither living any more.

He thought of his plan. Of the future. Of the things he now wouldn't have.

Blue sky. Green fields.

Love.

The emotion hardened. Became crystalline.

Keenyside.

He was responsible for all this. The one who should be punished.

Mikey felt the gun in his pocket, burning against his thigh, weighing on it like a hot brick.

There was nothing left, nothing to lose any more. No other way to fight back.

He left the café. Breath bad, hair and clothes dirty and smelly. Citizens dropped eye contact, moved aside.

Please don't stop and talk to me. Please don't make me acknowledge you exist.

He was now a citizen of that separate, invisible city.

The secret city.

He walked up Westgate Road, all the way to the police station. Stood on the opposite side of the road.

Mikey watched. Plotted and planned.

Waited for Keenyside.

His car in the car park. But no sign of the man himself.

That was OK, thought Mikey; that was fine. He would wait. He was good at waiting. He'd had a lot of practice.

Minutes to hours. Patrolling the same spot. Taking only short toilet or food breaks in a café with the same view.

Detaching his mind. Just watching. Planning: the walk up to Keenyside sitting in his car, a tap on the window, a smile and a shot. A walk away.

But no Keenyside.

Mikey thinking of giving it up, coming back the next day, when:

He appeared.

Mikey tried to hold down the sudden bubble of excitement that had risen within him. He looked around for a break in the traffic, attempted to cross the road.

No break came.

He put his hand in his pocket, curled his fingers round the grip of the gun in anticipation. Tried again to cross.

Traffic solid.

Panic welled: he was going to miss his chance. His perfect moment. Keenyside in his car and gone.

But Keenyside didn't head towards his car. He walked to the gate, looking to cross the road.

Heading straight towards Mikey.

Panic rose higher, threatened to burst into bloom. Mikey couldn't shoot him. Not here. Not now. It wasn't the plan. He had to get away. He turned, began walking up the road. Found a phone box. Hid behind it. Hoped Keenyside hadn't seen him.

He hadn't. He reached Mikey's side of the road, stood at the bus stop, checked his watch. Waited.

Mikey frowned. This wasn't right. Keenyside went everywhere by car. Enjoyed being conspicuous.

The bus arrived. Keenyside queued up, boarded it. Went upstairs.

Mikey took a chance. He ran forward, joined the end of the queue. Got on. Sat downstairs at the back. Faked looking out of the window.

The bus drove off.

Mikey's heart hammering, gun burning into his thigh.

Down Westgate Road. Along Corporation Street. Round Gallowgate. Pulling up by Grey's Monument in the city centre.

Mass embarkation. Keenyside among them.

Mikey stood up, surreptitiously joined the shuffling throng. Hit the pavement, looked around.

Keenyside had crossed the road, was making his way down Grey Street on foot.

Mikey followed. Down Grey Street. Over Mosley Street.

A crepuscular blanket dragged itself over the sky. Streetlights, vehicle lights, came on.

Down Dean Street. The Side. Headed towards the Quayside. All the way along, ignoring the eating, drinking, cultural distractions. Ignoring the cars, the noise. Crowds thinned, pedestrians became more sparse. Waterfront apartments were left behind.

Keenyside walked. Mikey followed.

Streetlights became more sporadic. Good for Mikey. He could drop back, hide in the pools of shadow between.

And on. Keenyside reached the Low Level Bridge where the Ouse Burn ran into the Tyne beneath the huge Glasshouse Bridge. Stopped.

Mikey, by a row of shuttered garages, stopped also.

Keenyside looked around.

Mikey flattened himself into the ridged metal of the inlaid shutters. Felt the shadow curl round him.

Keenyside, apparently satisfied that he hadn't been followed, took out a key and unlocked a padlock holding closed a rusting, chain-link double gate. A sign on the chain-link fence:

KEEP OUT. BUILDING DERELICT AND UNSAFE.

Keenyside slipped the lock and was in.

Mikey risked a look, stepped out. Walked towards the fence.

Behind it was a patch of weed-choked concrete. And on that, directly below the Glasshouse Bridge, was the building. Crumbling brick and sagging roof with missing tiles, it did indeed look derelict and unsafe. It stood on the edge of the Ouse Burn like it was about to crumble into it.

The whole surrounding area seemed derelict and unsafe.

Fronting the building were double doors with a smaller, inset door, also padlocked. Keenyside opened it, entered, closed it behind him.

Mikey frowned, interested.

He dropped back into the shadows.

Mikey watched.

Plotted and planned.

32

The late-autumn day had slipped away. Early night had stepped in as replacement. All along the Tyne the waterfront glittered and twinkled in come-hither picture-postcard prettiness. No sailors but still sirens, ready to entice the wary and the willing into Friday-night frolics.

But not yet. Five thirty p.m. Still time for culture and coffee at the Baltic.

An ex-flour mill from the mercantile heyday of the Tyne now reborn as cutting-edge contemporary art factory. A Tate Modern Mini Me nestling among the bars, restaurants, apartment blocks, hotels and cultural centres of the rejuvenated Newcastle/Gateshead waterfront, all twentieth-century reclamation, twenty-first-century aspiration.

Hammer stood in the gift shop. As incongruous as a nightclub bouncer in a *Swan Lake* chorus line. He had made an effort at camouflage: beige woollen beanie, black puffa jacket to soften his frame, faded carpenters and tan Timberlands. Fingerless gloves to hide the tattoos. The tooth impossible to hide. So no smiles.

Fake browsing a heavy Taschen hardback, eyes in reality on the entrance. Hoping to spot hostile faces, undercover cops laughably mimicking liberals, anyone he sensed was there to stop the deal.

Anything that screamed out 'setup'.

A roving brief covering the whole of the building. Scoping out and staying one step ahead of CCTV, making his body language as non-threatening as possible to staff and browsers. On duty all the time. Scrutinizing and scanning.

But, beyond art lovers, he had seen no one.

Because they were already there. And had been for most of the day.

Floor 2a. The administration block. The security suite. A small room to start with for only a two-person crew, now rendered cat-swingingly tiny by the inclusion of Nattrass and her team, plus Peta, Amar and Jamal.

Nattrass had been violently opposed to having them there, but Donovan had insisted. One of his conditions. Jamal, he had argued, could ID Hammer. And as a minor he needed *in loco parentis* guardians. Nattrass, seeing the logic if not the practicality, had reluctantly agreed.

No one had been allowed further than the rest of the administration block, and even then only with permission and for a limited amount of time. No police presence anywhere else in the building. Keenyside had taken part in enough operations like this to be wary. Despite being bent, Keenyside was still a copper. One of their own. And some may have sympathies. So the team was small and hand-picked: two techies, a four-man rapid-response team. Personal mobiles and phone calls had been banned. Communication only through official channels.

Minimum disruption to Baltic at all times.

Nattrass had got her wish: the four-man rapid-response team were from the firearms unit. Nattrass and Turnbull were also armed. The danger Keenyside and Hammer posed to the public, it had been decided, overrode any other concerns.

Her one regret: no marksmen. There was nowhere they could be securely lodged without arousing suspicion.

The team were focused, concentrated. Nattrass sat at the

CCTV desk, eyes on the monitors, headset beside her. Two techies, Rob and Charlie, alongside her. The shooters standing to one side, at ease, but ready to go. The Baltic security staff wide-eyed and butterflied. Like they had been dropped in the middle of a Hollywood shoot 'em up, just waiting for De Niro to walk through the door.

Turnbull kept sliding sidelong glances towards Peta, which she ignored. She and Amar were pressed against the back wall, out of the way. Jamal was by Nattrass, watching the screens with trepidation.

Turnbull sneaked alongside Peta. Spoke sotto voce. Skated on the surface tension.

'Wish this was still you?' he asked, smirk in his voice.

She turned, looked at him. Frowned. 'What?'

'This,' he said, flicking a gesture over the cramped room. 'The thrill. The rush.' He sighed, smiled. 'Can't beat it.'

Peta tried for as non-committal an answer as possible. 'I'm here, aren't I?' Her eyes averted from him, straight ahead.

'I know you're here.' His voice dropped further. 'But you're not on the inside. Not part of it. Not one of us any more. Not a real copper.' The last two words rolled out. Relishing the syllables.

Peta turned to him, eyes blazing. 'No, I don't miss it,' she said, voice rising, 'because the force is full of impotent little needledicks like you.'

Turnbull reddened, turned to face her. 'You bitch. You fucking bitch. You—'

'That's enough!'

Turnbull and Peta stopped, turned. Nattrass was staring at them angrily. The whole room was staring at them.

'Call yourself professionals?' Nattrass pointed at Turnbull. 'You, over there.' Turnbull slunk away into the corner of the room like a naughty schoolboy. She pointed at Peta and Amar. 'And you two, out.'

'What?' said Peta.

'I'm not arguing,' said Nattrass. 'This is a police operation and I'm in charge. Now get out.' She pointed to the
door.

Peta, not without difficulty, bit back what she had been
about to say and walked to the door, Amar with her. Jamal
detached himself from the screen he had been studying,
went to join them.

Nattrass looked at him. 'Where are you going?'

Jamal sniffed, shrugged. 'With me mates, innit.'

'You can't. You have to stay here.'

He looked between her and Amar and Peta. Being left
alone with police made him feel nervous. Past experience
taught him not to trust them. No matter what promises
they made him.

'Nah,' he said, sucking his teeth and aiming for nonchalance, 'I ain't Five-O material, y'get me?' He reached the
door. 'Don' worry. I see him, you the first to know.' He followed them out.

Nattrass sighed, shook her head. She opened her mouth
to speak, but the words had to be permanently delayed.

'We've got target on visual.'

Charlie, the techie watching the monitors, pointed. Alan
Keenyside was entering the café bar, finding a seat. He was
carrying an aluminium case.

The tension level in the room shot up to high-wire levels.

Nattrass got to the desk, jumped in the chair. She pulled
on her headset, flicked a switch on the desk unit.

'Helen to Faust and Mephisto. Helen to Faust and
Mephisto. Target is in place. Are you ready?'

Faust and Mephisto. Donovan's idea of irony.

There was a pause. It seemed to last ten hours. Then:

'Hi, Helen. This is Faust.' Donovan's voice. 'Ready as
we'll ever be.'

Nattrass looked at her watch. Two minutes to six. She took a deep breath. Then another. Opened the channel on the mic.

'Go,' she said.

Donovan and Sharkey walked from Newcastle to Gateshead over the Millennium Bridge, heading towards the Baltic.

Both suited, both carrying briefcases. Donovan striding, Sharkey hurrying alongside, trying to stifle the pain of his broken ribs.

'Stop grunting and groaning,' said Donovan as they passed a busker mangling an old REM song. 'They can hear it on the mics.'

'Couldn't be any worse than that . . . bloody awful racket,' said Sharkey between gasps.

They were both wired. Transmitter/receiver units in their briefcases, radio pieces placed deep in their ears. Donovan's was hidden by his hair. Sharkey would have to rely on body posture and placement.

Both focused, intense. A temporary cessation of hostilities. They had a job to do.

They crossed the square, approached the Baltic. The Riverside Café Bar was on the front to the right. Glass wall frontage with a door inset. Inside were people meeting after work, planning evenings with friends, family. Normal Friday-night relaxation.

And Alan Keenyside.

Two worlds side by side.

Donovan's heart was hammering. He didn't realize how pumped up he was until he saw his hand shaking as he grasped the handle. He took a couple of deep breaths, forced the nerves from his body. Kept the adrenalin. Controlled its use.

They went in.

Keenyside was sitting at a table, coffee before him, aluminium case at his feet. It matched the décor. He looked up as they approached, guessing correctly they were his contacts.

Keenyside rose, shook hands.

Donovan and Sharkey sat down. Sharkey angled his head away slightly.

No one spoke.

Donovan broke the deadlock. 'Where's the other one? The one we spoke to initially?'

Something flashed behind Keenyside's eyes. 'He's . . . indisposed. I'll be taking care of the negotiations.'

Donovan appeared to give the matter some thought, then nodded. Tension surreptitiously ebbed from Keenyside's shoulders.

'I presume you have the compound with you,' said Donovan, easing into the part he was playing.

Keenyside nodded, gestured to the aluminium case at his feet.

'Good,' said Donovan, remembering the script they had agreed on. 'Before any money changes hands, I'd like my colleague to test a sample. Authenticate it.'

Keenyside looked between the two of them. 'What d'you mean?'

'My briefcase contains portable testing equipment,' said Sharkey on cue. 'Give me a small amount. I'll run a couple of tests on it.'

Keenyside frowned, unconvinced.

Sharkey swallowed. 'Only a small amount. A couple of minutes.'

Keenyside scrutinized. Said nothing.

'It's standard procedure for this type of sale,' said Donovan, hoping a tone of authority tinged with irritation would keep things on track. He looked at Keenyside unblinking. 'As I'm sure you're aware.'

It worked.

'Yes, yes, of course,' said Keenyside, picking up the case, 'of course. I expected as much.'

Nattrass watched the action on the screen. The whole team did.

Keenyside opened the case.

The whole team stared, listened intently.

'Good work, Faust,' she said into her headpiece. 'Keep it going.'

Keenyside took out a small vial from the padded interior of the case. Two, Donovan saw, remained. He handed it over to Sharkey, who pocketed it and stood up. He let out a gasp. The other two men looked at him.

'Excuse me,' he said, rubbing his ribs. 'Cramp. Shan't be a moment.'

Picking up his briefcase, he walked off.

'Where's he going?' asked Keenyside.

'Toilet cubicle,' said Donovan.

Keenyside snorted out a laugh.

'He needs somewhere private,' said Donovan, face as blank as he could manage. 'Would you rather he did it here?'

Keenyside said nothing.

The two men sat silent. Waiting.

Donovan became aware of Keenyside scrutinizing him again.

'You look familiar,' he said, pointing a finger at Donovan.

Donovan's heart skipped a beat.

He cleared his throat. 'I don't think so.'

Keenyside was nodding. 'We've met before.'

Donovan struggled to keep his face stone-blank. 'No,' he said, 'we haven't.'

'Shit,' Nattrass said.

She looked around the room as if expecting to find answers there. Then pounced on the desk set, switched channels.

'Mephisto,' she said, 'get back in there, quick. You've tested the sample, it's turned out good. Now go.'

CCTV picked up Sharkey hurriedly exiting the Gents.

'But don't look like you're in a hurry,' she told him.

He slowed down, walked normally.

Nattrass sighed. Kept watching.

Sharkey walked back into the café bar, sat down. As composed as he could manage. He looked at Donovan.

'It's good,' he said.

Donovan nodded, turned to face Keenyside. 'Looks like you've got a deal,' he said. 'Let's talk money.'

Suspicion ebbed away from Keenyside's features. He smiled. 'Let's,' he said.

The room was completely dark. Deep black buried under tarmac dark.

Jamal stared. Fascinated.

He had left the administration floor along with Peta and Amar. The police movement ban, they had angrily decided, didn't extend to them. The atmosphere between them was dense, tension manifesting itself in different ways. Peta, furious with Turnbull, Amar attempting to calm her by making bitchy comments about him. Jamal could stand it no longer.

'Gonna have a look round, yeah? See what's happenin'.'

'Be careful,' said Amar. 'Stay out of the way.'

'Be on the lookout,' said Peta. 'You might meet—'

'Yeah, yeah,' said Jamal. 'Got my number, yeah? Call me.'

And off round the galleries. He thought it would be just paintings, sculpture and stuff, but it wasn't. Things in boxes. Dream diaries. A huge room with speakers hanging from roofbeams like crucifixes, the voices of alien abductees coming from them. Things he didn't understand, that didn't connect, but gave him some kind of *frisson* nevertheless.

Weird shit, he thought. Some fucked-up people out there.

But this one connected deep.

A huge gallery. Completely blacked out. A four-screen projection, two in front, two behind. On the enormous screens a Punch and Judy show. But not in kiddie seaside brightness. In grainy snuff movie slo-mo. Punch smashing down on Judy's head, eyes blurry blood-red smudges of papier-mâché hatred. His throaty laugh banged up to ear-bleed, distorted to primal scream level.

Smashing down. Down. Down.

Judy's body lifeless. Like war-torn newscam footage.

Violence stripped of entertainment. More real than real life.

Jamal stared. Fascinated.

Disturbed.

Why would people watch this? he thought. What do they get out of it?

'Kill the baby . . . kill the baby . . .'

This was even worse. Punch staving in the skull of a swaddled infant, accompanied by a bird-of-prey, wall-of-sound screech.

Smashing down. Down. Down.

Like a stone had been lodged in Jamal's heart. He felt for the baby. He was the baby.

It saddened him. Depressed him.

Down. Down. Down.

But transfixed him.

He didn't know how long he stood there. Time had stopped, was racing, or had gone into reverse.

The film, the experience, on a continual loop. Over and over.

A hangman's noose.

Justice for Punch.

A ghost to scare him. An executioner to kill him.

Jamal became physically uneasy.

There had been other people in the room while he had been watching. He was aware of them coming, staying, going when they had seen enough. But keeping to their own space.

Now Jamal felt someone behind him. Invading his space.

He turned slowly.

Punch being led to the gallows.

And fear shot through him.

A ghost to scare him. An executioner to kill him.

A smile. A blue, bejewelled tooth glinting in the darkness.

Jamal found his legs.

Jamal ran.

Donovan unsnapped his briefcase, took out his laptop. Put it on the table, powered it up. While he was waiting, he spoke to Keenyside.

'Give me the location and the number of your offshore account,' he said, voice as offhand and businesslike as he could make it, 'and I'll authorize the transfer of funds.'

Keenyside dug inside his pocket. 'I'd still have preferred cash.'

'Or a cheque, perhaps?' said Donovan, aiming for a dismissive tone. 'That's not how we conduct our business.'

'We don't like to leave a trail,' added Sharkey.

Keenyside unfolded a slip of paper, handed it over. Donovan read it, keyed digits into the laptop. Pressed RETURN.

Sat back.

'Now what?' asked Keenyside, pulling his shirt collar away from his hot and sticky neck.

'We wait,' said Donovan. 'For verification.'

Thinking: and I hope it comes fucking soon.

'You got that, Rob?' Nattrass said.

'I'm on it.' Rob, sitting on her right, wore a T-shirt with a picture of the Simpsons' character Comic Book Guy and the words I HAVE ISSUES written above it. He stared intently at his laptop, the numbers on the screen reflecting on the front of his spectacles, fingers moving swiftly over the keys. Deep in concentration.

The screen flashed up an acknowledgement box.

He smiled in satisfaction. Nodded at Nattrass.

'Good,' she said. 'We'll have a look at that later. See where his drug money's been hidden.' Then into the headset: 'Gone through.'

The acknowledgement box showed on Donovan's laptop. He smiled, tried to keep his sense of relief hidden.

'The funds have reached your account,' he said and turned his laptop round to show Keenyside.

Keenyside stared, almost overcome by the number of noughts on the screen.

Sharkey, suppressing a whimper of pain, leaned over and picked up the aluminium case.

Nattrass looked around the room. Everyone was by the door, ready to go.

'OK, everybody stand by. Wait for the signal . . .'

Donovan swivelled the laptop back round, snapped the lid shut.

'Well, gentlemen,' he said, replacing the laptop in his briefcase, 'that's that. Our business seems to have been successfully concluded.'

He was preparing to stand up, mouth opening to give the signal.

Keenyside sat back, looked at him. 'There's just one last thing,' he said.

Jamal ran. Avoiding the front entrance so as not to screw up the deal, looking for Peta and Amar, looking for another way out.

Not waiting for a lift or chancing dead-end runs, Jamal made for the stairs. Took them two at a time, heedless of the people he knocked out of the way, deaf to invocations and insults hurled in his wake.

He reached the next floor, looked around.

Nothing.

Up the stairs again, panting heavily, starting to slow down but refusing to: pushing himself further, making his legs pump harder.

The top of the stairs. Another look around.

The third-floor men's toilets right in front of him.

He ran inside.

Scoped the grey and white interior, thought fast. No way out. A toilet flushing, a man exiting. An empty cubicle. He jumped inside, locked the door. Pulled himself up on to the seat.

Tried to slow his breathing down.

With trembling hands, he took out his mobile. Speed-dialled Amar.

It rang.

'Come on . . .'

The main door to the toilets slammed against the wall.

Jamal heard shock and anger expressed by the ablutors.

'Shit . . . come on . . .'

Heard a cubicle door being smashed back on its hinges, the lock broken off. A shocked, angry voice. 'What the hell . . .'

'Come on . . .'

It was answered. 'Amar Miah.'

Another cubicle door being smashed open, another angry voice.

'Listen, man, it's Jamal.'

'Jamal, where—'

'Fuckin' listen. It's him. Hammer.' Jamal's voice was hushed, tamped-down hysteria. 'He's here.'

Another cubicle door. Jamal's stall shook. The next one along.

'He's here, man!' Jamal screamed. 'Here! The toilets! Third floor! Help, fuckin'—'

Jamal's cubicle door smashed open.

Hammer.

He smiled.

Mikey Blackmore stood outside the Baltic, looked up at it.

An art gallery. What could be more pleasant. Strolling round there on a Saturday afternoon, looking at the pictures, discussing what he saw with his companion. Using, but not showing off, his education. His understanding of art. His companion suitably impressed.

Then up to the rooftop restaurant for dinner. Fine wine. Maybe coffee and brandy to follow.

Then home. Together.

Mikey sighed. Stared through the window.

Saw people drinking coffee, wine. Bottled foreign beer. Eating sandwiches made with breads he couldn't pronounce stuffed with fillings he couldn't name.

Educated people. Prosperous people.

Secure people. Happy people.

Reading books he'd never heard of, papers too large to hold, gallery guides. Planning their evenings, their weekends.

Their lives.

And Mikey outside. A huge glass wall separating them from him. Cutting off what they had from him. Their lives sealed into the warmth.

Mikey outside in the cold.

He wanted so badly to be in there with them. Among them. One of them. Yearned for it.

But it would never happen. He knew that. Could never happen. Whatever thin thread of hope he had been clinging to was gone. For ever.

Pain tore at his heart.

Janine dead. Mikey no longer existing.

Pity and self-pity.

The glass wall would always be there.

Always.

Big, angry tears began to roll down his cheeks.

He had nothing left.

And the man responsible, Alan Keenyside, was sitting inside. Drinking coffee. Talking to his friends. Smiling.

Mikey felt his heart would break.

He drew the gun from his pocket.

Still crying.

Took aim.

'I know who you are now,' said Keenyside, sitting back, a look of cruel triumph on his face.

'What are you talking about?' Donovan hoped his voice sounded suitably dismissive.

'Your name's Joe Donovan. You're a journalist.'

Donovan froze.

Nattrass slammed the table hard with the palm of her hand.

'Shit! Fucking shit!'

She turned to Turnbull.

'Why didn't we know he knew him? Why didn't we know this?'

Turnbull, stunned, shrugged. Nattrass looked back at the screen.

'Shit . . .'

Donovan opened his mouth to speak. Keenyside stood up.

'Let's cut the bullshit. This is a setup, isn't it? A fucking setup.'

Sharkey stood up also. 'Of course it isn't.'

Keenyside stared at him, eyes like flint.

'Convince me.'

Sharkey glanced towards Donovan, moved towards Keenyside.

'Well, Mr Keenyside,' he said, 'it's been—'

The glass front of the café bar shattered.

No one moved, everyone calcified by shock and disbelief.

Then everyone moved.

Rapidly.

Screams and cries as people tried to hurl themselves beyond the range of spraying and raining glass.

Tables and chairs upended, thrown around. Food and drink flying.

In the chaos they learned things about themselves. Some ran for cover, dived out of the way; others pushed their loved ones to the ground, shielded them with their own bodies. Some pushed their loved ones before them as shields.

Chaos and confusion. Events occurring simultaneously in slo-mo and hyper speed.

More splintering glass. More horror-movie screams.

And behind the large-scale noise, small pops.

Mikey, blinded by tears, firing indiscriminately.

Nattrass ripped off her headset, looked at the rapid-response team.

'Go! Go! Get down there!'

They ran. She pulled out her radio, shouted her call sign. Requested backup. No need for secrecy any more. More police. Ambulances.

She turned to the two security guards, now standing dumbfounded and immobile. Told them to raise the alarm. Initiate evacuation procedures.

She put her head back, screamed to the heavens from the bottom of her lungs.

'Fucking hell!'

Then ran out to join her team.

Sharkey spun round, fell.

Straight away Donovan knew he'd been hit. Even before the blood began to soak through his pinstripe. He kneeled down beside him, looked up at Keenyside.

'Still think this is a setup?' he shouted.

Keenyside stood there, staring at him in hatred. Oblivious to the bullets.

'This is all your fault . . .'

'Call an ambulance,' shouted Donovan.

'Cunt . . .'

'Call an ambulance!'

Keenyside looked around, suddenly aware of what was happening. He kneeled down, prised the aluminium case from beneath Sharkey's body, checked for a way out, ran.

Dodging behind a pillar, towards the main exit.

And away.

Jamal screamed. Hammer grabbed him. Pulled him off the seat of the cubicle. His mobile clattered to the floor.

Pulled him face to face.

'We've got some unfinished business, little boy.' Hammer gave a leering smile. His breath stank of death and decay.

Jamal had never been so frightened in his life.

He was aware of people in his peripheral vision, standing watching. Hypnotized by horror: this can't be happening in front of me.

And the subtext: I'm glad that's not me it's happening to.

Jamal screamed.

'Help! Get him off me! He's goin' to kill me! Help!'

The words just documentation of a situation. No one, he knew, would help him. They would rationalize their inaction: undercover cop arresting teenage thief. Walk away.

Hammer began dragging him out. Jamal screamed and kicked.

The alarm sounded. The call to evacuate the building by the nearest exit. To use the stairs, not the lifts. To not run but walk in a calm manner.

Their audience immediately, hurriedly, left. A couple casting backward glances, but no more. Hammer stopped moving.

'Alone at last,' he said.

Jamal closed his eyes, expecting a blow.

It never came.

Instead, Hammer dropped him.

Jamal opened his eyes. Hammer was bent over by the

washbasins, holding a hand to his right kidney. Behind him stood Amar. Poised, ready to strike again.

Amar pulled back his arm, but Hammer turned, lunged at him. Amar jumped nimbly to one side, letting Hammer crash against the door. The wall shook. He turned, enraged.

Before he could make a move, Amar hit out hard with his fist, landing a perfectly weighted blow against Hammer's chest, upsetting his centre of gravity, knocking him back against the handbasins, cracking the mirrors.

Hammer, shocked at having been bested again, didn't move for a few seconds. Amar, expecting and exploiting that, grabbed Jamal and ran from the toilets.

They reached the landing. It was choked with people obeying instructions, trying to leave in as orderly a manner as possible. Despite that, a cloud of barely suppressed panic hung over them.

Amar turned to Jamal. 'You've got to get down,' he said hurriedly. 'Go through—'

His next words were lost. Hammer emerged from the toilets, punched Amar in the back. He crumpled to his knees. Hammer picked him up, punched him again. Amar was in too much pain to respond.

Hammer, having punched him beyond retaliation, pulled him back by his collar and pitched him forward into the descending crowd.

The barely suppressed cloud of panic broke as he collided with them.

Surprise turned to anger turned to shock. Some turned, saw Hammer, and that was enough for them. Screams and shouts competed with the alarms. Walks turned to runs. Self-preserving Darwinian nature reasserted itself. A human stampede began.

Jamal looked around. The floor was crowded. He had

nowhere to run. Knowing that, Hammer slowly turned to him.

'Now,' he said, 'where were we?'

Before he could make a further move, there was a tap on Hammer's shoulder.

'Don't you think it's about time you picked on someone your own size?'

Peta.

Amar tumbled downstairs. He was trampled and tripped, carried along, then left. The crowd dragged him down a floor, where he managed to spin free and fall to the ground.

He lay panting, hurting, the occasional kick or mis-step by a passing evacuee hurting him even more. He closed his eyes.

The kicking stopped.

He opened his eyes, looked up. People were still moving about him, but not over him. Kneeling before him was DS Turnbull.

'What happened, Amar?' he shouted over the din. 'Where's Peta?'

Amar managed a vague gesture. 'Up there . . . Hammer . . .'

He didn't have to say any more. Turnbull was off.

Amar managed to drag himself against a wall, get his breath back.

He couldn't move.

He hurt.

Feedback and static knifed through Donovan's head. Clawing at the side of his face he managed to rip out his earpiece. He looked around.

Chaos and carnage everywhere.

Screams and cries. Bodies moving and unmoving. No

more bullets. The sound of sirens getting louder. He looked at Sharkey, kneeled before him.

He lay twisted on the floor, blood pooling from beneath his left shoulder. Donovan took off his jacket, placed it under the wound, tried to prop his head up.

'I've been shot,' said the lawyer, more in surprise and anger than pain. 'Who the bloody hell did that?'

'I don't know,' said Donovan. 'Keenyside was as surprised as us.'

'Where is he?'

'He ran.'

'You've got to go and get him, Joe.'

'Will you be OK?'

'Course I bloody won't. I've been shot. Where's the fucking ambulance?'

Donovan took that as a yes. Gave another look around. People were beginning to move again. Assess the damage.

Alarms were still ringing, evacuation instructions still being issued.

'Go and get him, Joe.'

The entrance hall was starting to fill with people. Donovan stood up, ran to the doors. Following the route he had seen Keenyside take. Then outside on to Baltic Square.

He had on only a black short-sleeved T-shirt beneath his jacket, and the cold hit him hard. He shook it off; that was no more than most people wore in Newcastle on a Friday night. He scoped the square.

Police, ambulances, paramedics were arriving. Moving in, taking control.

He looked at the Millennium Bridge. Saw a figure almost at the Newcastle side, running, carrying an aluminium brief-case.

Keenyside.

Donovan pushed his way through the crowds, gave chase.

Keenyside had a good start on him, but Donovan was determined. He eye-tracked him, jumping out of the way of pedestrians, shouting at others to move for him.

Donovan reached the other side, checked on his quarry.

Keenyside was running along the waterfront, away from the bars and restaurants, the city centre, heading towards Byker.

Donovan, chest burning, legs shaking, gave chase.

Keenyside ran by some apartment blocks, jumped over a low fence, on to a grass verge. He ran beneath the Glasshouse Bridge, into shadow. Donovan, at a distance, followed.

Donovan reached the Low Level Bridge, Ouse Burn trickling beneath it. His legs were now liquid, his chest hot, raw meat. He looked around.

No Keenyside.

Before him a building. Derelict-looking, on a weed-choked stretch of concrete. Ringed by a rusting chain-link fence, on the fence a notice:

KEEP OUT. BUILDING DERELICT AND UNSAFE.

A padlock hanging loose from the gate. The gate open.

Donovan pushed open the gate, entered.

Walked slowly over the cracked concrete; listening, wary. He reached the front. Double doors. A small one, inset. Chained and padlocked. The padlock undone.

The door open.

Donovan, struggling to hear anything beyond his own ragged breath, pushed it open further, stepped in.

Inside was dark. He took one step, two.

The door slammed shut behind him.

He turned. Too slowly. Felt pain at the base of his skull.

As another kind of darkness claimed him.

33

Hammer stared at Peta. Then attacked.

She sidestepped, spun round, landed a kick in the small of his back. He turned, angry to be bested by a woman on the first blow. Swung at her.

Peta ducked, rolled. Sprang to her feet again. Smiled.

He was bigger, stronger and meaner, so she had to quickly adapt her fighting style, turn his strengths against him. Use guile, speed and precision-blows.

Hammer growled, lunged. Peta moved, but not quickly enough. He landed a glancing blow to her shoulder. It hurt. He followed through with another. It hurt even more.

Step it up, she thought.

Peta kicked, hitting Hammer in the solar plexus. He grunted, remained upright. She tried again, higher up. He grabbed her foot, held it firm.

She knew what he was about to do; he telegraphed the move. Twist her foot, snap her leg.

Before he could, she jumped up, pushing against him with her captured foot, using his body for leverage. Balanced on his chest. Clapped both hands over his ears.

He screamed in pain, let go. Blood began to trickle from his right ear.

She jumped back, looked around. The crowd had thinned on the different levels now, but the stairs of the building were still blocked. The three of them had this floor to themselves. They were standing by the entrance to one of the galleries. Peta caught a quick view of objects behind glass. She backed inside, away from Jamal, coaxing Hammer with her. Hammer, still in pain, charged.

'Getting tired, are you, Hammer?' she shouted. 'Not used to girls fighting back?'

She manoeuvred herself in front of one of the cabinets. Hammer growled and, snarling, let loose a punch. Peta ducked. The glass shattered round his hand.

Peta moved quickly behind him. Punched him as hard as she could in the kidneys. It hurt her hand. He was solid. She tried again.

Hammer spun round. His arm caught on broken glass. Shards gouged. Blood spurted. She took her eye from him, looked at it. He punched her.

The blow caught her on the cheekbone. She spun, hit the floor. Landed hard, winded.

He came at her.

She stuck her leg out, aiming a kick in his groin, but she was too slow. He grabbed her foot and, blood flicking and arcing from his damaged arm, twisted it hard. She felt something wrench in her knee.

She screamed and, going into the movement, not fighting it, spun her body round with it. Hammer let go. She was sprawled on the floor, panting, the pain in her leg, her face, like a hundred red-hot razors.

Hammer looked at her, then the doorway, where Jamal was crouching in fear.

Decided who to go for.

Jamal.

'No . . .' Peta tried to pull herself up.

Jamal stood, ready to run, but Hammer was on him and out of the gallery.

Peta, using one of the gallery's benches, pulled herself upright and, trying to ignore the pain in her right leg, half hopped, half dragged herself along behind him.

She reached the gallery entrance. Hammer was still standing there holding Jamal, his uninjured arm round the boy's throat in a choke-lock. The stairs were still blocked. He was looking for another way out.

There was a commotion on the stairs – someone fighting the tide, coming up while the majority were heading down. Peta recognized who it was.

'Paul!' she shouted, hanging on to the wall for support. 'Quick! Hammer's got Jamal!'

At the sound of her voice, Hammer turned. Frantic for a way out now. He scanned the floor, saw an open archway at the opposite end of the hall to the stairwell. Assuming it led to another set of steps, he made for it, dragging Jamal along with him.

Turnbull reached Peta.

'He's getting away . . .' She gestured to where Hammer had just gone.

Turnbull ran towards it, Peta, limping along, supported by the wall, following.

It wasn't a stairwell. It was an observation box. Out in the open air, walled in on three sides by glass, unroofed. The view was spectacular: the Tyne stretching away in both directions, the bridges and the waterfront lit spectacularly against the dark. It looked warm, exciting.

Like another city.

Hammer realized he was trapped. Stopped. Turnbull stood in the entrance way.

'Let the boy go,' he said, hands outstretched. 'Just let him go and we'll talk about it, OK?'

By way of a reply, Hammer pulled Jamal up, tried to push him over the glass wall. He would have managed it in one movement if his arm hadn't been damaged. And if Jamal hadn't struggled.

Jamal pushed and kicked against him, screaming, fighting for his life.

Turnbull drew his gun, aimed it.

'Let the boy go and step away,' he called. 'Or I'll fire. Do it.'

Hammer ignored him, pushed Jamal further. Jamal was balanced on the edge of the glass. He looked over. It was a long way down.

Jamal was too scared even to scream.

Peta arrived, clutching the doorway for support. 'Don't fire. You might hit Jamal . . .'

Turnbull looked between the three of them, weighing up his options. Speedily deciding what was the best thing to do.

Hammer pushed Jamal further. Smiled his blue-jewelled smile.

Turnbull fired.

'No!' shouted Peta.

Once. Twice.

Chest shots. The impact flung Hammer back against the glass. The bullets tore straight through him. The glass began to buckle and crack. Hammer crumpled, but stayed upright.

Turnbull fired again.

The third bullet killed Hammer. Head shot. His body banged against the glass, then began to sag downwards into a sitting position, leaving a huge red smear in his wake.

Jamal was left balancing on the glass wall. He tried to keep his balance, scramble back inside.

The fractures in the glass deepened. The wall began to sway.

Jamal began to slip, to fall.

'Jamal!'

Peta rushed forward and, ignoring the pain in her leg,

grabbed him, pulling him back inside. He tumbled into her and she lost her footing. They landed on the floor of the observation box in a heap.

She pulled the terrified boy close to her.

'It's all right now,' she said. 'You're safe.'

Donovan opened his eyes.

Head spinning, eyes pinballing in their sockets.

Tried to move his arms. Couldn't. Waited for focus to return, looked down. His arms were tied to the arms of a chair. No, not tied, taped. Bound tightly.

He tried his legs, his body; pulled them hard. Same story. Taped to a chair, upright, in a sitting position.

He sat back, head spinning, aching. He felt nauseous.

Deep breaths. Then a look around, attempting to work out where he was.

Saw old car parts. Tools. Smelled cold, fetid air. Squinted from harsh overhead lights. On the floor by his feet, motor oil stains. Others. Human oil stains.

A radiator on the far wall; two people, a man and a woman, cuffed to it, huddled under blankets. The man old, frail. Sick looking. The woman younger, wasted. Both with the pallor of hopelessness. What he imagined Belsen inmates looked like during the Second World War.

Then the shock of recognition.

Colin and Caroline Huntley.

'Colin Huntley . . .'

The old man looked at him, confusion in his eyes, as if hearing a name he hadn't heard in years. A name he was known by in a previous life.

'Caroline Huntley . . .'

The woman didn't answer. She looked to be in shock.

'Well, I'm glad you've made your introductions,' said a voice behind Donovan, 'Because you're all going to be together for a long time. Till death do you part, unless someone finds you.'

Caroline Huntley let out a little whimper.

Donovan turned, or tried to; pain flashed through his head when he attempted to move it, starburst fireworks exploded at the sides of his eyes. He waited for the speaker to come into his line of vision. He knew who it would be.

Alan Keenyside had changed out of his suit. He now wore a leather jacket, polo shirt and pressed chinos. He had a packed holdall by his feet, the aluminium case next to that. He stood in front of Donovan.

'Joe Donovan,' he said. 'Small world.'

'But I wouldn't want to shag it . . .' Donovan's voice, cracked and rough.

'Do what you like,' said Keenyside, straightening his jacket. 'I've got my money.'

'No, you haven't,' said Donovan, licking his dry lips. 'There was no money. You were right. It was a setup.'

'What d'you mean?' said Keenyside dismissively. 'I know you tried to entrap me. But the money was real. I saw it enter my account.'

'Smoke and mirrors, Alan. Smoke and mirrors.'

Keenyside became red in the face. 'You're lying.'

Donovan did his best to give a nonchalant shrug. Keenyside seemed to struggle not to hit him. Instead he smiled.

'Be that as it may,' he said. 'I've still got this little beauty. And how much is this worth on the open market?'

He brought up the aluminium case, gave it a pat.

Donovan could have laughed if the situation wasn't so desperate. 'Oh Alan, Alan,' he said, 'you're a study in self-delusion.'

Keenyside's face creased into an ugly frown. 'What d'you mean?'

Donovan turned his head to the side. Slowly. 'Tell him, Colin.'

Colin Huntley wanted to speak but was unsure whether to or not.

'It's all right, Colin,' said Donovan. 'I know what's been going on.'

'There is no compound, Alan.' Colin couldn't keep the sense of triumph from his voice.

'What?'

'There never was.' His eyes shone with vindication.

Keenyside swung his gaze between the two of them. He looked like a trapped animal searching for an escape route.

Donovan pushed the point home. 'The whole thing was a setup. Right from the start. Just to entrap you.' Then he added in his best John Lydon: 'Ever get the feeling you've been cheated?'

Keenyside was speechless.

'Was it worth it?' shouted Donovan. 'Everything you've done, every life you've ruined, every person you've killed. Eh? Was it? For nothing?'

Keenyside spun round. He wanted to lash out, strike at something, vent his anger.

'It's over, Alan,' said Colin Huntley. 'One way or another, it's the end.'

Keenyside's eyes were wide, staring. He was witnessing his whole world collapse around him. Close to breaking point, thought Donovan. Either that, or past it.

With a cry of near primal-rage, Keenyside hit the floor, went rummaging through his holdall, pulled out a gun.

'Over, is it?' His voice was shrill, hysterical. 'Finished? Well, if that's the case, you'll all be coming with me.' He swung the gun round. It pointed at Donovan. 'Starting with you.'

Donovan looked at Keenyside, about to come out with

another fearless quip to annoy him even further. But stopped.

There was the gun. Pointing towards him. About to kill him.

Donovan was scared.

Keenyside noticed. Laughed. 'Not so brave now, are you, Mr Clever Fucking Journalist. D'you believe in God? No? Yes? Think there's an afterlife?' He tightened his grip on the trigger. 'Well, you're in the mercy seat. You're about to find out. For yourself. Very soon.'

The Mercy Seat. The song back in his head, the hotel room flashing before him.

Donovan blinked it away, stared at the gun. Transfixed by the end of the barrel. Any second now, metal would be hurled from there towards him at a speed he couldn't measure. And it would be the last thing he would ever see.

This wasn't Russian roulette. That had only ever been a game of chance to take the pain away. This was different. Someone else was in control. Deciding whether he lived or died.

Donovan was powerless.

Faces, voices swam before him:

Tosher. *Think about it, Joe Donovan. Which of us would you rather be?*

Maria. Was this what it felt like for her? The disbelief? The useless struggle to not let go? The anger and injustice of having something taken from you when you've still got so much more to give?'

Johnny Cash kept singing in his head. *The Mercy Seat*. The condemned man only showing fear when confronting death. Finding truth for the first time in that same moment.

And David. Dying not knowing what had happened to his son.

Dying without finding him.

He didn't want to die.

That was the truth.

He didn't want to die.

Donovan stared at the gun. His world reduced to that one piece of lethal metal.

Saw Keenyside smiling, squeezing the trigger.

He closed his eyes.

'I want to live . . .'

The choice no longer his.

He waited, eyes screwed tight shut, for the shots. He heard them.

One. Two. Three.

He jumped. Gasped. They didn't hurt as much as he thought they would.

He remained still. He was breathing.

He opened his eyes.

Keenyside lay on the floor before him. Blood geysering from his spasming body.

He died. Donovan watched.

Then looked up. In the doorway stood a man he had never seen before. Dressed like a trainee tramp in overcoat, old jumper and trousers and filthy trainers. Youngish, but prematurely aged. He looked lost, homeless. He had a gun in his hand.

The man waited until the last flicker of life had left Keenyside then let out an enormous sigh.

As Donovan, Colin and Caroline watched, he began to cry.

The effort seemed to sap all the life from him. He rested his back against the wall, slid down it. Curled up foetally on the floor. His sobs threatening to engulf him.

He placed the barrel of the gun, still hot, into his mouth. Slowly, tenderly, like kissing a considerate lover. He winced from the heat.

'No,' shouted Donovan, 'Don't . . .'

The man either didn't hear or ignored him. He said something that Donovan didn't hear properly. Something about blue skies and green fields. Something about love.

'Don't!'

He pulled the trigger.

And Mikey Blackmore was dead.

Outside, distant but getting nearer, was the sound of sirens.

EPILOGUE

A SECRET GARDEN

Donovan put down his paintbrush. He stepped back, admired his handiwork.

Where once the wall had been rough, flaking plaster, it was now smooth, taking its first coat of paint. It was already an improvement. Brightening the room, giving hope to what would follow.

Outside, the rain was holding off. Inside, the house was warm, oil-fired central heating having been recently installed.

Changes. For the better.

He looked around. Jamal, in an old T-shirt of Donovan's that hung ludicrously down to his knees and an old pair of tracksuit bottoms, was applying paint to the skirting board in the far corner. He was working intently, tongue lodged in the corner of his mouth in concentration, eyes narrowed, making sure his paint distribution was even, that he stayed in the lines. Determined to do a good job.

Four weeks. Since that night at the Baltic.

Donovan had been led over the bridge back to Millennium Square, outside the Baltic. Ambulances, paramedics and police all milling about. The area had been cordoned off; Friday-night rubberneckers out in force, thrilled that this had brightened up their evening, TV crews arriving, making suppositions into camera.

In the middle of all this, Donovan had spotted Jamal. Peta and Amar had been taken off to hospital along with the other wounded. Donovan would see them later. As soon as he could. But there was Jamal, on his own. Sitting on the back steps of an ambulance, huddled beneath a blanket that made him seem even smaller, staring at everything going on round him as if he was in a dream. He seemed alone.

More than that, lost.

He walked up to him, sat next to him.

Jamal slowly started to tell him what had happened. Donovan had been told already but listened. Jamal needed to talk. He reached the end of his story, tears in his eyes.

Donovan sighed. 'Where you going now?' Donovan asked. 'What you going to do?'

Jamal shrugged. 'Dunno.' Kept his eyes averted from Donovan.

Donovan looked at him. Jamal had nothing to go back to, no home, just a drift back on to the street. More drugs and unsafe sex and an early, probably violent death. Donovan's heart went out to him.

Donovan looked around, checked that no one was in earshot. 'Let's get out of here. If the police want to talk to us, they can find us later.'

Jamal nodded.

They walked back to Donovan's hotel. 'Where you off to now?'

Jamal shrugged.

'I'll get you a room.'

Jamal's face brightened. 'Yeah?' He smiled. 'Thanks, man.'

Donovan booked Jamal into the hotel.

'You want something to eat in the restaurant? Or room service if you want to be on your own?'

'I don't wanna be on my own.' Jamal not able to look at him while he spoke the words.

'OK, then.' Donovan bought him dinner.

While they were eating, he looked at the boy sitting opposite him. Just an ordinary teenager. Or should be. He made his mind up, came to a decision.

'Listen,' Donovan said. 'If you've got nowhere to stay I've got a spare room.' He told him where.

'A cottage?' Jamal had said. 'In Northumberland? Is that in Scotland?'

'No, it's just up the road. Anyway, it's up to you. You can make the room your own but you'll have to help. The place needs doing up, making habitable.'

Jamal had frowned. 'Dunno how to do that, man,' he said earnestly.

Donovan smiled. 'Don't worry, neither do I. Be a laugh, eh?'

Jamal had tried to hide his pleasure at the offer, knowing it would be uncool to be too excited. But he gave a smile that almost threatened to split his face.

'Yeah, man,' he said, 'that be cool.'

Four weeks.

Donovan still had nightmares. Still saw ghosts.

More to add to the collection.

The deaths, the maimings. The funeral season, as Donovan thought of it.

Four weeks. Time for the dust to settle. Not enough time for wounds to heal.

Two people killed, six injured in the attack on the Riverside Café Bar. Not counting Hammer, Peta and Amar. Not mentioning Alan Keenyside and Mikey Blackmore.

Colin and Caroline Huntley had been rushed straight to hospital. They were recovering. 'Stable' was the catch-all phrase the hospital spokesperson at the infirmary used. There had been no decision made on what proceedings, if any, would be taken against Colin Huntley for his actions against the travellers and his other collusions with Keenyside. Whatever happened, Donovan doubted either of them would be fully whole again.

Peta and Amar were on the mend. They had been allowed out the next day, were recuperating back home. Donovan had been to see them and realized, while talking to them, that a bond had been established. Even in such a short space of time. They would keep in touch. Perhaps work together again. He really believed that.

However, their business, with no one to tend to it, was back in trouble. Despite their recent successes, Knight Security and Investigations was back to square one.

The *Herald* and the Northumbria police were at each other's throats. Each blaming the other for the débâcle. Neither backing down. Donovan knew it was just for show, a shouting match to indicate to the public how seriously they took these matters. More heat than light. He also knew, from experience, that once the public got sick of hearing about it and another story came along to take its place, that would be that. And matters of outrage, responsibility and blame would be quietly laid to rest.

Sharkey had been the *Herald*'s scapegoat. Sacked straight away, sacrificed to satisfy a supposedly outraged public. Donovan took a vindictive pleasure in hearing the news.

He also expected Nattrass to be demoted as a sign of public appeasement from the other side. But it hadn't happened.

'I've been carpeted,' she told him over a coffee at Intermezzo, a place she was developing a taste for, 'but mainly as a matter of course. No one blamed me. I mean,' she said, making an expansive gesture that masked a great degree of relief, 'the fact that a rogue element chose that night to target the café Bar wasn't my fault, was it?'

No action had been taken against her or her team. It had even been intimated that had the loss of life not been so great, a commendation might have been in order.

Keenyside's bagman and second-in-command had rolled

over. They knew about his network of dealers. Keenyside's empire was over.

Lip service was paid in the papers and on TV about a blow being struck in the war against drugs, but no one believed it would change anything. Not really.

Justice, in its skewed, sad way, had been seen to be done.

The first funeral was Mikey Blackmore's, the Social Fund covering the expenses.

The church in Scotswood, pollution-darkened almost to black. The vicar young, watch-glancing, speeding through as a matter of duty.

Donovan thought he would be the only mourner. But there were three college student types standing at the back.

Their presence puzzled him and they left looking disappointed. Donovan heard the words 'big-time gangster funeral' followed by a collective shake of their heads. The vicar looked at him almost in embarrassment.

'Friend, relative?'

'Neither,' said Donovan. 'He saved my life. I just wanted to thank him.'

Maria's funeral came a week after the night at the Baltic.

Donovan was still torn up inside. But he felt he had to go.

Amar, Peta and Jamal also wanted to go. Pay their respects. Amar and Peta on crutches, Jamal very uneasy. The service took place in Didsbury outside Manchester, where her parents had moved to. The trees were almost denuded, the last few curled and crinkled brown leaves blowing about as the mourners made their way into the churchyard. The church was old, picturesque. The surrounding streets pleasant 1930s semis. Almost impossible to believe, thought Donovan, that violent death could touch lives in an area that seemed as self-protected as this.

But it had. Lives could be broken anywhere. There was no protection. Donovan knew that.

The four of them stood at the back, listened to the service. Donovan became quietly enraged. All her work colleagues were there, or at least the ones who had bothered to make the trip up from London, but none of them seemed to be touched by her death to any great depth. There was a sense of sadness, but also of duty. Death meant promotion. And they all wanted to be next.

He tried to shake the thought away. Perhaps that was just his own sense of bitterness and loss manifesting itself. He hoped so. Because he couldn't shake off the feeling.

The new editor had already been appointed. Maria's hated old dep., the one who had made no secret of coveting her job. He came up to Donovan afterwards, shook hands, expressed his condolences. Smiling smugly all the time. Then, on behalf of the *Herald*, asked him to write his own account of what had happened.

'An eyewitness account from the eye of the storm,' he said. A phrase which, Donovan thought, didn't bode well for the future of quality journalism at the paper.

His first reponse was to punch the guy and walk away. But he didn't. Surprising even himself, he accepted the commission.

Back in Northumberland, he laboured on it day and night, determined to turn it into a truthful piece of work. He thought Maria's memory deserved full honour. And others who could no longer speak, the chance to have their story heard.

In doing so, it became more than that. Catharsis, writing as therapy; a piece that would exorcise the demons of the last few weeks, purge the ghosts from within. He created a safe working environment for himself out of the defined boundaries of the article. Then, taking his memories of events, and emotions concerning them, as raw ingredients, he began. He shaped and reshaped, striving for an emotional clarity and honesty, depth behind the words. In doing so he sculpted something that went far beyond the limit of his original brief. It became universal, a treatise on the nature of grief and anger, remorse and revenge.

It was undoubtedly the best piece of writing he had ever done, possibly the best he would ever do.

The *Herald* paid handsomely for it, realizing they had something special. In addition to that, they offered to broker him book deals, film rights. Anything to keep him writing. Donovan declined everything. While working on it, he had decided it would be the last piece he ever wrote. For them or anyone. He was finished with the *Herald*, finished as a journalist.

The piece had served its purpose.

Something else also happened at Maria's funeral. Just as the article was the past, so this could have been the future.

'There's Sharkey,' said Peta, pointing from the pew they sat in.

They were standing, collectively making their way outside after the service.

'Ignore him,' said Donovan.

They didn't need to be told. However, it was clear that Sharkey wanted to talk to them. As they made their way to the graveside for the final part of the service, Sharkey sidled up beside them.

He wore his usual immaculate pinstripe suit, with his left arm strapped up and a camelhair coat draped theatrically over his shoulders. Gave a respectful bow.

'You've got a fucking nerve turning up here,' said Donovan.

'We should find a spare hole and bury you as well,' added Peta.

Sharkey placed his good hand on Donovan's sleeve. Donovan turned.

'Please. Not here. I've come to pay my respects too.'

Donovan looked at him. There seemed to be genuine emotion behind his words. He looked to be grieving. Donovan gave him the benefit of the doubt.

They walked slowly on.

'The *Herald* chucked you out, then?' Donovan asked.

'They needed a sacrificial scapegoat,' Sharkey said. 'Someone to shoulder the blame and apologize in public. I am now, officially, a penitent.'

'Good. Because it's all your fault.'

Sharkey sighed as if about to argue. But said nothing.

They reached the graveside. Maria's mother, who so far had been stoical, let go all her tears as her daughter's coffin was lowered into the ground. Donovan looked away, trying to mask his own, private grief.

Afterwards, he turned down an offer to go back to Maria's parents'. He couldn't face it. Her mother saw his face, understood. As he, Peta, Amar and Jamal walked away, Sharkey found them again.

'Glad I caught you all,' he said. 'Wanted a word.'

'I can think of a good one,' said Amar.

Sharkey stood in front of them, blocking their path. 'Can we call a halt to hostilities and have a decent, civilized conversation? Please?'

'What have we got to talk about?' asked Donovan.

'I have a proposition for you which could be to your benefit.' Sharkey looked at Peta and Amar. 'All of you. Please hear me out.'

They said nothing.

'I'll take you to dinner.' He smiled. 'Can't say fairer than that, can I?'

★   ★   ★

Chinatown in Manchester. The Yang Sing restaurant. Gold and red décor. A round table piled high with dishes. The food excellent. Jamal ate like he had never been fed. Donovan, Peta and Amar picked. Sharkey tried valiantly with chopsticks, gave up and used a fork.

'So what was this proposition?' said Donovan, taking a sip of his gin and tonic, looking at the solicitor.

Sharkey put down his fork, settled back in his chair. Donovan sensed a lecture coming. He wasn't disappointed. The price he paid for the good food, he thought.

'Heavy industry,' he began, 'manufacturing. Mining. All the old industries. Here in the West, and particularly in Britain, they have declined to the point of extinction.'

'Anybody want the last chicken ball?' asked Jamal.

Donovan almost laughed out loud. He told him to take it. Sharkey, irked at having been interrupted, continued.

'What our blighted land of Albion now exists on,' he said, waving his fork as if that in some way emphasized his point, 'is information. It passes back and forth across the world at great speeds; it informs, if you will, every aspect of our lives.'

'Is there a point to this?' asked Peta. 'We've got a long drive home.'

'Yes, Peta, there is a point,' he said, angry now at his perfectly prepared speech being interrupted again. He indicated Donovan. 'Now you, Joe, I know you don't want to be a journalist any more. But you have first-class investigative skills. It would be a shame to see them go to waste. And you, Peta and Amar, you have a framework, a business structure already in place. Perhaps not as successful as you would wish, but the basics are there.' He sat back, looked at them.

'That's it?' said Donovan. 'The big idea? I should go and work with these two? Well, thanks, Francis.'

'Just hear me out. Not private investigators. Not investigative journalists, even.'

'Then what?' asked Amar.

Sharkey smiled. 'Information brokers.'

He explained. Information, he said, was sometimes hard to come by. Sometimes even deliberately kept secret. Sometimes not in the best interests of the majority. He proposed that they set up a company that utilized their individual skills for the express purpose of gaining information to sell.

'Who to?' asked Peta.

'Whoever wants it.'

'What if that doesn't turn out to be ethical?' said Donovan.

Sharkey shrugged. 'That's up to you. I'm sure a team with your collective intelligence could find a way to salve your conscience and maintain your company's integrity.'

'How will it work?' asked Amar.

Sharkey would make initial enquiries, use his contacts to find potential buyers. The three of them would get access to this information; Sharkey would sell it on. They'd all be paid. 'And handsomely,' he added. 'I am as in need of funds as you are. But this is the deregulated private sector in the twenty-first century. A very lucrative place to be.'

'Who has this information?' asked Donovan.

'Anyone and everyone. I doubt two jobs will be the same. It might be easy or it might be dangerous. But I'm sure it'll never be dull.'

Donovan stared. Sharkey had seen that look before. He swallowed hard.

'You've made promises before,' Donovan said. 'About David. Why should I believe you now?'

Sharkey looked suddenly hot. His features coalesced into a kind of frightened sincerity. 'I meant what I said about your son. I have contacts in the police force, the media, social services even. If I get to hear anything, a sighting, a body even –

God forbid – I will let you know. I'll even give you support in setting up your own investigation, if needs be.'

Donovan looked unconvinced. 'Why?'

All pretence seemed to drop from Sharkey's features. 'Because I believe it's something I owe you.' He sat back. 'And because I know what you'd do to me if I don't.'

Donovan almost smiled.

'Yeah, yeah,' said Peta, unconvinced. 'But can we trust you?'

Sharkey smiled. 'If there's money involved, then we're all on the same side.'

They all looked at him.

'Think about it,' he said.

They did. All the way back to Newcastle.

Argued about it, tossed the idea back and forth. Came up with an answer.

Yes.

And a name for the company. Because it couldn't be Knight Security and Investigations any more.

'What was that word he said earlier?' said Jamal, speaking for almost the first time.

'Which one?' asked Donovan.

'Albun, or something?'

'Albion, you mean?'

'Yeah, yeah. That one.'

They looked at each other.

'Albion it is,' said Amar.

'Albion?' said Nattrass, when Donovan met her for coffee next.

He nodded.

'Good name. Will we still have our reciprocal arrangement? Share mutually beneficial tips on ongoing investigations?'

'I don't know,' said Donovan.

Nattrass took a mouthful of coffee. Her eyes became steely over the rim of her cup.

'Are you going to play the cowboy like I warned you not to? Or are we still going to be on the same side?'

Donovan sighed. 'I hope so.'

She replaced her cup. Unsmiling.

'So do I. For your sake.'

Donovan looked around the room. A vast improvement. He looked at Jamal, still working furiously.

'You wanna break?' he asked.

Jamal looked up. 'Sure.'

He put down his brush, stood up and back. Admired his workmanship.

'You're doing a good job there,' said Donovan.

'Thanks, man.' Jamal's smile told Donovan that he knew that already. But it was still good to hear it.

Donovan went into the kitchen. Made tea for himself, got apple juice for Jamal. Took them back into the living room. Looked around. Yes, he thought, it's starting to take shape.

Jamal was settling in. It didn't look like he would be going anywhere soon. Donovan didn't know how he felt about that. The boy had a lot of problems. It wouldn't be easy. But in time, and with the right help, he hoped they would diminish. Disappear altogether, hopefully.

He crossed over to him, handed him his juice.

'Thanks, man.' Jamal turned, kept looking out of the window.

'What you looking at?'

'That bit there,' he said. 'In front of the house. Before you get to the road. That yours?'

Donovan nodded. 'You mean the garden.'

Jamal laughed. 'You call that a garden? Just weeds and stuff, man. That ain't no garden. Garden's got flowers an' shit in it. That's just a mess.'

'Well,' said Donovan, 'come spring, when winter's over, we can weed it and plant things in it.'

'You mean like flowers an' shit?'

Donovan laughed. 'Exactly that. Flowers and shit.'

'An' it'll grow, yeah? Be like proper?'

Donovan looked at the boy. Remembered Peta's words to him outside Father Jack's: *We can't do everything, Joe. We can't save everyone* . . .

And his response: *Just one . . . just one* . . .

Donovan smiled. 'I hope so, Jamal. I hope so.'

Jamal smiled.

Breaktime was over. They still had a lot of work ahead of them.

Acknowledgements

Thanks to Deb Kemp, Nick Kemp, Jane Gregory, Anna Valdinger, Kate Lyall Grant, Digby Halsby and my wife Linda.

Apparently there is a 'Get Carter' tour which features many of the locations used by the one in this novel but any resemblance between the two is entirely coincidental.

Joe Donovan will return in

THE BONE MACHINE,

to be published by Pocket Books in 2007.